MYSTIC DRAGON

BOOKS BY JASON DENZEL

Mystic

Mystic Dragon

JASON DENZEL

MYSTIC DRAGON

TOR

A TOM DOHERTY ASSOCIATES BOOK

NEW YORK

MYSTIC DRAGON

Map and ornament by Rhys Davies

A Tor Book
Published by Tom Doherty Associates
175 Fifth Avenue
New York, NY 10010

www.tor-forge.com

Tor® is a registered trademark of Macmillan Publishing Group, LLC.

The Library of Congress Cataloging-in-Publication Data is available upon request.

ISBN 978-0-7653-8199-6 (hardcover)
ISBN 978-1-4668-8569-1 (ebook)

Our books may be purchased in bulk for promotional, educational, or business use. Please contact your local bookseller or the Macmillan Corporate and Premium Sales Department at 1-800-221-7945, extension 5442, or by email at MacmillanSpecialMarkets@macmillan.com.

First Edition: July 2018

Printed in the United States of America

0 9 8 7 6 5 4 3 2 1

To

My sons,

Aidan and Andrew.

May you have the strength to move mountains

And the wisdom to meditate upon them.

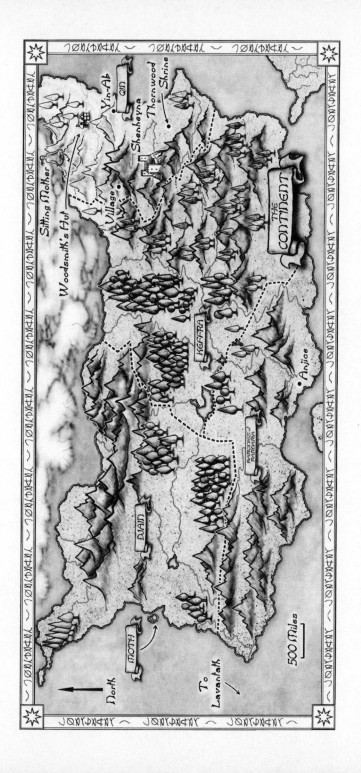

Listen Once,
  Hear Me thrice.
From stars to shore,
  Across paradise.
I cry, I call, I plea.
  My lost one,
Come Back to Me.
Come Back to Me.

MYSTIC
DRAGON

ONE

THE FORTRESS OF
SEA AND SKY

On the island of Moth, beneath a sweltering summer sun, Pomella AnDone lifted her hands above her head.

"I surrender," she said.

The two bandits pointing crossbows at her looked at each other in confusion. Pomella silently thanked the Saints that they hadn't loosed quarrels at her. She had intentionally made plenty of racket approaching them but still managed to surprise them. Not the best-trained bunch of bandits she'd run into, then. Not that the idea of handing herself over to these twerpers showcased her stunning intellect, either. Yet here she was.

As if to punctuate how blathering stupid this idea was, Pomella's horse shook his head and stomped a hoof.

"Easy, Quercus," Pomella soothed.

"Quiet!" one of the bandits yelled. He was dressed in a heavily padded cloth shirt. Greasy blond hair spilled out of his cap and plastered against the side of his head.

The other bandit, a man with an enormous gut and gray beard, shook his crossbow for emphasis. "Keep yer hands up!"

Pomella quirked an eyebrow at him. "They're already up," she said. By the Saints, with this heat they must be melting in all those layers. "Don't you want to come seize my horse and tie my hands?"

The bandits looked at each other again, uncertain of how to handle a volunteer prisoner. They were saved from having to use their brains, however, when all the commotion drew their captain, a sharp-nosed woman resembling a vulture. Unlike her underlings, she wore well-stitched leather armor that fit her long figure. She looked even more miserable in the heat than the crossbowmen.

"Who'n the dyin' hells are you?" Vulture-woman asked. Her accent was Rardarian, not Mothic.

Pomella kept her hands up but lowered her voice and eyes. "Forgive me, Mistress. I have no name."

The bandit captain eyed Pomella's ragged gray work dress and pulled-back hair. "You don't look Unclaimed. Why isn't your head shaved?"

"A thousand apologies, Mistress," in her meekest voice. The dress she wore was an old dress she'd made years ago, shortly before she'd left Oakspring to accept the invitation to the apprentice Trials. It had fit nicely back then, if a little tight in places, but now it barely fit the curves of her older body. "The watcherman banished me yesterday. I . . . I just c-couldn't do it." She scrunched her face up and hoped the performance would be convincing enough.

"You're Unclaimed but have a horse?" the captain said.

"He's my fathir's," Pomella said. "He said I should trade him for food."

The captain looked at her skeptically and Pomella could see her thinking it through. "Tie her hands, Stavin. Get the horse, Kel."

The greasy-haired bandit leaped to bind Pomella's hands while the other, bearded one kept his crossbow trained on her heart. "You sure 'bout that, Jeca?" said the bearded one.

"I gave you a jagged order, Kel," the captain said.

Kel reluctantly lowered his bow and spit into a nearby bush.

Pomella held her wrists out for Stavin, and waited as he struggled to tie them properly. Pomella bit her lip, forcing herself to not offer advice. Likely the bandit was trying not to touch her. She was Unclaimed, after all.

They led her east along a thin trail that hugged the southern edge of the Ironlow Mountains. With the sun blazing, Pomella wished for the shade of her traveling cloak. She considered asking for water but thought better of it.

After nearly an hour on the trail, the captain directed them north, in the opposite direction from the main road. She brought them to a camp surrounding a nearby spring. Pomella's eyes widened. The camp was far larger than the rumors had said. At least twenty bandits milled around, grooming their horses, moving prisoners, or walking on patrols. Three large tents stood near the spring.

But what really surprised Pomella was the number of prisoners she saw. More than a hundred disheveled men and women shuffled around in large groups, letting themselves be herded like cattle.

The Unclaimed.

The lowest of the low in every society, the men and women being held by these bandits—these *slavers*—had each received a punishment that ostracized them from society forever. By law and tradition, the Unclaimed could own nothing beyond what they could carry. Nobody could touch them, speak to them, or give them shelter. It was a disgusting part of their culture. Nobody was born to this lowest caste.

Rumors had reached Kelt Apar that there was a large enclave of Unclaimed in the area and that it had been raided recently by bandits. In theory, each Unclaimed person had committed a horrible deed to earn this irrevocable title. But the reality wasn't that simple. The nobility generally bristled at the slightest perceived offense from those they saw as beneath them, and handed out horrible punishments for "crimes" as simple as leaving the barony, or owning a more beautiful horse than the baron, or having a more beautiful wife. The lives of the Unclaimed were bad enough, but in the past year somebody had begun rounding them up to sell as slaves to the Continent.

The captain led Pomella and the other bandit Stavin toward one of the tents. At the entrance, a short bald man wearing a leather vest over a loose shirt snapped directions to another bandit. "Brigid's tits, man, I don't care what kind of mudshite hovel you find them in, get those filthy culks cleaned! I won't have them dyin' on the ship 'cause they're covered in their own shite! You don't have to touch 'em, but get 'em to scrub themselves and each other."

The man he'd been berating knuckled a pathetic salute and

practically ran away. The bald man turned and saw Pomella and her captors. "Who ya got here, Jeca?"

"Fresh meat, Paks," said the bandit captain, not bothering to dismount. "Turned herself in."

Paks eyed Pomella. "Ain't even shaved yet? Have ya touched her?"

The captain narrowed her eyes. "Course not. I ain't no animal."

"You don't look like you're from Moth," Paks said to Pomella.

"Where I come from doesn't matter," Pomella said.

Pomella knew it was her dark skin that made him say that. Her parents were native to Moth, but her grandmhathir on her fathir's side, whom she strongly resembled, had come from the distant nation of Keffra.

Paks sneered. "Haven't learned how to speak to your betters yet, eh?" He nodded to Stavin. Pain exploded across Pomella's jaw as the bandit slapped a pole across her cheek. Pomella stumbled but managed to stay on her feet. Blood dripped from her lip, but she quickly caught it with her bound hands. She'd hoped to avoid getting hurt like this, but sometimes you had to invest in a little pain. Pomella rose carefully to ensure none of her blood landed on the ground. She didn't want to draw Oxillian's attention.

"Careful," Jeca said, still sitting atop her horse. "We'll get less if her pretty little face is mangled. The Shadefox won't be happy."

"She'll heal up on the voyage," Paks said. "Besides, her hands still work. The Shadefox won't have to know."

"You won't be giving me to the Shadefox," Pomella said, dabbing her face again. "Nor will you be selling any of these other people."

Paks stepped toward her. "I don't think Stavin hit you hard enough," he said. "Looks like you're too much of a *hetch* to even be Unclaimed."

Pomella narrowed her eyes. She hated that vulgar term for a filthy, lowborn woman.

"Get rid of her," Paks said, and turned away.

Pomella closed her eyes and inhaled. All around her, the Myst, the invisible energy of the universe that lay everywhere, permeating everything, swirled like a cloud caught in a wind. According to her teacher, Grandmaster Lal Faywong, the Myst was the only thing that truly existed and it was alive and supremely aware. The whole island, its people, Pomella, these bandits, and all of their feelings and thoughts were simply limited expressions of the Myst.

That was the theory, at least. At the moment, what concerned Pomella was completing her task.

Silver streaks of light circled her like a Springrise ribbon. A tide of energy arose within her. She opened her eyes just as Stavin yanked on the rope binding her wrist. She yanked back at the same time, and used the Myst to hurl the bandit over her head and across the ground.

"Shite!" Paks screamed.

Pomella lifted her bound wrists above her head, then willed the Myst to wind itself around the rope. As the tiny threads of Myst settled into it, she ignited them with a mental command, and they vaporized into dust.

Time to bring in her helpers.

Pomella stilled her mind and silently summoned her hummingbirds, Hector and Ena. Quick as luck'ns they appeared, zooming through the air, trailing silvery smoke behind. They crossed above her head and dropped a polished oak staff into her hand. As her grip tightened around it, the Myst surrounding her *focused* and surged.

"She's not Unclaimed, you culks!" Paks roared. "She's a—"

Pomella silenced him with a sweep of her staff, wrapping him in a binding of Myst and stuffing his mouth to shut him up. She spun and threw a barrier up just as a crossbow bolt sounded behind her. It had come from Kel, the fat bandit who'd first found her. Pomella tied his feet together with the Myst and threw him sideways into Stavin.

She didn't really consider herself a warrior, but after shutting down a double handful of slaver operations she'd picked up a trick or two.

A wave of panic rippled across the camp as bandits abandoned their posts and ran. One by one Pomella wrapped them up and dragged them together into a pile of grunting and struggling bodies.

"There now," she said. "Let's talk business. Who's in charge? Is it you, Paks?"

Paks' jaw worked in a vain attempt to curse past the silvery gag. Pomella twitched a finger and it dissolved, releasing his voice.

"When and where were you going to meet the Shadefox?" she demanded.

"Choke on gunkroot," Paks said.

Pomella sighed. She hadn't expected to get a lot of information from the bandits by asking nicely. Very likely they knew little about the Shadefox. Few people did. It seemed as though he operated within carefully contained cells and used proxy representatives in order to limit exposure.

All around the camp, handfuls of Unclaimed had gathered to watch. No matter how many times she saw them, her heart ached at seeing their filthy state. Most wore rags that barely passed as clothes while some were outright naked. None of those noticed or cared about their nakedness, though. When you were Unclaimed, even your bodies were worthless.

Pomella straightened her back. Hector alighted onto the top of her staff while Ena landed on her shoulder.

"All of you are free to go. These men and women won't hurt you," she promised. "My name is—"

"The Hummingbird!" an Unclaimed woman said. She was around Pomella's age, in her early twenties. A mote of light sparked in her otherwise-dull eyes.

"That's what they call me, I guess," Pomella said. "I am going to Port Morrush tonight. There will be food for you there."

Paks chuckled behind Pomella. "What're ya gunna do, *Hummingbird*?" Pomella peered over her shoulder at the man. "Yah can't feed 'em all. They're Unclaimed. You're as far above 'em as you can be. Their lot won't change. Besides, look at 'em. They don't *wanna* change! You can lord over them all you—"

Pomella made a cutting motion with her free hand, stuffing Paks' mouth again with the Myst.

A thundering of hooves sounded on the far side of the camp. A full complement of the baron's Shieldguard stormed toward them. The burning afternoon sun glinted off their plate armor and lance tips upon which the ManHinley banner flew. They didn't bother to slow down for the Unclaimed, who had to scramble to make way.

The riders circled Pomella and the bandits and brought their horses to an easy rest. One of the soldiers, the captain according to his additional knotted shoulder rope, removed his helmet, revealing a dashing face with a square jaw and well-groomed red beard.

"I hadn't expected to find one of your kind in charge here," he said, inclining his head only the barest amount. He held a sword in his gauntleted hand.

"You arrived just in time, Captain," Pomella said. "But you won't need those weapons."

The captain hesitated only a heartbeat after her command. "As you command, Mistress." He sheathed his sword, but Pomella noted that none of his soldiers did. "My name is Captain Lucal Daycon. I'm sure you understand that I have orders to fulfill. I've been commanded to arrest every one of these people and submit them to the baron's justice."

"You may arrest the slavers," Pomella said, "but the Unclaimed are free to go at *my* command."

"The baron and baroness do not take kindly to Unclaimed loitering on their lands," Lucal said.

"And if none of the barons welcome them, then where do they go? It's a problem, isn't it, Captain? But don't worry. I'll be speaking to the baron and baroness this evening anyway. You may proceed with taking these"—she gestured to the bandits behind her—"to Port Morrush. We'll see what *justice* the baron and baroness have in mind."

"As you say, Mistress," Lucal said. Pomella knew he wouldn't disobey a direct order from her. The deep, centuries-old rules of society forbade it. But once she was out of sight, she worried Lucal would take justice into his own hands.

"You will escort me and these criminals to the Fortress of Sea and Sky," Pomella said. "Learn what you can from their leaders, but do not harm them or you will answer directly to me. I expect a report this evening. I'm especially interested in whatever you can learn about the man known as the Shadefox."

"You are quite the vigilante, Mistress . . . ?"

"Pomella. My name is Pomella AnDone. And I am not a vigilante. I am a Mystic."

Well past highsun, as the caravan of soldiers and arrested slavers approached the mighty Fortress of Sea and Sky, a familiar tingling sensation tickled Pomella's senses. She peered into the startlingly blue sky and caught sight of a silver bird.

It was a fay eagle, soaring like a festival kite. Wispy trails of mist drifted off the bird's wings, as if they painted clouds with their passage. It lingered for a full minute, drifting in the air, which struck Pomella as unusually long for a fay casually drifting into the human realm. Finally, like passing thoughts, it vanished, returning to the invisible world it had come from.

Pomella waited until the last of the eagle's misty presence faded before turning to Lucal. "Did you see that eagle, Captain?"

From atop his brown gelding, the young soldier shaded his eyes and looked up. "No, Mistress. Most of them nest along the eastern edge of the Ironlows. Few come this far south."

"Yah, I suppose so," she muttered. Most people usually couldn't see the fay, but there had been increasing rumors of occurrences in which they did. Anybody could be taught to attune themselves to the Myst, but generally only Mystics and rare individuals who had a natural affinity for the Myst were able to perceive

the fay without training. She herself had been one of those individuals, before fate and chance had conspired to lead her to a
life as a Mystic.

Putting thoughts of the eagle aside, Pomella turned her attention to the imposing stronghold looming in front of them.
For nearly five hundred years, the Fortress of Sea and Sky had
dominated the southern tip of the Mothic Mountains. During
those centuries, it had welcomed countless wandering Mystics,
and on rare occasions played host to the island's High Mystic.
But on this day, Lucal led his company and Pomella beneath the
front gates and into the open courtyard beyond, the first time
in the fortress's storied history that it had welcomed a common-
born Mystic.

Pomella kept her hood up despite the day's heat. She found
comfort in the hidden depths of the cloak, which she'd re-
trieved from her saddlebag along with a proper riding dress.
The hood also ensured that everyone in the fortress wouldn't
see her drenched in sweat from the long ride. She resisted the
urge to knuckle her back. Someday, she'd learn how to ride a
horse properly. Maybe, anyway.

Lucal signaled his soldiers to break off and take the prisoners to wherever it was they were to be kept. He motioned for
Pomella to follow.

A pair of mailed guards holding pikes stood on either side of
the inner keep's double doors. The guards turned in unison and
pulled at the heavy iron rings bolted on as handles. The doors
opened, yawning like the maw of a great beast opening into a
gullet of shadows.

Lucal bowed in farewell and left Pomella to cross the keep's
threshold by herself. She dismissed her hummingbirds, who flew

up and away into the higher portions of the keep. Pomella entered the fortress and sensed the Myst stir, an unseen rush of energy swirling in the entryway, dancing with delight by her presence.

The guards stood at attention, hands on their long weapons. Beyond them, the baroness and her husband waited inside the foyer. Pomella's attention turned to Kelisia ManHinley, the ninth-generation ruler of the southern Mothic barony, wringing her hands nervously. The baroness bowed to her, followed by her husband, Pandric. Even after all these years, Pomella still felt a rush of anxiety when a noble bowed to her. She fought the urge to bow back, even lower.

"Welcome, Mistress Pomella," Pandric said. "I understand you rescued some unfortunate victims from the cruelty of slavers. The baroness and I thank you for your efforts. The recent rise of slave trading in our barony is a thorn in our side." He peered at his nervous wife. "Although I am sad to say that we have more personal matters to discuss."

Normally, it would've been unusual for Pandric to greet her first, since the line of nobility ran through Kelisia, but a quick glance at the circles beneath the baroness's puffy, bloodshot eyes was enough to tell Pomella that she was barely able to keep her emotions in check. The baroness had dark wavy hair that cascaded down her back all the way to her thighs. Pomella wondered if she'd ever had her hair cut in her life. She had remarkable cheekbones, and stunning brown eyes. But there was a hollowness to her eyes, and a gauntness to her features. Pomella had heard it had been a hard week for the baroness, and for the entire House. Almost certainly the baroness had asked her husband to lead the pleasantries.

Pomella observed the easy manner with which Pandric spoke,

as well as his terribly handsome features. Although she'd not met the couple until now, Pomella had heard of their youth and renowned charm. Despite the baroness's emotionally vulnerable state, the reports of her beauty not only were apparently true but also perhaps fell short. Time would tell, however, whether the noble couple would uphold the old ways of heavy discrimination against the lower castes, or embrace newer ideas.

Pomella slipped her hood back, revealing long dark hair that hung well past her shoulders. The baron and baroness had pale skin, common on Moth, several shades lighter than Pomella's. "Thank you, Lord Baron. And greetings to you, Lady Baroness." She inclined her head to each. "What a beautiful home you have here by the sea."

"You're too kind, Mistress," Pandric said. He wore a dark-blue coat, representing the ocean that the fortress overlooked, along with gray trim for the clouds that on most other days cloaked it. Pomella guessed the baron was in his mid-thirties, a little more than a decade older than herself. His short, neatly trimmed hair and beard had a couple of gray hairs just beginning to show. "The landscape is beautiful," he said, "but the fortress itself can be cold."

The baroness stepped forward, her anxiety clearly taking precedent over protocol. She took one of Pomella's hands into her own.

"Please, Mistress," Kelisia said. "Our Norana. Can you help her?"

Pomella squeezed the baroness's hand. "Call me Pomella," she said. "I will do what I can. Tell me what you know."

"She's been asleep for five days," Kelisia said. "Her nurse put her to bed, as usual, and she hasn't woken since."

Pandric slid an arm around his wife. "Norana's very much alive. We can see her breathing, and often smiling or grimacing from her dreams. But no matter what we do, we cannot rouse her."

The anguish on the baron's and baroness's faces broke Pomella's heart. Unbidden, a memory floated to her of her young brother, Gabor, from when the Coughing Plague had swept through their home village of Oakspring. Not everyone caught the disease, and nobody understood why some folk were affected and others not. Gabor had begun coughing, right when the scare was worst, and Pomella remembered the terror that had gripped her grandmhathir at the thought that his symptoms would progress into the full horrid nightmare. Even their hardened fathir, who normally gave no quarter to his emotions, lingered his hand upon Gabor's tousled hair a little more often than normal. It turned out that Gabor had just come down with the common chills, thank the Saints. But Pomella remembered the fear her family had shown, and she remembered her own.

"Take me to her," Pomella said in her most reassuring voice.

Kelisia squeezed Pomella's hand before practically running to the carpeted stairwell, which led to a landing that ascended to the upper rooms of the keep.

Pandric walked beside Pomella at a more normal pace. "My wife barely eats or sleeps," he said as they passed a set of massive stained-glass windows overlooking the landing. The artwork depicted the iconic Saint Brigid shouting commands across a ship's deck to sailors as they struggled against a storm. "I'm afraid I might lose them both."

The stained-glass artwork caught Pomella's attention because she'd never heard of Brigid sailing a ship before. The Saint and her years-long hunt for her son was the defining epic of Moth, and was frequently told on the Continent as well. Pomella knew the *Toweren* by heart, and often sang it when she visited commoner inns, a pastime she enjoyed but generally kept from Lal and Yarina.

Pomella pulled her attention from the glass artwork as she stepped onto the upper stairs. She focused her mind, easing it into that place where the Myst revealed itself more easily. As she climbed, she called to the Myst, pulling it from the building's stones, the wooden guardrail on the stairs, the carpet, and even the clothes she wore. The Myst swirled in her vision, like smoke churned by a passing breeze. It whispered wordless secrets with a voice she heard in her heart rather than her ears or mind. Secrets that it had witnessed through the centuries, hinting at what may yet come to pass.

Vague shapes took form within the silvery haze, existing only for moments before disappearing like water vapor on a hot day. Pomella watched as the Myst shaped itself like a painting on the wall, but it vanished as she turned her head to examine its details. Tree branches and vines dipped from the ceiling, making it appear as though for a moment she were walking in a shimmering likeness of the Mystwood.

All of these visions were a reflection of Fayün, the land of the fay, the world that reflected their own, like the opposite side of a coin. They were glimpses of a different realm, one in which the Fortress of Sea and Sky did not exist or, if it did, it existed in a different, unfamiliar form.

Up ahead, Kelisia looked back over her shoulder to ensure Pomella and Pandric still followed. She led them down a hallway that overlooked the entry chamber they'd stood in earlier before cutting into an adjoining passage. Several doors stood along either wall, and it was one of these that the baroness headed for.

Pomella knew which room the child was in before Kelisia approached it. She tightened her grip on her staff. Silver light, blazing bright, seeped from beneath the nearest doorway. Vines and ivy crawled across the door, invisible to everyone except Pomella with her Mystic eyes.

The baroness led them into the room. To Kelisia and her husband, the room likely appeared to be a normal nursery, albeit a wealthy one worthy of the eldest daughter to the nobles living in the Fortress of Sea and Sky. A crib stood against the far wall, which had been painted with a mural depicting the Mystwood, with the green conical tip of Kelt Apar's central tower rising above the tree line. Soft candles lit the room, while thin drapes rippled from a breath of sea breeze blowing in from a southern-facing window. An elderly nurse rocked in a chair beside the crib, knitting.

But that was not the entirety of the room Pomella beheld.

Instead, she saw the world of Fayün bleeding across into the human world. Usually it was just a single creature or plant that crossed over the veil into their world, and then only briefly. But rising before Pomella was an entire jungle of trees and vines and creatures, running and scattering as she and the nobles walked into the room. Silvery moss-covered boulders rested beside Norana's crib. It was as if the stone had been carved to fit the baby's crib.

There could only be one reason to explain the unusual lingering glimpse of Fayün. In recent months Mistress Yarina, the High Mystic of Moth, had been preparing her apprentice,

Vivianna, and Pomella for the coming of Crow Tallin, a rare celestial event in which the fay would linger longer than usual in the human world. Pomella only understood a little about it but could think of no other reason for such a phenomenon.

Pomella crossed the room and peered into the crib. Little Norana, not even a year old, lay on her back beneath a thin blanket with her fists balled up beside her cheeks. Her chest rose and fell with slow puffs. She looked like any other sleeping tyke except for four ragged scratches running down her face, across her eye, from her forehead to her neck. The scratch marks weren't normal. They shimmered with silver light, and lay etched into her skin.

Pomella bit her lip. Norana's parents wouldn't be able to see the scratches. Something from Fayün had caused them. Just as Mystics could Unveil the Myst and Fayün to manipulate it, so could the denizens and environment of the fay realm sometimes affect the human world. It was extremely rare, happening only a few times on Moth every year, which was high compared to other nations because, of all places in the world, the island was said to be where Fayün overlapped the most with the humans' own world.

The old nurse stood and silently bowed her way out of the room. She closed the door as she left. Leaning her staff against the wall, Pomella placed her hand over Norana's head. The little girl had no fever, but Pomella found herself remarking at how soft the child's hair and skin were.

She glanced around the crib, looking for signs of the fay creature that might have caused the scratches. Silver walnut shells, leaves, and broken twigs lay scattered around the baby. Turning her gaze upward, Pomella glimpsed a pair of silver eyes lurking in the branches of a large tree. The eyes blinked once, then faded into the tree.

Kelisia approached Pomella. "Do you know what ails her?"

"She's been injured by a fay creature," Pomella said. "The veil between the fortress and Fayün is thin here. In the fay realm, this very spot isn't a child's nursery, but a den to some sort of wild animal."

Kelisia's eyes narrowed in fierce determination. Pomella admired how, upon learning this information, the baroness didn't wail or despair.

"Then how do we purge this infestation?"

Pomella shook her head. "That isn't an option. There are ways to strengthen the veil to prevent this from happening, but for the moment, it would be best to move the nursery elsewhere and lock this room off from the rest of the fortress."

Kelisia's eyes burned. Before she could speak, though, Pandric placed a calming hand onto his wife's shoulder. "Please, Pomella. We will do anything to help her."

Pomella gestured to the tyke. "May I?"

"Of course."

After easing her hands beneath the child's neck and lower back, Pomella lifted Norana into her arms. She remarked at how wee the child was, so thin and frail. She cradled the tyke in her arms and bounced her lightly. "I'll need a handful of moments alone with her, please. She is safe."

Kelisia seemed as though she was about to protest, but Pandric patted her arm and pulled her toward the hallway outside.

"Oh, and Baron?" Pomella said in a quiet voice. He paused at the doorway. "There is a large enclave of Unclaimed outside your city who need food. What I do here is given freely, but I hope you will consider acting generously on their behalf as well." She gave them both a reassuring smile.

Pandric nodded in understanding, then closed the door.

"Oh, you sweet warrum," Pomella said to Norana, using the old term her grandmhathir had used for small children. "What scratched you?"

Pomella closed her eyes and reached out with the Myst. She sought the child's emotions, and perhaps, if she was lucky, a glimpse of her memory of what had happened. Like most of her skills, reaching into memories was one talent she'd somehow taught herself over the years. She'd never done it with a child, however.

Pomella began to hum a gentle lullaby. Singing had always been at the heart of her relationship to the Myst. In her years as a Mystic apprentice, it helped her Unveil the Myst and grow. And today, seven years later as a full Mystic, she was still empowered by singing.

Her footsteps sank into the soft rug that filled most of the room. Pomella walked around it, gliding around the whole room with Norana in her arms. She sang an old lullaby she remembered from her grandmhathir. It was a song she'd never forget because it had been sung to her throughout her early life, and that of her brother. Supposedly, the song was another one associated with the Brigid legend, a lullaby the Saint supposedly sang to her infant son. Pomella wondered if that was true, or whether it had been adopted and assimilated by the people of Moth who could never get enough of their beloved Saint. Whatever its origin, Pomella measured her footsteps to the slow rhythm of the song.

> *"Bab-bie wonder*
> *Bab-bie light*
> *How'd you fall into my sight?"*

As she walked and sang, Pomella willed the Myst to accompany her with a gentle tune. It was something she'd taught herself to do during her apprentice years. She found that she could make the Myst play music only she could hear and, because it came from her, it was always in perfect harmony with what she sang.

> *"Bab-bie star*
> *Bab-bie night*
> *Let me hold you under moonlight.*
> *With eyes so gentle*
> *Soft and down*
> *Take me with you into town.*
> *Bab-bie wonder*
> *Bab-bie light."*

Before Pomella could begin the next stanza, Norana twitched in her arms. The child remained asleep, but her face scrunched up as if to cry. Pomella let her Myst music continue, but she shifted from singing to humming in order to concentrate on what was happening.

Silvery light rolled off Norana now. The scratches on her face pulsed angrily. Pomella pinched her fingers just above the child's face and pulled, as if she were tugging an invisible string. As she did so, she willed the Myst to bring forth the child's recent memory.

A tendril of light rose from the center of Norana's forehead, twisting around Pomella's fingers. Rising with it came blurry memories. In that moment, Pomella was able to recall, as if it were her own memory, a time when she—as Norana—lay in her crib, sucking on her fist. A cat, striped with different shades of silver, slinked across the crib. It hissed at her, and Norana cried. The cat came closer, and Norana flailed, smacking it with a tiny fist. The creature dodged and hissed and fled, but not before taking a hard swipe at the child.

Pomella steadied herself with a deep breath. Even if Norana could somehow see fay creatures at this early age, it was unlikely she could affect or hurt them.

Or so Pomella had believed.

She looked upward into the silver tree growing above the crib, searching for the pair of eyes she'd seen earlier. Sure enough, as she peered into the branches they appeared. Pomella reached out with the Myst, and pulled the creature forward. It was the same cat from Norana's memory, twice as large as the child herself.

The cat hissed and spit, but Pomella pinned it down with the Myst. "You will leave this child alone," she said to the cat. "I will have her relocated to a new room, but this is the human realm. Remain in yours. Go."

She released the fay creature, and it fled into the branches before misting away.

"There. It shouldn't hurt you again," Pomella said to Norana. "And I will keep this memory so it no longer haunts you. Now, let's do something about those scratches and wake you up."

She hummed again as she summoned the Myst. She touched Norana's face, gently rubbing the wounds. Slowly they faded, soothed away by her touch. It wasn't that the baby had received a physical wound, or that Pomella had been able to heal her directly, but rather she was able to erase the connection that bound the child to the wound that linked her to Fayün.

Sometimes it all made Pomella's head hurt. Being a Mystic wasn't easy.

When the scars vanished, Norana opened her eyes. Deep brown pools stared up at her.

Pomella smiled. "Hello." Norana's chin quivered and then she began to wail.

Pomella figured this was a good time to hand her back to her parents.

TWO

THE WOODSMITH

A grizzled hermit, known to the few scattered villagers in the area as the Woodsmith, strode through the hidden paths of Broken Fist Mountain in northern Qin. He hiked with confidence, his stride optimizing his pace while conserving energy. Layers of animal skin and fur covered his body. Two chest-high walking sticks served as extensions of his arms, helping him blaze a trail.

Angry red and purple rashes covered his exposed skin, but the Woodsmith paid them no mind. Long hair and a scraggly blond beard hid most of the blemishes on his face.

His eyes swept over every bush and every stone that crossed his path. A white fox watched him from a nearby shrub. The Woodsmith couldn't see the fox, but he knew it was there because of the faint tracks in the snow, along with partially buried scat dotted with iceberry seeds. Ignoring the fox, he sniffed the air.

The smoke he'd smelled earlier was stronger here. He followed it south.

As he trekked through the thawing snow, he glimpsed White-paw and the rest of the pack following the same course further up the mountain's slope. The wolves were as curious as he was about the scent. Before he'd caught it on the wind, it had been the pack who had alerted him to the unusual activity.

Few visitors came to the northern highlands of Qin, and that was how the Woodsmith liked it. For four years he'd lived here alone, avoiding humans as much as he could. On the rare occasion that a passing band of travelers came near, he'd vanished into the woods and watched silently until they were gone. If an overeager youth from one of the nearby villages dared to investigate his hut, he'd scare them off. And on the rare occasion where somebody became lost, he'd guided them home from afar, leaving obvious clues they could see and follow, but never interacting with them directly.

All his time alone in the highlands, the Woodsmith had never seen a massacre like the one that awaited him when he approached the rarely used cart path cutting through the valley.

Flames feasted on a ruined wagon that had been overturned in the middle of the overgrown road. Six bodies lay chained to the wagon. The Woodsmith expected there was at least one more buried beneath the wreckage. The fire wasn't new. It had moved past the main course and now smoldered on the after-meal. Most of the bodies were charred beyond recognition.

The Woodsmith flicked his wrists and his walking sticks became finely sharpened blades. Memory in his left hand,

Remorse in his right. He reached out with his senses, and stepped out of the forest to approach the ruined caravan. White-paw and the other wolves watched him from the unseen shadows of the forest.

The first thing he noticed upon reaching the dead bodies was that they hadn't died from a bandit ambush, or even from the fire. They'd been slaughtered by animals. A chill crept up the Wood-smith's spine. Nothing native to these parts would cause this sort of damage.

The fay had been here.

This wasn't the first fay attack he'd seen. As recently as a month ago there'd been another. A pair of mountain goats had come down the mountain to get his attention. He'd followed them to a corpse that had belonged to a local, middle-aged man who'd likely been out gathering iceberries. He'd been gutted by a tusk the length of a man's forearm. Small, silvery rodents were crawling on his body when the Woodsmith had arrived.

He circled the burning wagon and confirmed his suspicion that a seventh body lay beneath the overturned wagon. Normally, he'd recognize it as a merchant cart, headed west for its seasonal visit to the villages located in the mountain interior. But the chains attached to the six bodies told another story. Those people had been prisoners. They were the merchant's wares. These were slaves.

Unclaimed.

The Woodsmith used the tip of his blade to turn one of the lesser-burned faces. His grim expression took in the short hair, the patch of pale skin that had fallen against the snow, and a single milky-blue eye. A pair of red-tinged hairs lay beside another body.

The Woodsmith spit the foul taste from his mouth. These Unclaimed were from Moth, far away across the world. Likely the merchant had been taking them to Yin-Aab, where such *wares* were valued. He moved on to search the rest of the wreckage.

He used his foot to break open a partially burned wooden chest. Inside he found a bolt of woolen fabric, metal cups, pins, scraps of iron useful for repairing homes, and two formerly fine lace dresses suitable for young noblewomen seeking feast-day attire.

The Woodsmith relaxed and sheathed his blades. He faced the forest where he suspected Whitepaw was and raised an arm. He wanted to let the wolves know it was safe. The fire was not a danger to the surrounding forest.

Covering his face with a clean strip of the wool fabric, the Woodsmith dragged the seven bodies into a line. He had to break the chain from the cart to free them, but the fire had done most of the work for him. His hand lingered only half a heart-beat above the Unclaimed before he shook off his old habits and moved the bodies. It felt strange to touch another human after so many years, even though they were dead. These people might be the corpses here, but in some ways the Woodsmith felt that he'd died long before them.

He buried the Unclaimed together in a single grave but left the slave merchant to burn. When he was done he stood silently over it, giving each person some peaceful attention before sorting through the caravan's wares.

He gathered as much as he could, but not for himself. He'd certainly keep some of it—perhaps a scattering of useful tools

or one of the bolts of cloth—but he planned to deliver the rest
to the mountain villages under the cover of night. The villagers
would wake up and find gifts in their central square waiting for
them. Perhaps he'd carve some elderberry flutes and leave those,
too. He loved hearing the villagers play the wind instruments
whenever he left some for them to find. It was the flutes that
inspired the villagers to give him his name.

As the Woodsmith assembled a makeshift litter to carry the
goods, a chill wind tickled the back of his neck.

Instinct took over. He dropped everything in his arms and
spun around, whipping Memory up into a ready position. In
his years living alone he'd practiced the fundamental combat
stances he'd learned from a man now long dead. Although he
no longer had a teacher to guide him, daily effort combined with
a cultivated will to survive gave him confidence that he could
defend himself.

He also realized that whatever lurked here in the forest could
likely easily overwhelm him.

Nothing stirred in the underbrush.

The Woodsmith rotated, slowly dragging his gaze across
every tree and shrub. A long minute passed without further incident. The Woodsmith wondered if he'd imagined the strange
sensation. Slowly, he lowered his blade, but did not sheath it.
He kept his senses alert as he went about gathering some of the
more useful things scattered throughout the ruined wagon.

The Woodsmith tied a small pouch of salt to his belt and
set off to return home. He took only one step before coming
to a halt.

A pile of stacked stones rested in the middle of the path.

The hairs on the back of his arms stood on edge. Fear gripped his chest. There was no mistaking the stack. The rocks had been placed in a precise and familiar manner.

"*Sim*," whispered a voice.

The Woodsmith spun around, looking for the source of the voice. He found nobody, and whipped his attention back toward the pile of rocks.

Whoever had placed them knew his old name, the name that he'd practically forgotten.

Slipping back into the forest, the Woodsmith fled.

THREE

THE ROLLING FORGE

Heavy rain drenched the Rolling Forge Inn. Pomella sat in a shadowy corner, listening to the storm patter against a nearby windowpane. She sighed. She'd heard stories of other countries where it hardly ever rained in the summer. But on Moth, even during the hottest part of the year, you could count on at least a handful of storms.

She wore her well-worn cloak, once vibrant but now faded to a dull green, to conceal her face and long hair from curious eyes. Her staff rested on the ground beneath the table, out of sight for the moment.

Beyond the foggy window, on the nearby peak of Sand Hill, the Fortress of Sea and Sky loomed in the darkness. Clusters of lanterns illuminated it like lantern bugs glowing in its walls.

Pomella had been vague about her reasons for not accepting

the ManHinleys' offer of hospitality, even when the baroness and her husband had insisted. After Pomella had awoken their child, they had lavished Pomella with praise, offers of payment, and anything else she could've asked for. Pandric went so far as to press two reigns into her hand. It'd been hard for her not to gape. Those two coins were worth two hundred stands, which was akin to two *thousand* clips. Money like that was unheard of back in Oakspring. You could buy a horse for everyone in the village with that!

Pomella had gently pushed the money back into the baron's hand but did remind both of them about the enclave of hungry Unclaimed that would soon descend upon the city. She'd also mentioned the importance of paying their seasonal tithe to Kelt Apar, a tradition that the three baronies of Moth had done for centuries. It baffled the baron and baroness that she wouldn't accept their money or hospitality, but their overall gratitude had been plain.

Laughter and hollering from the common room rolled over her in waves, surging and rising as drinks flowed. As it was one of two major port cities on Moth, Port Morrush's inns rarely lacked for a variety of patrons on a stormy evening. It seemed to Pomella that every dockhand and sailor from Moth and the Continent packed its walls. At least a hundred commoners filled the room, extending into every corner, crowding themselves into any space that could hold them. A mixture of candles and oil lanterns lit the room, except for the corner where she lurked. Pomella let the sounds stream like wind through a willow. She smiled. It reminded her of home, and it was a nice change from the lonely days of living in Kelt Apar.

She didn't recognize anybody except the glowering bouncer

standing at the door with her meaty arms crossed in front of her chest.

Mags. The tall, thick-muscled woman had been one of the Black Claw bandits who had harassed Pomella seven years ago. Mags stared at everyone with an expression that made her look like she'd just swallowed gunkroot. She was one of the inn's owners, although you wouldn't guess it from her sour expression and lack of human interaction.

A round face with a bald head and neatly trimmed goatee popped into Pomella's dark corner. Dox, the other owner of the Rolling Forge, finished wiping his hands on his apron, then scratched his forearms. "Doing well, Mistress?" he asked with only a hint of teasing in his voice. He spoke with a heavy Rardarian accent that hadn't faded in the seven years he'd lived on Moth. The former Black Claw had convinced Mags to open the Forge after selling off their former gang's equipment and horses. An actual forge wagon hung from the high ceiling above the common room, representing the only remnant from the Black Claws' past.

"As well as rain," Pomella mused in reply.

Dox patted his sweaty forehead with his apron. A smile blossomed on his face. "Aye, the good Mothic weather booms our business."

"Perhaps you could turn your extra profits from tonight to provide free meals to the poorest families living in the city," Pomella suggested.

Dox wiped his sweaty forehead. "Always the Mystic of the Commoners, aren't you?" he said, but not without affection. "Are you sure I cannot introduce you to everyone? Let them see you."

"I'm content here. I've had a long day. Thank you, Dox."

"Anything for you, Mistress. Always." He bowed slightly and returned to the bustling room and his patrons.

Aside from experiencing a change of pace from the quiet days at Kelt Apar, Pomella enjoyed watching people go about their regular lives. Most of these men and women struggled through their lives. They may not be *content* with their lives, but they were certainly resigned. Few, if any, had been given opportunities like her to rise above the caste they'd been born to. She wished she could do more for them. To show them how it was possible. Yet here she sat, lurking in a quiet corner, wondering if the gulf between her and the commoners had finally grown too vast for her to reach out.

"Perhaps the brandy's affecting my sight, but is it possible that this lonely corner hosts an even more lonely lady?"

Pomella looked up to see a well-dressed man with a short, scruffy beard and brown eyes politely holding a cap in his hands. He spoke with a Mothic accent and had curly brown hair. His smile exuded a winning charm. He bowed to her.

She was about to tell him to scamper off when he continued. "Berrit Lorndrew. It's quite packed in here. May I join you?"

Pomella sighed inwardly. A little company never scared happiness away, her grandmhathir had always said. "Of course," she replied.

He slipped into the chair across from her and mimed trying to peer into the depths of her hood. "And whom do I have the pleasure of sitting with?"

"Pomella," she replied, slipping her hood off. Berrit's eyes widened at seeing her long hair. She wore nothing that outright stated she was a Mystic, but she also lacked jewelry and rich attire that would mark her as a noble.

"I beg your pardon, Mistress," he said. "I assumed you were a merchant-scholar like myself. Please forgive my brash introduction."

"Nonsense," Pomella said. "I was beginning to feel a bit *too* reclusive over here."

Berrit leaned toward her. "Wait a moment. I've heard of you. You're the one they call the Hummingbird. The Commoner Mystic."

Pomella's cheeks heated. She was suddenly glad the shadows hid them. "People love to admire symbols. I'm happy to provide one, if it helps them, but most days I trudge in my garden's mud and tend goats."

"That's a humble living for one whom nobles bow to," Berrit said.

"What are you a merchant of, Master Lorndrew?" Pomella said, changing the topic.

"Please, Mistress. Call me Berrit."

"Then call me Pomella."

He inclined his head in agreement and smiled again. There was a slight suggestion in the curve of his lip. "Your wares?" Pomella prompted.

In reply, he withdrew a musical instrument as wide as two hands from his inner coat. It was a set of nine slightly curved pipes, each tube a bit longer than the one beside it.

"A singer?" she asked, her interest piqued.

Berrit shrugged. "A minstrel," he said. "I trade in music. My fathir wanted me to take over his successful furniture business, but I"—he flourished the hand holding the pipes—"I find contentment in the crafting and performance of the musical arts."

His eyes twinkled at her, but before Pomella could reply a wind howled through the inn. On the far side of the common room, the door opened, spilling in rain. The cold gust charged in like an angry bull in a stall. The flames of the candles shook. An awkward silence overtook the crowd as three hunched figures slipped silently into the inn and closed the door. Hushed murmurs greeted the strangers.

Pomella vaguely recognized the two men and the woman who had entered. These were Unclaimed from the enclave she'd rescued this morning. There were no physical marks, no Mystical aura about them, that declared it, but nobody—not even the grubbiest commoner farmer on Moth—wore rags as filthy as theirs, or had bald heads and hollow sunken eyes set into uncomfortably thin, sore-lined faces.

The crowd, already crammed too tight into the common room, somehow backed away until there was a gap around the three newcomers as wide as Pomella's outstretched arms. The woman whispered something that Pomella could not hear. It sounded like a request.

Mags cracked her knuckles and stepped toward them.

Pomella gave Berrit an apologetic smile, then stepped around the table and out of the shadows. "Hold, Mags," she said. "There's room for more. Come forward, friends."

In the relative silence of the inn, Pomella's voice carried across the crowd, and soon every face gaped at her. One by one people raised their glasses to her in salute, while the more sober ones actually stood and bowed. A handful of elegant, dark-skinned merchant-scholars nodded to her from one of the larger tables near the inn's blazing hearth.

So much for a quiet evening in the shadows.

The Unclaimed slowly shambled forward. Pomella couldn't imagine the courage it took for them to come to a public place and enter unannounced. They could be killed for such a brash act. But she had encouraged them this morning, and her presence clearly bolstered them.

Chairs scraped across the floor and several people squeaked in worry when one of them brushed by too closely. The gap around them followed them as if they were encased in a bubble. Pomella studied each of them. The men were unshaven, with pale blotchy skin, and touches of red in their gray beards that revealed their Mothic heritage. Their eyes leaped everywhere, like feral animals wondering if the food they were being offered was actually a trap. Pomella forced herself not to look away. Even after all these years, it was hard not to. Old habits were difficult to overcome, even for a Mystic.

"Dox, bring these people a meal. They've had a long day."

Dox opened his mouth to protest but thought better of it. He rattled his hand in the air to get the cook's attention. The cook, an old woman who had stuck her head out from the kitchen when everything went unexpectedly silent, saw his gesture and vanished back into her domain to prep something.

At her gesture, the Unclaimed shuffled to the dim corner where Pomella had been sitting at moments before. Berrit backed away to give them room. The Unclaimed hunched awkwardly, not knowing how to handle themselves. Pomella gave them a reassuring smile before realizing that now everyone had returned their gaze to her.

"Sing for us, Lady!" somebody called.

Pomella sighed. Whenever she found herself recognized in a public place, something like this happened. "It's late," she told them, "and you're all having plenty o' fun without me."

"Please, Lady!" said another voice, this time coming from a young woman who looked like she hadn't even seen twenty springs yet.

Pomella found herself looking around for help and caught Berrit's grin. He shrugged at her as if to say, *Why not?*

"Oh, buggerish," she mumbled to herself. Then more loudly to the crowd, "What do you want to hear?"

A storm of suggestions tumbled over her like the surging wind from outside.

"Sing 'The Nightingale's Dream'!"

"'Old Gimmish's Lament'!"

"'Steamy Jinny's Walking Pants'!"

The crowd laughed at the last suggestion, which was a raunchy ballad that would barely be appropriate at an inn long after dark. Pomella laughed with them until she realized the idea came from a gangly teenage boy no older than thirteen. How did he even know about such things? And what was he doing here anyway?

Berrit's voice came from behind her. "Perhaps the *Toweren*, Lady?"

In true Mothic fashion, the crowd immediately rumbled in agreement. Pomella supposed you couldn't walk into a crowded inn on the island without eventually hearing Brigid's saga retold.

Pomella nodded, and more cheers washed over her.

"Hey, Dox," she called, "how about something sweet to get me started?"

But before Dox had a chance to fulfill her request, a pint of hard honey cider got passed to her from the crowd. She accepted the mug from the same teenage boy who'd asked for "Steamy Jinny." He winked at her as she took the mug. Winked at her! He was, what? Thirteen years old at most? That would make her ten years older than him. She took a long pull at the drink, glad for the sweet calm it offered.

A round of cheers sounded as she set the drink aside. The large gathering made room for her, and quieted.

"Earlier today," Pomella began, "I visited the Fortress of Sea and Sky, just outside of town and up Sand Hill. The baroness's wee tyke required assistance, so she called upon the High Mystic for aid. Well, as her reputation rightly portrays, the High Mystic, Mistress Yarina, was eager to help. Normally she would send her apprentice, Vivianna Vinnay, but she was caring for a mhathir up in the north who'd just borne three warrums at once. So I went to help the baroness instead, and had the privilege to hold little Norana ManHinley, may she one day reign in sunshine. That night, I soothed a wound from her body, and sang her a song."

As Pomella spoke, the tension melted from her body, and she sensed the Myst rise through her. She strummed the Myst gently, breathing a silent whisper across the room. One by one the candle flames puffed away, and the oil lanterns dimmed. Even the fire in the fireplace seemed to settle as if it were ready to listen to her sing. None of the people appeared to notice the changing light.

Unbidden, soft music emanated from Berrit's strange flute, perfectly setting the tone for Pomella's story. It drifted along with her words like a quiet companion at her side.

Since becoming a Mystic apprentice, she'd finally had the freedom to practice and develop her singing without fear of her fathir shouting at her. Even without somebody to run harmonies with her, like her grandmhathir had done, Pomella's singing had grown stronger, along with her mastery of the Myst. Grandmaster Faywong said it was the Myst that taught her to sing, that it was forever reminding her that she and all people were already expressions of the Myst, that they were all perfect songs, and all she had to do was remember how to express her music.

Across the room, faint wisps of silvery light drifted. Out of the corner of her eye, vines coalesced and twisted around the exposed beams of the roof. A huge oak tree wrapped itself around the inn's fireplace.

The crowd murmured their approval. Several people pointed at the phenomenon materializing around them, and one man let out a tiny yelp and nearly fell out of his chair as a silver beanstalk crept up the wall beside him. Because Pomella had explicitly Unveiled these phenomena, and wanted them seen, everyone present could.

She noted how easily Fayün became Unveiled. It was as if it *wanted* to drift into the human world, and that felt unusual to her. Pomella would have to be careful not to Unveil too much, lest it rush in.

"It occurred to me," she went on, "that our island knows of another tyke that encountered the fay. You cannot have lived on Moth and not know the story of his mhathir, whose sad tale has been passed down for centuries, whispered or sung beside every hearth, and in every inn on our island. It tells how she lost her son, then searched the farthest corners of our land, before traveling into the silver realm to find him. This"—Pomella waited to build tension—"is *our* story. Our blood, our heritage. *This* is the story of our beautiful, our terrible, our mighty Saint Brigid."

Without missing a beat, Berrit launched into the familiar opening notes to the *Toweren*. Eager applause sounded, but was quickly shushed by other patrons as Pomella began.

> *"Come follow me*
> *On memory free*
> *Of Brigid old*
> *And tales long told*
> *Of abandoned hearth*
> *And tiresome trails*
> *In soaring Tower*
> *Her child pales*
> *Caught by death's dark power"*

As she sang, she stirred the Myst, Unveiling silvery apparitions that danced in the air above the crowd and depicted the story she told. She sang and showed Brigid desperately looking for her stolen child, how she went to the lagharts and convinced them to help her. The silvery illusions shifted to form the likeness of Lor Gez, the Hundred-Eyed, All-Seeing tyrant, who challenged Brigid to a duel and fell to her despite his dishonesty but still awarded her Dauntless. The nature of the prize changed from barony to barony, with some versions of the tale claiming it was a sword, others a bow, and a handful claiming it was her Mystic staff. Pomella had grown up hearing the mighty artifact was a sword, so her swirling play above the common room had Brigid spinning and cutting down jealous kings and the all-powerful Corenach until at last she came to the dwelling of the Nameless Saint, and into the final stanzas of the tale.

Not a sound could be heard anywhere in the Rolling Forge as everyone from the merchant-scholars to the Unclaimed—and even the mice—leaned forward to hear. Emotion welled in Pomella's heart, but she keep her voice steady, trying not to let her own song overwhelm her.

> *"Come die with me*
> *Upon the fire tree*
> *Broken and beat*
> *But far from defeat*
> *Of master and scale*
> *And wounds that will not bind*
> *From a window leap*
> *Desperate to sleep*
> *His memory forever will she keep"*

Pomella let the silence linger as she readied herself for the end. She extinguished the swirling lights and smoke to depict a lonely Brigid huddled alone in a prison, where some claim she died, and from which others claimed she escaped and spent her final days in hiding.

Berrit gave Pomella a soft look as he continued to play his pipe, leading her to the final stanza.

> *"Come fall with me*
> *My Brigid free*
> *Her heart now cold*
> *And all foretold*

Of accomplished quest
And purpose begotten
A scorned master crossed
Mother and child forgotten
In death's dark Tower, lost"

Pomella lingered on the final word, and when she finished she finally let a tear drip down her cheek. The tragic song moved her, of course, but even more moving was how at this moment a gathering of people from nearly every caste sat in rapt attention, not thinking about how they compared to the person beside them, and not caring about anything except a song that spoke to them all. *This* was her purpose, as a Mystic. To unite, and bring people together.

Berrit sounded the song's final flourish, and the crowd erupted into applause.

FOUR

THE THORNWOOD

Eleven Years Before Crow Tallin

A blazing summer sun baked the rocks that Shevia and her older brothers scrambled over. Shevia furrowed her brows in concentration as she reached up and climbed the steep bank. Sweat made her silk dress cling to her skin. It tickled her, but she ignored it. She was determined to prove to Tevon that she could make it by herself, and she was not going to let a sticky dress stop her. Her friend had told her that Tevon and her other brothers would like her more if she kept up with them.

Above her on the slope, her triplet brothers scrambled arm over arm toward the top, each trying to reach the summit first.

The slope was the only accessible route to the top of the ledge, which would give them a wider view of their family's estate. Tevon arrived first, as usual, but only half a hand ahead of Typhos. Tibron was three full hands behind them, but only because he kept stopping to check on her. Shevia was pretty sure that if he wanted to he could have beaten his brothers.

Seeing Tevon and Typhos at the top, Tibron glanced down at her. Sweat plastered his dark hair to his forehead. "Are you well, Shay-Shay?"

Shevia nodded and kept climbing. It wasn't that difficult except for the ridiculous dress. Her gangly-long legs kept getting tangled in it. Two years ago, when she was seven, she had asked her mother how long it would be until she grew to be as tall as the estate guards. Mother's cold glare had rained over her from the other side of her embroidery. "Our family is not known for our height, Shevia," she said. Her fingers punched the embroidery needle through the lace. "You should not desire to grow tall. Long legs and brute muscle are commoner traits. They need that strength to complete their physical labors. The Minams are merchant-scholars. Our superior lineage and intellect set us apart."

Shevia was not sure how the Minam family lineage would help her climb the slope in this dress. Besides, Shevia couldn't help that she'd been cursed with long, skinny legs.

Tibron hesitated only a moment before joining his brothers. Shevia climbed after him, and finally accepted his hand to reach the top. She dusted herself off.

"Stay low," Tevon said in his usual commanding tone.

Shevia dropped to her belly. She wanted to ask why they had

come. Her brothers had not invited her. Just minutes ago she had been practicing her painting in the garden when she saw them storming out of the main house and running toward the estate entrance. Something exciting must have been happening and Shevia was not about to miss it. Tevon had protested after she caught up with them, but Tibron convinced him to let her come.

"There," Typhos said, pointing. It was the first time Shevia had heard him speak all day. His eyes were focused on the road below on the far side of the ledge, down the opposite slope they had climbed. Typhos was the middle triplet, quiet, and the one who always focused most diligently on the task at hand.

The three brothers leaned lower to the ground, staring like hawks with their dark eyes.

The rattle of a carriage rolled toward them. Moments later, it came into view, emerging from a bamboo grove farther up the road. Its bright lacquer screamed with bold colors. Six armored riders trotted beside it.

"The Obais," Tevon said. "You were right, Tibron."

Shevia's eyes widened. The Obais were the most powerful merchant family in Qin. Recently, she had overheard Unmuth, the captain of her father's caravan guard, say that they even had more influence than some of the noble houses. They were even said to have a Mystic living in their household to tutor the children. But not in the ways of the Myst, of course.

"Five warriors, plus a laghart," Tibron said.

"A laghart!" Shevia said, a smile bursting on her face. She craned her neck to try to glimpse the lizard-creature, or perhaps the Mystic or the mighty merchant-lord himself. "What are they doing here?"

The slap came fast and hard. Tevon hardly looked at her as he retracted his hand. "Hush, girl. Your noise bothers me and will carry down to them."

Shevia covered her slap mark with her hand. Tevon would one day inherit the Minam business and therefore must always be treated with the greatest respect. Tears trembled at the corners of her eyes, but she held them. Tears were weakness, as Mother said. She refused to look at Tibron, but she knew he looked at her with concern. Tibron was weak, too.

"They are guests of Father and Mother," Tevon said, watching the procession. Shevia noted his voice was louder than hers had been. But as he was the eldest of the triplets, his wisdom was greater than any of theirs.

"Father is expecting us," Tibron said. Nothing else had to be said. As a single mind, the brothers slid down the slope. Shevia followed, running to the orchard as fast as her legs could manage. It was the long way back to the house, but the only way to get there without being seen by the Obais from the road cutting through the estate.

As they approached the rear of the house, Tibron looked back over his shoulder and slowed for Shevia to catch up. "Are you well?"

"Yes," Shevia said. "Stop asking."

"I need to find Father. Go to your room and put on a clean dress in case Mother summons you."

Shevia nodded and brushed past him. He caught her by the shoulder, then lifted her chin and turned it so he could see where Tevon had slapped her.

"Tell Cilla to put ointment on it."

Shevia shrugged him off and strode toward the house. Why

couldn't Tibron see that he had insulted her further by reminding her of her failure? She yanked the door open to the back foyer and ran into her mother.

"In Mountain's eye, where have you been?" Mother said, looming over her. She was as thin as bamboo, with high cheekbones that Shevia had been told she would be fortunate to one day inherit.

Shevia lowered her eyes. "I climbed the slope with—"

"Your dress is torn. The Obai family is here for the evening meal. I do not want you seen. Go to your room and do not come out. I shall punish you later. Two strikes."

"Yes, Mother. Thank you for correcting me." Shevia thought of a horrible curse word she had once heard Cilla use, and was tempted to use it to berate herself.

Mother lifted Shevia's chin, just like Tibron had done earlier. But unlike his touch, her hand was cold and hard. Shevia felt as though she were being examined like a gemstone under the scrutiny of one of her father's collectors.

"Make that three strikes. You blemished your face."

"Thank you, Mother. I am sorry."

"Go. Do not further ruin your face with tears."

"Yes, Mother."

Shevia ruined her face with tears.

She lay on her bed, sobbing into her pillow, hoping her noise would not invade anybody's ears. With each shuddering breath, she further marred her face, causing herself to feel worse and cry more. What a weak and stupid child she was. She itched to claw at her arms and let her stupidity flow out.

Across her room on the dresser, beside her hairbrush and half-finished painting of a horse, sat her glass statue of Sitting Mother. The holy woman stared at her with compassionate eyes. Shevia pulled a pillow over her head to hide from them.

A knock sounded at the door. Shevia froze. The knock came again.

"Shay-Shay?" said a soft voice.

Cilla.

"May I come in?" the House Maintainer asked.

Shevia peeked at her white-painted door. She wiped her puffy eyes, slipped off her bed, and moved toward it.

But her hand faltered at the door handle. She was not a baby anymore. Cilla had always cared for her, and comforted her during hard times. The House Maintainer would want to hug Shevia and help her pick out a fresh dress. She didn't need that. She needed somebody who understood her and would tell her how to do better.

She needed her friend.

"Shay-Shay? I heard you moving. May I come in?"

"No!" Shevia yelled, surprised at her noise. "Go away! I forbid you from entering."

"I just want to help."

"You can't! Go away!"

"Shay-Shay, I—"

"Do not call me that!" Shevia screamed. "I forbid you from calling me that ever again! Leave or I will have Unmuth beat you!" She doubted she could convince the captain to flail the

House Maintainer, but she was probably within her right to at least try.

Only silence came from the other side of the door. Moments later, Cilla's clothing rustled as she walked away. A sudden urge to rush out and grab Cilla before she left came over Shevia. But she forced herself to be strong, and pulled her hand back from the painted-white door. She turned her back to it. Sitting Mother still gazed at her with an infinitely patient expression on her face.

"Stop," she grumbled at the statue.

On the opposite wall, a large window looked out to the western side of the estate. Shevia approached and looked out. The sun lowered toward the horizon, dimming her mother's garden—a bewildering maze of hedges, carefully pruned trees, and rosebushes—which lay just outside the window. An ivy-covered stone wall encircled the garden.

Beyond the garden wall was where her friend lived.

Brushing the last of her tears away, Shevia threw open the door to her wardrobe and pulled out a clean dress. This time, she chose a sturdier one. The window latch flipped open with the smooth ease of much use. Her feet found familiar holds as she climbed down the vine trellis, which was positioned just outside. She hardly had to think about this climb anymore.

Shevia drifted through the garden, using the dimming light and tall shrubs to hide from anybody who might be looking. She ducked low, cursing her height again. A sweet rose fragrance filled the air, familiar and comforting. She was used to the aroma as it drifted through her window at night on warm evenings where she left her window open.

When Shevia reached the stone wall at the far end of the

garden, she slipped behind a large potted fig tree and found the little divot, sized just right for her foot. She lumbered up the side of the wall, following the familiar grips and footholds, and rolled across the top on her belly. She fell to her feet on the other side, lithe as a kitten.

Shevia dusted herself off. The wall hadn't always been her method of getting out of the garden. Two seasons past, she and Cilla had discovered rabbits eating the leafy vegetables they had planted. Shevia had tracked the rabbits to a little hole tunneling under the wall, with mounds of fresh soil piled up on either side. She recalled the fresh scent of the season's rose blossoms mixing with the damp dirt.

It smelled to Shevia like freedom.

She convinced herself she had just gone to look for the rabbits. What she had found was something entirely different.

Shaking off the memory, Shevia hurried down the hill that sloped away from the garden and her parents' walled estate. She ran on her tiptoes, deftly finding the flat rocks that jutted out of the hillside's wild grass like islands in a wavy sea. She counted her leaps and noted each familiar landmark.

The hills rolled beneath her feet, taking her down to a narrow valley filled with thornbushes and huge boulders. She was well past the home of whatever critter had been eating her vegetables, but she did not care. There was no wind, and no watchful eyes other than the setting sun.

The thornbushes grew denser as Shevia descended toward the bottom of the valley. At last she found the gap in the dense wall of thorns. She slipped in, carefully avoiding the sharp branches. The world darkened as the thorny shadows consumed her. Even with her height, the bushes towered over her, so it was like walking in an eerie forest. A few times, Shevia had pretended she was Saint Brigid, bravely marching through the Mystwood on the faraway island of Moth. Perhaps next time she came, she would bring a fallen branch and have it be her staff, Dauntless.

The ground continued to descend. Shevia tiptoed along the path, ducking low and squeezing between branches. It was easier going than the first few times she had come. After she had been punished for ruining several dresses, Shevia had taken the time to carefully break off the worst obstacles. Now, if she was careful, she could come to the heart of her little Thornwood without any rips or smudges on her outfit.

At last she approached the heart of the valley. The thornbushes grew high above her head, creating a vaulted ceiling that reminded her of a smaller version of her family's banquet hall. Stepping farther in, she imagined this was Kelt Apar, and her friend, the High Mystic.

A branch cracked behind her and she heard a familiar voice curse. Shevia whirled around and saw Tibron shaking his arm, trying to unhook his long-sleeved shirt from a thorn. A flash of panic rushed into her. Her first thought burst from her mouth before she could stop it: "Don't tell Mother or Father!"

Tibron yanked his arm free and glared at her. "Ancestors, Shevia! What are you doing here?"

"What are *you* doing here?" she demanded.

"You weren't in your room. I looked out the window and saw you climbing the garden wall. Mother's going to punish you!"

"Not if you don't tell her! Please, Tibron, please say you will not!"

"How did you you find this place?" he asked. "It looks dangerous."

Shevia watched him marvel at the vaulting ceiling of thorns. It seemed to loom over him as a warning. The Thornwood belonged to her friend, and Tibron was not welcome.

"My friend lives here," she said before she could stop herself. "She says I'm welcome anytime. She gets lonely, so I come to visit." Shevia always thought of her friend as a "her," although she wasn't sure why.

Tibron's hand drifted to his belt where she saw he wore the dagger Father had given him last summer. His eyes darted around, clearly afraid something would jump out and attack them. She put her hand on his arm to reassure him.

"Come on. I will introduce you." She took his hand.

She found the pile of rocks where they always were. They rose in a waist-high mound. Beneath them, a wide hole descended into the ground. Tibron's eyes widened.

"Is that a pit? How did it get here?"

Shevia shrugged. She sat at the edge and dropped down, feet-first. She fell a distance not much greater than her own height. She was in a tiny cave as wide as her outstretched arms. A large crack gaped on the ground between her feet.

Tibron slipped into the pit and crouched down to his heels, looking around. "I don't like this, Shay-Shay."

Lowering herself carefully, Shevia bent low over the gap until her face hovered just inches above it. Once, she'd put her arm down the crack to try to feel the bottom. She hadn't found one.

"Hello, friend," she whispered into the crack.

The warm scent of her friend's breath wafted over her. She breathed it in, enjoying the sour mixture of burned sandalwood and holly. She smiled, and felt her mind relax.

"Shevia," said Tibron, his voice more tense than before. "What's that smoke? Back away."

More smoke rose from the vent, and Shevia gladly breathed it in. Her eyes rolled back in her head, and a strange, happy feeling tingled across her body. She sat up and looked at Tibron. Colors swirled around him, along with a silvery mist. She saw him age as he sat there, looking at her with concern. His face filled out, then grew wrinkles. Gray hair spread through his black, and a matching beard grew upon his face. She felt sadness come from him, followed by a mournful and deep love.

"Shevia," he said. "Come away from—"

"My friend says you're the best of my brothers," she said. "You should try more. You let Tevon control you too much."

Tibron's eyes narrowed. "We're going home." He grabbed her wrist, but without thinking Shevia rolled it and shoved his arm away with her free hand. Tibron snatched his bruised wrist away, shocked by her quickness and strength. The smoke from the vent filled the little cave now, silvery and bright. It filled Shevia's lungs, and her mind. Her friend's voice filled her. She didn't speak words that Shevia could hear, but her mind was suddenly filled with her comforting presence, and with that came understanding.

As the smoke filled her lungs further, the cave melted away. There had never been this much before. A small trickle in the past, enough to make her dizzy and hear her friend, but not much beyond that. Now, as her mind fuzzed, she floated above her little Thornwood, looking down on it as a bird might. To the east her parents' house towered on top of the hill. The skies raged in confusion as the sun and moon spun around, each dancing and competing to shine longer than the other. Lightning flashed, and storms raged for mere seconds before the cruel sun blasted them away.

She breathed in again, and rushed to her parents' home. In the ballroom she saw a feast laid out on a table. Her friend nudged her, whispering urgently to her. Shevia gasped and her whole body shook. She wanted to scream but couldn't. Her father's face lay on his dinner plate, his mouth opening and closing like a caught fish trying to breathe. He convulsed as inky green lines clawed up the sides of his neck and across the backs of his hands. Mother lay nearby on the floor, also gasping for air.

Shevia's body shook once more, and suddenly she saw Tibron, holding her by the shoulders. The cave coalesced back around her.

"Shevia!" Tibron screamed.

"Tibron," she managed.

"What happened? Your eyes turned . . . I-I cannot describe it. What is this smoke? What were you thinking in coming here?"

"Tibron, listen to me."

Her brother began climbing up through the hole above, pulling her close to his body as if afraid she would slip away. "I should never have let you go in. We won't tell Mother or Father of this, but I will make sure they know to bury this cave."

"Tibron!" Shevia screamed, and slapped him, hard. He was bigger than her, and already thick and strong for his age. But her slap snapped his head around, dazing his eyes. He stared at her, gaping.

"We have to warn Mother and Father," she said, strangely calm. "The Obais are going to murder them."

Mustering her courage, Shevia burst into the dining hall, Tibron behind her. She had expected him to argue with her the whole way back to the estate, but he'd been strangely subdued. Whatever it was, she could not worry about him right now.

A chandelier hung from the high ceiling, casting lights across the long table. Cilla's staff had set out the family's best feastware. One of her parents' house servants—Miqo, a girl just a few years older than Shevia—moved between the Obais, pouring drinks. Unmuth, tall and imposing even in his old age, stood guard with his hands behind his back.

Shevia's mother spied her immediately, her eyes narrowing until they were as sharp as daggers. Moments later, the rest of the hall's occupants looked up. A pang of fear raced through Shevia. So many powerful adults were here! Her gaze was drawn, as if pulled by a strange force, to a figure standing against the distant wall, drowned in the fading light of the early-evening sun. He loomed from the corner in black robes trimmed with gold, and held a wooden staff half again his height. Gold studs gleamed in both his ears, matching other pieces of jewelry that surely made Shevia's mother twitch with envy.

A Mystic.

Beside him, equally as dazzling and strange, stood a lizard-like creature in padded armor. The laghart! Its slitted eyes pierced her, and its tongue flicked out, whipping the air once, twice, before vanishing back into its scaly face.

Shevia heard her father clear his throat. She tore her attention away from the intriguing guests and looked at him. "Ah, Shevia, my little swan," he said, "I missed you today."

Shevia knew her mother would be glaring at her still, so she avoided looking at her. Four richly dressed men sat at the table. The oldest and fattest was glaring at her from behind a thick beard. He must be the one in charge.

"I believe your little swan was asked to remain in her room," Mother said in a cool voice. "She ruined one of her dresses earlier today, and it appears she did so again."

Shevia looked down at her dress and saw that, indeed, her effort to flee the Thornwood had caused her to catch her dress and, in a few cases, even draw blood.

"Father," she began.

"Your daughter is quite precocious, Chovin," the old, fat Obai man said. His cheeks wiggled as he spoke, but the amusement in his voice didn't reach his eyes.

"Father, I need to talk to you. It is about—"

"Whatever you need to tell him can wait," Mother interrupted. Her tone was dangerous now, and normally Shevia would have realized she had gone too far. "And you, Tibron. I expect more from you. I am disappointed."

Father waved a dismissive hand. "It's fine, Ivushen," he said to Mother. "What is it you want to tell me, Shevia? Make it quick. Master Obai and I have business to settle this evening."

"He is going to kill you."

Mother's gasp was the only sound before silence gripped

the dining hall. A tense moment passed; then Father laughed, nervously looking at his guest and then giving his daughter a hard stare. "You've had your fun," he said. "Now apologize to our guest, and go back to your room. We'll speak of this later."

"Children and their silly games," Obai said with a chuckle.

Shevia's cheeks burned. "Keep your noise in your fat face!" she snapped.

Mother burst to her feet, eyes aflame with rage. "Unmuth, take this child out of this hall!" The punishment would be severe, perhaps worse than anything Shevia had ever received.

She didn't care.

Matching eyes with the old, fat man, Shevia found a new strength she'd never felt before. It came from knowing that she was right. That, no matter how much Mother whipped her later, there was a certainty that she knew beyond all doubt: if she didn't stop him now, Master Obai would kill her whole family before the night was done.

Unmuth closed in on her.

"I saw it," Shevia said, surprised at how calm and grown-up her voice sounded. She could feel her friend's presence, not beside her exactly, but back in the Thornwood, watching, encouraging her. "They poisoned the wine. It's already in your cup, Father. And yours, Mother. They came here to kill you."

"Careful, girl," Obai said to her, his tone dangerous. "I'll forgive your foolish youth, but you tread on dangerous territory."

Unmuth reached for her, but Tibron stepped in and blocked his path. "I'm sorry, Unmuth," he said. "My parents need to hear this." It was the first time her brother had spoken since she'd told him of her friend's revelation. Did he really believe her?

Her mother was beyond words. Her stony face had turned purple with rage.

Shevia snatched up her father's wine goblet and shoved it in Obai's face. "Drink it. Prove me a liar."

Shevia's father stood up. His loving exterior melted away. "Take her, Unmuth! Tibron, stand down or you'll share your sister's punishment."

Little beads of sweat formed at Obai's hairline. His eyes darted, just briefly, to the corner where his Mystic and the laghart warrior stood.

"I will not be part of this ridiculous game! Chovin, if your children are this grotesque, then I daresay I am inclined to believe they learned it from you."

"Drink the wine, Lord Obai," Tibron said.

Obai slammed the table with his fist and hefted himself from his chair. "I will do no such thing! You go too far! Let's go, Ahg-Mein! Xather! Get the carriage."

Shevia straightened her spine. "My friend says you never intended to sell the Darkmire Mines to Father. That once you poisoned him, you would blackmail Duke Yinto in order to claim Father's resources. My friend says you are a coward. And she says you will not survive this night."

Obai lifted his arm to backhand her, but Unmuth leaped forward and caught it.

"You have destroyed your family, brat!" Obai spit.

Why did nobody believe her, ever? Was it because she was young? She would prove to them that she was not just a silly little girl.

The merchant-lord's eyes bulged as Shevia tipped her father's wineglass to her lips and drank a heavy sip. The wine tasted disgusting, but she forced herself to swallow. Why did adults drink this? It tasted like—

Her stomach clenched and she gasped, dropping the glass.

Her mother screamed.

It felt as though a creature with sharp claws tore at Shevia's stomach. Her throat clenched, denying her air. She reached to her neck, and saw deep green lines inking their way across the backs of her hands, creeping like vines toward her fingers.

Around her, the hall erupted into chaos. She sensed people fighting, and swords flashing. She couldn't follow any of it, but she sensed Tibron standing above her, wielding his dagger protectively.

Shevia wished she could be in the cave, in the heart of the Thornwood, with her friend who spoke to her, and helped her see things nobody else could see. As her vision faded, Shevia saw Obai's Mystic watching her calmly. He did not move to help her, nor did he seem concerned with the fighting erupting around him. He cocked his head sideways, as if observing a bird with a broken wing.

Shevia struggled for breath, but she was not afraid. Her friend had promised she would live past today. This, no matter how scary, was just the beginning of their friendship.

FIVE

LAGNARASTE

Pomella and her horse crested the low-rising hill outside of Oakspring. She tugged Quercus' reins, pulling him to a halt. The gelding shook his mane, clearly glad to be resting. Sweat rolled down Pomella's forehead and the back of her neck.

She hadn't planned to return to her old home, but the night of her visit to the Rolling Forge she'd received a message in the form of a flamebird.

In the deep hours of the night, she'd awoken to an urgent *pressure* upon her consciousness, similar to the feeling of being watched by an unknown observer. At first she'd tried to dismiss the warning, but the sensation grew until she'd slipped out of bed, trying carefully not to disturb Berrit, and gone to the shuttered window. Within moments beams of light shone through the window slats, visible only to her Mystic eyes. She threw open the shutters and a line of fiery smoke blazed into the room.

Not unlike her hummingbirds, the flamebird was larger, about the size of a canary, but formed entirely from living silver flame. Pomella had known immediately who sent it. Only Vivianna could conjure such a fay creature and harness it as a messenger.

Alighting onto her palm, the flamebird had chirped once, twice, then released Vivianna's voice, which filled Pomella's mind.

Pomella, I hope you are well. Word reached Kelt Apar this evening that there's trouble in the village of Oakspring. Somebody there is seeing fay creatures. Normally, I would look into it, but with Crow Tallin approaching, Mistress Yarina needs me here to prepare for the arrival of the High Mystics. She asks you to handle this issue immediately. Grandmaster gave no objection. May the wind and Myst go with you.

Its task complete, the flamebird had leaped from Pomella's hand and puffed back into Fayün, leaving her to fret over her return home.

Seven years had passed since she'd left home, and other than a single letter to her fathir to let him know she'd become a Mystic apprentice, she'd communicated in no way with anybody from her old life.

A storm of fears churned in her stomach. The last time she'd seen her fathir, he'd been enraged. He'd called her stupid, worthless. If he'd had his way, she would've never left home, and quite possibly never sung again. She remembered that night she'd left. To illustrate how foolish she was for wanting to become a Mystic's apprentice, her fathir had told the story of how when he was a young man he'd found a wandering Mystic and begged him to let him become his apprentice. The Mystic responded by threatening, and possibly beating, her fathir. Pomella had never understood how any Mystic could do such a thing. It seemed to go against all the lessons she'd been taught.

Noting the tension in her body, Pomella took a deep breath and brought focus to herself. She sensed the Myst stirring around her. *True knowledge of the Myst comes through letting go,* her master Lal sometimes said. *And letting go hurts.*

She dismounted, nearly twisting her ankle in the stirrup. Quercus turned to look back at her with irritating patience.

"Don't look at me like that," Pomella grumbled to the horse. She'd grown more accustomed to riding over the years, but it still didn't come to her as easily as it did to Vivianna. Likewise, the gelding had miraculously learned to be tolerant of her clumsy habits.

Pomella lifted her hair off the back of her neck, hoping to catch a cool breeze. A fluttering feeling of dread rippled through her as she gazed down on her old village. The little farm community sat nestled not far from the wide and swiftly flowing Creekwaters, which drifted out of the Mystwood and the towering slopes of MagBreckan. A cluster of homes encircled what she recognized as their village green, although its grass had browned for the summer. Farther out, a loose ring of dwellings marked the only real border Oakspring could claim. The top of Ilise AnCutler's waterwheel peaked above the tree line near the Creekwaters, and Pomella could hear the slow plodding sound as the wheel dipped and lifted from the current.

It was definitely Oakspring. But beyond the familiar markers, it didn't look like *home* anymore. Several new houses stood where none had been before. Hinder AnMere's farm in the northeast appeared divided now, partitioned evenly by a low stone fence. Perhaps he'd died and there'd been an inheritance dispute? More sheep dotted the hillside than Pomella remembered, but no sounds came from the smithy.

She thought of Sim, and as always, a rainstorm of emotions surged through her as she recalled his familiar face. Oakspring couldn't be home without him. It seemed like it had been the life of the stars since they'd strolled together across these very hills, mingling hands and shy glances before growing comfortable enough to share their thoughts and hopes. Nobody had known her as well as Sim had. She'd forever appreciate how he'd followed her when she went to the apprentice Trials. It's possible she wouldn't have survived those nightmarish few days if he hadn't been there to inspire her.

Now he was gone, far away on the Continent. She hadn't heard from him since her apprentice Trials. Her last memories of him were the few stolen kisses they'd shared the morning he left, just days after Grandmaster had taken her as his apprentice. It had been for the best, she supposed. Had he stayed, he would've been a distraction.

Not that it had made it any easier to lose him.

Pomella adjusted her cloak and set thoughts of Sim aside. She allowed her gaze to wander toward her fathir's house. Usually, on a day like this, he'd be out working on barrels, or perhaps a piece of furniture. But an eerie sense of emptiness floated around the distant house. The windows were shuttered tight. More disturbingly, her once vibrant garden that surrounded the house was now nothing more than a trampled patch of brown weeds.

Best to get through this as quickly as possible. Fumbling with the straps on her horse's saddle, Pomella removed her staff. "Let's go, Quercus. I want to walk the rest of the way."

Familiar scents danced around Pomella, bringing memory forth. The acrid smell from the tannery made her think of the time she and Bethy had snuck there in order to gobble honey pies. Goodness AnCutler's farms, believed to be the oldest in Oakspring, still had the stench of countless generations of cows. Familiar as they were, Pomella wrinkled her nose.

Word of her arrival caught fast, so by the time she'd walked across the few hills and approached the village a crowd of familiar folk had gathered to greet her. Pomella hadn't expected to receive much in way of greeting. But here stood Goodness AnCutler and her husband, staring in wonder besides the Watcherman, Goodman AnGent, who patted his sweaty bald head with a handkerchief. Old Hinder AnMere glared at her through his one good eye. A few tykes—far too young to remember Pomella—hid behind their mhathir's skirts.

Pomella's mind raced as to what she should say, but a familiar voice called out first. "Oh sweet Brigid, Pomella!" Bethy AnClure burst through the line of people and threw her arms around Pomella's neck. The gathered crowd laughed and applauded.

Bethy clung to Pomella's neck, squealing high-pitched sounds of joy. Pomella hugged her back, unable to keep herself from laughing as well.

"It's been so long. I've missed you," Bethy said.

They pulled apart and Pomella studied her. Bethy's red hair had grayed a bit, even at her young age. She'd cut it even shorter than she'd previously had it, as most women of Oakspring eventually did. Pomella remembered coveting her friend's hair color when they had been children. Glancing down, Pomella immediately saw her friend was swollen with pregnancy. "Bethy! You have a wee tyke on the way!"

"Aye," Bethy said with an amused eye roll. "This'll be my fourth. With my luck, the Saints'll see fit to give me another boy. They haven't spared me yet."

"Four!" Pomella said, eyes popping. "You've been blessed! I can't wait to meet them. Who's the lucky papa?"

Bethy leaned forward conspiratorially, and for a moment she looked seven years younger, like Pomella remembered. "Danny AnStipe."

Pomella gasped. "Danny! Oh, Bethy, you married up!" she teased.

Bethy's girl-like smile slipped just a bit, but she continued, obviously trying to keep a positive tone. "I—I suppose I did. But, just so you know, I go by 'Bethilla' now."

Pomella realized, too late, the awkwardness of her comment. As young girls, she and Bethy had always joked about how they aspired to marry somebody from a higher caste. They would tease each other that the most handsome boys were always "a class above" and that if they married one of them they'd be marrying up. Considering Pomella's new position in the society, the joke didn't float as well anymore.

"Bethilla. Yes. Of course," Pomella said.

Watcherman AnGent cleared his throat. "Lady Pomella, may we take your cloak and horse?"

"You're too kind, Watcherman," Pomella replied. "But please. Call me Pomella. And this is Quercus. I'd appreciate it if he could have some fresh water and hay."

"Of course, Lad—uh, Pomella," said the Watcherman. He bowed awkwardly and snapped his fingers toward a gaggle of young boys who lurked near one of the nearby houses. His

threatening look summoned them in an instant. Before the be-
wildered boys could stare any longer at Pomella, the Watcherman gave them tasks: to fetch hay, lead Quercus, prepare a stall,
and brush the gelding down.

"Pomella?" came a voice behind her.

Pomella turned to see the familiar warm face of Cana An-
Clure, Bethy and Sim's mhathir. Her husband, Lathwin, stood
just behind her, resting one of his meaty hands gently on his
wife's shoulder. Lathwin had grown a thick beard since Pomella
had last seen him.

"Dear girl," Goodness AnClure said, her lined face shining
with affection. "'Tis grand to see you. We've missed you and
prayed for your health. You look wondrous. Radiant, even." She
dropped her gaze and wrung her hands. "Lathwin and I were
just wondering if—" She opened her mouth to say more, but a
sudden wave of emotion caught her.

Goodman AnClure patted his wife's shoulder. "We told
ourselves we'd wait awhile to ask," he said to Pomella. "But seeing you . . . it's too much. Could you . . . Maybe, perhaps, you
could tell us about . . ."

"Sim?" Pomella finished. Saying his name out loud was like
being bitten by a stinger-fish. She suddenly realized she hadn't
spoken his name in years. And she realized, too, that Cana
and Lathwin had now lost two sons in their lifetime. First they
lost Dane to the plague when Pomella was not much older than
a tyke. Then they'd lost Sim, who, as far as Pomella knew, had
run away with even less warning than she had and clearly never
returned home. Now they only had Bethy and her children.

"I last saw him seven years ago," Pomella said, her face

softening, "shortly after I was taken as an apprentice. He went with a friend to the Continent, to become a ranger. I've not seen or heard from him since."

Cana buried her face into her hands and burst into tears.

"Thank you," Lathwin managed. "We received only one brief letter. Jus' a handful of words. Sim could read well, but not write."

"'I am well and seeking my future outside Oakspring,'" Cana quoted. "That's all he said. Those words've burned in my heart all these years."

"Nobody could tell us if he was even alive," Lathwin continued. "After he ran off with you, we didn't know whether he'd ever come home."

A lump rose in Pomella's throat. As it always did when her emotions soared, the Myst stirred within her. Pomella gently cupped Cana's face. "He was a hero," she said. "He helped defend Kelt Apar from people with horrible intentions. His bravery won't be forgotten."

As she spoke, she coaxed the Myst to arise and carry a memory from her mind to Cana's. It was a simple memory, but one that hadn't faded over the years. The memory was of Sim, smiling at her one last time as he left Kelt Apar. His shaggy blond hair tumbled down his forehead, framing his deep blue eyes. He wore a simple shirt, with a leather vest over it, along with brown pants and ankle-high traveling boots. He had a small bundle of clothes slung over his back, along with a sheathed sword—the same one his fathir had forged and Sim had left home with.

It was the last time Pomella had seen Sim. She drifted the memory toward Cana on the wings of the Myst. As it settled into Cana's mind, her eyes lit up with surprise. Her expression took on a distant look, as if the world around her had just melted away.

"Keep that safe," Pomella said. "It's yours now."

Cana blinked back tears, and slowly brought Pomella into a hug. "Tell me he'll return," she whispered into Pomella's shoulder.

"He'll come back to us," Pomella assured her.

Us.

She hadn't expected to say it that way.

Pomella caught Bethy's eye. A terrible fear gripped her chest, but she had to know. "Where's my fathir? And my brother?"

Bethy's smile faded.

Wild marigolds and lilies grew upon his grave.

Staring at those yellow flowers, devoid of other emotions, Pomella recalled the first time she'd met with the High Mystic in the central tower of Kelt Apar. There'd been marigolds in a vase atop the table that day. Strange, the memories that arose at unexpected times.

She thumbed the familiar texture of her staff, letting the wind catch her cloak and hair. Only Bethy stood with her, along the slope of Reyman's Hey, the hill where the villagers of Oakspring traditionally buried their dead. Pomella's mhathir was there, too, right beside her fathir.

"I-I'm sorry for your loss, Pomella," Bethy said. "You must be devastated."

Sadness swam within her, but Pomella let it pass through

her and beyond, not allowing it to take hold or linger where it would gnaw and do damage. "I'm a Mystic. To us, death is just another stage of life. It is a gateway to a deeper experience of the Myst."

She said the words, and betrayed no outward emotion. But she wondered if she honestly meant them. Shouldn't there be more to how she felt? She wondered how Bethy saw her, standing at her fathir's grave, having just learned of his death. No tears ran down her cheeks. She wasn't clutching her staff with a white-knuckled grip. She felt nothing. Not even the numb feeling that comes from shock or sadness. If anything, Pomella felt *balanced*.

"Why didn't anybody tell me?" Pomella asked.

Bethy bit her lip. "We didn't know how to get ahold of you. And I . . . some of us . . . weren't even sure you would want to know. You have to understand, Pomella. Don't you remember? You hated him when you left. He smothered you. In the months and years after you ran away, he only grew more withdrawn. By the time he died, he hardly saw anybody. He didn't even live in your old house anymore. We aren't sure where he spent most of his days. The Watcherman says he'd been . . . dead . . . more than a week when he was found by the Creekwaters."

Pomella understood. It was more than what Bethy explained, though. The villagers of Oakspring were simple people. For all their lives, and the lives of previous generations, the commoners of her village lived in awe and fear of Mystics. By becoming one, Pomella had put herself out of their reach. No matter how much the High Mystic strove to make Kelt Apar freely approachable for all people, most days its paths and guesthouses remained empty. The people of Moth relied on the presence of Mystics but feared their attention.

"What about Gabor?" Pomella asked. Her brother had been only twelve years old when she left for the Trials.

Bethy fidgeted with the lace on her shawl. "He left for Sentry, heedless of the baron's laws, along with the traveling merchants the spring after your fathir was found. Nobody has heard from him since."

Pomella closed her eyes and evened her breathing. It had broken her heart to leave her little brother behind. But she couldn't be responsible for him. He'd still had Fathir, and the AnClures, to look after him. It wasn't like he had been alone when she left.

So she tried to tell herself.

"Your brother became an angry young man," Bethy went on. "He got violent a few times. He refused to work, and picked fights with his friends. Lissybette AnGrove, who was run'n the river with him at the time, came to me last fall saying her flow was late. Said she was 'fraid to tell anybody 'cause she didn't want to marry him. She got her bleed'n a few days later, thank the Saints, but it just shows how people saw your brother."

Pomella sighed. How quickly the simple innocence of childhood was lost. She'd achieved her dreams of becoming a Mystic, but at what cost to others? Did her fathir and brother wilt in the shade while she stole the sun? She realized now why she'd avoided coming home. She'd known that everything would be different and that there wouldn't be anything left for her anymore.

"Thank you, Bethilla," Pomella said, "for everything. I never had a chance to say that to you before. You were the one who gave me the push out the door, all those years ago."

Bethy looked away. "I'm glad one of us managed to get out. Most of the village wanted you to go. Looking back, it was as if we always knew it would be you. You never saw so many Goodnesses weave together a Common Cord that quickly to inspire you." She gestured to Pomella's faded green cloak. "Giving you the cloak was Sim's idea."

"You could leave, too. I'm sure there's—"

Bethy shook her head and scoffed. "Have you really left us that far behind, Pomella? Look around. I'm a commoner, living on somebody else's land, in little more than a thatch hut. I don't know anything about the Myst, I'd be useless as a ranger, and I don't want either. I have children to raise. You made your choices, and I stayed."

"But was it enough for you?" Pomella asked.

"Yah, I guess it has to be."

They stood beside each other, not making eye contact. The wind shivered across the marigolds and lilies.

"I'm very tired from my travels," Pomella said, her voice even. "I'd like to rest. But before I retire, tell me, who petitioned the High Mystic for help?"

"I did," Bethy said. Pomella noted the iron in her voice. "It's my boy Dav. He caught something."

Pomella frowned. Vivianna's flamebird had mentioned a problem with the fay. "Caught what?"

Bethy shook her head. "I think it's one of those silver animals you used to go on about."

A chill ran through Pomella. She thought of Norana and the fay cat she'd banished. "Can you see this creature? Can others?"

"Yah. Everyone can. We're all scared of it. But Dav . . . he's been acting different lately. Can you help him?"

Pomella suppressed a wave of fear. She'd never heard of a fay being trapped by someone. She didn't think that was even possible, even for a Mystic.

"I'll do my best. Take me to him."

The warm smell of fresh bread wafted around Pomella as she stepped into Bethy's home. Bethy bustled ahead, sweeping wooden toys out of the entryway with an exasperated sigh. The house was small, like all the others in Oakspring. Hand-placed stones encircled the foundation, with oak beams rising to support wooden shingles.

Four faces turned to stare at Pomella as she entered. The first was familiar to her. Danny AnStipe had hardly changed in seven years. His face was still boyishly handsome. He brightened into a smile.

"Pomella, welcome!" he said, coming forward and bowing. Two of his children cowered behind his legs, while the smallest one fussed to be held.

Pomella opened her mouth to return the greeting, but a little boy crashed into her leg and hugged it. "Oh, hello, warrum," she said. She patted the child's back awkwardly.

"Engle!" Bethy scolded. "Treat Mistress Pomella with respect!"

Pomella didn't bother to hide her smile. She freed her leg and crouched down face-to-face with the boy. He had a mop of his mhathir's red hair, and a scattering of freckles across his nose and under his blue eyes.

"You're Engle?" Pomella said. The boy nodded. "You look like your mhathir. Do you like to explore the forest?"

Engle nodded again, more vigorously. "Dav trapped a monster!"

"Well, is Dav here? Can I talk to him?"

Bethy walked over and roused the tallest boy from behind his fathir's legs. Like Engle, the boy had red hair and freckles, but his eyes seemed distant, as if they weren't focused on anything in the house. He stared in Pomella's direction, but he may as well have been looking through her rather than *at* her. Several holes gaped along his line of teeth.

"This is Dav, our eldest," Bethy said, putting her hands on his shoulders. "Dav, can you tell Mistress Pomella what you found?"

Dav shook his head.

Still crouched on her knees, Pomella shifted so she faced him. "Hi, Dav. I'm Pomella. I'm an old friend to your mhathir."

The boy looked at his feet.

Pomella leaned in and whispered, "Did you know that I'm a Mystic?"

Dav's eyes widened and met hers.

Pomella held up her palm and swirled the Myst above it. A handful of silver leaves, drifting like wind-shaken fog, descended into her palm. Pomella offered up her hand. "Go on; you can touch it."

The leaves were a simple illusion, conjured to offer a soothing sense of peace. Dav reached a hand toward the silvery leaves but snatched it away as his fingers grazed the edge of the fluttering shapes. He buried his face in Bethy's skirts.

Pomella let the leaves fade. "Do you have a secret you want to tell me?"

Dav eyed her from behind the skirt. "Can you talk to animals?" he asked. He had a slight lisp, possibly on account of all his missing teeth.

Pomella smiled. "I might. Do you have a special animal you want to show me?"

Dav looked up at Bethy, who smiled and nodded encouragingly. "Go show her," she said.

"It's over there," Dav said. He pointed past the supper table toward the back wall that contained the family's few dishes and large food chest. It took Pomella a moment to realize he was indicating outside, beyond the wall of the house.

Pomella stood and took Dav's hand. He led her out the back door and down the steps toward a clearing behind the house. About twenty steps into the yard, a gnarly oak rose up out of the ground. At the tree's base a rectangular apple crate was turned upside down, pinning a burlap sack to the ground. The sack wiggled, as if something was caught inside.

Pomella bent closer to the crate, peering as if she could see through the rough fabric. She focused her attention and stretched out her senses as she'd been taught, reaching with her mind and heart toward the contents shifting in the sack. "What have you got here, Dav?"

The Myst swirled and trembled around Pomella. An animal, native to Fayün, lay in that bag, trapped, and probably terrified.

"He's been coming every night," Dav said, "after supper when Mama sends me out to play. He likes when I give him blackberries from our bush."

Pomella motioned for Dav to stand beside Bethy, then lifted the crate aside. The creature in the canvas bag stilled. Pomella mentally readied a defense, then lifted one edge of the bag's opening, and peeked in. "Come out, friend."

The fay generally became agitated when they were trapped within the human world without an anchor to fixate on and help them remain grounded. Some fay, such as Pomella's hummingbirds, or the creatures Vivianna regularly summoned, remained docile and friendly when brought from Fayün. But if they became lost, or somehow trapped, they could turn hostile. Pomella had seen it happen a handful of times, including a time when a pack of wolves had been trapped and subsequently abused by Ohzem, the iron Mystic who'd caused so much trouble during her first journey to Kelt Apar.

The bag shifted, and then a shining, silvery nose poked out. Pomella held out her hand, and quick as a luck'n a fay critter ran onto her palm. The children gasped. Even Bethy made a sound and took a step back. It was a silver pineten, no larger than a squirrel. Pomella stroked the pineten's head with her finger. The poor little thing trembled, seeking the protection Pomella offered.

"I'm surprised you can see her," Pomella said. "It's rare that anybody except Mystics can see the fay."

"I named her Lagnaraste," Dav said.

The name struck Pomella as unusual and oddly specific. She shivered, unable to help herself. "That's a funny name. How'd you think of it?"

Dav shrugged. "She told me."

Pomella pursed her lips. "It seems like you have a natural affinity for the Myst," she said.

"Really?" Dav said, suddenly brightening.

"Now, Pomella," Bethy said, "no need to fill his mind with

blather. Dav likes helping his fathir with the goaties, and told his grandfathir he wants to learn how to forge iron. Didn't you, Dav?"

Dav wilted but nodded. "Yah."

"Things are changing, Bethilla," said Pomella. "At least, I'm trying to change them."

Bethy's look could have seared rock. "Nothing truly changes in Oakspring. Even when it looks different than before."

They held gazes for an extended heartbeat, but Pomella sighed and nodded. "OK. Well, your friend is a little scared, Dav," she said, dropping the subject. Little Lagnaraste scrambled up her arm to her shoulder. "I'll release her, so she can return home and—ouch!"

The pineten bit her shoulder, and Pomella yelped. Bethy also let out a tiny cry of surprise.

Lagnaraste leaped from Pomella's shoulder and ran toward Dav. Pomella summoned the Myst. She could see the subtle bond, as thin and fragile as thread, chaining the fay animal to Dav.

She snapped the Myst toward the thread and extinguished the link between them.

But instead of misting away as Pomella expected, the pineten darted in a new direction, and scampered into the oak tree, not disturbing a single leaf with her passage.

Pomella frowned to herself but quickly masked it with a smile. "There. Everything is fine now, Dav. She'll go home and won't be scared anymore. Just don't set out any more berry traps."

Bethy hurried over to Dav and picked him up. She looked from Pomella to the tree. "Are you sure?"

"Yah," Pomella said. "I doubt you'll see her again."

Somehow, the boy's kindness and his homemade berry trap were enough to link the two of them together. She wasn't sure what would've happened if the pineten had remained chained to Dav over a longer period, but it wouldn't have turned out well. Not all fay creatures adapted well to humans. Pomella couldn't imagine the fits Bethy would have if her eldest son had a fay critter running around her house every day.

"Well, I certainly hope we don't see *it*," Bethy said. "Those creatures have no place in Oakspring. They can stay in the Mystwood if they feel the need to visit."

Pomella's mind raced. The pineten *should* have vanished as soon as the bond was removed. Why were the others still able to see her? Pomella didn't expect the pineten to harm Dav or the rest of Bethy's family, but she didn't understand why the creature didn't return to Fayün.

"Will you be staying for supper?" Bethy said in a tight voice.

Pomella looked into the oak tree, toward the fay creature whose presence she could not see but could still faintly sense. At the mention of dinner, her stomach grumbled. "Actually, I'm sorry, but I need to return to Kelt Apar."

"I'm sorry to hear that," Bethy said, sounding anything but.

"I am, too," Pomella lied. "But I should return home."

Home, to Kelt Apar. Because Oakspring was no longer her place.

SIX

THE COLOR OF BLOOD AND FIRE

Three days later, Pomella drifted in a sky of her own making, letting the gentle tides of Myst carry her like a cloud caught in a gust of wind. She focused only on her breathing, and gently diverted stray thoughts that sought to invade her mind. Somewhere distantly she was aware of her body, sitting cross-legged in the corner of her cabin in Kelt Apar.

Even as the Myst carried her mind through an infinite void, she sought a state where she touched both Fayün and the human world at once. Grandmaster spoke of it sometimes, and required her to sit every morning and evening in meditation, trying to search for it. The Crossroads, he called it, or the Joining, the place where worlds met.

Pomella breathed in, filling her body with not only the

familiar smoky scent of incense and her cabin but also the Myst itself, where she held it, then released, exhaling the air and Myst around her.

When Pomella managed to find the Crossroads—where she existed both nowhere and everywhere at once—she found the Myst most readily available, most powerful, and most easily shaped.

Today, unfortunately, was not such a morning.

A barrage of thoughts assaulted her mind, each one trying to knock her off that delicate balance between worlds. She thought of Norana, and the fierce scratch she had on her face. She thought of how easily non-Mystics were seeing the fay, and with more frequency. She worried about the growing number of Unclaimed who were being captured by slavers, and what that meant.

Fatigue was another concern, a deep one she felt after her weeklong journey between Port Morrush, Oakspring, and now Kelt Apar. It seemed to her that her head had hardly touched her pillow before the sky lightened and her hummingbirds, Hector and Ena, had arrived at her window, buzzing and tapping the windowpane to wake her. She'd grumbled and waved them away in a very un-Mystic-like manner, before finally dragging herself out of bed to begin the morning routine.

Further distracting her now was the unusual company crawling across Kelt Apar. Normally only four people lived there on the grounds. Grandmaster, Vivianna, Mistress Yarina, and herself each had their own dwellings. Oxillian, the Green Man, and several rangers came and went, but generally, Pomella's mornings like this were filled with quiet solitude.

A loud rattling, like a pile of firewood being shaken, sounded outside as a laborer pulled a wagon past her cabin. Pomella tried to ignore it, but the clatter pulled her out from her meditation.

She sighed. She wasn't going to get much more done during this morning meditation. Beyond the rattling carts and road exhaustion, the one overriding fear that crawled into Pomella's gut and shook her off-balance was Dav's fay creature. It shouldn't have been unusual, but for some reason Pomella couldn't explain, the little pineten felt wrong. There'd been an unusual number of fay creatures in the Mystwood of late, which Yarina said could be expected with Crow Tallin approaching. But there was something else that made Pomella afraid. The name Dav had given the silver animal.

Lagnaraste.

Pomella bit her lip. It wasn't unusual for tykes to give strange names to critters they encountered. As a young child herself, she'd scampered about, naming trees and other landmarks on the edge of the Mystwood. She'd once given the surname Buttersnatcher to an entire family of rabbits she'd come across, as well as proper names to every one of them.

A loud clicking noise sounded at her window. Hector had jammed the glass pane hard.

"OK, OK, I'm coming," Pomella said.

She pushed her worries about the fay pineten to the back of her mind. Nothing good would come from dwelling on them.

The scent of flowers and a bright sun greeted her when she finally stepped outside with her Mystic staff in hand. Pomella smiled. *This* was home. Her garden surrounding the cottage burst with roses and daisies and sunflowers. White lilies, too, which only bloomed in the summer. She'd planted them because they were Lal's favorite. Her strawberries were red and ripe, so she picked one off the branch and wolfed it down. Glancing up, she saw a flock of geese flying in formation over Kelt Apar's central tower. As always, the tower, with its green conical roof, was the focus of their community, the heart of the Mystwood, and the most iconic location on Moth.

As Pomella exited the little gate encircling her garden onto soft grass, Hector and Ena greeted her, swirling around her with their trails of silvery light.

"Hello, dear ones," she said, holding out her fingertip for Hector to alight onto. The little bird's silvery feathers shone as brightly as always. Hector and his smaller sister were seven years old now, which Pomella understood to be older than most hummingbirds from the human realm lived. But her birds didn't seem to age like normal birds. They stayed forever young, eager as always to please her and cause mischief.

"What's your secret, huh?" she asked the bird. Hector buzzed his wings. Not wanting to be left out, Ena zoomed past her brother, trying to harass him into a game of chase. Pomella could feel the siblings' rivalry dancing around them. She'd never been able to truly explain her connection to the birds. She'd saved them from a fay crow when they were babies, and ever since they'd followed her around, seemingly attached to her in such a way that she could often distinguish their emotions. Grandmaster once told her it was rare for Mystics to permanently bond with fay creatures. Even Vivianna, who had a strong affinity for the fay, never managed to form a full bond.

As if summoned by Pomella's thoughts, Vivianna emerged from around the corner of her nearby cabin, a storm of thoughts and nervous energy plain on her face. Her raven-dark hair was tied into a loose bun, but several strands hung loose. Shady bags circled her eyes, making it plain that sleep had eluded her. Yet despite Vivianna's apparent fatigue, Pomella was amazed at the grace and competence her friend showed. Like Yarina, Vivianna exuded an aura of intelligence and confidence that had been bred into them with their noble upbringing. They both seemed to drift across the ground rather than walk. Perhaps it had to do with their noble upbringing. As children of wealth and privilege, both the High Mystic and her apprentice had been taught from an early age to display elegance with every action.

Pomella wiped her runny nose with her sleeve. She had no such upbringing. "Not much sleep, yah?"

Vivianna brushed a long twist of hair from her oval face. "Not a moment's rest. I hope you enjoyed sleeping in your cottage last night," Vivianna said.

Pomella's eyes narrowed. "Why?"

Vivianna gave her a long stare. "Because all our cottages are being given to the visiting High Mystics for their stay."

"Oh, shite," Pomella said. She'd forgotten that.

Crow Tallin occurred only once every sixty years. For centuries, the High Mystics of the world gathered in Kelt Apar to observe a rare celestial event. Yarina had placed Vivianna in charge of overseeing many of the logistics. Pomella had offered to help, of course, but Grandmaster had surprised her by insisting she stay focused on her meditative studies instead.

"What did you expect would happen?" Vivianna said. "You don't expect High Mystic Bhairatonix of Qin to sleep in a tent, do you?"

"Don't they bring their own fortresses and towers and hidden fay realms to retreat to? These are High Mystics, after all."

Vivianna's expression didn't change. Clearly she wasn't going to lower herself to Pomella's sarcasm.

"Fine. I'll sleep on Lal's floor," Pomella said. "They won't push a boot against a grandmaster's back. Where will you be staying?"

"In the tower, attending Mistress Yarina."

Pomella quirked an eyebrow. She and Vivianna were rarely invited into Kelt Apar's central tower. When she'd begun her apprenticeship, she'd imagined that she would live in the tower with the High Mystic. But in all the years studying here, she and Vivianna were only brought into it for certain rituals, or for private meetings with Yarina. Vivianna, on account of actually being Yarina's apprentice, saw the inside of the tower far more than Pomella, but still not on a regular basis. An overnight stay was all but unheard of and, in Pomella's case, had never occurred.

Vivianna glanced at her forearm. Faint runes glowed on her skin. Vivianna traced them with her finger. It appeared to Pomella to be some sort of list.

"It's tradition to wear red during the days leading up to Crow Tallin," Vivianna said. "The 'color of blood and fire,' according to the old writings in the tower's library."

"That doesn't even make sense," Pomella said. "Blood and fire are different colors."

"If you want to object, talk to the past masters," Vivianna said. "Mistress Yarina approved some gowns for us to wear. I had them brought from Port Morrush, and they arrived this morning. The merchants from that town nearly came to blows over who would have the privilege of making them for us. I'll have yours sent over to your cabin before highsun."

"Thanks," Pomella said, her mind still on the strange fay occurrences.

"How did the summons to Oakspring fare?" Vivianna asked, still not looking up.

"About as well as milk and mudshite stew," Pomella said.

Vivianna raised an eyebrow.

"Something strange happened with a fay there," Pomella said. She didn't feel like explaining her interaction with Bethy. "A child somehow trapped a fay. A pineten. The entire family could see her, and the little critter didn't dissolve back to Fayün after I severed the thin bond she had with the tyke."

Vivianna rolled her forearm to stare at some runes on the opposite side. She pursed her lips as she consulted the information there. "There have been three other instances of fay that were visible to everyone in the area. One of those reports claimed a swarm of rats was seen in the streets of Sentry. In each instance, the fay lingered far longer than expected."

"Have you ever heard the name Lagnaraste?" Pomella asked. "That's what the boy named the pinten. It sounded strange to me."

Vivianna shook her head. "Sounds like the fruit of a child with an active imagination."

"I suppose," Pomella said. Hector, who had lost interest in their conversation, leaped from Pomella's hand and flew away.

Pomella noticed Vivianna watching him go. If Pomella possessed one thing that Vivianna desired, it was her bond with her hummingbirds.

"Perhaps your birds can teach us something about these other fay," Vivianna said.

"How?" Pomella said.

"I don't know exactly. But Mistress Yarina says all of the fay are connected. Perhaps, by better understanding the ones closest to us—to you, I mean—we can better understand their nature."

"Perhaps," Pomella said, glancing at her hummingbirds as they chased each other around. As far as she was concerned, these two just liked to stir up trouble.

"Just because a creature or object from Fayün looks like something you're familiar with doesn't mean it will behave that way," Vivianna said. "There are many classes of fay. The ones that most commonly cross over are animals, like your hummingbirds or the pineten. But there are other, more intelligent, sometimes malevolent, creatures."

Pomella quirked an eyebrow. "Such as?"

"Well, there's the axthos, for instance," Vivianna said. "I've never seen one, but I've seen references to them in the tower library. They're supposed to be nasty little creatures that delight in harming others."

"Sounds lovely," Pomella said, frowning.

"Then there's worse things, such as wivans," Vivianna said. "They're extremely rare. They're what you get when a fay creature ensnares—or possesses—something from the human realm. Individually the fay and the human might be fine, but when they're merged together it's supposed to be awful."

Pomella thought of Dav and the pineten. The creature certainly hadn't *possessed* him, but Pomella shuddered to think of what that would have been like if the pineten had.

"Awful in what way?" Pomella asked.

Vivianna shrugged. "The books I read are pretty vague. What I understand is that our world and Fayün naturally repel each other. They are content to exist beside each other, but facing apart. If something from one world becomes stuck in the other, the resulting friction aggravates its emotions, causing it to be aggressive or unbalanced."

"Unless it has an anchor," Pomella said, thinking of her hummingbirds and how they bonded early in their existence with her.

"Yes," Vivianna said. "Like that."

A familiar figure approached. Pomella and Vivianna turned at the same time as Vlenar, the laghart ranger, joined them. He wore his usual set of padded leather clothes over his scaled body. Pomella had become used to his strange, almost surreal, way of moving that was the result of both his biology and years of training.

He bowed his head as he reached them. "Misstressses," he hissed in greeting to them both.

"Hello, Vlenar," Vivianna said. "Any news from beyond the tree line?"

Vlenar's tongue zipped out, its tip tasting the air, before returning. "The number of people gathered is far beyond what we expected. We are keeping them outside Kelt Apar's borders for now, but I don't know if we'll have enough rangers to enforce that for very long."

"What people?" Pomella asked.

Vivianna tucked a stray tendril of hair behind her ear. "Mistress Yarina sent proclamations to Moth's three barons, declaring that the days of Crow Tallin would begin soon, and culminate at the next full moon. She told them to expect an increase in fay sightings, and provided a list of precautions everyone could take. The barons, of course, did a poor job of conveying that to their commoners, and now many of them are flocking to Kelt Apar for protection." She jabbed at some runes on her forearm as if annoyed by the addition of more work.

"What is she doing to provide that protection? Will they need it?" Pomella said.

"We are hosting the largest gathering of Mystics in the world," Vivianna said, "including all seven High Mystics. There's a tide of rangers, and possibly more than a hundred soldiers. I think they'll be well protected." She pursed her lips and turned to Vlenar. "Do you have an updated count of rangers and soldiers?"

Vlenar shook his head. "I will gattther that."

"Thank you," Vivianna said. "I need to make sure the other cabins are ready for the High Mystics. Oh, and, Pomella, Grandmaster's robes arrived as well. Since you have little else to do, can you remind him to wear them to the ceremony tonight?"

Pomella tightened her jaw. She knew Vivianna was overwhelmed with all her duties, but it wasn't her fault that Lal didn't want her helping. "I'll take care of it."

"Thank you," Vivianna said. "Now, where's Oxillian?" She looking up from her forearm. "I need him to—oh, never mind." She flicked the air with her finger, and the sound of a silver bell filled the air.

The ground rumbled and churned. Calm as tea, Pomella took a half step backward. Oxillian, the fabled Green Man known throughout Moth, rose from the ground near their feet. His massive form rolled upward, shaping itself into a towering, broadshouldered man. Dirt and stones and grass from the nearby ground formed his body. His eyes were made of polished pebbles that had, until moments before, rested deep beneath the ground. A long beard, formed from the nearby lawn, swayed in the breeze.

"Hello, Ox," Pomella said.

The Green Man bowed to them both. "Mistress Pomella, welcome home," he said. His familiar deep voice rumbled like an avalanche in Pomella's stomach.

"Any new reports?" Vivianna asked.

Pomella looked at Oxillian expectantly. As the guardian of Kelt Apar, and having the unique ability to sense certain kinds of activity across the entire island, Ox was often the first source for knowing if something unusual was occurring. Between him and the handful of rangers roaming across Moth, Kelt Apar was reasonably well informed of happenings.

"No, Mistress," Oxillian said. "But all of the rangers have returned. They report that the High Mystics are arriving on time."

"Has there been anything to indicate more slavers are slinking around the island?" Pomella asked.

"There are always groups of people who ride with horses and carts," the Green Man said. "But I cannot determine their plans or intentions."

"OK, thank you, Ox," Pomella said. "Where is Grandmaster Faywong right now?"

The Green Man shifted his bulk, and for a moment a distant look crossed his face. "He is returning to his cabin from the south woods. Would you like me to pass a message to him?"

"No, thank you," Pomella said. "I will find him myself. Besides, I think Vivianna could use your assistance." Turning to her friend, she added, "I'll take care of the robes."

"Thanks," Vivianna said, returning to the list of runes on her forearm.

Grandmaster's cabin was as dull as ever. Pomella slipped her shoes off as she crossed the dwelling's lone threshold. The familiar scent of incense and spices mingled in the air. Broon, the old brown dog, struggled to stand from where he'd been lying.

"It's just me," Pomella said to the dog. "Don't get up. I don't want you to hurt yourself."

As usual, Broon ignored her, licking her feet and wagging his tail.

Lal sat straight backed on top of a blue cushion. He sat as though meditating, with his legs crossed and tucked beneath him. Chillybumps rippled over Pomella's arms. Whenever she was around her mentor, the Myst stirred in subtle yet powerful ways. By being in his presence, it was as if the Myst sang to her more loudly.

Lal lived a humble and unusual life. It bothered her that he insisted on keeping the most ragged hut on the grounds as his dwelling. He was a grandmaster. Pomella had grown up in a wooden house not much larger than this, so she understood his choice to live simply, but sometimes she wished he'd allow himself to accept at least a little more prestige. She, Vivianna, the rangers, and Oxillian had built a newer, larger cabin last year, which they'd offered to Grandmaster, but he'd declined.

She pressed her palms together, touching them to her forehead, and gave him a small bow. "Hello, Grandmaster."

Lal opened his eyes. "Ah, Pomella," he said in his thick, breathy accent. "Welcome back. How'd trip go?"

"Exhausting. Lots of problems with the fay."

She stepped carefully around clutter lining the floor. Lal had very few possessions, but lately he tended to neglect small things. Broon's wooden water bowl was overturned. A wooden vase held a bouquet of wilted lilies. The one cabinet in the dwelling that contained dishes was open, with its contents sitting on top, flecked with crumbs.

Pomella picked up one of the dishes and dusted the crumbs off. "How has everything here been?"

"Loud. Lots of people. I stay out of way."

Pomella set the dishes into a bin that to be washed later. Checking his food container, she saw it was empty. She made a mental note to refill it, and to include strawberries from her garden, too. "Are you ready for tonight's ceremony?" she asked.

"Not going."

Pomella paused. "What? Why not?"

"Retired."

Pomella narrowed her eyes. "Every High Mystic from the Continent will be here. Retired or not, you're still a grandmaster."

"I just Lal."

Frustration welled within Pomella. He could be so stubborn. She loomed over him. "Yes, I know. But with respect, you're also my master, and Mistress Yarina's former teacher. From what she's told Vivianna and me, this is the most important ceremony in the century. You can't miss it."

"Won't miss. Crow Tallin happens everywhere."

Pomella stared at him, incredulous, before huffing away to stack more dishes. "I wish you would let them honor you. They'll probably want to see you."

"Crow Tallin important. No time to . . . what do you sometimes say? . . . 'shiver my ego with kisses.'"

Pomella flicked another jagged crumb off the plate. She loved Lal, but he could be so damn frustrating. "It's 'skiver.'"

"Still make no sense."

Pomella plunked a plate down, hard. "What makes no sense is that you're one of the foremost Mystics in the world and you're going to hide in your cabin when you should be seen by your peers, who all aspire to be like you!"

She realized, too late, that she'd gone too far.

"Shite. I'm sorry, Grandmaster. I—"

Lal sighed. "Sit down, Pomella. Bring tea."

Pomella closed her eyes and took a calming breath. "I'm not good at making tea." She almost added, *I'm not Yarina*, but thought better of it. Apparently, Lal had become used to Yarina's ability to masterfully craft perfect cups of tea during her years as his apprentice.

"Please," Lal said.

Pomella suppressed a grumble and dropped a pinch of tea leaves from a nearby wooden container into Lal's only cups and filled them with the last of the water from his pitcher.

Lal gestured for Pomella to sit next to him. "Tell me about trip."

Stirring the leaves in her cup with a finger, Pomella told Lal about the fay she encountered at the Fortress of Sea and Sky, and at Oakspring.

"Mm, Crow Tallin comes," Lal said when she'd finished. "The veil between this world and Fayün thins."

"So what does that mean?" Pomella asked.

Lal shifted off his cushion. He looked out the window and his eyes took on a faraway expression. He sat there for a long minute. Pomella knew to wait. This was Lal's way.

Finally, he returned his gaze to her, and she could see the depth in his eyes. The Myst surged in her body, tingling her.

"When I apprentice, sixty years ago, all High Mystics met in

Kelt Apar. Sixty years before that, they did, too. And sixty before that they came, and sixty before that, all the way back for
centuries. Each time, they come when Treorel passes the night
sky."

"Treorel?" Pomella asked.

"A star. Mystic Star. But not like other stars. Treorel not
flicker. It shines steady, and shines red. Like blood and fire.
It moves opposite way from other stars. Some Mystics say it
another world, like ours."

Well, that explained the meaning of blood and fire. "Another world? Like Fayün?"

"No. Not Fayün. Not mirror world. Maybe another place,
with different oceans, different lands. Different people. Maybe
like us, or like lagharts, or very different. Nobody know."

Pomella tried to imagine a different world, with other people
and creatures and who knew what else. She'd only begun to
understand the idea of Fayün, but now it made her head spin to
think there could be other worlds you could walk on.

Lal must've seen her mind buzzing with the ideas, because he
waved a hand to dismiss it. "Treorel important for other reason.
When it comes, human realm and Fayün come closer. The veil
thins until, in some places, it becomes hard to tell difference between worlds. At peak time, Treorel passes behind the full moon.
When that happens, Crow Tallin—Mystic Twilight—begins,
then . . ."

He shook his head.

"What?" Pomella urged.

Lal stared at his teacup. "When that happens, the veil van-
ishes. Fay roam our world freely. People get lost in Fayün. Worlds
merge."

Pomella's chest tightened. "So this is why there's been a surge of fay sightings across Moth," she said.

"Will see more," Lal said. "Soon."

"Why do the High Mystics come to Moth then?" Pomella asked.

"The veil always thin on Moth. Especially thin. As days of Crow Tallin arrive, whole island and Fayün become one. Very chaotic."

"So what do we do?" Pomella said.

"Yarina and High Mystics keep peace. You help. Do as they say. I retired."

Pomella perked up. "Really? I thought you didn't want me involved."

"The Myst stirs, Pomella," Lal said. "You will feel it change soon, if you haven't already. Listen to it. Follow it, even if it leads you away from normal path. Besides," he added, "you not listen to me anyway. I tell you to focus on finding Crossroads. You ride to help Unclaimed."

Pomella's stomach roiled. "They were being sold as *slaves*, Master."

"Huzzo," Lal said, taking her hands and using her Mystic name. It was a name he'd given her when she'd become his apprentice, shared only between the two of them. "I know you want to make difference in world. But you only tend a single tree. I try to show you how to change whole forest."

Pomella didn't see how. Most days, all she did was sit and meditate. While it was true that helped her have better mastery of the Myst, it was just a tool. "But I *am* trying to change the forest," she said. "Many commoners and Unclaimed look up to me because of the opportunity you've given me. I really feel like I can make a difference in their lives."

"Change, by its very nature, reflects impermanence," Lal said. "The Myst is unchanging, fixed, eternal. Strive for *that*. Find it, and you find yourself. Find everything that could ever be. Fix everything for everybody. Make impact that lasts forever, in all places and times."

"But *how*?" Pomella said. "I don't see it."

Lal's face softened. "My Huzzo, you never will if your eyes are looking only at *this* world."

Pomella had to force herself to not squeeze the fragile cup in her hand too hard. "Is this how you taught Mistress Yarina when she was your student?"

"Yarina is still my student. She has different role than you. Requires different methods."

"Well, I'd love to know what my 'role' is," Pomella said.

"Don't know," said Lal. "For you to discover. Crow Tallin be good for you. Do as Yarina say, show respect to other High Mystics, and be one with the Myst. When Crow Tallin comes, best opportunity to seek the Deep."

Pomella looked away. Meditating and connecting with the Myst was fine, but she still felt she needed to have a practical connection to the world. And if she needed to do that on her own, she would. "I'm sorry for my outburst earlier," she said after a long moment of silence.

"It's OK. I was young once, too."

Pomella swirled her cup of cold tea and changed the subject. "Vivianna ordered dresses for her and me to wear to the ceremony tonight. Mistress Yarina wants us to all wear red. *All* of us."

"Yes," Lal said. "Red important. Match energy from Treorel."

It surprised Pomella that Lal didn't put up more of a fight. "So you'll go?"

"No."

Pomella looked at the ceiling, not sure how to put this delicately. She supposed it was best to just lick the petals and see what stuck. "At least do it for tradition's sake?"

"I'm sorry, Pomella. I cannot."

Pomella clanked her cup onto the floor and stood. "Do you remember how you made me run around the perimeter until I could barely walk? You said it was important for me to be present in my body. Well, I think it's also important to be present in the world you lived in. You aren't dead yet, Master. Nothing prevents you from following your path while also demonstrating support for those that need or respect you."

"Mmm," said Lal. "Be careful during these days of Crow Tallin, Pomella. Dangerous."

Pomella sighed. She gathered the bin of dirty dishes into her arms and moved to the door. "Good night, Lal."

She left without waiting for a reply.

SEVEN

THE HIGH MYSTICS

Icy water coursed around Pomella's hands as she mindlessly scrubbed Lal's dishes at the river.

Lal's description of Crow Tallin worried her. Pomella couldn't imagine the whole island merging with Fayün. As a Mystic, she had a certain familiarity with the silvery land and its denizens, but how would all of that appear to everybody else? Likely there would be panic, not to mention people hurt if the fay animals became scared or threatened. And according to Vivianna, there were other, worse, denizens of fay beside forest animals.

She took a deep breath. The river always calmed her. It ran north to south through Kelt Apar, dividing the grounds into two parts. The western portion housed the cabins where she and Vivianna lived, and the eastern part was where the central tower stood in the middle of a wide lawn, encircled by a ring of wildflowers. Today, of course, that open area around the tower was dominated by tents and people milling around as they prepared for that night's ceremony.

A tiny stream of silver appeared in front of her, followed by several more, streaking above the river before fading from the human world. Pomella watched them dissolve. Such visions weren't uncommon to her in Kelt Apar, but this one felt different.

A large fay bird misted above the water. Pomella stared in wonder. The bird was unlike anything she'd ever seen before. It was twice her height in length, with magnificent plumage that ripped through an unseen wind. It had the head and beak of a falcon, but its body was more exotic, with individual tail feathers that were longer than her arm. It glided above the river, beating its wings once to propel itself upward into a looping arc. On the downward rush, it dipped its wings below the surface but did not stir the water.

It seemed to Pomella that the bird was dancing around her and the river. She looked toward the cabins, hoping to catch Vivianna, but her friend was nowhere in sight. Pomella wanted to reach out to see if she could touch the bird's plumage. But as she lifted a hand, the bird rolled itself to the side and flew west, toward the treetops. She waited for it to fade, as most fay typically did after a few seconds.

But the bird continued to fly, and, if anything, seemed to become more opaque as it flew away from her.

Pomella bit her lip. If Crow Tallin was coming soon, she wanted to better understand the fay. And the bird was so beautiful, how could she not want to follow it?

She slipped her shoes off and hitched her skirt above her knees. There were several bridges that crossed the river, but none were close enough to get to without risking losing the bird. She stepped into the water and sucked her breath in at the cold. She waded across, barely managing to hold her skirts, shoes, and Mystic staff out of the water. She stretched to her tiptoes to keep as much of herself out of the water as possible.

When she reached the far shore, she shook her legs out and ran after the bird. It dipped below the treetops, close to the monument of past masters. She could hear soft music now, just a single haunting note coming from the same direction.

Pomella emerged into the small clearing and came to a stop. A gray-scaled laghart wearing red robes and holding a curved Mystic staff stood beside the tall bone-white pillar of the past masters. The Mystic turned his head toward her, and slipped his hood off. Green and gray scales accented the Mystic's eyes and other features. Pomella had only met a handful of lagharts in her lifetime but knew well enough that their scale coloring differed just as much as human skin tone. Like all lagharts, this one, which she identified as male, had the same three-swirl pattern of scales inherent to everyone in their species. This was the first time, however, that Pomella had ever seen a laghart Mystic.

"Hello," Pomella said, bowing. "I'm sorry to disturb you. I was following . . ." She gestured to the large fay bird now resting beside the laghart. ". . . Your fay bird."

The Mystic bowed in return. "Itt isss ffffine," he said. His tongue zipped out, tasting the air. "You are nottt disssturbing me. I am admiring your monumenttt."

"Oh," Pomella said. "Of course." She approached and gave the laghart a warm smile.

"Hhhow mannny generationsss back doesss ittt reccccord?" the laghart asked, still considering the pillar.

Pomella walked to the monument and put her hand on it. Engraved on the pillar were the names of Kelt Apar's past masters. Moss covered large portions of the lower half, having appeared in late spring. After Crow Tallin, Yarina would probably require her to scrub it clean, just as she did each year. Pomella plucked a piece of moss with her fingers and flicked it away.

"There are thirty-six names on the pillar, accounting for eight hundred years of our lineage," Pomella said, "but we believe there are more names that have been worn away stretching back further."

"Are thhhey all human?" the laghart asked.

Pomella gave him quizzical look. She'd never considered that. "I don't know. I believe so, however. I've never heard of a laghart High Mystic on Moth."

The laghart stepped closer to the pillar, his slitted eyes still studying it. "Befffore humansss, there were laghartsss on thisss island. Befffore High Mysticsss, there were *Zurntas*."

"*Zurntas?*"

The laghart finally took his gaze away from the monument and looked at her. His elongated pupils reminded her of double-edged daggers. "*Zurntas* are what we laghartsss call our Mysssstic masssters. It isss from thhhem thhhat humansss firssst learned of the Myssst."

Pomella smiled, not wanting to contest the claim. "I clearly have much still to learn," she said. "But forgive me, I don't know your name. I'm Pomella."

The Mystic's long tongue flicked several times. "Pomella AnDone, the ffformer *kanta*. I'vvve heard much abouttt you."

"*Kanta?*" Pomella said. She wasn't terribly surprised that

he'd heard of her. In the years since Lal had taken her as an apprentice, word had supposedly spread beyond Moth.

"In my land, Lavantath, acccross the wessstern ocean, all laghartsss are hatchhhed indentured. We mussst ssserve the Bronze Ones, who in turn ssservvve the Golden, and they the People of the Sky, who livvve in Indoltruna, the Endlesss Palace."

"I was born a commoner," Pomella said, "but we were not indentured."

"You were born ttto a way of lifffe that you couldn'ttt essscape. You exisssted to elevate the vvvalue of your better's holdingsss. That isss what it isss to be *kanta*."

"I *escaped* just fine," Pomella said, not without some bite in her words.

"As do mossst *kanta* from Lavantath. After thhhirty-thhhree years a *kanta* may choose ttto become one a Bronze One. Buttt here, it isss harder to rissse, and unheard of to asssccend to becoming a Mystic."

"Well, I suppose I never was good at following rules," Pomella said.

The laghart's long face shifted into a sort of smile. "Indeed. What you did wasss remarkkkable. We—the Mysssstics of Lavantath—ressspect you. I am Hizrith."

"Welcome to Kelt Apar, Hizrith." Until now, Pomella had very little knowledge of what lay to the west, across the ocean. The Continent to the east represented the only other geography she was knowledgeable about. She'd heard vague stories about the western lands where the lagharts came from, but she'd never heard of Lavantath before. Nor had it occurred to her to ask anyone about it. The lagharts seemed to be a quiet people, mostly living alone on Moth. From what she understood, they weren't a very populous race.

The silver bird flapped its wings once, and Hizrith placed a clawed hand on it. Pomella remarked at how the scales on his claw shone silver as they touched the bird. The bird adjusted itself, pushing against the claw as if eager for his scratches.

"You can touch the fay?" Pomella said.

Hizrith's tongue flicked out, and his long snout curled into what Pomella recognized as a smile. "Yesss," he said. "Hemosavana isss my fffamiliar."

Pomella thought of Hector and Ena. They would often land on her palm or shoulder, but touching them felt like touching a cold puff of air.

"I have a pair of familiars," she said, "but I don't know if they can feel my touch."

"The fffay are generally bound to Fffayün. Buttt under cc-certain cccircumssstances, they can affecttt ttthis world. Thisss isss essspecially true if they havvve a bond with a massster, or hossst."

"You seem to know a lot about the fay."

"In daysss long passsttt, it was laghartsss that firssst disss-covered Fayün and bonded withhh the fffay. The *Zurntass* are peerlessss in thhhat regard."

"Are there many *Zurntas*?" Pomella asked.

"More than the ssstars," Hizrith said.

Pomella quirked an eyebrow at this. As she opened her mouth to politely reply, Hizrith swished his tail and shrugged.

"True masssters of the Myssst never die. The *Zurntass*. Seer

Brigid. They livvve on in the Myssst, evvven afffter they die and their bodiesss decay."

A rush of excitement surged over Pomella at the mention of Brigid. "I didn't know Saint Brigid was well known beyond Moth," she said.

"Seer Brigid isss more thhhan a Sssaint," Hizrith said. "Ssshe isss the Myssst itself made flessssh. She wasss the firssst human Mystic. The *Zurntass* taughttt her, but in time ssshe sssurpasssed their power. To lagharts, she isss beyond everyone who hasss come sssince. She isss the *Zurnta* to all other *Zurntas*. Sssomeday, ssshe will return to fffree the *kanta*. We wait fffor her."

His eyes closed as he spoke, and his voice took on a reverent tone. Pomella sensed the Myst stirring around him. A soft breeze swept through the clearing. It was strange to Pomella that the lagharts worshipped Saint Brigid, who had been human. While it was true that the *Toweren* was full of stories of her and the lagharts adventuring together, they always portrayed her as a human woman with red hair and fair skin.

"Do you believe she was a laghart?" Pomella asked.

"Perhapsss," Hizrith mused in his hissing voice. "Sssome offf my pppeople do."

Pomella circled the tall pillar, dragging her fingers across the mossy surface. The grass surrounding it was kept short by Lal's goats and sheep, but right now it bunched up at the very base of the marble. "Her name doesn't appear on this pillar that we know of," Pomella told him, "but some believe she was the first High Mystic of Moth, before Kelt Apar was founded."

Hizrith approached the monument and held up a clawed

hand beside its marble surface. He glanced at Pomella as if to ask permission to touch it. Pomella nodded.

The laghart ran a clawed finger slowly across the marble. A warm aura radiated from the monument. Silvery tendrils of smoke coalesced and swirled around the the pillar, spiraling upward. The names on the pillar shown with a steady golden light.

"What are you doing?" Pomella asked. Whatever Hizrith was Unveiling, it didn't appear to be harmful, but that didn't put her at ease.

The laghart closed his eyes, and the silver swirls spun faster. The golden letter-runes forming the names of the past masters faded away, only to be replaced by different shapes, hard angled and shining green. The new names emerged from *behind* the one she knew.

"The passst *Zurntass!*" Hizrith hissed softly.

Pomella marveled at what she was seeing, but a heartbeat later the shining letters and Myst faded, leaving the pillar as she remembered. She saw no traces of what must've been the laghart's language. She took an inward breath, finding calm.

"The island of Moth has a rich history and many mysteries indeed," she said.

The large bird, Hemosavana, stretched itself to its full height, and spread its wings. It craned its long neck and opened its beak as if singing.

"My massster calls me," Hizrith said. "I mussst go."

Pomella swallowed the flood of questions she had for the laghart. A pang of guilt stabbed her as she remarked at what a good apprentice Hizrith must be to his master. She doubted he badgered his master like she'd done to Lal earlier.

"I hope we can speak again soon," Pomella said, bowing slightly to him.

"Yesss," Hizrith said, returning the gesture. "It isss fortunate that Crow Tallin bringsss usss togethhher. I hope that in yearsss to come, we can continue ttto havvve sssuch dissscussions."

"Yes," said Pomella. "I would like that. Perhaps we could be friends."

"Indeed," said the laghart.

That evening, as the sun set beneath the western Mystwood treetops, Pomella emerged again from her cabin and walked toward Kelt Apar's central tower. She nervously smoothed her dress. The dressmakers Vivianna hired had outdone themselves. The long dress was entirely dark-red velvet, with cap sleeves that just barely spilled over the curve of her shoulders. A row of gold buttons ran up the front of the dress from her navel to just below the square collar. Although it was slightly more utilitarian than she'd hoped, she gave the design no second thought. It was a remarkably comfortable dress and she was honored to be wearing something that somebody had worked on for many hours just for her. That, and it fit her just right.

The first stars emerged above her in the warm night sky. Pomella felt strangely alone walking toward the tower. Kelt Apar had been transformed into a bustling camp of Mystics and strangers. Normally the tower stood in the middle of the wide, quiet clearing, which was filled with neatly trimmed grass and a few meandering paths. On most days, other than Vivianna and Pomella's hummingbirds, Lal's sheep and goats were the only company she had on the grounds.

Tonight, however, the grass and paths were nowhere to be found. A ring of tents encircled the entire clearing. Firelight flickered from within the circle, but Pomella couldn't see its source. A scattering of servants and apprentices scurried about handling last-minute tasks.

The clearing was wide enough that there was still open space between the outermost tents and the tree line. Pomella caught movement at the edge of the Mystwood. Squinting against the rapidly dimming light, she saw the graceful stride of what could only be a ranger on patrol. Sure enough, moments later she recognized Vlenar moving in his odd way with his back bent nearly parallel to the ground. She remembered her conversation from earlier with him and Vivianna about how the rangers and soldiers might not be enough to keep the crowd of commoners off the grounds. She frowned at the tree line, not liking the entire situation. With that many terrified people in one place, things could easily get out of hand.

She made her way past the line of tents with her Mystic staff in hand. A familiar buzzing rippled over her as Hector and Ena arrived.

"Not tonight," Pomella told them. "I need you to stay home."

Ena hovered right in front of her face, clearly disappointed.

"I don't think the High Mystics will—"

Hector flicked past her ear, clipping her hair.

"Hey!" she said. "Look, it's an important event and—"

The two hummingbirds spun in a circle and hovered aggressively in front of her again.

"Oh, fine," she said. "I suppose all the other Mystics will

have their familiars." She thought of Hizrith and Hemosavana, and wondered if the massive bird would be present. "Behave, though, and stay close, OK?"

Ena danced with joy in the air, while Hector seemed irritated that he'd been told to behave. Pomella shook her head and entered the clearing.

A crowd of Mystics, perhaps more than a hundred, stood on the lawn, chatting and mingling among each other. There were both men and women in roughly equal numbers, some dressed richly and others in rags caked in dust. All of them held a Mystic staff, as varied as their owners.

But as interesting as the Mystics themselves were, more amazing to Pomella was the raw, tingling sense of power that emanated from the collective crowd. The Myst hummed all around her. Chillybumps rippled up her arms. She couldn't help but smile. A hundred Mystics gathered together. This might be the only time for nearly a century that so many came together.

A few faces turned toward her, studying her with interest or curiosity. Pomella kept her expression neutral. Despite seven years as a Mystic, she had to fight the urge to lower her eyes and slink away. She reminded herself that their opinions of her didn't matter. She belonged here. This was her home.

Pomella searched the faces for Vivianna. She found her standing between two other Mystics, chatting easily. One of the Mystics was older and stooped, with a beard divided into three parts. Vivianna seemed completely at ease. Her dress was beautiful, more elegant than the one Pomella wore. Her dark hair spilled down her back like a waterfall, setting off her light skin. Vivianna was a natural in social situations. Most Mystics were, or at least pretended to be, because they'd all come from noble families who had raised them to be part of society at an early age.

Seeing Pomella, Vivianna excused herself from her companions. The bearded Mystic bowed his head to her and turned to find other company.

"There you are," Vivianna said to Pomella. "I was beginning to worry you wouldn't show. How's the dress?"

Pomella held her arms out to show it off.

"It's beautiful," Vivianna said, smiling. "Did you convince Grandmaster to wear his?"

"He's not coming," Pomella said.

Vivianna stared at her. "What? Why not?"

"Because he's being Lal," Pomella said.

"He's a grandmaster," Vivianna said. "He should be here."

"I tried to convince him," Pomella said. "But you know how he can be." She looked around at the gathered Mystics. They mostly kept to small clusters, no more than three or four speaking together in low voices. A few loners stood on the outskirts, their faces expressionless, clearly uncomfortable being near so many people.

One particularly large group located on the far side of the clearing drew Pomella's attention. It had as many as perhaps a dozen Mystics standing together, their attention on something, or someone, Pomella couldn't see. She tilted her head and only had to wait a moment before one of the Mystics shifted aside, revealing a tall girl with dark hair and lightly tanned skin at the center of attention. While she was certainly pretty, it struck Pomella as unusual that so many Mystics would fawn over an attractive girl.

Maybe some of these Mystics had been *too* reclusive lately.

As if sensing her attention, the girl turned and looked right at Pomella, whose spine tingled. For a brief second they held each other's gaze and Pomella felt a sense of pain and familiarity. She tore her gaze away as a wave of dizziness came over her.

When she recovered, she flicked her gaze back, but the girl had already turned her attention back to another dark-skinned Mystic with black stripes slashed across her face and other exposed skin. A virga. The unusual skin pattern reminded Pomella of Rochella, the ranger who had helped her during her apprentice Trials. Thinking of Rochella made Sim come to mind.

The familiar pang of missing him crept up again, but she gently let it pass. "When does the ceremony begin?" Pomella asked.

"Very soon, at full dark," Vivianna said. Light from torches that were scattered around the lawn cast a warm glow across her face. "Oxillian will greet everyone and make introductions. Then the High Mystics will arrive."

"Will there be wine?" Pomella said.

Vivianna quirked an eyebrow.

"I'm just teasing," Pomella said, but Vivianna gave her a knowing smile. "How many Mystics are here?"

Vivianna consulted her forearm where a column of runes illuminated. "One hundred fifty-seven Mystics including you and me, sixty-four apprentices, and seven High Mystics."

"And Lal," Pomella added.

"And Lal," Vivianna agreed.

"There's so much power in the air," Pomella mused. "Do you feel it?"

Vivianna nodded but kept her attention on her forearm. Pomella paid her no mind. She excelled at planning, organizing, and Unveiling the Myst in a traditional manner. For Pomella, the Myst was like a voice, whispering to her constantly, calling her, inviting her. She heard it in the wind. She felt it in the sunshine, and in the filtered moonbeams that slipped through the trees of the Mystwood. Grandmaster spoke of the Myst being alive and self-aware. It had no goals, no motive, other than to draw people toward it, calling them to connect and fulfill their potential.

Tonight, more than any other night in her life, Pomella could tangibly feel the Myst dancing around her. Surely Vivianna felt it, too?

The ground near the tower entrance rumbled, drawing over two hundred pairs of eyes. The soil bulged upward, forming a large mound, like a bubble rising from below the lawn until it towered above everyone's head. As the small hill came to rest, another shape rose from its pinnacle. The Green Man's familiar form and face rolled and twisted into existence. He wore a cloak of grass and summer flowers, and crowned atop his head was a laurel of twisted red leaves. Even Oxillian was dressed for the event, it seemed.

"Mystics and guests," the Green Man boomed, "arise and lift your hearts, make way, for the High Mystic of Moth!"

The door of the stone tower opened and out stepped Yarina, as beautiful and elegant as ever. Even though Pomella saw her frequently, the moment resonated with her, and she couldn't help but stare in awe. It was a familiar moment to her, much like the first time she saw Yarina, all those years ago.

The High Mystic crossed the lawn toward the hill. The ground rose as she walked, lifting her toward the summit. She wore a stunning gown of red and pink, with a sheer shawl of woven lace. In her right hand she carried her twisted Mystic staff that was nearly a full arm's length taller than her. Yarina's hair lay flat down her back, which surprised Pomella. Generally, the High Mystic liked to keep her hair up. Pomella turned to Vivianna to ask her if that was her idea. She stopped short when she saw her friend's admiration for her master. Pomella had never seen two people more connected. Yarina and Vivianna thought alike. They had a way of communicating that required few, if any, words. Watching the way in which Vivianna learned from Yarina, a person might think that Unveiling the Myst was easy. Vivianna progressed steadily, and even when the lesson called for patience she excelled where Pomella typically found initial frustration. The High Mystic and her apprentice even dressed alike. There was no doubt in Pomella's mind that Yarina had chosen the right person to become her successor.

As Yarina crested the newly formed hill, Vivianna touched her palms together and tapped her forehead and heart. All around her, the other Mystics were doing the same, or something similar. Some bowed; others curtsied. Pomella mimicked Vivianna, sending Mistress Yarina a genuine surge of gratitude for being a mentor and guardian for the past seven years.

Yarina lifted her free palm to indicate everyone should rise. She swept her eyes across everyone gathered, then turned her attention to the distant tree line straight ahead.

The Green Man spoke again: "In the name of the Saints and past masters, Mistress Yarina Sineese calls upon and welcomes the delegation of High Mystics of our world. Come forth, great masters, and grace us with your presence."

A massive wave of energy rippled through the crowd. Pomella couldn't help but smile, and felt a lump form in her throat.

A path opened among the gathered Mystics leading from the edge of the crowd to the hill Yarina stood on. The burning torches scattered throughout the crowd brightened. The Myst sang to Pomella. She could hear its music, as clearly as one hears a bell. Her heart yearned to sing that perfect song.

From the shadows, a figure emerged and walked toward Yarina. He was a short man, round and bald and dark-skinned, carrying a staff no taller than he was. He walked on sandaled feet, and wore a dark-red robe, thrown over one shoulder, exposing his arms. He smiled at those he passed, and again, every other person genuflected in some fashion.

"Be welcome, Master Ollfur of Keffra!" intoned Yarina. "Your presence illuminates us."

Pomella beamed. Her grandmhathir had been born into a noble house in Keffra but had given it up for a simple life of a commoner on Moth many years ago.

Master Ollfur joined Yarina on the top of the hill. Yarina bowed, but the other High Mystic chuckled a jolly laugh and hugged her instead. The gathering of Mystics laughed with him.

Serene as ever, Yarina smiled and hugged him back. She slipped from his embrace and looked back down the path he'd just walked before Oxillian called out, "By the grace of the Myst, welcome Master Angelos and Mistress Michaela of Rardaria, who each bless us with their presence!"

A pair of High Mystics, a man and woman, equal in height and stature, with matching Mystic staves, strolled down the path. Their faces were reflections of each other. Both had long platinum-colored hair that did nothing to diminish their majestic beauty.

"They are twins," Vivianna murmured to Pomella. "My parents were on a diplomatic visit to the Baronies shortly before I was born, and had the opportunity to meet them. Mistress Michaela touched my mother's swollen belly and blessed it. My mother believes it stirred the Myst within me."

The twin High Mystics came to the summit of the hill and exchanged greetings with Yarina. Ollfur hugged each one.

The next High Mystic the Green Man announced was Master Willwhite from Djain, a thin wisp of a man with pale skin, white hair trimmed short, and a piercing gaze. He carried a short Mystic staff like a baton, tucked in the crook of his elbow. Pomella had to peer carefully at him to see his features because they seemed to *shift* as he walked. It was as though one moment he had a rounded nose and the next it was more pointed. His lips and eyebrows changed slightly, too, but always remained delicate, almost effeminate.

Following Master Willwhite came Ehzeeth, an ancient-looking laghart with many missing scales. He leaned markedly on a heavily curved staff, and was escorted by Hizrith, who seemed ready to catch his master if he stumbled. Hizrith stopped short of the low hill, allowing Ehzeeth to ascend alone. Yarina greeted him, "Welcome, *Zurnta*."

Ehzeeth did not speak, but his tongue zipped out and licked the air many times as he studied each of his High Mystic peers. He, too, received a hug from Master Ollfur.

"And finally," Oxillian intoned, "with great respect and admiration, the High Mystic of Moth sends her greetings to Master Bhairatonix of Qin. Be welcome, great master; your brilliance lights our paths!"

A towering man, taller than anybody Pomella had ever seen before in her life, strode toward the other High Mystics. He was pale skinned and reed thin, and carried an enormous staff even taller than his head in his right hand. His left hand was lost in the folds of his robes. He kept his dusty gray hair trimmed short, but his beard spilled down to his stomach. He walked with his back straight and his head high.

Yarina and the other High Mystics bowed to him as he ascended the hill. Master Ollfur reached to hug him, but something in Bhairatonix's expression brought him up short, causing him to settle for a bow.

Seven High Mystics now stood before the central tower of Kelt Apar. The air *rumbled* with energy.

With the arrival of the final High Mystic, the crowd filled in the path they'd walked in on. An assortment of rangers and apprentices, all of whom had arrived with their masters, joined the gathering to watch the ceremony unfold.

The familiar presences of Hector and Ena swooped around Pomella. She shooed them away with her hand, giving them a look that promised a nasty scolding later if they didn't behave.

"By the grace of the Myst," Yarina said, spreading her hand and staff to the gathered crowd, "we are gathered. We come together to attend to the ancient and urgent business of Crow Tallin. As the Mystic Star Treorel passes over us, we—"

She cut off as the crowd near Pomella stirred. Pomella looked around, trying to see what the disturbance was.

Suddenly she was aware of her hummingbirds circling around her skirt. "What the skivers is it?" she whispered to them.

But the murmuring in the crowd answered for them. Pomella looked over those gathered and saw a familiar figure walking humbly forward.

It was Lal.

His poorly fitted robes stood out in an awkward fashion.

His expression and the lines on his face told Pomella he was unexpectedly nervous, an emotion Pomella hadn't seen on him before. Her heart swelled with emotion for him. He'd come. By the Saints, he'd actually shown up. As he noticed attention on him, he straightened. Pomella smiled. Here was a Grandmaster. The seven High Mystics upon the hill should fall to their knees before him! He was practically a living Saint!

Yarina cast a cool stare at her old master, her expression flat but clearly still considering what to do next. The other High Mystics had similarly blank expressions except for Master Ollfur, who, of course, grinned from ear to ear. Most Mystics in the crowd looked at Lal with a confused expression, and Pomella understood why. Despite his robes, he appeared Unclaimed. He kept his head and face shaved, and he generally walked with a slightly stooped posture.

Most striking of all, however, was that he carried no Mystic staff. Pomella had never seen him hold one, and while she'd wondered about it before over the years, she had just become so used to the idea that he didn't carry one. Now, as he stood among a crowd of over a hundred other Mystics holding staves, she wondered for the first time whether he even *had* one.

Master Willwhite, the slight, straight-backed High Mystic from Djain, broke the silence.

"You've been harboring an unexpected guest, Yarina," Willwhite said.

"An old friend," Master Angelos added.

"Yes," said Angelos' twin sister, Michaela. "But one whose path diverged many years ago."

Pomella narrowed her eyes. What did the High Mystic mean, diverged?

Master Ollfur smiled and clapped his hands once before speaking for the first time. "Just in time for the fun!" he said, and his voice had the tone and inflection of one who had just landed a joke. The crowd laughed.

"No," said a cold, hard voice, and the laughter faded. "He has no place here," said Bhairatonix.

Pomella clenched her fist. All Mystics deserved respect, especially the great High Mystics. But after that comment, she thought Master Bhairatonix was a culk. How could Lal not have a place at Kelt Apar?

She shot a glare at Yarina. Why was the High Mystic not standing up for him? She returned her attention to Lal, whose face had hardened. Her heart went out to him. He looked scared. Alone.

"Your time is past," Bhairatonix said. "Crow Tallin shall be handled by those of us gathered here already."

A thick tension hung in the air. Yarina said nothing, although Pomella could almost see her willing herself to maintain control. Anger boiled within Pomella. Mistress Yarina had been Lal's student, but now she refused to stand up for him.

But Lal had another student.

"He has a name!" Pomella called out.

Vivianna gasped beside her. Fear gripped Pomella as every face turned to look at her. By the Saints, what was she doing?

"This man is Ahlala Faywong," Pomella said, plowing forward. "Former High Mystic of Moth, and a Grandmaster of the Myst. This is his home, and all of us are graced by his living presence."

She touched her palms to her heart and forehead and bowed low, which proved to be wise, because she could feel her cheeks burning red.

Somebody needed to have said something. If Yarina wouldn't, then Pomella had to. She didn't care if it broke custom for her to speak up, but Lal deserved this.

All around her, and spreading outward like a pond ripple, the gathered Mystics bowed to Lal. There was no variety in the gestures this time. Every Mystic touched their palms together and bent at the waist, just as Pomella had. She felt the Myst surge within her, and at that moment she felt as though she could move a mountain.

Rising, she saw Lal's face soften as he give her a sad but loving look. Upon the low hill, the seven High Mystics studied her with mostly neutral expressions. Master Ollfur smiled, of course, and Yarina remained unreadable.

But it was Master Bhairatonix who held Pomella's attention. His cold stare was pure rage honed to a fine point.

You go too far, his look seemed to say.

Too far.

EIGHT

THE ORACLE

Eight Years Before Crow Tallin

Snow drifted around the Thorn-wood Shrine. From her oversized cushioned chair, Shevia watched it float lazily, as if time had stopped, seizing the flakes in the air, temporarily halting their descent. Her breath curled in front of her face, consuming a mote of snow.

A shiver of cold pebbled her arms, but she hardly felt it. Shevia only felt exhaustion these days. Before the tingling sensation faded, Miqo placed a heavy blanket over her shoulders. Once it was settled, the girl backed away a step and bowed, eyes lowered.

Shevia flicked a glance at her. Even in her bulky servant's attire, Miqo's curves were noticeably visible. The girl was fourteen years old now—two years older than Shevia—but she looked completely different from Shevia. Shevia wondered if she'd ever have hips or breasts like Miqo.

The sound of heavy footsteps crunching atop fresh snow drew her attention. Tevon, Typhos, and Tibron ascended the steps to the Shrine, their fur-lined cloaks catching snowflakes. Following them were her parents, dressed in flowing silks and lacking only the gold jewelry allowed by custom to the nobility. Solemn expressions covered their faces as they escorted the esteemed family from Keffra forward.

Ahg-Mein tapped Shevia's chair with his Mystic staff, indicating she should stand. Shevia forced herself not to glare at the man. She could no longer muster the strength to have contempt for him. Even though he had been the one to pull the poison from her body on the night her parents were almost murdered, she had never felt even a thumb's worth of gratitude for the former Obai House Mystic. She was beyond hating the thin-bearded man with his slicked hair, gold jewelry, fine fur cloaks, and smelly oils. Shevia suspected that as long as money flowed to his pockets the Mystic was content to stand in the corner and observe. Ahg-Mein sought profit above all else, even if murder was happening in front of him, or even if a little girl was drinking poison.

Gliding obediently from her chair, Shevia graced her finest curtsy to the Keffrans. "High-Pellan Uteen. High-Pellar Sutir. Welcome," she said, carefully navigating her way as best she could in the awkward Continental language. "I am humbled by your attendance. How may I serve you?"

The High-Pellan and his wife were a magnificent couple, tall, with deep brown skin and impressive physiques. They inclined their heads to Ahg-Mein but otherwise ignored him. Uteen Bartone was said to have been a champion duelist before he inherited his family's lands. The only duelist of more renown than him was Sutir, his wife. Dark, swirling tattoos—indications of their accomplishments—covered most of their exposed skin below the face, including their necks and the backs of their hands.

High-Pellar Sutir examined Shevia with a critical eye. "My gracious ancestors," she said, "you truly are a child. I hardly believed the reports."

"Do I displease you, High-Pellar?" Shevia said.

"No, of course not. It is a pleasure to be a guest at your Shrine."

Like most nobles who visited her, the High-Pellar seemed uneasy at the idea of a girl from a merchant-scholar family commanding such an unusual power. Shevia was not a Mystic, nor was she a noble. The very idea that a person born into that caste was involved in such things seemed impossible to them. More questions would likely have been asked if not for the presence of Ahg-Mein. With a Mystic present, even nobles would hesitate to ask those questions in public.

"Your kindness is greater than its wondrous reputation," Shevia said to the High-Pellar, keeping her voice meek. She spoke the words but hardly knew what she said. She didn't care at all about these nobles or anybody else. Most of the time she didn't care about anything. Her body felt like a shell, and the real Shevia—the little girl who used to scamper through the thorny hills outside her parents' estate—had been hollowed out and replaced by the fumes of the vent, and the demands of her ambitious family. Her mother assured her it was for her own good, and that perhaps the Minams would even rise to the nobility someday.

But Shevia knew the truth. Even if her family did become noble, she would forever be required to breathe in the fumes and speak the visions she saw. The Bartones were just another petitioner, come from far away, to demand and receive a prophecy.

Every noble came in person because the visions were always personal to the requester, and always significant, the sort of knowledge that generally people didn't want heard by others. Shevia's prophecies had launched more feuds than she cared to remember. At least one all-out war had been sparked by a tiny secret she'd spoken to the King of Rardaria. Shevia had heard he ordered his wife executed because of the secret she had kept from him.

Mystics, too, came from afar, curious to understand her power, and to try unsuccessfully to replicate it for themselves. The harder they tried, the more spectacularly they failed. Shevia stifled a shiver at the most recent memory of an attempt. She was content to let Ahg-Mein handle the few Mystics who decided to investigate her.

The remainder of the Bartones' entourage walked up the steps behind them. There were six guards, all wearing layered black and silver armor. Vicious swords hung at their sides, and each carried a shield on his forearm decorated with the crest of a crouching sand leopard. In between the six guards walked a boy and a girl, clearly the son and daughter of the nobles standing before her. The girl was about Shevia's age, with the same smooth, dark skin as her mother, but with her father's strong chin. The girl had the beginnings of curves to her body, too. Shevia barely cared anymore. Everyone would surpass her in everything.

It was the boy who snared her eye. He was tall and muscular, with long braided hair and hints of his own tattoos underneath his shirt. He was much older than her, maybe by as much as six or seven years, but his face was heavenly. Looking at him, Shevia felt an uncomfortable rush of emotion—the first she had felt of anything except spite in a long time. She forced herself to keep calm on the outside, and face the boy's parents.

"This is our daughter, Ellisen," said Uteen, "and our son, Quentin."

Shevia bowed her head to each, grateful that she was not required to make eye contact with the boy.

"So how does this work?" Sutir asked. "It is frightfully cold out. I trust there is not much ceremony, considering the weather?"

"I apologize for the weather, High-Pellar," Shevia said. "It is an unfortunate consequence of living this far north." Uteen snorted a laugh at this. Shevia kept her face blank. Her parents encouraged her to make such disparaging comments about the weather, their small estates, Shevia's young age, or even her unusual height. It made the nobles more comfortable, they said.

Ahg-Mein stepped forward. "The Oracle of Thornwood is honored to speak the truth of her vision to you. It is customary that a tithe is first given, in order to support her modest dwelling."

Shevia waited, hands folded within her robes. There was nothing modest about her dwelling. Her family had become unprecedentedly wealthy over the last three years because of her visions. The nobility paid incredible amounts of gold to learn secrets that could change the course of their Houses forever. The Minam fortunes now exceeded those of many of the nobles they served.

"Ah, yes, of course," Uteen said. He patted his cloak a few times as if trying to remember where he kept something, and finally pulled out a gilded scroll case, undoubtedly containing papers declaring that the Minam family was now entitled to a vast sum of money. He handed it to Shevia's father without a second glance. "Now what?"

"I will commune with the Thornwood," Shevia said, "and speak to you of its vision, High-Pellan."

Ahg-Mein had told her family it would be unwise to explain the nature of her visions. Shevia had wanted to be honest about her friend, but the Mystic and her parents crushed that idea immediately. It was too childish, they said. Equally unacceptable was if they spoke of the Myst in any way. Nobody, especially not Shevia, understood who her friend actually was, or whether the Myst was involved. If Ahg-Mein had any theories, he kept them to himself. It surely might be related to the Myst, of course, but it would be indecent for somebody of their station to outright declare they could commune with it. Tibron had been the one to suggest they use the name Thornwood, and link her visions to that.

"My husband will not receive a vision," Sutir said. "Our son and daughter will."

Shevia stifled a shrug. It mattered not to her. Every noble who came before this had demanded a vision related to their personal future. This was the first request for somebody other than themselves.

"I apologize for bearing unfortunate news, High-Pellar," Shevia said. "The Thornwood only grants visions for a single person."

"Then you shall read the vision for Quentin now," said the High Pellan, his eyes narrowing with annoyance. "Then tomorrow, or however long it takes this thorny forest to rest, we will have it for Ellisen. Don't worry, Chovin," he said, turning to Shevia's father. "I will pay your fee again. Half again more, if you have to reschedule another caller."

Shevia waited for her mother's nod from behind the nobles before continuing. "As you wish," she said. Her father would probably have to make alternative arrangements for the family coming tomorrow. Even among nobles, few stood higher than the Bartones from Keffra.

It was all the same to Shevia. Tomorrow morning, an hour before sunrise, Cilla would wake her and assist her in donning the bulky ceremonial robes her parents had designed and purchased. Most of their former lessons together had come to a halt following the Obai incident. Certainly, all of her free time had vanished.

After she had been shamefully dressed by somebody else, her brothers would escort her down the newly paved path that led to the center of Thornwood Valley. The sharp bushes that had once caught on her dress and hidden the entrance to the underground cave where her friend lived were either long gone or trimmed back to make room for the Shrine. Other, larger trees with thorny vines had been brought in and planted at great expense to enhance the Shrine's atmosphere. Day after day Shevia sat atop her chair and breathed the fumes from the vent. And day after day she saw visions that changed people's lives, while hers remained eternally empty.

The handsome boy Quentin stepped forward. Shevia suppressed a shiver in her chest. He wasn't really a boy, she supposed, although he wasn't an adult, either. She wondered if he just saw her as a little girl. He smiled at her, and waited.

"Come," she said.

Shevia led him forward a few steps until she was at the base of her seat. Typhos and Tibron bent to lift the heavy chair. A deep grinding sound shivered through the air as they slid back the marble base on which the chair rested. As soon as the seal was removed, silvery smoke from the vent wafted into the cold air. A faint hissing sound, like water turning to steam, sounded around them. The familiar scent of sandalwood and holly filled her nostrils, immediately triggering the start of her trance.

Shevia extended her arms for Miqo to slip off her outer robe. Her skin pebbled in the cool air, but she ignored it as she stepped down the marble steps, and stood directly above the wide crack in the ground. She turned to Quentin, the only person she could now see. The smoke billowed around her, and she let the familiar dream take hold. Her eyes rolled back, and it began.

A presence rose around her. As always, there was nothing to see or touch, but Shevia felt her friend rise as surely as if she were standing beside her.

Her friend looked at Quentin with formless eyes, weighing him. The falling snow around her shifted to rain. The Shrine and its remaining thornbushes stretched upward, reaching toward the sky until they became tall trees. The hard ground softened into muddy grass. She stood somewhere else now, in a forest.

About fifty steps ahead, the trees opened into a wide clearing, with a stone tower in the middle. Men and women walked and talked, prayed and died, endlessly coming and going in and out of the unchanging tower. Years and single heartbeats passed. One of the passing figures turned, and it was Quentin, but his skin flowed like molten stone. Beside him was another person, a girl, who wore only a cloak made of silver wind. Maybe four years older than Shevia, the girl had light-brown skin and hair cut short like a commoner.

She turned and stared at Shevia, her eyes burning with hatred.

Angry storm clouds gathered overhead. A searing-hot gust carrying glowing red embers howled from the direction of the stone tower. The wind stung Shevia's eyes, but she could not turn away. Quentin and the unknown girl screamed soundlessly and turned to ash.

The top of the tower exploded and in the vacant space sat a woman sitting cross-legged in the air. Her long, shimmering hair stormed all around her.

Shevia shielded her eyes, but after a moment the roaring-hot wind soothed her. She lowered her arms and looked again at the woman. She could not make out the woman's face or other details, but recognition dawned on her. She thought of the little painted-glass statue in her room.

Sitting Mother. Her friend.

A smile tugged at Shevia's lips. At last, she knew. She tilted her head back and let the gusts consume her. Tiny motes of ash flashed against her skin. She breathed deep. She wanted to ask a thousand questions.

Sitting Mother spoke, not with words exactly, but with understanding that simply arrived in Shevia's mind. *Ask that which burns within you*, she seemed to say.

Shevia opened her eyes and leveled her gaze. The tower, the grassy clearing, and the forest were all gone, replaced by an entrance to a deep cave. The wind rushed out from the dark hole, searing hot but alive with power.

Ask that which burns within you. Shevia thought of her life, and the Thornwood. She saw the long years ahead as nobles came to her over and over, demanding visions. She wondered if she could ever have more than that. Could somebody like that boy, Quentin, ever see her as a woman and not a hideously tall and skinny girl? Would her parents ever see her as more than a puppet? And above all, why could only she, and nobody else, receive the visions?

For the first time in many years, complicated emotions stirred within her. It was as if they had been frozen by time and circumstance, but now melted away by the heat of her friend's whispers.

Anger was the first to emerge from the thaw.

"How can I be free?" Shevia said.

The wind shifted, honed and focused like a knife, biting into her right shoulder. Shevia cried out and looked at the place where she had been struck. Her shirt burned away, revealing raw, pinkish skin. A series of red and black marks lashed her shoulder. It appeared to be one continuous line, twisting over and around itself in a swirling pattern resembling a snake.

The world exploded in silvery light. Shevia screamed and opened her eyes. Snow drifted around her. Mother and Father stood nearby, staring at her with fear. Behind them, Quentin and his family looked uncomfortable.

Ahg-Mein gazed at her from behind his Mystic staff, his head cocked to one side. Shevia remembered seeing the exact same expression on his face three years ago as he watched her fight poison.

Tibron knelt beside her, holding her head up. Her other two brothers waited nearby. "Shay-Shay," Tibron said. "Are you well?"

Her hands trembling, Shevia gently pushed Tibron away. She rose and directed her stare at her parents. Her mother's eyes were wide, and her father gaped at her. Anger, as cold and fresh as the falling snow, still coursed through her.

"A new High Mystic of Moth has been anointed," she declared, turning to the High-Pellan and High-Pellar. "She will seek an apprentice." As with all visions given to her by her friend, Shevia knew with an absolute certainty that her words were true. The events she witnessed in the trance weren't literal, but she always awoke understanding their meaning with perfect clarity.

The High-Pellan's face broke into a smile. "At last! A worthy master for our son. Tell me, how can Quentin succeed at the Trials?"

"He will be blocked by another candidate. A commoner."

Stunned silence answered her. For a moment, it was almost as if Shevia could hear the drifting snowflakes land upon the ground.

"Are you joking with us, child?" the High-Pellar asked.

The High-Pellan's face darkened with anger. "If you are lying to us, girl . . ."

Shevia's anger broke. "I do not lie! I am not a child! Within two swollen moons the High Mystic will invite a commoner girl to attend the Trials. Beware the doors she could open. The secret eyes of the world watch."

Shevia's father cleared his throat. "Please forgive her agitated state. It is often like this when she awakes from the trance."

"Do not speak for me, Father," Shevia said. "You will never again do so."

"Shevia!" her mother snapped. "How—"

She cut off as Shevia turned her searing gaze at her. Her

mother must have seen something terrible in her expression, because she took a step back.

"Begone," Shevia said in a quiet voice that she knew all of them could hear. It had been so long since she'd felt anything. Now, thawed by the unusual trance, her anger turned molten.

Nobody around her moved. "*Go!* All of you! This is *my* Shrine. I am the Oracle of Thornwood! Leave or I will burn you to ash!" She screamed the last.

A cold hand clutched her shoulder. Without thinking, Shevia snatched it away, twisting it with her clawed hands. Ahg-Mein screamed and fell to a knee under her grip. Her mother gasped. Somewhere, buried in the back of her awareness, Shevia knew that by harming a Mystic she forfeited her hand, if not her life.

"I do not fear you, Mystic. You are a charlatan like the rest of them. Test me and you will feel my friend's wrath."

The Bartones' guards drew their swords, but only moments ahead of Shevia's brothers. A wave of heat rose up Shevia's spine, starting at her tailbone, slithering up toward her head. As the warmth spread, so did an intense pressure, lighting her skin aflame. A silvery fog rose around them. Nobody else seemed to notice it except Ahg-Mein, who stared with wide eyes.

"*Go!*" Shevia screamed, throwing the Mystic away from her.

The Bartones fled, trailed by Ahg-Mein and Shevia's family. She screamed and screamed until she was alone with her tears. Her skin burned with heat. She clawed at her heavy robes and pulled them away. She stood, half-naked in the heart of the Thornwood. The strange fog swirled and mixed with the fumes rising from the nearby vent. Shevia heaved through her breaths and looked at her shoulder.

Rising from the skin, like a tattoo, was the woven image of a red and black snake.

Hours passed. Shevia's anger steamed around her well after sunset.

It was Miqo who finally returned from the house, carrying a bundle of fresh clothes for Shevia. When the girl approached Shevia, she bowed, and informed her of a guest's arrival.

"I do not care. Tell whatever disgusting noble it is to go back home. They will get nothing from me."

"Your pardon, Lady Mistress," Miqo said, using a term she had previously only used for Shevia's mother, "normally, Unmuth and the rest of the guards would turn him away, but under the circumstances, they had no choice but to let him pass."

"Out with it, girl!" Shevia snapped. "Who is he?"

Even in the dim light, Shevia could see Miqo blush. "The High Mystic of Qin."

Cold fear gripped Shevia. The High Mystic. Was this because she'd touched and hurt another Mystic?

"What does he want?"

"He did not say. But he insists on speaking to you immediately. He awaits you in your father's library."

The fear with her swirled in her stomach, but she suppressed it. Sitting Mother was with her. She could feel her through the twisted shape on her shoulder. The tattoo didn't move, but she could feel it *writhe* beneath her skin.

She would face this High Mystic.

"Lead me to him."

"Please, Lady Mistress, your robes. They are . . ." Miqo hesitated, likely too afraid to say anything Shevia might consider as criticism.

Shevia realized she still wore her torn Oracle robes. "I will change," she said.

Miqo handed over the clothes with trembling hands and turned her back to give Shevia privacy. After she changed, Miqo led her to the library. The house seemed unusually quiet. Dusk approached, but no evening lanterns had yet been lit.

The heavy doors to her father's library creaked open, revealing the familiar desk and shelves where he kept his business records. Both of Shevia's parents, as well as Ahg-Mein and her three brothers, stood within. All stood with their heads down and backs to the wall, waiting in silence.

In the center of the library stood a towering man, easily the tallest person Shevia had ever seen. He held a staff that was as gnarled as his back was straight. He faced away from Shevia but turned as she entered. His hair and beard were white like snow, as was his skin. He kept his other hand hidden in the depths of his bloodred robes.

Shevia's father cleared his throat. "Shevia, this is High Mystic Bhairatonix. He traveled all the way from Shenheyna to see you. His presence is a blessing upon our house." He said the last with a not-so-subtle hint that she should speak with civility around him.

"So you are the girl," Bhairatonix said in a deep, resounding voice. He glanced at Miqo. "Leave us. See that we are not disturbed."

Miqo squeaked a fearful reply and shut the doors behind Shevia. For a long moment, nothing but silence danced around the
room.

"I am the Oracle of Thornwood," Shevia said, mustering her
courage.

The High Mystic laughed. "Indeed. But you are still just a
girl." Before Shevia could react, he shifted his staff to lean
against his shoulder and shot out his hand to clutch her chin.
He studied her, turning her cheeks back and forth, and finished
by holding her gaze. There was intense interest in his eyes, and
perhaps something else, too, although Shevia wasn't sure if she
recognized it properly. She willed herself not to shudder.

"Your visions have caused quite a stir," Bhairatonix said. "It
remains to be seen if you're a clever liar or something more. Tell
me, can you summon the Myst?"

"I—I am not sure, High Mystic. I am not—"

Bhairatonix silenced her with a glance. Shevia's mouth snapped
shut. She could not tell if he did something to silence her, or
if she simply obeyed out of habit. He looked sideways toward
Ahg-Mein. "Can she use the Myst?"

"I do not know, Master," Ahg-Mein said. Shevia noted the
fear in his voice. A Mystic, feeling fear.

Bhairatonix nodded at the air, and a circle of spinning light
formed in front of him. "This is a wind flower," he told Shevia.
"Use whatever power is at your disposal to extinguish it."

"Apologies, Master," Shevia said. "I am not a noble or—"

"I will not ask again," Bhairatonix said.

Shevia caught a glance from her mother, who nodded slightly.
She stared at the wind flower and tried to put herself back into

the trance-like state she felt when she was with her friend. She closed her eyes and willed herself to remember.

Nothing happened.

Shevia concentrated on her tattoo and silently begged Sitting Mother to come forth and give her power.

Again, nothing happened. Bhairatonix watched her carefully. The wind flower continued to spin.

Bhairatonix dismissed it with a casual wave. "Today, girl, you made a bold declaration about the High Mystic of Moth. I had not foreseen this. You will tell me what you saw, and I will know if you're lying."

Was that why he was here? Was a commoner becoming a Mystic such a large concern that it warranted the attention of Qin's most powerful Mystic?

Shevia clenched her hands to prevent them from shaking. She steadied herself and told the High Mystic about the vision she'd had earlier in the day. She told him everything, except about her attraction to the Bartone boy, and Sitting Mother appearing to her. When she finished, she waited, not knowing what to expect. Spoken aloud like that, it sounded foolish.

Bhairatonix considered her for a moment, then frowned and brushed past her toward the door. "You are a foolish girl with no power," he said. He turned to her parents. "You will tear that Shrine down tomorrow. Bury whatever you found in the ground."

Shevia's father sighed and nodded.

Ahg-Mein stepped forward. "I do not believe that is wise, Master. The girl's visions have always been true. I've studied many of the subtle evidences in its favor and—"

"You are a greedy fool, Ahg-Mein," Bhairatonix said. "You

spend too much time surrounded by luxury. Perhaps a few de-cades as a wanderer will teach you humility granted by the Myst."

"With respect, *Master*, I will do as I please. I have seen what this girl will do. In fact, I claim her—"

Without warning, Ahg-Mein's Mystic staff snapped out of his hand and flew toward the High Mystic. Bhairatonix caught it in the same long-fingered grip that held his own staff. The stolen staff shone with a cold, silvery light, the twists of wood shining bright.

"You will claim nothing, boy."

Ahg-Mein's eyes bugled. "No! Master, I—"

The stolen staff flashed with light and exploded into gray ash. Ahg-Mein screamed.

"I declare you Unclaimed," Bhairatonix said. "From this day forth the Myst shall be denied to you."

Ahg-Mein fell to his knees and ran his hands through the ash drifting onto the floor of her father's library.

With a final glance at Shevia, Bhairatonix pushed the library doors open and walked away.

Shevia looked from her mother and brothers to the sobbing Unclaimed man on the floor. Her mother took a small step away from him. Ahg-Mein looked up at Shevia. The memory of her poisoning came to her mind. Shevia cocked her head side-ways, just as Ahg-Mein had. The anger she had felt earlier in the evening rose again.

Shevia smiled. A cold, cruel thing that she hoped was like a knife twisting in the former Mystic's heart.

The Unclaimed man saw her smile, and Shevia saw the rage build within him. He snarled and looked toward the departing High Mystic. He reached into his robes and pulled out a short dagger. With a snarl he shoved past Shevia and threw himself at Bhairatonix.

Without thinking, or knowing why she did it, Shevia screamed. It was not a normal scream, but one formed of power. Her tattoo burned on her shoulder. The scream exploded out of her, shaking the room and knocking both the Unclaimed and High Mystic off their feet. The dagger clattered across the floor.

Bhairatonix found his feet first. He lifted his staff, and as he did so the man formerly known as Ahg-Mein rose off the floor as well. He clawed at his throat as if a hand held him there. His boots kicked at nothing in the air.

"Becoming Unclaimed was too good for you," Bhairatonix said. He tilted his staff slightly, and the Unclaimed man's spine bent with it. Shevia gaped. The man's back went farther and farther until it finally *snapped* with a loud popping noise.

Bhairatonix lowered his staff and dropped the corpse. He looked at Shevia.

"So there is power in you. Good. I claim you as my apprentice."

Shevia gaped. Her father rushed forward and fell to one knee.

"Master," he said. "I would gladly give you my daughter if you command it, but please, understand. We are but humble merchant-scholars. It would bring shame and ruin to our house if it was known that our daughter dabbled with the Myst. The Mystic—I mean . . . Ahg-Mein—he assured us it was of no concern because nobody could prove her visions came from the Myst."

Bhairatonix considered him. "Very well. From this moment forth the blood of the Minam family is noble blood. You may tax those who live on your land, and you are charged with their well-being. May you and your House rule with wisdom.

"I also claim your so-called Thornwood," he added. "None are to trespass on it, under penalty of becoming Unclaimed. Set a guard, night and day. I shall return to study it from time to time."

He flicked a finger through the air and the gold jewelry that had been around Ahg-Mein's neck snapped free and floated to Shevia's mother.

"Your first gold jewelry, Lady Minam," Bhairatonix said. He turned to Shevia. "Come, girl. Your true education begins now."

Shevia's mother looked from the gold necklace—the mark of nobility—to her daughter. For the first time in her memory, Shevia thought she saw something that resembled affection in her face. But a heartbeat later it was gone, lost as she bowed low to Shevia.

"You served your family well, Daughter."

Tevon, Typhos, and Tibron looked at one another.

"So that's it," Tibron said, stepping forward. "You're just going to take her?"

Tevon yanked Tibron back. "Know your place."

Bhairatonix looked from her brothers to her parents. "Three twins? Bad luck indeed." His tone sounded amused.

Shevia's father stammered, "M-m-master, I apologize for my sons. They are good men, if a bit overprotective of their youngest sibling."

Bhairatonix considered. "No man should ever apologize for his sons, especially a noble. They seem hearty. I will allow them to come with us. I will see their training completed, but not as Mystics."

Shevia's father bowed. His voice cracked as he spoke. "I would be honored, if that is their choice."

Tibron spoke first. "I'll go."

Tevon sighed. "I go with my brother."

Typhos shrugged and nodded his agreement to go.

"Then it is settled. Come. Bring nothing. New possessions will be provided when we arrive at Shenheyna."

He crossed toward the entrance, stepping over the mangled body of the man he'd killed. The man was not important. He had been Unclaimed. Her parents would have to arrange for another Unclaimed to come and drag the body away. After that, Shevia wasn't sure what would happen to it.

Despite her long legs, Shevia had to hurry to match his even longer stride. "Master," she said, the word sounding strange on her tongue, "are there formalities we must—"

Bhairatonix gestured with his staff to dismiss the idea. "Needless ceremony."

"But what about my staff?"

He halted and loomed over her. "You will never question anything unless given leave to do so. *I* decide what you need. But if a staff is what you desire, then so be it."

He peered at a nearby servant closet, whose door banged open. A mop with a long handle flew toward them. Shevia jolted in surprise and caught the mop. Bhairatonix snapped the air with the top of his staff and the bottom portion of the mop disintegrated, leaving Shevia with nothing but a long handle in her hand.

"Congratulations, apprentice," Bhairatonix sneered, and continued to the manor exit.

Shevia stared in disbelief at the pathetic handle in her hand. Tibron put his hand on Shevia's back, urging her forward. She tried to look back at her father, or even her mother, but Tibron and her other brothers blocked her view.

NINE

VISIONS OF PAIN

Flickering fire from a multitude of torches illuminated Pomella's face as she returned Master Bhairatonix's hard stare. Every part of her mind screamed to look away, to yield to her superior. This was a High Mystic! He was one of the most powerful people in the world, and one she'd been taught to give respect to at all times.

But by the Saints, if he wasn't going to properly acknowledge his superiors then neither would she. Somebody had to stand up for Lal. Because that's what a student did when her master was treated with disrespect. Pomella wondered what sort of grudge Bhairatonix had against Lal.

"Thank you, Pomella!" Yarina intoned. As always, her voice was a melody, carried easily over the gathered crowd. She shifted her gaze to Lal. "The High Mystics welcome you, Grandmaster.

Your wisdom and experience will be an asset to us during Crow Tallin."

Pomella noted that Yarina still did not invite him to join the other High Mystics on the raised hilltop. She bit her lip, resisting the urge to demand that Lal take his rightful place among them. The High Mystic addressed the crowd once more, as if to move on from the uncomfortable topic.

"Mystics and guests," she said, "for the safety of everyone gathered, Kelt Apar shall be sealed against outsiders until Crow Tallin concludes." She nodded to the Green Man, who stepped forward and lifted his arms.

The crowd shifted as the gathered Mystics exchanged glances. Pomella frowned. What did Yarina mean?

A deep rumble answered her. The ground trembled beneath her feet. A cracking noise sounded in the distance. At the edge of the Mystwood, a thick wall of wood, dirt, and stone rose from the ground. Even at this distance, Pomella could smell the freshly churned soil as it was torn from the depths of the ground and fortified upward. The wall spread north and south and curved to encircle the entire compound. Its uppermost edges dwarfed most of the surrounding trees so that only the tops of the tallest could be seen. A chorus of angry cries rose from beyond the wall until they were drowned out by the thick hedge.

"By the Saints," Pomella whispered.

A figure sprinted across the lawn, coming from the distant shadows near the wall. Pomella couldn't see who it was, but she suspected it was a commoner or other person who, intentionally or not, had found themselves on the inside. A second, hunched figure streaked after the first. Vlenar.

Pomella stared in horror as Vlenar tackled the runner. In

the dim light she could only perceive a tumbling of shadows, but quickly Vlenar had the person pinned to the ground.

It was just one person, but the implications worried Pomella. In the days approaching Crow Tallin, the High Mystics should be helping to comfort and protect people, not push them away with walls. A brief, irrational worry crossed Pomella's mind. What if the man struggling on the ground against Vlenar was somebody she knew? What if it was Berrit, the minstrel she'd met at the Rolling Forge? There was nothing to indicate that it was him.

Yarina went on, as if nothing was amiss. "For nine hundred years we have gathered to protect the world. At times like these, some sacrifices must be made for the greater good."

Pomella gave Vlenar and the intruder a concerned glance. She wasn't sure the greater good was being served, but there was nothing more she could do about it right now.

"Treorel's passing is a time of transition and change," Master Ollfur said with his constant smile. "It burns old ways, and ignites conflict. But we are called to rise above that. We are gathered here to bring unity and guidance to the world."

"Master Ollfur is correct," said Master Willwhite. He turned his shifting face toward the crowd. "There is no time for strife among ourselves. Without us, Moth may fall into chaos, and if that happens, so might other civilized lands."

"The time to unite is now," said Mistress Michaela. A wind shuddered through the clearing, flickering the firelight and the High Mystic's white hair. Shadows danced across her and her brother's face. "The days of Crow Tallin begin tonight. Already Treorel rises in our night sky. Soon, it will be visible, both day and night."

"In eleven days," said Master Angelos, "Treorel will briefly drift behind the moon, during which time Fayün and the human realm will overlap completely. The fay will roam our world freely, and ordinary people will find themselves stepping into the silver realm."

"Be mindful of your studies!" Yarina intoned. "These next days will stretch our resources. The world looks to us, the guardians and custodians of the Myst, to guide them to safety and assure them that the hardships will pass. To address these needs, you will be dispersed, beginning tomorrow, across Moth to where the need is most. Already we're receiving daily reports of unusual phenomena that call for our attention.

"Oxillian"—she gestured an upraised palm toward the Green Man—"and my student, Vivianna Vinnay, will give you specific instructions as needs arise."

Bhairatonix lifted his staff, and its long shadow stretched across the hill. He kept his other hand hidden in the folds of his robes. "I propose an alternative solution!" he intoned. Pomella shifted uncomfortably. The High Mystic's haughty tone grated on her nerves.

"A different solution to the dangers of Crow Tallin?" Master Ollfur said, and chuckled.

A scattering of chuckles arose from the crowd at the High Mystic's good-natured joke, but Pomella saw a shadow darken across Bhairatonix's face.

"An oracle has arisen in Qin," Bhairatonix said.

The last of the crowd's laughter died. Pomella glanced at Vivianna, who frowned. Just beyond her, Lal stood behind the rest of the crowd, all but forgotten. He listened to Bhairatonix without expression. Pomella wondered what Bhairatonix was getting at. There were occasionally reports of certain individuals from the Continent who could see the future, but most ended up being false or exaggerated reports surrounding the exploits of a local Mystic.

Bhairatonix gestured toward the rear of the crowd, which parted as it had earlier. Three rangers, tall, young, clean-shaven, and well-dressed with bloodred capes billowing behind them, strode down the path. They moved with confident assurance, backs straight and eyes darting everywhere, constantly monitoring for danger, even here. Pomella couldn't help but admire how handsome they were. Each carried a curved sword at his hip. They had tanned skin, jet-black hair, square jaws, and sharp facial features. Their faces were polished reflections of one another. They had to be brothers. Triplets.

The brothers made an impressive procession down the line. They moved with graceful ease, keeping their attention straight ahead. As handsome as they were, their expressions told Pomella that they were as sharp and as deadly as the swords they carried and undoubtedly knew how to use.

Another figure emerged behind them, drifting in the wake they left with their passing. She was unusually tall, skinny, with long dark hair and a short Mystic staff that was as thin as its owner. The crowd buzzed as she glided down the path. The Myst stirred around Pomella. It was the woman she'd seen earlier surrounded by the crowd of Mystics.

The rangers arrived at the base of the hill and waited, hands on sword hilts and eyes turned down.

"Is this sort of parade normal?" Pomella whispered to Vivianna.

Vivianna shook her head. "I wasn't alive for the last Crow Tallin. But I didn't see anything in the old books about the introduction of anybody besides the High Mystics."

The newcomer joined her ranger escorts. As one, they bowed before the High Mystics. The rangers bent at the waist while the girl spread her arms wide and eased downward into a slow and graceful curtsy.

Each of the High Mystics examined her, weighing her as a noblewoman might eye a feast-day tribute brought forth by the commoners working their land. Pomella was reminded of a time during her apprentice Trials when she'd encountered a unique fay creature with the ability to speak. Mantepis had spoken of how true masters could instantly see beyond a person and discover the potential they possessed. *They could Unveil you with a glance*, he had said.

The woman at the center of Kelt Apar now bore the judging gazes of seven High Mystics, not to mention those of over a hundred other Mystics. Even Master Ollfur's smile had slipped, leaving behind a serious and concerned expression. Master Ehzeeth's slitted eyes narrowed and his tongue flicked out as if to taste the woman's potential. Pomella knew how she felt, having had the same attention only minutes ago.

"I found her in the rugged valleys of the highlands," said Master Bhairatonix, "in a prestigious House. For ten years I've trained her, focused her, and she has become one of the foremost Mystics of the land. I give you Shevia Minam, the Oracle of Thornwood."

The woman, Shevia, turned. Her sleeveless red dress had a scooped neckline, baring skin with the same tanned shade as the ranger brothers'. The wind fluttered her dark hair across her face. Upon her upper right arm and shoulder was an intricate tattoo of a clawed serpent, shaped in the style of a Mothic knot. Again, Pomella thought of Mantepis, who looked like a massive snake with four thin legs. The creature depicted in the tattoo had a barb-ended tail that coiled around Shevia's arm and ended at her elbow. Its head curved up and over her shoulder to rest below the base of her neck. Shevia projected calm and confidence, perhaps even arrogance. She seemed entirely unconcerned with the most powerful individuals in the world staring at her. Now that the angle and light provided Pomella with a better view, she saw the woman had unusually colored eyes, off-blue, drifting toward lavender.

Lavender eyes. Where had she seen that before?

"A true, living oracle, you say, Bhairatonix?" said Master Willwhite. "The world has not seen an oracle in centuries. Are you certain?"

In reply, Bhairatonix leaned his staff against his shoulder and used his right hand to withdraw a carved, ornate box from his voluminous robes. "Apprentice!" he commanded. Shevia ascended the hill and stood below her Master, bowing in deference. The High Mystic towered over her, despite her unusual height.

He held the box out, and a wisp of light snaked around it and lifted the lid. A cloud of silver-green smoke wafted out. Shevia bent her head and inhaled deeply.

Pomella narrowed her eyes. "What is that?" she murmured to Vivianna.

"I don't know," Vivianna said. "Some kind of incense, it looks like."

Bhairatonix snapped the lid shut. "Now. Unveil the pain of this island," he said. His words shuddered through Pomella.

"As you command, Master," Shevia said with a thick, clipped accent that sounded like Lal's.

Shevia curtsied again and then descended the hill. The three rangers stepped back, as did the crowd, to give room. In the firelight, Pomella saw Shevia's eyes glaze over. She stood straight, slowly arcing her Mystic staff in a wide circle until it was above her head, parallel to the ground. Then, faster than Pomella thought possible, she whirred it downward and jammed it into the ground.

Warm wind wafted through Kelt Apar, wafting Pomella's hair. With it came the Myst, building intensity.

Pomella glanced at Vivianna, who stared in wide-eyed wonder.

Shevia stood rooted to the spot, with her head tilted back. The Myst *rumbled* around Kelt Apar. A fist of fear arose in Pomella's gut. Normally, when the Myst stirred powerfully around her she felt compelled to sing, to harmonize with its essence and join with it. But now she wanted to cower. It was if she were watching an avalanche tumble down a mountain. She wondered if the rest of the gathered Mystics held their breaths as she did. Pomella looked at the High Mystics to gauge their reactions.

With an almost inhuman voice, Shevia called out to the night. She spoke quickly and with force in a language Pomella didn't understand.

Like a thunderclap, the Myst responded.

Brilliant silver light erupted from Shevia's staff, momentarily blinding the crowd. The avalanche crashed over them, carrying Pomella along whether she wanted to or not.

Muffled whispers filled the air, riding the storm of energy. They came from every direction. The gathered Mystics looked around, trying to find the source of the voices. It sounded to Pomella as though they were surrounded by a charging army.

Silver lines of light streaked into the clearing, only a small handful at first, but then quickly gaining in number. Each beam of light zoomed toward Shevia but stopped short, exploding into a puff of smoke. Within each cloud was the billowing, silvery image of a person. The first was a commoner by her appearance, dressed in a Goodness' work dress and stained apron. A gentle wind tugged at her hair and the smoke surrounding her.

"It came from the sky, without warning," the woman said, addressing Shevia. "As big'n mighty as a stampedin' ox, I never saw such a sight. It tore my arm, and it still lives outside my house. Help me."

Before the words faded, another image spoke, this time coming from a teenage girl, also wearing commoner work clothes and her hair cut short. "I saw it in the loch on the far side of the hill from my grandfathir's sheep pen. As wide as my arms, with scales like a snake. Help me."

A storm of images appeared. They spoke over one another in a jumbled assault of reports and requests for help. Shevia stood in the center of it all, catching her breath. Steadying herself, the girl turned to face the High Mystics.

"As you command, Master, so I obey."

The beams of light and the voices continued to materialize. A merchant guard spoke of a creature on the road. A baker from Sentry claimed his cat had gone missing and now he saw strange rats everywhere. On and on the stories came, each telling of a problem, and each implying that the fay were at the heart of it.

"Blessed Saints," Pomella whispered to Vivianna. "You ever seen anything like that?"

Vivianna shook her head. "No, and certainly not from an apprentice."

Pomella frowned. Lal and Yarina had always taught her that despite their reputation to the contrary, most Mystics rarely displayed grand Unveilings such as this. Using the Myst was not about spectacle or might. There was a good chance that the majority of Mystics gathered in Kelt Apar tonight were better known for their use of ritual, meditation, and subtle Unveilings of the Myst. By most standards, the display Pomella had put on at the Rolling Forge Inn was extravagant.

But nothing Pomella had ever done could match the sheer spectacle that Shevia displayed.

A hundred voices called to the young Mystic, each pleading for assistance. More appeared every second, adding their plight to the list of woes faced by the people of Moth.

Upon the low hill, Bhairatonix turned to his peers. "As you can see, my apprentice is more than capable of assisting us. The voices you hear are real. But unlike the petitions you receive, which require a person to find enough courage or desperation to reach out to us, these pleas are shared only to their loved ones, or to the quiet shadows in their home. My apprentice *sees* where no others can."

"She is impressive, Bhairatonix," said Master Willwhite. "We will make use of the girl."

"Indeed," said Yarina. "We will speak with her now, in private, before we attend to our . . . other duties."

Pomella caught the slight pause in Yarina's voice. It was subtle, and she wondered if anybody else had noticed.

Bhairatonix nodded to Shevia, who slowly waved her staff in front of her, as if wiping a dirty window. The multitude of images and pleas vanished, leaving the clearing in a heavy silence.

Yarina continued. After the assault of sound, the High

Mystic's melodious voice carried like a dove flying over a ruined battlefield. "Tomorrow beginning at dawn, we shall receive each of you in the tower. Oxillian will provide you with specific instructions."

"Rest deeply tonight," Mistress Michaela added. "For the days and nights of Crow Tallin are long."

As one, the High Mystics turned away from the crowd, and followed Yarina into the tower. Oxillian gestured for Shevia to follow. The younger woman began to do so, but not before she peered over her shoulder, searching through the crowd. Her eyes fell on Pomella, and suddenly Pomella felt a warm shudder coursing through her. Shevia locked gazes with her, and again an overwhelming sense of connection gripped her. Where had she seen this girl before?

Pomella's heart hammered. Shevia's expression betrayed nothing, but she stared at Pomella far longer than would normally be comfortable. She turned away, and took a calming breath. So much was happening that she didn't understand. Crow Tallin. Shevia. Lal.

Thinking of Grandmaster made Pomella wonder where he was. The crowd of Mystics had begun to disperse. She searched for Lal but couldn't find him.

"What's wrong?" Vivianna asked.

Before Pomella could answer, Hector and Ena flew in front of her, buzzing with excitement.

"I— What now?"

The birds circled her once, then zoomed over the clearing. A handful of Mystics glanced up at the birds as they passed overhead. They flew to the far side of the clearing, on the outer edge of the firelight opposite Pomella. They hovered beside a man standing with his back to the thinning crowd.

In an instant, she knew. She didn't need to sense her hummingbirds' excitement, or see his face as he turned his attention from the birds to look across the clearing at her. Her heart clenched.

"By the Saints," Pomella whispered. "Sim."

She fled the gathering outside the central tower. With everything else happening tonight at the ceremony, she couldn't bring herself to face Sim.

There had been a moment, right as she recognized him, when he'd turned his attention to her. But before they could lock gazes, she spun and left the clearing.

Seven years ago, Pomella had convinced herself that parting ways with Sim was emotionally manageable. And at first, it had been. There'd been much to learn and adapt to in the early days of her apprenticeship. Lal and Yarina kept her busy with an abundance of chores on top of lessons focused on meditation, and how to consistently sense the presence of the Myst. Yarina allowed her to plant a vegetable garden and had given her materials to make work dresses for both herself and Vivianna. All of these tasks helped distract from the pain of losing Sim.

For a scoopful of weeks, anyway.

As she hurried from Sim's gaze, the familiar grip of anxiety threatened to creep into Pomella's stomach. She thought she had already dealt with this. But after he'd been gone a year,

Pomella had come across the Common Cord given to her by the Oakspring Goodnesses. It was a series of colored cords, all twisted with various Mothic knots representing each family in the village. The memory triggered an avalanche of pain of losing her home and Sim. That night, alone in her cabin, she'd let the emotions overwhelm her. She'd sobbed, purging herself of the last remnants of Sim. But doing so had left her awash with guilt for letting him go. She didn't tell anybody, and especially hid it from Vivianna, who, back then, still had occasionally treated her with disdain on account of their upbringings and the tumultuous beginning to their friendship.

That had been the one and only night she'd cried for Sim. It had been a release before she grounded herself and refocused on her studies.

So why now, she wondered as she hustled away from the clearing, six years after finally letting him go, could she not face him? Perhaps you couldn't ever truly let go of the people closest to you in your life. Or perhaps it was just Sim she'd never be able to expunge from her heart. Or even want to.

And what did it say about her that she didn't miss her fathir like she missed Sim?

The answer to that last one was simple. For years Sim had been the one who'd been there for her in a way her fathir never had. Sim had been one of the few people from Oakspring who seemed to understand her, and who sought to spend time with her in the edge of the Mystwood. He'd been the only one who hadn't called her a nutter for claiming to occasionally catch glimpses of the fay lingering between trees or across the Creekwaters.

Now, tonight, amid all the chaos and intrigue, Sim's presence had proven to be too much for her. Pomella needed to be alone.

She pushed open the gate leading to her cabin and garden but stopped as her hummingbirds looped around her, radiating confusion.

"I'm not going to talk to him tonight," Pomella told them. "I need to think."

It was only then that she noticed two servants in simple red robes standing outside her cabin. One of them shook out a blanket near the door, while another eyed her curiously. Pomella remembered now that her cabin was being reserved for one of the High Mystics.

Suppressing a grumble, Pomella turned around and headed for Lal's dwelling. Bright stars shone bright above her, dimmed only by a waxing half moon. A warm feeling washed over her, and she paused atop the bridge spanning the river. She could feel something stirring the Myst. She glanced all around but saw nothing except darkness and the shimmering water.

Her hummingbirds were nowhere to be found. "Hector? Ena?"

Suddenly something massive erupted from the river, lurching into the sky directly over her. A silvery fish, or some other huge sea creature, leaped above her, arcing from one side of the bridge to the other. Pomella stared and smiled. The fay creature had at least seven large fins, and a long tail that forked at the end to form twin flippers. A huge mouth yawned open as it leaped over her. Two eyes on either side of its body gazed down at her as it twisted and plunged to the far side of the bridge.

As the fay vanished into the river, Pomella's gaze drifted

upward again, toward the starry sky. She'd seen something that caught her attention as the fay passed over her. It didn't take her long to find what she was looking for.

Treorel, the so-called Mystic Star that was not a star, blazed in the sky above her. It shone red like the color of blood, casting a pinkish aura around it. Other, lesser stars faded away in that pink haze as if being consumed by its fire.

"So you're what's causing all this fuss," Pomella said to the star. "Try not to stir the night pot too much, OK?"

Pomella knocked on her master's door and pushed it open when nobody answered. Broon popped up from his corner and came over to greet her.

"Yes, hello," Pomella said. "Go lay down." She quickly tidied up some of the clutter, then prepared for bed. A jumble of thoughts clanged in her head; at this point, she just needed sleep.

A knock sounded at the door. Her heart raced as she opened it. She knew who it would be. Lal wouldn't knock on his own door.

Moonlight spilled into the cabin revealing Sim.

He looked older than the seven years they'd been apart would seem to account for. Gone was the softness in his face, the lingering innocence that he'd managed to hold on to before he'd followed her into the Mystwood all those years ago. His face was harder, but his eyes hadn't changed. Those stunning blue eyes.

He was clean-shaven except for a trim tuft of hair on his chin. His scraggly straw-colored hair spilled over the tops of his ears. A sense of loneliness and solitude radiated from him. He'd changed greatly, no doubt, in his time apart from her, just as she had.

Without a word she let him slip into the cabin, closed the

door, and wrapped her arms around him. She buried her head into his chest, noticing how lean he'd become. Sim had always been a tall, strong boy, but whatever softness he'd had before had been streamlined into a hard exterior.

Slowly, as if trying not to scare her away, she felt his arms wrap around her, too. They stood there, holding each other, steady as a boulder in a river of emotions, for what felt to Pomella like the life of the stars.

Pomella breathed in his scent. Beneath the smell of pine and dirt, of roads and mountains, there was a trace of what was uniquely him. "I never thought I'd see you again," she said at last.

"I never thought I'd return."

She pulled away to look at him, trying to take in everything that was new about him. "Where did you go? How did you get here?" she asked.

His face hardened, but it was subtle enough that Pomella wouldn't have noticed if she hadn't been beside him and watching. He looked away from her and his eyes grew distant.

Another long silence stretched. Gently, as if coaxing a rabbit from its burrow, Pomella touched his cheek and pulled his attention back.

"I'm here," she said. "Tell me."

"The places I went," he said in a quiet, rough voice, "I will not take you, even in memory."

"Sim . . ."

He muttered something apologetic, and pulled away. Before she could protest, he was out the door, walking with withdrawn, almost feral movements.

Pomella released the breath she didn't know she'd been holding. She looked at Broon, who'd returned to his corner. Upon his seeing her attention, his tail thumped happily against the floor.

Pomella bit her lip. "Buggering shite, Sim," she mumbled, and ran out the door.

He was halfway across the field, heading toward the cabins. She ran a handful of steps, then called out, "I saw your mhathir and fathir!"

He stopped but turned only his head slightly back in her direction.

"Bethy, too," Pomella continued. "She married Danny An-Stipe and they have three warrums and a babe coming in the fall. They all miss you. I gave my last memory of you to your mhathir."

Treorel glowed behind him, above Kelt Apar's central tower.

"You were there for me once," she said. "Your story is your own, but you don't have to carry it by yourself."

Sim considered her with an expression that was as familiar to her as rain. For a heartbeat she thought he would return with her to the cabin, but then he shook his head once, and continued away across the field, leaving Pomella alone to wonder where he'd been for seven years.

TEN

THE EYESTROM

Seven Years Before Crow Tallin

Sim vomited over the side of the ship.

He waited until his stomach calmed, then wiped his mouth with the back of his wrist. He closed his eyes and tried to catch his breath. His forearms itched. He scratched them without thought.

Despite having been at sea for three weeks, he was still learning just how different life aboard a ship was. The rolling, dizzying motion of the *Eyestrom* made him retch anytime he was on deck, although it seemed to occur less often of late. Rochella didn't offer him any sympathy, but neither did she look entirely at ease, either. Sim thanked the Saints that the ship, at least, hadn't sunk immediately as he'd half-expected it to. He longed for the familiar comfort of Moth's soil. So much water, with no land in sight, jumbled his stomach.

Come on, Sim, he imagined his brother, Dane, saying to him. *This is the price of a little adventure!*

As a child, Sim had talked with his older brother, Dane, about all the places they hoped to visit across the world. *In Qin, the mountains reach past the clouds,* Dane had said, getting that faraway look in his eye. *They make MagBreckan look like a little hill by comparison!*

Even then, Sim hadn't entirely believed his brother. How could Dane possibly know about those other places if he'd never been there? Dane never got a chance to leave Moth, as the Coughing Plague had taken him, along with more than half of their village. Dark dreams of Dane's final days haunted Sim during those first nights at sea.

"You sure love feeding those fish, Thudfoot," Rochella said from behind him. Sim turned to look at his mentor. He hated the nickname she'd given him. In the bright, midday sunlight, her thick black stripes contrasted more strongly than usual against her brown skin. Thin white lines outlined the black markings.

"What I wouldn't give for a real bed," he told the virga ranger.

"We had one at the inn back in Port Morrush, right after we left Kelt Apar," she said.

"I slept on the floor that night. You got the bed," Sim reminded her.

Rochella brushed a lock of her short-cropped hair away from her eye. Despite its dark color, it shimmered in the daylight. As a ranger, she stood above commoners but made the deliberate

choice to keep her hair short, not caring about the confusion or
frowns it brought to others when they learned her profession.

"Right," she said. "Well, I hope you enjoyed it, 'cause you won't
see another for a long time."

Sim shook his head. Rochella's demeanor had hardened after
leaving Kelt Apar. She'd made him carry the saddlebags, tend
their horses, cook their meals, and set their camp. It wasn't very
different than when he was a prisoner with the Black Claws,
except that he wasn't chained up at night. But despite this, he'd
learned a lot from her. She had an uncanny ability to read his
mind, especially when it came to his feelings for Pomella.

Pomella.

He'd been gone from her a handful of weeks, and already he
missed her. During all the troubles surrounding the apprentice
Trials, Sim had gradually come to accept that she couldn't be part
of his life. But during the sparse couple of days they'd had together afterward, strolling through the grass in Kelt Apar, steal-
ing kisses in her cabin, he'd opened his heart and let her get close
again.

"Let her go," Rochella said. "You have enough to carry. Don't
bring her memory with you."

"I wasn't—"

Rochella held up a finger. "You asked me if I'd take you along
with me to the Continent and teach you to become a ranger.
That's fine, so here's your first lesson. Don't talk. Listen. Always
listen. Shut your mouth, and don't scare the forest animals."

She waited for him to say something, but Sim knew better
than to reply. This was her fifth "first lesson" for him since they'd
left Kelt Apar.

"Good," Rochella said. "You can be taught."

"Sssim!" called a hissing voice.

Both he and Rochella turned to see Mizzka, the laghart first mate of the *Eyestrom*, walking toward the front of the ship where they stood.

The bow, Sim reminded himself. The front of a ship was called a *bow*.

Despite having weeks to acquaint himself with her, Sim still marveled at Mizzka's scale markings and how they differed from those of Vlenar—the only other laghart he'd ever met. While both lagharts shared the swirling vortex pattern supposedly common to all of their kind, Mizzka's color patterns were lighter and more streamlined. Light-blue scales contrasted with darker, almost purple ones. Mizzka's eyes were different, too, narrower, more almond shaped. It had initially taken Sim a moment to realize upon boarding the *Eyestrom* for the first time that Mizzka was female. She didn't have breasts or curves, like a human would, but her size, frame, and tone of voice suggested a certain feminine quality.

"Yah?" Sim replied, wiping his mouth once more to ensure it wasn't dripping.

"The captttain wantsss to sssee you," the laghart said, her tongue flicking out to lick the air.

Sim scratched his forearms again. They'd sprung a rash recently. He'd rarely seen the captain, who generally kept to his cabin. The only time he'd interacted with Sim directly was when he eyed him up and asked Rochella if she'd allow Sim to help crew the ship. Rochella had gladly given permission for the captain to work Sim raw, which he did, all under Mizzka's vigilant eye. He'd been paired up with a boy named Hormin, who, Sim recognized, had been one of the Black Claws. Apparently the High Mystic had ordered him to return home on the *Eyestrom*, along with Saijar, one of the other apprentice candidates that had given Pomella a bundle of trouble. At first Sim had wanted to throw Hormin overboard as they worked together in silence, but the kid's quiet demeanor softened his anger. Hormin was a handful of years younger, making Sim wonder how the boy had gotten tied up with the Black Claws. Hormin wore a patch over one eye, which he hadn't before. Sim decided to let it go.

Wondering what the captain could want, Sim considered asking Rochella if he should go. But all he'd done since he'd left Moth was follow other people's orders. This time, he would do it on his own terms.

"Aye," he said, and deliberately did not look at Rochella as he followed Mizzka.

He knocked on the small door leading to the captain's cabin, and ducked through when he was called in. Captain Zeph peered over a map while swirling a bottle of amber liquid.

"Ah, Sim. Come in. Have a seat." He gestured to a chair along the wall. A small window—which Sim had learned was called a port—stood near the spot Zeph indicated. Sim moved to the chair but didn't sit.

It had surprised Sim to see that the *Eyestrom*'s captain was a lean, muscular man with wavy hair not much older than himself. He wore a vest over his otherwise deeply tanned bare chest, along with loose trousers tucked into shiny boots. An embroidered yellow sash, which Sim had learned was a sign of rank among seafaring people, hung off his waist.

"How do you like it aboard the *Eyestrom* so far?" Zeph asked.

Sim scratched his forearm before clasping his hands behind

his back, trying to hide the unsightly rashes. "I prefer being on land, uh, sir."

Zeph waved a hand at him. "Call me Zeph."

"Thank you, but it wouldn't be proper. You're a merchant, the captain of our ship."

"Whatever you prefer. I understand we all have our own unique tastes and ways of doing things. Drink?" He indicated the bottle.

"No. But thank you," Sim said.

Zeph splashed a bit of the alcohol into a glass cup anyway, and walked it over to Sim. His offer plainly left Sim with no choice. Sim accepted the glass, marveling at its weight and craftsmanship. He'd never actually seen a real glass cup before. He'd rarely seen real glass at all. Supposedly, crafting something like this took great skill. As a former blacksmith, Sim suddenly felt clumsy and brutal compared to the craftsman who had created this item.

"I can see you're a good lad. Your mathir raised you properly. Mizzka tells me you work hard with the others. That you don't mind breaking a sweat. *Hoom!* If I'm not careful, I'll end up having to pay you, or take you on for our next voyage?"

There was a slight questioning tone to that last statement.

"I'd be very lucky if you did, Captain. But I'm committed to learning from Rochella right now."

"So young, and already you have commitments. Careful with those, Sim; when you commit young, you may learn to regret it later." He lifted his glass. "To the voyage," he said, and drank. Sim saluted in return and drained his glass. He coughed, and nearly spit the drink out. It tasted like shite. How could anybody like this?

Zeph clapped him on the back. "I had my first shot of chi-uy when I was fourteen. Ol' Captain Byrnlox insisted I take one when we landed on the shores of Qin. By the ancestors, that was a good night! Took my first tumble with a woman that night, too. A local girl, about my age. She was just a common field girl. . . ." He paused to wave his hand. "You know what I mean, and she was supposedly chosen specifically for me. Ah, Sim. I'm sure you remember your first. She was shy, naturally, and I hardly knew what to do with my snake, but we got by." He grinned as he poured himself another drink.

Sim stared into his empty glass. "May I ask why you called me in?"

Zeph nodded. "Ah, of course. You don't want to hear me ramble about my old conquests! I want to hear about you. You intrigue me. Tell me, how did you come to be with that pretty ranger?"

"Rochella?" Sim said before he could help himself. He supposed she was pretty, even though she was nearly twice his age. He'd just never thought of her in that way. Often, anyway. "She helped me when I was sick," Sim said.

Zeph nodded with a knowing smile. "No need to say more, I understand." He leaned across his desk. "I've never had a virga. Are they as good as their reputation? I hear they can be . . . primal . . . once aroused."

Sim set his glass down. He wanted to leap across the table, break every glass bottle, and smash his fist into this boyish captain's pretty face. But that wouldn't be a good idea not simply because Zeph was the captain of the ship, but because the man was a merchant-scholar. There'd be severe punishments if Sim lifted a hand toward him.

"I wouldn't know," Sim said. "It's not like that. She's my mentor."

"I meant no offense," Zeph said, raising his glass in an apologetic salute. "Teachers provide a variety of lessons in their own ways. Where are you traveling to?"

"To the Baronies," Sim said. "The High Mystic ordered us to escort Lord Saijar home safely. After that, I'm uncertain. Rochella has a contact there she needs to find afterward." As soon as he said it, though, he remembered one of Rochella's "first lessons": to keep his mouth shut and not reveal too much about himself. Enemies lurked everywhere, and every snap of information, no matter how innocent seeming, could be used against you.

Zeph nodded. "Well, if you change your mind, or fancy more . . . profitable . . . ventures, then I believe I could find work for you here. I've recently taken on a new contract through Port Morrush, and your knowledge of the island would be useful to me. But in the meantime, you are always welcome aboard the *Eyestrom*."

Sim set the glass onto the desk. He wanted to ask more about this offer, but Rochella's advice to stay out of trouble kept him quiet. He settled on another topic in order to not let the silence stretch. "Why do you call it that? The ship."

"Ah, I named it after *my* mentor, Captain Byrnlox Eyestrom. The finest sailor of our era, regardless of what his jealous rivals would say. He was like a father to me. So much so that after he died I took his last name as well. Like you, I, too, came from humble origins. Perhaps we are not unalike, you and I. This is another reason why I like you."

Something about the captain's tone didn't sit well with Sim. "Thank you for the drink, Captain."

He made for the door, but Zeph stopped him. "Oh, and Sim?"

Sim turned back.

"Do put in a good word for me with Rochella?" The captain's smile sent chills down Sim's spine.

About a week later, as sunlight yawned into the below-deck quarters, Sim awoke to the sound of a man coughing. Sim groaned and rolled away from the sound. It was coming from Hilash, one of the other swabs Sim had been matched with to work.

He tried to close his eyes and go back to sleep, but the rolling, endless movement of the ship churned his stomach. He hoped he didn't have to vomit again. He'd finally stopped three days ago, but his stomach never quite settled right. He hoped this first sea voyage would be his last.

Hilash's coughing continued. Sim peered across the narrow aisle to the other set of bunks. Rochella lay with her back to him, a single ratty blanket pulled up over her shoulders. Because her hair was short, Sim could see the exposed nape of her neck. Her skin was a deep brown, darker than Pomella's. He could see the white-edged line of a black stripe running across the back of her neck. Sim knew very little about the virga people, but he had to admit that her skin was alluring in its own way. He found himself wondering what the stripe pattern looked like farther down her back, and across the rest of her body.

Those thoughts brought forth his recent conversation with Zeph. He shook his head. No. Rochella was a mentor, and was old anyway. She was probably in her mid-thirties.

His thoughts drifted again to Pomella. He closed his eyes

and remembered her lips on his. The way she'd melted into his arms when they were alone.

Sim groaned and sat up. Rochella was right. Thinking of her just made it harder. But he couldn't stop.

He reached over to his small pack and opened it up. He kept a needle and some thread, a few clean cloths, a waterskin, and a bit of food in there, stashed away at Rochella's suggestion. Also inside was *The Book of Songs*, given to him by Pomella. He could only read the fragments that used the common runes, but that was fine. Inside was a wealth of imagery and other things he didn't understand. But it reminded him of her.

The last item in his bag was a vial. Zeph's glass cups couldn't compare to this vial in terms of elegance and craftsmanship. It was about the size of his palm, rounded at the bottom, and smoothly curved to a tapered top. A silvery-green liquid was sealed within by a wax seal. It was another gift from Pomella. She hadn't told him where she'd gotten it, but she'd told him what it was.

Poison.

Sim hadn't been comfortable accepting the gift, but Pomella had insisted he take it. It repulsed her for some reason. He wasn't sure when he would need—

Suddenly Hilash sat up in his bunk, just two beds down from Rochella. The older, sun-baked man leaned over the edge of his bunk, legs spread wide, bent double as he hacked. He coughed again and again, his face turning different shades as he did. Two other sailors peered at him from their bunks. One of them mumbled, "Shut'm up."

Hilash keep coughing. Seeing nobody else offering to help, Sim moved toward him. "Hilash?"

The man lifted his bone-tight face, and a sudden pang of

fear charged through Sim. Bloodshot red cracks lined Hilash's eyes. His lips were bright red from coughing up blood. Upon seeing him, the other crew members scrambled over the bunks and raced up the ladder to the deck above.

Sim slipped his feet onto the cold floor planks and stood. As he approached the ill sailor, Hilash scratched at his arms and coughed some more. Blood splattered across the floorboards. He lifted his eyes to Sim.

"Gett'way!" Hilash rasped.

Sim stared, the fear raging in his chest. Red rashes covered Hilash's face. Rashes like Sim's. A hand touched his shoulder.

"We need to go," Rochella said. Sim hadn't seen her wake up or get out of the bunk. She dragged him toward the ladder and practically shoved him up through the portal. Once on deck, Rochella slammed the hatch and placed her foot on it as if to lock Hilash away and anyone else still in there.

"On your guard," she murmured to Sim.

He was about to ask why, but then he saw the crowd gathered around them. A silent crew of men encircled them. Most covered their mouths and noses with their hand or an old scarf. Some brandished makeshift cudgels in a threatening manner. Behind the sailors, a line of armed soldiers stood with their arms on forearm-length swords. They stood in front of a young man with blond hair, who Sim understood to be Saijar, one of the candidates who had competed against Pomella in the apprentice Trials. Sim hadn't seem him at all during the voyage until now. They'd mostly stayed belowdecks, as far from the rest of the crew as possible.

Mizzka pushed past the sailors, her forked tongue zipping out in furious jabs. "What issss happening?"

Saijar mumbled something to one of his soldiers. Sim only caught the word "laghart," but his sneer made it clear what he thought of the *Eyestrom*'s first mate.

One of the regular sailors, Eshan, a lanky red-haired man with a Mothic accent, jabbed his finger at the hatch Rochella stood on top of. "There's a scuttlin' nasty down there, Mistress. This boy has the red rash!"

Sim crossed his arms, trying to hide his blotchy forearms.

Mizzka's slitted eyes slithered toward him. "Lettt me sssee, boy."

Wilting beneath the hard look of the *Eyestrom*'s first mate, Sim held out his arms.

Mizzka's long tongue whipped the air. "Ttttake your sssh-hirt offfff."

"He's under my protection, Mizzka," Rochella said.

"He'ssss a thhhreat to our ssshhip!"

Rochella was about to respond, but Sim put his hand on her shoulder. "We can't hide it," Sim whispered to her.

She glared at him, eyes blazing anger that he hadn't let her handle the situation. Or perhaps anger because he hadn't told her sooner. But it was too late. She nodded.

Sim set his jaw, and lifted his shirt over his head. The cool air pebbled his skin.

A collective mumble of fear passed through the sailors. Every man shuffled a step back. Sim wasn't sure who, but somewhere in the gathered crowd somebody whispered, "Plague."

The word sent a chill down Sim's spine. He looked down at his skin, and this time he couldn't deny what he saw. His entire torso was covered in angry red blotches. He'd seen them before.

As a child, he'd watched his brother break out with the rash, followed by the more extreme symptoms, like Hilash suffered from down in the hold. Everyone from Moth, and most people not from the island, knew what those red rashes meant.

The Coughing Plague. The rotting disease that supposedly no Mystic could heal.

"Get him off my ship," came a voice from behind Sim. They all turned and saw Captain Zeph standing at the rail outside his upper hold. He glared down at the gathering, his face set in stone.

Nobody moved to apprehend Sim. Each sailor looked away, unwilling to be the one to touch him unless ordered to.

Sim attempted to appeal to Zeph. "I have the rashes, but nothing else. I can still work fine."

Rochella shoved him aside. "May the Saints spare me from loudmouth dunders. Zeph—"

"Mizzka," Zeph said, his eyes cold. The laghart darted forward, quicker than most humans could move. Before Sim could react, her clawed hand snatched his wrist and twisted it backward and toward the sky. Sim cried out as pain shot up his arm and into his spine. He bent over double, trying to ease the arm twist.

"Stop!" Rochella said. "Release us both peacefully, Zeph, and we will leave now."

"I intend to let you step foot off this ship peacefully right now, actually."

"Give us a raft."

Zeph shook his head. "If you think I'll part with one of my—"

"You were paid handsomely to deliver us safely to the Continent. If word reaches any Mystic that you threw a ranger and her apprentice overboard, you'll never be welcome in a respectable city again. At the least, our fare covers the cost of a tiny raft."

"*Hoom!* You are a danger to my ship and my crew, and I won't part with anything. You can swim to the Continent."

"Then he and I will fight, and bleed, and bite every one of your men until this ship becomes a walking infestation. Let us go now, and we'll walk to your raft and not touch anybody."

"It may already be a plague den!" Zeph shot back.

"Or it may not, but are you willing to risk it?" Rochella said. Zeph considered her.

"And let me be clear," Rochella said, her eyes narrowing. "There will be much blood if you try to throw us overboard."

Zeph held her gaze, then nodded to Mizzka. The laghart's grip on Sim relaxed. He straightened, and looked to Rochella.

"Ready a raft," Zeph said to the crew. "Quickly."

Mizzka leaped into action, hustling several sailors ahead of her.

"Our gear," Sim said.

Zeph glared at him, and Rochella put her hand on his shoulder. "Let's go."

They moved aft and portside toward the place where Mizzka's sailors were lowering one of the small rafts. They stepped away so that Rochella and Sim could climb aboard.

The crew on the ship was silent as they were lowered down. As they neared the water, Zeph appeared at the side rail and motioned over the edge with his hand. One of the sailors threw two bags, containing Sim's and Rochella's travel provisions as well as a single canteen of water.

Just as the small vessel touched the water, a figure leaped over the edge and splashed into the water.

"Jagged shite," Rochella grumbled.

The figure flailed in the water, clearly unable to swim. He screamed, his words indecipherable, but clearly begging for assistance.

"We have to help him," Sim said. He stood and balanced himself, ready to jump in.

"Sit down!" Rochella roared.

"He'll die!" Sim yelled back.

Rochella cursed under her breath but grabbed an oar and shoved it into his arms. "This is on you, Thudfoot. Get us closer and I'll grab him. Knowing you, you'll get dragged in and you'll both drown. It would be what you jagged deserve, though."

Sim snatched the oar and fumbled with it enough until they were a bit closer to the panicked man. Rochella leaned over to grab him, but the man clawed at her arm, throwing her off-balance.

"Stop floundering, you blind culk!" she yelled.

The man didn't stop his mad scrabble.

Rochella lifted her fist and smashed him across the temple. The man's desperate flailing stopped. Rochella dragged him onto the boat, which immediately made Sim realize there would barely be enough room for all three of them. Sim looked at him. It was Hormin, the boy who had been traveling with Saijar but had spent time with Sim and Hilash. He was awake but unfocused. Already a large lump was forming on his head.

Rochella was breathing hard from her efforts. She glared at Sim, then pulled Hormin's shirt open. Across the boy's chest was a cluster of festering red rashes.

"I hope you're happy," Rochella said to him.

They drifted away from the *Eyestrom* until the ship grew distant, and they saw from far away that somebody was thrown overboard. Hilash.

Sim looked away from the ship, unable to think of what he'd left behind. "I don't understand how I became infected," he said.

Rochella turned away from him and stared eastward, toward the Continent. "Get rowing."

A lump formed in Sim's throat. There was a more immediate concern. "Won't you be infected?" he asked.

Rochella kept her eyes on the horizon. "Virgas are immune to the plague."

A wave of relief spread through him. He'd never heard of anybody being immune. "So now what?"

Rochella stood up, naturally finding her balance in the rocking boat. The ocean wind caught her short hair, tousling it behind her like dark flames. Her eyes were locked on the eastern horizon, perhaps seeing more than Sim could understand. "We are rangers. We do what we always do. We move, and we survive."

ELEVEN

THE UPPERMOST CHAMBER

"Mistress Pomella?" a booming voice said.

The voice, followed by a dog barking, startled Pomella out of her dream-filled sleep. She bolted upright, disoriented, still lingering in that place between slumber and wakefulness.

Her mind scrambled to hold on to the dream she'd been having, but it drained away like water through fingers. Pomella brushed her hair from her eyes and tucked it behind her ear. She'd been dreaming of Sim, and a ship of some kind. There'd been a laghart, and that boy, Hormin, from the Black Claws all those years ago.

Dreams could be as strange as snow in spring.

"Mistress Pomella?" Oxillian said again. He tapped at the

shuttered window near Pomella's head. "You are summoned by the High Mystics."

Broon was up now, sniffing the door, his tail wagging as eagerly as ever.

"OK!" Pomella called, trying to rub the sleep from her eyes. Seeing her awake, Broon ran between her and the door, eager for her to open it. "I'll come in a moment."

She peered toward the shuttered window, trying to gauge the hour. Bright light shone through the window frame, telling her it was at least past sunrise. She groaned.

"Also," said Oxillian, "there's a man here to see you. He is waiting for you outside."

Memories of Sim flooded back to Pomella from last night. She bit her lip. "I'll be out in a moment. Thank you, Ox."

Pomella leaped from her bed and scrambled to sort herself out. She threw her Crow Tallin dress back on, and raked fingers through her hair to try to tame it. Steeling herself to face Sim again, she opened the door.

It wasn't Sim. It took her a moment to recognize the short-bearded man who stood there. It was Berrit, the minstrel she'd met at the Rolling Forge. He smiled at her, rakish in his fine clothes.

"Good morning, Mistress," he said, sweeping his hat off and bending a flawless bow.

Pomella looked around in surprise. "Berrit? Where's . . . Ox?" She'd caught herself before asking about Sim. "And how did you get into Kelt Apar?"

And what, by the blathering skivers, was he *doing* here? She peered past the minstrel to see Oxillian now standing several dozen steps away from the cabin, presumably waiting for her to follow.

"A group of us managed to slip past the rangers last night before the wall went up," Berrit said. He plunked his hat back on his head. "The Green Man found us, but I convinced him that I knew you and it was important to talk to you."

Pomella bit her lip, trying to find a polite way to proceed. "Look, Berrit, it's nice to see you again, but this is a really bad time. There's a lot happening and you're really not supposed to be—"

"I have information about the Shadefox," Berrit said.

With some effort Pomella managed to keep her expression neutral as she considered him. With all the chaos of Crow Tallin happening, she realized she'd let her attention from the slaver bandit ringleader waver.

"What makes you think I have any interest in the Shadefox?"

Berrit fixed her with a knowing expression. "You asked me not to waste your time, Mistress. I'm a minstrel and hear many things. It's no secret that you—the Hummingbird, the Commoner Mystic—have been hunting poachers who've been rounding up the Unclaimed. Also, I bought some drinks for one of Baroness ManHinley's shieldguards a few nights back and he talked my ear off. Apparently, Captain Lucal was able to gain some information from the slavers you captured outside Port Morrush."

"Go on," she said, eyes narrowing.

"Uh, may I come in?" he asked.

"No," she said.

Broon shuffled past Pomella's legs to sniff Berrit's feet.

Berrit awkwardly patted the dog's head. "Does he bite?"

"Only culks," Pomella muttered. "Now what did you learn about the Shadefox? Do you know where he is?"

"Not exactly," Berrit said. "The rumor around the camp surrounding Kelt Apar is that the Shadefox is here in person."

"Inside the wall?" Pomella said.

"I don't know," Berrit said. "It only went up last night. The information I have is from yesterday before the ceremony. Supposedly, he plans to feed off whatever chaos comes from Crow Tallin and use it as an opportunity."

"An opportunity for what?"

Berrit shook his leg to try to push Broon away. "Likely to collect more slaves."

"How can we find him?"

"I don't know exactly," Berrit said, "but my guess is that he won't make a move until there's more people. The roads into the Mystwood are packed with caravans, as people are seeking out Kelt Apar. Nobody knows what to expect from Crow Tallin, but they know from older generations that it gets bad. People are scared. They're talking about Crow Tallin, wondering what it means for them."

"Mistress Yarina will release information to the public about what they can expect," Pomella said, although she wasn't certain at all whether that would actually happen.

Berrit sighed. "I realize we only met recently. I had an . . . enjoyable . . . night with you. I understand it may be hard to trust me, but please know, I'm trying to help."

Pomella tensed and readied a retort but then sighed. "You're right; I'm sorry. Crow Tallin is a difficult time, and the truth is that I don't know exactly what to expect. The fay will become visible, if they haven't already done so. There's some danger, but not if everyone remains calm and trusts us Mystics to do our jobs."

"I trust *you*," he said. "It's the other Mystics I'm wary of. You remember how it was when you were still a commoner. Most of us feel like the Mystics ignore us and see us as an annoyance. They leave us to the nobility to be dealt with. They say they want to offer assistance, but most folk are terrified of approaching a Mystic. And when they finally dig up the courage to do so, they're often ignored or told their problem isn't important enough. I know you're not like that, and maybe High Mystic Yarina isn't, either, but in many people's view most Mystics are . . . well, they're the kind of people your dog would bite."

Unfortunately, Pomella knew what he meant. Her fathir had distrusted Mystics. Sim had, as well. Even Bethy had shown she didn't entirely have a comfortable view of them. It had been difficult for her to see that before, but now, the more time she spent as a Mystic, the more she tried to see somebody else's point of view, and to understand their experience. She thought of Lal, who lived his life similar to an Unclaimed, partly, she thought, in order to better understand them.

"I'll speak to Mistress Yarina and encourage her to communicate with the people beyond the wall," she said. "You should speak to one of our rangers about the Shadefox. If there's anything else you know, tell them."

"The only other tidbit I've heard is that he's young," Berrit said. "He rose through the ranks fast. But everyone agrees that he's ruthless. Cruel."

"I need to go," Pomella said. "Thank you for this information."

"It was my pleasure, Mistress," said Berrit, bowing again.

When he straightened, he winked at her, and Pomella couldn't help but smile.

"Come on, Broon," Pomella said. "Leave him alone now."

Berrit gave her an expression of thanks. After Pomella grabbed her cloak and Mystic staff, he licked his lips and addressed her once more.

"Maybe when this is all over we could see each other again," he said.

Pomella looked from him to the central tower across the lawn. There was so much to do, her mind tumbled with new thoughts of Sim and what it all meant.

"Perhaps," she said.

The musty scent of Kelt Apar's central tower washed over Pomella as she stepped through the familiar doorway leading to its foyer. Vivianna looked up from where she sat behind a small wooden desk.

"Good morning," Vivianna said. "They're waiting for you upstairs in the upper chamber."

Pomella quirked an eyebrow. "The upper chamber, huh?" She'd never visited there before. As far as she knew, it was the one place in the tower she'd never visited. She couldn't be certain, however, because after all these years she was still learning the secrets of the tower, and of Kelt Apar in general.

"I only went in there recently for the first time as well," said Vivianna. "Just mind your formalities and you'll be fine."

Pomella leaned in close to Vivianna. "I just heard the Shadefox is lurking outside Kelt Apar."

"Really?" Vivianna said. "How did you hear that?"

"It doesn't matter right now," Pomella dodged. "I just wanted you to be aware of it, in case something comes up while I'm away."

Vivianna rolled her forearm over and traced new letter-runes onto the list that illuminated on top of her skin. "I will alert the rangers and let you know if I hear any more."

"It would be so much easier if Ox could just appear every place there's a problem," Pomella mused. "He does that easily enough."

"He's not a Mystic," Vivianna said. "With all the strange occurrences happening with Crow Tallin, he could get trapped again like he did during our Trials. Besides, Mistress Yarina told me that every Crow Tallin his ability to sense trouble throughout the island becomes clouded. He becomes disoriented."

Pomella sighed. "Well, I suppose it's our job anyway, not the Green Man's, to be seen by the people." She ascended the spiral staircase with nervous excitement

Drifting, glowing lights lit the stairwell, each shining with steady radiance born of the Myst. The first time Pomella had seen these, as an apprentice candidate, she'd marveled at the idea that the world contained such wonders. She now understood that they were incredibly difficult to permanently Unveil and not just any Mystic could conjure such wonders. The lights used here in the central tower had been Unveiled as a gift from a master Mystic and artisan in Djain nearly a century ago. Lal had told Pomella how his master, Mistress Joycean, had been an apprentice when that occurred.

She passed one of the floating orbs in the staircase. It hovered in midair and shone with a steady white light. Pomella reached her hand out to feel its warmth, but no heat radiated from it.

Leaving the little wonder behind, she strode up the steps,

passing the familiar doors and landings that she'd been to many times before. She glimpsed inside the open door to the library as she passed, noting its familiar shelves and cushions scattered throughout. Climbing these steps reminded her of her second apprentice Trial, which, at the time she'd taken it, she'd been unaware even was a Trial. She hoped this meeting with the High Mystics would go more smoothly than that meeting with Yarina had gone.

The stairs leveled off on the top floor, revealing a single door Pomella had never been through. The tower was at its narrowest at this height, with the top room not much wider than four or five spans of her arms across. The door before her was made of old wood, splintered in a few places. A faded rendering of what Pomella supposed was a moth, or perhaps a butterfly, was carved into the door.

She knocked, and when she heard Yarina say "Come," she turned the wooden handle and entered the room.

A ring of glowing lights, identical to the ones she'd passed, illuminated a small room. Heavy oak beams curved upward above her head to form the rafters of the tower's famed conical top. Framed artwork featuring portraits of long-dead past masters decorated the walls, spaced evenly around the perimeter. A single square window, currently open, provided the only ventilation in what was sure to become stifling heat later in the day. Pomella had often gazed at that window from the outside, wondering what lay within. Like most of the tower, the floor was made of stone. Where the stone had originated, and how exactly it had been laid, was beyond Pomella's knowledge. But if anybody in the world knew, it would be one or more of the people sitting closely together before her.

The High Mystics sat on cushions arranged around the curve of the wall. Bhairatonix sat in the center of the group, with Yarina and the twins, Angelos and Michaela, to his right and Ehzeeth, Ollfur, and Willwhite to his left. Near Master Willwhite, almost casually forgotten, was Shevia, who sat by herself cross-legged with a straight spine, keeping her eyes downcast.

Pomella's attention was drawn not to the seven High Mystics waiting in the room for her, but to the far end of the room beside Yarina, where there stood a waist-high podium with a glass sphere atop it. The sphere was as large as her head, perfectly round, and filled with silvery smoke that slowly churned within. She saw flickering movement inside the sphere but didn't have time to look more closely.

"Hello, Pomella," said Yarina.

Pomella bowed, suddenly remembering her formalities. "Blessings to you, Masters," she said, touching her palms to her forehead and heart.

"Please, sit," said Willwhite, gesturing to the empty center of the room. As before, his voice shifted as he spoke. Pomella forced herself not to stare as she knelt in the middle of the room. The High Mystic's pale skin seemed to glow with the Myst, with silvery smoke gently streaming off it. His effeminate features seemed more pronounced in the daylight, to the point where Pomella glanced at him again. Had she not known him, she might have mistaken him for a woman.

The narrow curvature of the room made the High Mystics form a tight arc around her. For a moment, the only movement in the room was the flickering from the glass sphere. Pomella thought she could hear the faint *tink* of something tapping inside the glass.

"Master Bhairatonix," said Yarina. "Would you be so kind as to ask your apprentice to Unveil a need on the island for Pomella to assist with?"

"Not yet," Bhairatonix said, not looking at Yarina, but staring directly at Pomella. "So this is the commoner girl."

Pomella stilled the surge of anger that spiked in her chest. She reminded herself that she was in the presence of Yarina, and six other High Mystics.

"She is no longer a commoner," said Master Willwhite in his drifting voice. "In this life, our natures change. Only the Myst is constant."

"Tell me, girl," Bhairatonix said, ignoring Willwhite, "how are your studies?"

Pomella forced herself to remain calm. "They are well, Master. Thank you for your concern."

"Do you find the gardener to be a worthy teacher?" Bhairatonix said.

Anger roared within Pomella, but Yarina spoke before she could snap a retort. "Pomella has exceptional potential that shines brightest when she channels her emotions in a positive way."

Pomella snapped her mouth shut.

"Grandmaster Faywong," Yarina continued, "who was *my teacher* as well, has taught her well. She was bathed in the waters of Kelt Apar two years ago and emerged a full Mystic. I oversaw the ceremony myself. We are proud to have her here at Kelt Apar."

"It is very unusual for a grandmaster to take an apprentice so late in life," Mistress Michaela said.

Master Ehzeeth, the laghart, hissed several times, and tapped his clawed hand on the floor to indicate he had something to say. Everyone waited patiently while he found the strength to speak.

"A *Zzzurnta* likkke Fffaywong ssshould nottt be quessstioned."

"Let the girl be, Master," Ollfur said to Bhairatonix. "She doesn't deserve to be picked on. I've heard very good things about her. The people of Moth love her." His Keffran accent reminded Pomella so strongly of her grandmhathir that it was as if she were reaching across time to remind Pomella of her presence.

"Of course they do," Bhairatonix said in a cold voice.

"I hear you have a marvelous singing voice," Master Angelos said to Pomella. He and his sister, Mistress Michaela, both had pale skin and a narrow facial structure. Pomella estimated that they were in their sixties, although their smooth skin and pure white hair made them seem far more youthful.

"Will you share it with us?" Michaela added.

Pomella inclined her head. "Of course, Mistress. What would you like to hear?"

Michaela smiled, and it warmed Pomella's heart. She was reminded of Vivianna's admiration for the twins, and shared that affection with her.

"Do you know the song 'Into Mystic Skies'?" Michaela asked.

"Yes, I do," Pomella said. "My grandmhathir used to sing it to me when I was a tyke. I would be delighted to sing it for you."

She took a deep breath and cleared her throat before beginning the song she'd learned from her old *Book of Songs:*

> *"The night has gone,*
> *The sun lifts and flies.*

Always I'll follow you,
Into Mystic Skies."

The Myst rose around Pomella. Here, in the tower, surrounded by seven High Mystics, it surged, filling her with strength. She rode that wave but coaxed it just enough to Unveil musical notes to accompany her singing.

It was like when she performed at the Rolling Forge, but rather than a crowd of half-drunken commoners, her audience consisted of the world's High Mystics.

She played the Myst like a harp.

"Around every corner,
The road always bends.
Leading to you,
My journey never ends.
Now as we go
Out of the past
I'll hold you once more
Forever, at—"

"Thhhheyyyy came like sssilver fffire!" hissed a voice, cutting into Pomella's song like a knife to the throat. "Blood aaand blade, cuttting, ssslaying our own."

All eyes turned to Shevia, who sat, upright, looking toward the roof. Her eyes were glazed over, as if seeing beyond the wood and stone roof. Her voice was her own, but she licked and hissed in the manner of a laghart.

Shevia's head thrashed to one side as she continued. "Come to usss, High Myssstic. The fffay. The ffaay burn us!"

Still sitting, Shevia screamed and threw out her hands. Streams of silver wind rushed from behind her and raced toward Pomella. Pomella threw her hands up and ducked beneath her arms, but nothing hit her. Instead, when she opened her eyes she saw the ethereal image of two lagharts bent over the body of a third. They appeared to be licking the wounds of the corpse.

Then, abruptly as it came, the image vanished and Shevia gasped and leaned forward, trying to catch her trembling breath.

If any of this seemed strange to the High Mystics, none of them showed it. The only reaction they showed was to calmly turn to Ehzeeth. The laghart master appeared no more agitated than the others, although his slitted eyes narrowed slightly and his tongue snapped the air and hovered there, its forked tip wavering.

"A vvvelttten," Ehzeeth said.

"The fay are crossing the veil faster and sooner than we expected," Michaela said.

"We must help them if we can," said her brother, Angelos.

"There are several veltens on Moth," Yarina said to Ehzeeth. "Can you tell which one these people belong to?"

Ehzeeth shook his scaled head. "I do notttt know enoughhh of the cusssstom here to identifffy their communittty."

"I can ask Vlenar," Pomella said. "I'll describe what they were wearing and ask him if he knows where they might live. As a laghart ranger from Moth, he would know best."

"They live in the eastern shadow of the iron mountains," Shevia said. Her voice was hoarse, but it was her own again. She eased herself to an upright position, back straight, and tucked back a strand of her long black hair behind her ear. As she did so, she looked at Pomella. "The fay came from the mountains, and attacked them."

Iron.

A sudden memory rushed to Pomella. *The mountain shakes and the moon is wrong. Fear the iron and awake the Mystic song.*

Her memory was from a dream she'd had, seven years ago, on the slopes of MagDoon, which was part of the Ironlow mountain range, which Shevia undoubtedly referred to now.

In that dream, a little girl had appeared to her, and given her a warning she hadn't understood. A girl with lavender eyes.

"Pomella?" Yarina asked.

Pomella ripped her gaze from Shevia. "Yes, sorry, Mistress."

"There is a velten in an eastern valley of the Ironlow Mountains," Yarina said. "Go there, and ensure the fay are settled and the lagharts are safe, then return home at once. Take no more than three days if you can."

"Surely she should not go alone," Ollfur said. "An entire community was attacked."

"Take the ranger you mentioned with you," Willwhite said. "There could be danger, so it will be good to have one of his kind with you."

"She will need more assistance than one ranger can provide," Michaela said. "Especially if whatever attacked the lagharts still lingers."

Yarina pursed her lips. It struck Pomella as unusual for the High Mystic to express even the slightest outward sign of distress.

"There is nobody to spare," Yarina said.

"I will go," said Shevia in a quiet voice.

"You are needed here," Bhairatonix said, his voice cold.

"I can join her after the other Mystics have been distributed across the island," Shevia said, not looking at her master.

"You will do as you are told," Bhairatonix said.

Yarina broke the tension. "Thank you, Shevia, for your offer. I will send Vivianna to go with Pomella. They have worked together for years. I had planned to keep her here at Kelt Apar to help manage affairs, but Master Ollfur is correct that this need is very great."

"Well then, it looks like you have your assignment, Pomella," said Ollfur with a smile. The light from the room's lone window shone off his bald head.

Pomella stood and bowed to the High Mystics. "Yes, Masters. I won't disappoint you." She flicked her gaze toward Shevia, who had her hands folded in her lap and eyes downcast.

The smoke within the glass sphere cleared just enough at that moment for her to see a palm-sized silver moth fluttering within. It leaped toward the glass and bounced back before hovering in the center. A wave of sadness for the moth came over her. What was the glass, and why was the moth trapped within it?

As she descended the stairs, Pomella caught one final look at Shevia, who peered up at her. Pomella found herself wondering more about the girl and the moth, and wishing she had more answers than questions.

TWELVE

FINDING BITH YAB

Five Years Before Crow Tallin

Sim's breath misted in front of him as he and Rochella entered the mountain village. The cluster of thatch-roofed homes looked nothing like the great city of Yin-Aab they'd recently visited but looked identical to every other frozen homestead they'd been to here in the mountains over the past several months.

Snow drifted around him and the virga ranger, signaling an earlier than expected arrival of winter. It seemed to Sim that each season since he and Rochella had left Moth two years ago seemed off schedule. It was as though they had rushed through the rainy months, skipped over summer and autumn, and barreled right into winter. Up here, in the highlands of Qin, where snow never melted and stony peaks scraped the sky, it seemed as though the world wanted to sleep.

A handful of villagers noticed their approach and shied back into their homes. It had been the same in the previous villages. Visitors were rare, rarely bringing good omens. The locals only trusted the regular merchants who came seasonally, and it was plain to all of them that Sim and Rochella didn't carry goods to barter. They seemed to know that the two rangers would only bring trouble, or worse.

Sim pulled his scarf up over his nose and mouth. He slowed his pace ever so slightly, letting Rochella take the lead. He didn't like to be around people. Not while his plague rashes were visible on his skin. Rochella assured him that after this long he probably wasn't nearly as contagious as he feared, but Sim still felt more comfortable with his face covered.

The rashes were a major reason they'd come to Qin, which was about as far away from Moth as one could get and still be on dry land. After being thrown off the *Eyestrom* two years ago, they'd drifted for six days before landing on the rocky Continental shore. Sim had no idea what became of the ship or its crew and passengers. They could've died of the plague for all he knew.

After their inglorious arrival at the Continent, the plan changed. According to Rochella, every ranger needed a task, a path to follow that served the will of the Myst. The task they gave themselves was to find a Mystic who would sympathize with them, seek to understand Sim's ailment, and possibly cure it.

There wasn't any doubt in Sim's mind that he was infected with the Coughing Plague. The rashes still grew and spread, and although they faded after a time, they would give way to new ones. But beyond those unsightly blemishes, he had no other symptoms. Hormin, the teenager who had jumped ship with them, hadn't fared so well. Sim had cradled him as he died four days after joining them on the boat. He and Rochella had done their best to save him, but even with Rochella's advanced knowledge of herbs and medicine, they were powerless to stop the plague. Sim shed a couple of tears when they let Hormin's body go into the water. The last glimpse of him sinking into the water—just a boy, younger than Sim—promised to stay locked in Sim's mind forever. Not because Sim had been close to him, but because he knew that somehow he'd caused that death.

During their travels across the Continent, they'd heard rumors that perhaps one of the Mystics of Qin could cure any disease. Their search had taken them to the capital, where they'd learned of a scarred Mystic named Bith Yab living in one of the highland villages.

"Are you sure this is the place?" Sim murmured from behind his scarf.

Rochella glared at him, giving him his answer.

Sim shrugged in apology. He should've known better. Rochella *always* knew where she was going. In the years he'd known her, she'd never gotten lost and always found what she sought. Early in their time together, during the week they'd drifted at sea, Sim had asked her how she could be so certain where to go.

"When you've been lost enough times," she'd said, staring eastward across the waves toward the Continent, "you learn to find yourself. Know where you are in your own context and you'll never be lost."

It made as little sense now as it had then. Sim had learned to trust her, and that was enough.

Rochella unslung her hunting bow and handed it to him. "I'll handle this," she said. Sim nodded, glad to let her walk forward without him.

"Hello!" Rochella called to the quiet village. Then she called out a greeting in Qina, a language Sim couldn't speak but recognized as the same one she'd used in all the other villages.

Silence answered her. The last of the villagers had scuttled into their homes. The buildings were erected from stone and wood, each carefully supporting a steeply sloped roof meant to accommodate heavy drifts of snow. Nearby, a wooly ox with massive horns groaned at them from behind a pen that was far too small for it.

The sound carried out of the otherwise-quiet village, and echoed across the towering mountains surrounding them. Sim felt eyes watching him, coming from both inside the homes and the mountains themselves, questioning why he and Rochella intruded.

Rochella made her way to the largest home and knocked on the door. The biggest house usually belonged to the person in charge.

"No," said a voice behind Sim.

Without thinking, Sim dropped his walking stick and Rochella's bow. His hands flew to his belt knife, which he brandished in a defensive stance. Rochella had taught him to favor small weapons. Speed and utility mattered to rangers. They weren't soldiers marching in an army. A sword was great, but not if you had to haul it across a massive land filled with mountain ranges. The sword Sim had brought from Moth was long gone away, left aboard the *Eyestrom*.

The voice that had spoken belonged to a young woman around Sim's age. She was short, light-brown skinned, with black hair cut to a commoner's length. She wore leather and fur clothing, decorated with beads. Dark eyes stared at him with wide-open fear. Her hand trembled.

"No," she repeated, and pointed toward Rochella.

Sim didn't lower his knife. "No what?"

The girl shook her head, confused. Then Sim remembered they didn't speak the same language.

"Rochella!" Sim called, not taking his eyes off the girl. He knew better than to trust her. In a similar remote village in Keffra last year, they'd been attacked by a group of children, who threw rocks at them when they saw Rochella's striped skin.

Rochella approached and eased his knife down. "You're frightening the poor girl." She smiled to reassure the girl and spoke to her in Qina. The quick, clipped-sounding words rushed by, and Sim wondered how anybody could keep up.

The girl flicked her gaze between Sim and Rochella but finally relaxed. Sim realized it must've taken her a great deal of courage to approach them. She began speaking, even faster than Rochella. As she did so, the ranger's face hardened. Rochella's hand drifted to her own knife, still resting on her hip.

"She says the Mystic we seek isn't here," Rochella said. "He was taken, eight days ago, by a demon. The village has been living in fear ever since."

Sim darted his gaze around the village, suddenly alert, as if expecting something terrible to jump out from behind one of the stone huts. The girl continued her story, while Rochella listened.

As the two women talked, Sim approached the large house Rochella had knocked at and pushed the door open. There was no lock because remote communities like this saw no need for such things. Or so they'd believed.

Sim eased into a cluttered house, and wondered why, after eight days, the villagers hadn't cleaned it up. There was clear indication of a struggle, but no blood that Sim could see. The owner's possessions lay scattered about, and a few simple wooden pieces of furniture were toppled, but that was the extent of the destruction.

Sim let Rochella's training take over. He used all of his senses to learn what he could. His gaze swept over every corner of the room, while he listened and sniffed the air. The Mystic they sought had lived here. Nobody else was likely to have such a collection of books like the ones that lined the wall on shelves, or a cushion for sitting and meditating by the window.

Sim heard footsteps, and turned to see Rochella and the girl approaching.

"What did you learn?" he asked.

"Bith Yab was attacked at night, and dragged screaming from this house," Rochella said.

"It may have been night, but he was awake," Sim said.

Rochella cocked an eyebrow at him. "How do you know?"

"Because his bed isn't disturbed."

Rochella nodded. "Something very dangerous took him."

Hilash's and Hormin's dead faces stared at Sim from the depths of an ocean of memory. "We need to find him," Sim said in a quiet voice. "He's the only lead we have for finding a cure."

The girl from the village waited in the doorway, unwilling to cross the threshold.

Rochella stood a long minute, then stared through the western wall of the house. Her eyes had a faraway look. Sim recognized that look. It usually meant she'd come to a decision, and there'd be no going back once it was made. Without breaking her gaze from the wall, she spoke to the girl in Qina. The girl nodded and ran off.

"What's our plan?"

"Swiko is bringing us food and other supplies. We hunt."

Sim nodded. That was all he needed. He moved to exit the house, but Rochella stopped him. She leaned in and breathed into his ear. "The Mystics of the highlands are powerful. Whatever it was that took Bith Yab is unlike anything you've faced." She paused. "More than anything I've faced."

"Do you know what it is?" Sim whispered back.

"Not yet, but I sense it," Rochella said, "like a hound sniffing prey. Whatever it is, the girl was right. It is not normal, and I cannot say more with any certainty."

When they emerged to the center of the small community, the girl, Swiko, and some others had come out. Three of the village women offered food. A little boy and girl were sent to top off the rangers' waterskins. Last, an old man limped forward. He had the longest beard Sim had ever seen, dangling down to his shins. He wasn't ancient, as far as Sim could tell, but nonetheless old, perhaps in his sixties. Sim was terrible with estimating ages. The man carried two walking sticks, and offered them to him.

Sim bowed in thanks but shook his head in polite decline. "We already have walking sticks," he said.

Rochella nudged him. "Not like those."

The old man gripped one of the staves with two hands, and twisted. Immediately the lower two-thirds of the staff fell away, revealing a long, slightly curved blade. "Onkai," the old man said, grinning through crooked teeth.

Sim had never heard of an onkai before but could immediately see their utility. He bowed lower than before. "Thank you," he said, and accepted the staves. He handed one to Rochella, who bowed in thanks as well.

Sufficiently equipped, Sim and Rochella walked westward through the far end of the village. Just as they found the trail leading deeper into the mountains, Sim heard running footsteps coming from behind them. He and Rochella turned as Swiko caught up to them.

The girl smiled at Sim with an expression he instantly recognized as something more than friendliness. A part of him felt suddenly awkward, but the more focused part, perhaps the ranger in him, guarded his emotions and kept his face blank.

Swiko said something quick to Rochella, then reached for Sim's hand. He snatched it away. He didn't like people touching him anymore. Swiko flinched at his recoil but reached out again anyway, more slowly this time. Carefully she handed him a wad of rags.

Sim examined the strange gift. It was a cotton doll, wrapped in course canvas, resembling a woman sitting with her legs crisscrossed. A stream of pure white hair flowed from her head. Sim touched the hair with his fingers and his eyes widened.

"*Silk*," Swiko said, emphasizing the word as best she could with her thick accent.

"Yah, silk, I suppose," Sim mused. He'd never felt it before. Back home, only merchant-scholars and the nobility were allowed to own such fine fabric. He didn't know if that law applied here as well. "Thank you."

He allowed himself to favor Swiko with a smile, and she returned it, radiant. She directed some more words to him that he couldn't understand. Then she gave him a knowing look, touched his shoulder with her hand, and walked back toward the village.

"She said Sitting Mother should go with you," Rochella said. "And that she'll await our return."

Sim watched Swiko for a moment, then looked at the doll. "It's not much of a Saint."

Rochella considered him for a long moment. Sim could see she was debating how to respond. Finally, she shook her head. "You have a lot to learn, Thudfoot. Come on. No more talking. Let's hunt."

It took three days for Sim to actually see evidence that they were chasing something real. As always, he simply trusted Rochella, never questioning her ability to somehow know the proper way. On this occasion, it was the scattered remains of a cook fire that convinced him they were most likely chasing a person.

Rochella held her hands over the charred ash. "No heat. We're still days behind. But we're getting closer."

Sim looked at the surrounding evergreen forest, packed with snow. He resisted the urge to comment that of course the embers would be cold up here in the wintery mountains. By the Saints, *he* was perpetually cold.

Cold, and hungry, although food wasn't something he worried about much. They always found it. Sim set traps exactly where Rochella suggested, and always, without fail, there was game caught when he went to check it.

"Something else happened here," Rochella said, looking at the ground surrounding the remains of the campfire. She stood and carefully stepped backward, eyes scanning the ground.

Sim tried to follow her gaze, and sure enough, he soon saw unusual swirling patterns in the ground. There were footprints, too, but that was to be expected near a campfire. But there was something more. Wide, sweeping arcs traced across the snow and dirt. When he looked carefully, Sim could see fallen pine needles in the snow all pointed in the same direction, as if they'd been swept that way.

"Covering up his tracks?" Sim said. "If so, he did a poor job of it."

"No," Rochella said. "There was a struggle."

"A struggle? I don't see it."

Rochella's face hardened. "We should leave now. We'll camp away from here for the night."

The note of worry in her voice made Sim shiver. He followed her deeper into the woods, wondering what would unnerve her like that.

She pushed hard for the remaining hours of daylight. Neither of them spoke, but Sim could clearly sense an unusual air of worry about her. Before the sun set, Rochella insisted that Sim gather as much cloudcap and silverbane as he could find. She directed him to an overgrown slope sheltered from heavy doses of snow by towering evergreens. Sim was used to gathering cloudcap. He'd been gathering it as often as they could find it. Rochella brewed it into a tea whenever she could. He thought the bitter brew tasted worse than gunkroot, but Rochella didn't mind it. Sim imagined it may even have been her one delicacy that she looked forward to, although he never asked directly.

"I'll take first watch," Rochella said after they'd brewed the tea and settled in.

Sim slept, and awoke in the deepest part of the night, when both shadows and silence were at their strongest. The moon was nearly full, so a soft light covered him like a blanket. The campfire, small to begin with, had burned down to just glowing embers.

He lay there, staring at the stars managing to peek through the treetops. Up here in the mountains, they were clearer than anywhere else he'd ever been. As he often did at times like this, he thought of Dane, who'd always wanted to travel. Sim liked to think that his endless days on the road were a kind of tribute to his brother. He hoped Dane would've been proud of him.

But tribute or not, Sim wished he had a proper bed again. It had been far too long since he'd slept in one.

"Sim?" Rochella said, her voice barely more than a whisper.

Sim turned toward her. She stared westward into the woods, lost in thought. There was no need for him to reply. She knew he was awake.

"Your vial of poison," Rochella said.

Sim's chest tightened. "Yah?"

"If things go poorly tomorrow, take its contents."

Sim stood, looming over her. "Why are you talking like this?"

"We're close. I don't think I'm matched for this."

The fear radiating from her unnerved Sim. "What are we hunting, Rochella?"

"I'm not sure."

"Don't hide things from me."

Rochella closed her eyes. He could see her trying to regulate her breathing. She was scared, very scared.

Sim hunched down to her eye level. "What is it? Whatever it is, if it's too much, we can abandon our hunt."

Rochella shook her head. "No, we can't. Our path goes through it."

"What do you mean?" Sim asked, letting a note of irritation into his voice. "How can you say things like that? I don't understand."

"You will, someday," Rochella said. "I've tried to train you as best I could. I hope it's been enough."

"Stop talking like you're going to die," Sim said. "Whatever it is, we don't have to face it. And if we do, we'll overcome it."

Rochella finally looked at him, and for once, to him, she looked young. Maybe it was the softness in her face, but something in her eyes made her more vulnerable. More beautiful.

She met his gaze. Even in the dim starlight, he could see her eyes shimmer. "Never lose that part of you, Sim. The portion of you that always sees a way through a problem. Hold on to that, always."

"What are you so afraid of?" Sim asked. "Tell me, please."

Rochella's eyes narrowed in familiar anger. It did not make her less beautiful. "The truth?"

Sim nodded. "Yah."

She looked away, then back at him. "I'm afraid of being alone."

They held each other's gaze; then Sim cracked a smile and laughed.

Her face hardened. "What?"

"You? Afraid of being alone? You're a *ranger*!"

Rochella leaned forward so she was closer to Sim. "It's one of *everyone's* greatest fears," she said. "Search within yourself, and someday, you'll see it staring at you. Someday, you'll have to conquer it."

Silence stretched between them. Sim realized how close they were. "I will if you teach me."

"I have only one lesson left for you," she whispered, and Sim saw something else in her eyes. Something like what he'd seen in Swiko's, yet more intense.

Sim swallowed. "What lesson?"

"How to let go," she said, and slowly pulled him into a kiss.

Sim held back only a moment. Then he felt a fire roar to life within him. She kissed him slowly, deeply, and he found himself moving his hands across her. Rochella kissed him with certainty and with control, just as she did everything else.

She directed his hands, and soon Sim found himself lying on top of her. One by one the layers of their clothes slid off until the embers of their fire faded, and nothing but moonlight was left to see by.

The next afternoon, they cornered their prey.

They approached with caution, coming to a clearing in the woods where a cave entrance yawned against the side of the mountain. Heavy snow had begun falling shortly after sunrise. Sim and Rochella didn't bother to conceal their final camp. Rochella had led him directly to the clearing, moving with speed and confidence. She only said two words to him as they set out: "Focus today."

Rochella stepped out into the clearing, and motioned with her hand for Sim to circle the opposite way around.

Their prey waited for them.

He was a laghart, dressed in shredded bits of cloth that might once have been robes. He seemed to be male. His scales formed the familiar three-swirling circle pattern all lagharts shared, but his coloring was all white and red. His tongue flicked out into the freezing air as he watched Sim and Rochella approach. The laghart stood still otherwise, like an animal wary of a predator.

The laghart held a tall wooden staff in one of his clawed hands. Sim's heart sank. The laghart was a Mystic.

Rochella nocked an arrow and held it ready. Her eyes never strayed from the laghart. "A wivan," she said. "Don't hesitate."

Sim didn't have time to ask what a wivan was. The laghart lurched in a strange, jilted way. He hissed and snarled like an aggressive animal.

Sim flicked his wrist and the bottom portion of his staff dropped away, revealing the onkai blade. He walked the opposite direction from Rochella, weapon ready. He tried to ignore his shaking hands.

The laghart leaned over at the waist until his spine was parallel with the ground. He hissed, showing rows of sharp teeth. Slitted eyes blazed with an inner fire that seemed more primal and raw than those that would belong to a normal, sentient being.

The laghart Mystic spun his staff, swirling it until the falling snow flurried around it.

Rochella launched an arrow, but either the laghart's blurry

staff deflected it or something else knocked it aside. Rochella pulled another arrow, drew, and launched again but was met again with the same result.

"Stay back!" she yelled at Sim. She readied another arrow.

The laghart was still spinning his staff, but now Sim could see that he was somehow using the Myst. Clumps of ice and snow lifted from the ground, mixing with the fresh powder falling from the sky. The laghart continued to pull them together until spikes of compact ice hovered in the air.

"Rochella, look out; he's going to—"

The laghart screamed, and the spikes of ice flew toward both Sim and Rochella. Sim dove out of the way. A quick glance at Rochella showed she'd done something similar to avoid injury.

The laghart readied more ice darts. "We have to get close!" Sim yelled.

"No!" Rochella retorted. "Take cover!"

Sim thought fast. With just his onkai blade and his belt knife as weapons, his attack options were limited. He was useless this far away. With Rochella's bow being ineffective, he'd have to get closer.

He stalked sideways, away from Rochella, trying to outflank the laghart and get to his blind side.

Rochella loosed another arrow just as the laghart released another volley of ice. She dove out of the way again, this time losing her grip on her bow. The laghart sent a second, having kept some in reserve for a follow-up assault.

With the laghart distracted, Sim leaped, and swung his onkai downward.

The wivan moved like a shifting wind and caught him midair by the throat. Sim gagged and struck at the claw wrapped around his neck. The onkai blade clattered to the ground. He felt as though his head was about to be yanked from his body.

The laghart's tongue flicked from his face. He studied Sim with slitted eyes. Then the tongue touched his skin, tasting him.

Sim spit in the laghart's face. He recoiled, just as Rochella charged forward with her onkai blade.

The Mystic blocked her attack with his staff. He dropped Sim, who sucked air into his lungs. Rochella kicked the creature in the stomach, buying her enough time to strike again with her onkai. The blade dug deep into the laghart's neck, but no blood emerged.

Rochella's eyes widened at what should've been a killing blow.

The laghart moved, faster than any human, knocking away Rochella's onkai blade, and yanked the back of her hair.

Then he tore Rochella's throat out with his mouth.

Sim screamed.

Blood drained and spurted from Rochella's ruined neck as the laghart dumped her onto the ground. He turned to Sim and hissed.

Sim scrambled to his feet and found his onkai blade. He circled the beast as snow continued to fall around him. He refused to look in Rochella's direction. He couldn't think of her. Couldn't go there yet. By the Saints, the image of her blood spraying out—

His stomach churned, but he forced himself to focus on the laghart. He was a dead man standing unless he could get closer.

The Mystic's tail slashed back and forth against the ground, forming patterns like the ones Sim had seen by the campfire yesterday. The laghart leaned over double at the waist again and hissed again, showing bloody teeth and dripping saliva.

Raising his onkai, Sim screamed and rushed toward the laghart, irrationally hoping his brute strength would overwhelm the creature. The laghart sidestepped with his incredible speed. Sim knew he was outmatched for speed, but he was ready for the sidestep. The moment the laghart leaped, Sim shifted his attack and swung ahead of where the creature's momentum was taking him.

The blade sliced right through where the laghart's head should have been, but somehow, impossibly, he ducked and caught the onkai, tearing it from Sim's grip. The laghart roared, a sound that buried itself deep into Sim's bones.

The laghart punched his clawed fist into Sim's gut, knocking the wind out of him. He gasped and fell to his knees, trying to suck in air. The laghart loomed over him.

This was it.

Sim had faced death before. He'd been cut open by a hateful bandit with a sword. He'd been forced to march up a mountain under the wrathful gaze of a Mystic. He'd watched his brother die slowly, and seen Rochella die in an instant. Sim relaxed his muscles and looked up at the crazed laghart Mystic who wanted to take his life.

It was his moment to die.

The Mystic swung a clawed hand at Sim's head, intending to take it off. Sim ducked, barely avoiding the blow, and snatched his small belt knife from his hip. He jammed the knife straight up, letting the laghart's arm drag across its edge. The cut wasn't enough to harm the laghart, but it was enough to draw blood across the creature's claw.

The laghart howled in frustration, which gave Sim enough time to scramble backward.

The laghart glanced at his hand and then fixed his crazed, yellow-slitted eyes on Sim. Slowly, as if to show how little the wound had hurt, the laghart lifted his claw in front of his face. His long black tongue snaked out and licked the wound. Around the Mystic, dozens of ice darts rose and formed.

Sim's heart pounded.

The laghart pointed at Sim, then stopped. His claw trembled. The Mystic looked again at the claw. Sim watched as the claw turned blackish green.

The laghart screamed, shaking his arm as if to fling the venom out.

Sim rose to his feet, his grim eyes never leaving the murderous creature. Desperately, the laghart screamed again and leaped at Sim, coming at him low from the ground. But the laghart's movements were desperate and weak. Sim kicked the laghart in the face, knocking him to the ground.

The laghart thrashed and screamed as the poison worked through his body. Sim pulled the glass vial Pomella had given him from his pocket and tossed it into the snow. It had served its purpose.

The beast thrashed in agony as the poison worked through his body. Somehow, he twisted his head and fixed his gaze on him once more, and spoke.

"Lagnarassste!" he hissed.

Sim lifted his onkai from the ground. It gleamed in the

morning light, colder than the surrounding snow. He kept it in check, however, and watched until the laghart finally died.

Sim buried Rochella beside the cave. The ground was frozen and rocky, but in his grief he didn't know what else to do. It took him most of the day to dig the hole using only stones and heavy branches. The few tears he shed froze on his face.

When he finally went to lower his mentor into her grave, he forced himself to look at the wound that had killed her. After the laghart had died, he'd backtracked a little ways to find Rochella's cloak so he could cover her while he dug. But now, lifting the edge of the cloak, he saw what remained of her neck.

He vomited into the snow.

Knowing she'd want him to do so, Sim removed everything from her body that he could use. Her remaining rations, some fresh paper, a tiny wooden vial of ink, and her hunting knife. He never wanted to touch his own knife again.

He stripped her body naked and buried her in the ground. As a ranger, he knew she loved the land. This way, she'd forever be a part of it. As he placed her in the grave, he stopped and stared at her chest and shoulders. Less than a day ago, her body had breathed and moved with slow passion against his. Now, with the blood draining away from her chest, he saw something he hadn't noticed before.

Faint red sores, too dim to be seen against her dark skin, spread across her body. Sim's heart broke again. All this time, and she'd been infected with the plague as well. She'd lied to him about being immune. His mind raced. How could she've stayed alive this whole time? Something would have had to keep the plague at bay.

The cloudcap tea. It was the only thing Sim could think of that she'd had regularly, and that they'd gone out of their way to find. Another frozen tear dropped from his face.

The sun was well past the western mountain peaks before he finished covering her. He lay on top of the fresh grave, hungry and cold, and stayed there all night, using his cloak to stay warm.

The next morning, hunger got the better of him. Moving by habit, feeling nothing, he set traps to try to catch game. He tried to think of where Rochella would want him to place the trap but couldn't decide where that would be. He chose a place at random, and hoped for the best.

While he waited for food to kill itself in his trap, he finally explored the cave. Inside lay the corpse of an older man who had presumably once been Bith Yab. He wore ruined clothes that matched the style of the mountain village. Upon the back wall of the cave Sim found the image of a snake, stylized like a Mothic knot, painted in blood. It made Sim sick, so he avoided looking at it.

For the second day in a row, Sim spent the majority of the short daylight hours digging a grave. He carefully laid Bith Yab to rest, climbed out of the hole, and found the little Sitting Mother doll Swiko had given him. If the Saint was real, she wasn't watching over Sim. He tossed the doll into the hole with the corpse, and covered them up.

Finally, Sim burned the laghart's body. He checked his

hunting traps and wasn't surprised to find them empty. Famished, he ate the rest of his and Rochella's provisions, then slept as the laghart's body burned and kept him warm.

It took him twice the time to find his way back to the mountain village than it had taken him and Rochella to hunt down the laghart's location. Exhausted and famished, he managed to stay on his feet only with the help of both onkai staves, and finally collapsed into Swiko's arms when she ran down the path to meet him.

Sim tried to push her away, worrying that even with his covered face he'd infect her. But Swiko ignored him and led him to Bith Yab's old house.

The villagers fed and cared for him for a week. Swiko hardly left his side, and even at night he saw her sleeping on a cot beside his door. Nightmares filled with Rochella's dead face haunted him.

During the daytime, the old man with the long beard showed Sim some basic techniques with the onkai that he could practice on his own. By now, he'd picked up a scattering of words from their language and used them to try to express his gratitude. The old man smiled and bowed, making Sim certain that whatever he'd attempted to say had been a pile of jumbled nonsense.

On the evening before Sim left the village, the entire community came together under the full moon. They built a bonfire and nearly everyone stood and told stories. He wasn't sure, but Sim suspected they were all telling stories about Bith Yab. The villagers rolled with laughter as an old woman told an animated story that Sim had no chance of understanding. Normally the woman's expressions would make him smile along with everyone else, but the humor lasted as long as a thin cloud in a summer sky.

Swiko told a story that made most of the villagers cry. She glanced at Sim afterward, but he avoided her gaze and stared at his boots. He wondered if he should tell them a story about Rochella, but what was the point? Even if he could speak their language, what stories would they care about? Sim couldn't think of any good ones. The only story that came to mind was how Rochella had recently bought him the boots he was currently staring at. They had been in Yin-Aab, the nearby city that made Port Morrush seem tiny.

Take care of your feet, Thudfoot, she'd told him. *A ranger never stops moving.*

He'd come to like the nickname she'd given him, even though he'd never discovered the specific thing he'd done to earn it.

Finally, at the end of the night, the whole village stood, and the old onkai man began to sing. His voice, surprisingly deep and resonate, chanted, *"Huzzzz-oh!"*

Sim lifted his head to listen. He'd heard that chant before, but where? The village echoed the old man: *"Huzzzz-oh!"*

For some reason, it made Sim think of Pomella.

The villagers chanted again, *"Huzzzz-oh!"* and the word echoed off the mountains around them. A flood of Pomella memories came to Sim. He wondered what she was doing, and whether she ever thought of him. But all those thoughts accomplished was making him feel more sad.

He readied to leave the next morning, before sunrise. His bags were loaded with food, and both his waterskin and Rochella's had been filled. As he'd anticipated, Swiko was awake and insisted—using gestures and the half-speak they'd devised as their own form of private communication—that she walk with him.

Sim preferred she not accompany him, but he didn't have the language or energy to explain that he wanted to be alone. As they left Bith Yab's house, Swiko gestured for him to follow her up the path toward the summit of the mountain the village rested on, rather than down and back toward Yin-Aab where he and Rochella had come from. Sighing, Sim followed.

It took the better part of the day for them to reach their destination. Not because of the distance, but because of the snow. All of the paths leading to the heights were blocked by a wall of ice and snow taller than Sim. But it wasn't the summit Swiko led him to. It was a cliff that overlooked the village, now far below them. Seeing his confusion, the girl took the onkai from Sim's hand and set them aside. She looked him in the eyes, and when he turned away she gently pulled his face back with her hands, and removed the scarf that he always kept around his nose and mouth.

"Swiko," Sim began. "I can't; I—"

She placed a finger on her lips, then stepped aside and pointed across the valley to the northeast. There, far distant across the cold, clear sky, was a massive mountain, plainly visible, towering above all others in the range.

"Sit-ting Mother," Swiko said in her thick accent. "Go. You."

Sim opened his mouth to protest, then closed it. "Why?" he said after a while.

Confusion swam in Swiko's eye, but she replied, "Sitting Mother. Find. Heal. After snow."

His excuse died on his lips. *Heal*, she had said.

Heal.

Rochella was gone. Pomella was gone. Dane was gone. Sim was alone, without any purpose.

We are rangers. We do what we always do. We move, and we survive.

Rochella's words, returned to him from across time and death.

Sim gazed to the distant, cloud-wreathed mountain. Swiko wanted him to stay until the snow melted. But he was a ranger now, and rangers didn't stay in one place too long.

But heavy snow already blanketed those mountain slopes. Swiko was right. Part of what she was trying to tell him was that he couldn't go there now even if he wanted to. Without Rochella to guide him through these unfamiliar winter lands, he would have as much chance of surviving as a flower blooming in snow. Maybe even with her help they wouldn't have been able to survive. There was no shame in wintering here.

He nodded to Swiko. "Yah, OK," he said.

A wide smile bloomed on Swiko's face. "OK," she said. She took his hand, picked up the onkai staves, and led him back down the mountain.

For some reason he couldn't understand, Sim felt as though he'd failed.

THIRTEEN

BEFORE THE THIRD NEW MOON

Three Years Before Crow Tallin

Shevia swept the floor of the kitchen like a good apprentice. Above her, sour-scented ropes of garlic hung from the rafters beside iron pots and wicker baskets. A cauldron of soup bubbled over a fire, slowly steaming until the time it was ready to become supper.

Shevia worked the broom back and forth, her mind numb, not caring whether the floor was spotless. She paused to fold a lock of long hair behind her ear. Master Bhairatonix did not like when her appearance was short of perfect. "Master yourself before you can master the Myst," he would say.

A wave of bitterness lapped at the shores of her mind. More and more she wondered whether the previous four years of her life were typical. Did all Mystic apprentices slave over meaningless chores all day? Back home, her family had had servants. She had been free to paint and study language. Now she was little more than a scullion.

Shevia set the broom aside. With the amount she used the ugly thing, it was appropriate that her Mystic staff had once been a mop. With the sweeping done, all that remained was to wash the highsun meal dishes and finish preparing dinner. Perhaps afterward, if she pleased him enough, Bhairatonix would give her a lesson about the Myst.

Flicking her gaze out the kitchen door to ensure she was alone, Shevia summoned the Myst and reached out her hand. The Myst rose reluctantly around her, and she willed it to carry her *actual* Mystic staff across the room to her. The staff glided through the air smoothly, wobbling only once. She frowned at herself. She would have to do better and eliminate the wobble next time.

As the staff touched her hand, the Myst surged around her. She didn't fully understand it, but somehow, whenever she touched her staff the Myst seemed more powerful, more immediate. Bhairatonix had declined to explain why when she asked. In fact, he rarely taught her anything. Probably because she was the worst apprentice in all of Qin, despite having the greatest of masters. She would have to try harder to be more perfect.

Closing her eyes, Shevia sought stillness within herself. She'd long ago mastered the ability to hide her emotions, eventually finding that if she didn't have any there would be nothing to repress. She found the Myst was most powerful when it wasn't filtered by weaknesses such as sadness, excitement, or anger. This was one lesson Bhairatonix taught her soon after taking her as his apprentice: that emotions clouded your ability to command and manipulate the Myst.

Raising her staff an inch above the ground, Shevia tapped it downward, releasing the Myst and willing it to scour the soiled dishes and then dry them when they were clean.

The familiar silvery light swirled around the dishes, obeying her command. Foamy water rushed across their surfaces, swishing back and forth until they were clean. Tiny bubbles drifted in the air.

She risked a moment of distraction to peer out the kitchen door, hoping Bhairatonix wouldn't see her using the Myst for her chores. He'd caught her once using it to clean rugs. The resulting punishment had left her sobbing and limping for days after. After that, Shevia had learned to be a better apprentice. Or, at least, in those moments when she failed to be good, she learned to be better at hiding her poor choices.

Shevia allowed herself a small feeling of triumph at having saved herself more tiresome work. She returned her attention to the sink and had to stifle a gasp.

Challop, her master's black cat, sat beside the dishes, watching Shevia and swishing her fluffy tail. The cat's green eyes pierced into Shevia, seemingly looking for faults.

Shevia immediately released the Myst. The dishes dropped back into place, and at least one clay bowl shattered.

Shevia froze, waiting to see what would happen. She couldn't prove it, but somehow she suspected that Challop knew everything that happened at Shenheyna and reported back to Bhairatonix. When she was a child, Cilla had told her stories of Mystics who bonded with animals, giving a portion of themselves to the creature in exchange for companionship, service, or secrets. Challop looked like a normal cat, but Shevia couldn't be sure. She watched the cat glance at the dishes and even lift a paw to swipe at a drifting soap sud.

"I am leaving on a journey."

Somewhere in the numbness of her mind, Shevia felt a surge of what must have been fear. She turned to see her master's unusually tall body framed in the kitchen doorway. As always, he held his staff in one hand, and his other was tucked away in his robes. Challop glided across the counter toward him. Seemingly without thought, Bhairatonix reached out and stroked the cat with the same long, bony fingers that gripped his staff. Shevia had become used to his abrupt way to appear and address her. He saw no point in simple greetings.

"Yes, Master," Shevia said. "What do you require of me?"

Bhairatonix's eyes searched her as if trying to find evidence of wrongdoing. Shevia gave away nothing.

"Keep my home tidy while I am away. Disturb nothing. I will return within—"

He cut himself short as he saw the broken dish. He tapped his staff once and the bowl's shards shot out of the soapy water and hovered between them. His face remained expressionless as it rotated in the air, dripping water. Bhairatonix tapped his staff again and the bowl spun itself back together, good as new. It drifted back onto the counter, gently tapping the surface as it settled.

Bhairatonix lifted a bony finger in front of his face, and twitched it. Shevia blinked, and realized she was lying on the floor. Everything around her was blurry. She gasped for air but found it difficult to inhale. She touched a trembling hand to her nose and found blood on her fingers. Her first thought was that she shouldn't get blood on the floor.

Shevia did her best to steady herself and stand. The blow had spun her fully around, and she had disturbed a table when she fell back. Shevia forced herself to turn around and face her master again. She dared not speak until given permission.

"The life of a Mystic is not easy, girl," Bhairatonix said. "As the keepers of the Myst, we have a responsibility to maintain perfection in all we do. Sloppiness like this"—he indicated the repaired bowl—"is the mark of careless commoners."

Shevia kept her eyes lowered. She felt blood trickle down her upper lip.

Bhairatonix stepped forward and put his hand on her shoulder. "But I forgive you, Shevia. You were not raised a noble. These missteps are to be expected."

"Yes, Master. I'm sorry I am a disappointment."

Bhairatonix moved his hand to lift her chin. She let him. He ran a chilly thumb across her lower lip, wiping the blood away. It lingered just a moment longer than necessary, pressed against her flesh just a little harder than expected. Shevia could not bring herself to shiver.

His hand drew away, his face stony. "See to your face. I will return before the third new moon."

He swept out of the kitchen, bloodred robes swishing behind him. Shevia remained motionless, letting the blood flow from her nose. Time seemed to still around her. She thought of that last day in the Thornwood, where the snow had drifted motionless in the air.

Challop watched her with a curious expression. She wondered if the hateful beast was entertained.

Shevia didn't move, fearing that if she did time would grab hold of her again and her emotions would overwhelm her. Here, in this frozen world, she was in control. She was beyond pain.

Shevia thought of her friend Sitting Mother, now long lost.

A drop of blood pooled on her chin, wobbled, then fell. She caught it without thought before it could splatter on the floor.

Before the third new moon. That meant Bhairatonix would be gone for nearly two weeks. She would use that time to become a better apprentice.

By evening, the main house was clean. Shevia mindlessly wiped her hands on a rag, then folded the cloth thrice, making sure to match the corners perfectly. She allowed herself a relaxing breath, and straightened her robe. Her nose still stung, but the bleeding had stopped. She'd been able to conceal the wound with makeup, something Bhairatonix allowed her.

Silence enveloped the manor as Shevia walked through each room, hunting for chores. The silence was nothing new to her. She welcomed it. She ended her rounds in her master's astronomy tower, privately one of her favorite places. Full-sized windows encircled the entire room, looking out on the rocky, evergreen-filled terrain surrounding Shenheyna.

Only she and the High Mystic lived in the manor atop Mount Hinya within the Saychin Mountains. Bhairatonix kept to himself, welcoming few visitors, leaving only the crisp air and multitude of evening stars to keep Shevia company. She loved the stars but carefully concealed that affection from the High Mystic. She counted them each night from the secret comfort of her bed in her tiny room. That counting awakened her love of numbers, allowing her to add and multiply levels she had never done before. With Cilla no longer around to teach her, she began figuring out the mathematical puzzles herself, even giving names to the factors she had never been taught. Hundreds, thousands, then tibrans, typhons, and so on.

Shevia examined the large telescope dominating the center of the room. The long tube pointed upward out one of the western windows, stretching as long as her arms were wide. Shevia wondered what was inside it. Her fingers itched for her to look through the eyepiece. She'd been allowed to, once, when Bhairatonix had let her gaze upon the moon. Her hands had shaken with excitement when she saw its cratered surface up close. Now she wondered if she could look again tonight while the moon was near full.

Sweat trickled down Shevia's back. Her hands shook. She took a tiny step toward the telescope, then fled the tower back to her room.

She lay on her bed, not daring to be caught in a part of the manor she should not have been at this hour. Thirteen days. That's how long it was before the third new moon of the year. She could be a good apprentice for at least that long.

As the night deepened, she played a game with herself, opening and closing her eyes, trying to see if she could feel weightless and invisible in both worlds, sighted and dark. With the silence of the manor, and her loneliness, she imagined herself to be the only person in the world. Maybe the moon was a world, like the one she lived on? Maybe there were people living there? But how far away must a place like that be to appear so small in the sky? Her mind boggled as she attempted, poorly, to comprehend the distance. She lay there for an hour, calculating, and decided that the next factor after tibros and typhons would be tevons.

Her names for those units brought to mind her brothers, whom she had not seen since shortly after arriving at Shenheyna. Bhairatonix had sent them away to become rangers. He had told her that if they survived she would likely see them again. He had not said when that would be.

Shevia eased herself to a sitting position. She pulled her long hair away from her neck, trying to cool it. The noise in her mind overwhelmed her. She had to focus on something else. Had to *do* something. But after the incident this morning, she was more determined than ever to behave. She had to find something to do that her master would approve of.

A bath. She could take a bath.

But as she stared at the small, crude tub in the washroom a minute later, another idea crawled into her. She glanced around for Challop. She had not seen the cat since this morning. Briefly, she wondered, then dismissed, whether Bhairatonix had taken her with him. Feeling safe, and before she could stop herself, she grabbed her Mystic staff, left her room, and found herself facing the imposing double doors leading into Bhairatonix's bedroom.

Her hand hesitated over the handle. She had been inside the room many times to clean, but always with her master's permission or supervision. This was clearly different. A good apprentice did not do what she planned.

But Bhairatonix would be gone for thirteen days. She turned the handle and pushed the door.

The High Mystic's private chambers opened before her. Shadows consumed most of the room. A high vaulted ceiling rose above, boasting a mural of Mystics and fay twisting in elaborate dances outside a tower. Peering through the darkness, Shevia wondered if they were actually fighting a battle. The depicted tower had a single window and a ring of stars surrounding it. A hand, covered in blood, protruded from the window as if its occupant was trying to claw their way to freedom. The darkness mostly hid an elaborate glass chandelier hanging above the center of the room, directly over a circular floor rug.

Against the nearest wall sat a huge four-poster bed with heavy wine-colored drapes. The stillness of the perfectly woven curtains assured Shevia that her master truly was gone.

An old wardrobe that smelled of musky cloth and candles dominated the wall opposite the bed. Between the bed and wardrobe was a large window offering the best view in the manor aside from the astronomy tower. Thick curtains that matched the bed's concealed the landscape beyond, but Shevia had seen it before, and knew it looked over a sheer drop in the mountainside, and on to the valley beyond.

She drifted on bare feet across the rug and used a finger to open a tiny slit in the curtains. The valley on the other side was dark except where the moon shone its light. It reminded her of Thornwood. The echo of old memories ached in her heart, but Shevia let them slip. She retracted her finger from the curtain, letting the view vanish.

Her master's wardrobe was the next place she examined. Her hands shook as the heavy mahogany doors opened silently, revealing musky robes, shoes, and other clothes. She found nothing of interest until, as she began to shut the door, she caught sight of an intricately carved box, about the size of her hand.

Shevia's heart beat faster. She recognized that box. She knew she should leave it alone, but a moment later she found herself carrying it through an open archway beside the wardrobe, leading her to her master's washroom. Inside she found what she sought. Bhairatonix's huge bathtub, built for an enormous person of his size. Not daring to hesitate for fear of changing her mind, she lifted her staff and summoned the Myst. Silvery mist swirled inside the tub, slowly filling it with water. She shifted her weight and churned her staff as if stirring a large pot. It took nearly twenty minutes, but eventually the foggy light within the tub shone brighter, and the water steamed with warmth. She added more heat until the whole room fogged over.

Setting her staff aside, Shevia disrobed. She glimpsed her ghostlike reflection in the washroom's vanity mirror through the steam. The figure in the mirror with a twisting snake tattoo on her shoulder peered back at her, sad and skinny.

Shevia didn't bother to toe the water but submerged herself completely into the huge tub, reveling in the heat. It was as though she lived in a sea of fire, and it felt . . . rejuvenating. She submerged herself until only her mouth, nose, and eyes broke the surface. She inhaled deeply, letting the searing heat consume her. Her black hair floated around her face.

As she lay inside the steamy tub, she remembered the trances the Thornwood Vent had pulled her into. Shevia thought of Sitting Mother, her friend, whom she missed. Dwelling on her seemed like a violation of her relationship with her new master. She belonged to him now, and Sitting Mother was far away.

Shevia floated on her back and examined for the carved box she's taken from Bhairatonix's wardrobe. The carvings depicted a repeating series of serpents, each biting the tail of the one beside it. She shivered at their similarity to the twisted snake imprinted on her shoulder. Every three or four months, Bhairatonix brought the box to her and opened it, releasing scented vapors from the Thornwood Shrine which pulled her into the familiar and inescapable trance. Shevia would then obediently tell her master of her visions, none of which she could remember the next day. She didn't know why those visions left her memory afterwards, but she suspected Bhairatonix perhaps had a hand in wiping them away.

Steadying her trembling hands, Shevia ran her fingers over the carved box. She dreaded the visions as much as she craved them. Each time she breathed the fumes, she did it for the benefit of another person. Today, just once, she would do it for herself.

She eased the hinged lid of the box open. Familiar greenish smoke wafted out, and Shevia breathed it in. The mixed scent of sandalwood and holly washed over her. The anxiety she'd been feeling washed away. Her eyes rolled back in her head. The water grew warmer, then hot, bordering on uncomfortable. She shifted, trying to rise, but found she couldn't move. A tinge of fear rose within her, but now the heat was increasing, faster. The water danced with energy, and pulsed with silvery light. Her panic rising, Shevia wondered if Bhairatonix had come home and caught her.

The water churned. Streams of bubbles rose from somewhere in the depths.

She lurched her body upward, but it wouldn't break the surface. It was as if an invisible rope, or tentacle, grasped her from below, not letting her rise or fall. Her breathing accelerated. Her whole body burned.

Then suddenly, like a hot iron brand stabbing her flesh, her right shoulder erupted in fiery agony. All the heat in the bath raced to that spot, igniting it with pain. She screamed and arched her back.

Her chest and shoulders broke the surface. The serpent-shaped tattoo twisted with energy and life as if it were alive and trying to consume her arm.

As the water boiled she instantly became aware of another presence. A familiar and comforting one. Within the pain, Shevia felt Sitting Mother embrace her, with hands that simultaneously held her within the fire and above it.

Nothing was said, as always, but Shevia's mind was filled with understanding. Sitting Mother had never abandoned her, she suddenly knew, just as she had said she would not. Shevia need not fear, for power and understanding were within her grasp. True power was inside her, not waiting beyond her reach where she needed it to be given to her by another person, whether that person was a High Mystic or anyone else.

Sitting Mother's presence swam around Shevia, circling her. Empowering her. Her friend would teach her to find that power. She would teach her to find the Myst. All Shevia had to do was allow it.

The tattoo writhed, and Shevia reveled in the burn. She hungered for it. Power would help her not fear. It would bring her answers. And maybe, freedom to make her own choices.

As the beautiful, searing fire-water torched across her, Shevia screamed. The noise exploded out, rattling the entire washroom and cracking the mirror above the sink basin.

The heat vanished, burned away in an instant along with the entire tub of water.

Shevia bolted upright in the tub, panting. Heavy fog filled the entire room. She remained there, naked and shivering. When the steam cleared enough for her to see, she looked down at her tattooed shoulder. Rather than covering just the rounded slope of her shoulder, the tattoo now spread wider, reaching from the midpoint on her collarbone down to the middle of her biceps. The twisting serpent's spine now sprouted small, triangle-shaped spikes, and two claw-sized wings—similar to a bat's—rose out of its back. The head was larger, and now teeth jutted out. The serpent's body twisted in an even more elaborate way, snaking in loops around itself and her upper arm.

Shevia smiled. She ran her fingers across the enlarged creature. A new wave of power surged within her, like a tide of water rushing against a cliff.

Thirteen days.

She had thirteen days to explore her new skills, and explore the manor.

The clouds coursed through the sky above Shenheyna for a full week while Shevia combed the manor. Carefully and methodically she examined every room, every shelf, and every drawer in order to learn their secrets.

The days passed as if in a dream. She ate sparingly, not caring to prepare meals each day. Not wanting to leave tasks undone, Shevia made sure to complete her daily chores, using the Myst at every opportunity. It obeyed her commands more easily now. Sweeping a room required only a wave of her staff while just a tap was needed to repair simple objects, such as the cracked bathroom mirror.

With mindless ease Shevia purged the house of dust and insects. Challop eventually returned from wherever the vile creature had skulked off to. Shevia kept a watchful eye on the cat, making sure not to explore a forbidden place with the beast present.

By the evening of the eighth day, only one room remained unexplored. She made herself a full meal and went to bed early. On the morning of the ninth day, she approached Bhairatonix's bedroom once more with staff in hand. Although she had been inside many times, her intuition told her there was *something* hidden inside his chambers. The mystery whispered to her, luring her in.

She strode into the room, and closed the double doors behind her. Her eyes took in the whole room: the painted ceiling, the rug, the chandelier, the bed, the tall wardrobe, and the archway to the washroom. The secret was in here. She did not know what it would be, but it was important.

She began with the rug, looking under it, and within the fibers. She studied the pattern for messages. She examined every glass shard in the chandelier, using the Myst to break any illusions around it. She searched every hidden corner of the bed, and found herself wondering if Bhairatonix ever shared it with anybody. He was old, perhaps in his sixties or seventies, but that did not mean he was celibate. Did he enjoy the company of women or men? A shiver rippled her spine as she remembered the way he had sometimes looked at her, and the intimate way he sometimes touched her back, or thumbed her lips.

The bed, and wardrobe, and even the night pot yielded nothing. But still, the mystery called to her.

Standing again by the door, Shevia trailed her eyes across everything in the room, catching every detail. She had searched everything, including the exotic mural on the ceiling. What was she missing? There was nothing else to search, no furniture, no other paintings on the wall.

Shevia's heart skipped a beat. Paintings. There were no other paintings. Here, or anywhere else in the manor.

Every Mystic, by tradition, kept an image of their master—or many masters from their lineage—in their home or dwelling if they had one. It defied possibility that the High Mystic of Qin would not have a painting or drawing of his masters somewhere in the house.

Shevia closed her eyes and took a calming breath. She relaxed into herself, and went to the inner place in her mind where she most often felt Sitting Mother. She floated there, in conscious rest, and summoned the Myst. It rose around her, and she stirred it. She moved it with her staff and arms. She stepped with it, circling it around the room, like a whirlpool of energy until it spun and raced on its own.

"Sitting Mother!" she shouted, realizing it was the first she'd spoken aloud in nine days. "Come forth and share the secrets of Shenheyna with me!"

She summoned more of the Myst, willing it harder to swirl and reveal the secrets of Bhairatonix's manor. If her master would not reveal them, then Sitting Mother would.

Her tattoo warmed, giving her more power. A snarl curled her lips. "I am the Oracle of Thornwood! Hear me!"

A rushing wind filled the room, disturbing only her hair and robes. The wind followed the path of her whirlpool, then funneled upward, toward the ceiling. The Mystics and fay in the tapestry seemed to come alive, continuing the violent dance they were locked in.

Shevia watched as the whirlwind narrowed and focused until it centered on the hand that protruded from the mural's tower window. The hand erupted with silvery light, and in that moment the wind, and the funnel of focused Myst, vanished.

Unprepared for the abrupt shift in energy, Shevia lost her balance and stumbled. Silence and stillness enveloped the bedroom. She regained her footing and tucked her stirred hair behind her ear.

Above her, the ringed constellation of stars surrounding the tower shimmered. Shevia stared at it. A long moment passed before she lifted her staff above her head and touched its end against the hand.

A rumble filled the room, coming from the wardrobe. When it stopped, Shevia lowered her staff and approached the wooden cabinet. She eased open the doors and pulled aside her master's robes. Previously when she had looked here, she'd only found a solid wood backing. But now the wood panels were gone and a long stone hallway descended impossibly out the back. By normal logic, the tunnel should run out of the house and down the sheer cliff below the manor. But somehow, the passage before her led to a subterranean chamber that should not exist.

Shevia allowed herself a rare smile. Stilling her nerves, she descended the path.

The tunnel led to Bhairatonix's laboratory. It was a cave hollowed out of a mountain. Because of the strange nature of the tunnel, Shevia could not be sure if it was deep beneath the manor, located in another part of Mount Hinya, or someplace else entirely.

A dozen steadily burning candles encircled the chamber, illuminating a handful of bookshelves loaded with dusty tomes. The smell of melted candle wax mingled with mildew. Shevia wondered why the High Mystic would keep so many books in such a moldy and humid chamber. Perhaps he kept the pages preserved using the Myst.

Large paintings of men and women hung against the rough stone walls, encased in elaborate golden frames. *Here* were the past masters. She had been right! She recognized none of the faces but did not expect to. Bhairatonix had never spoken of his previous masters.

A large, sturdy table rose before her. Upon it sat glass flasks filled with unusual liquids and powders. A bookstand atop the table held a decaying tome containing an annotated illustration of a glass sphere encasing what looked like a butterfly, or perhaps a moth. The labels were written in a language Shevia did not recognize except for a single word.

"Reunion," she whispered.

Her fingers itched to flip the pages and explore the book's contents. But her eyes widened as she caught sight of an open space on the far side of the table. A wave of fear swept over Shevia. She tried to tuck it away but could not keep her hands from trembling.

The book and other objects forgotten, Shevia wound around the table carefully, approaching the wide empty area of the cavern as if she were approaching an agitated snake.

Her heart raced. She had to leave. Now. But the sight before her gripped her in a trance.

Chalked in a wide circle across the bumpy cavern floor was the image of a serpent, elaborately knotted around itself, with claws and wings and triangular spikes on its back.

The urge to flee the laboratory fought against her need to wipe the image away. Bhairatonix had seen her tattoo before, but not often or long enough to reproduce it here so accurately. And he certainly had not seen it in its latest, more evolved form.

Shevia decided to flee, but before she could take a step back toward the passage a cat meowed.

In that instant, Shevia knew. She didn't need to see Challop sitting at the base of the tunnel, swishing her black tail. Shevia didn't need to see the hideously tall, lanky form dominating her only escape route.

"You go too far, girl," Bhairatonix said.

Shevia's mind raced. It had not been thirteen days yet. It had only been nine!

Her master strode forward, taking his time.

"I have spared you these years and given you opportunity to observe and learn. And this is how you repay my generosity?" The calm in his voice underscored the danger Shevia knew she was in.

Shevia looked desperately for another way to escape but knew she would find none.

"Don't touch me," she said, holding her staff up between them. She wished her hands weren't shaking. She called to the Myst, and its power rose within her.

"You dare summon the Myst against me?" Bhairatonix snarled, sweeping Shevia's staff away with a hard wave of his hand.

The memory of Ahg-Mein's horrible ending flashed in Shevia's mind. Bhairatonix leaned his staff against his shoulder and snapped his hand outward. An invisible force yanked Shevia across the room and into his grip. She choked as his fingers squeezed her throat.

For a panicked heartbeat, Shevia considered unleashing her new power against him. She could save herself!

Tears fell from her eyes as he bore down on her face.

"You will learn your place," he said.

He threw her over the table, across the room onto the chalked floor. Shevia tried to scramble to her feet, but an invisible force crashed her back to the floor. She begged Sitting Mother to help, and in response power rose within her.

But the sight of her master striding toward her trampled her newfound hope. The humble, fearful apprentice within her realized she'd been a terrible pupil. She deserved what was coming. How could she, a pathetic wretch, a gentle gust of wind, compare to her master's hurricane of power?

He lifted his fist and she broke under his fury.

FOURTEEN

A MOTH IN GLASS

Shevia opened her eyes, leaving the dark memory of the past behind. She brought herself back to the present, within the tower at Kelt Apar.

The dark-skinned girl from multiple visions left the chamber, leaving Shevia alone with the High Mystics. A moment passed and Yarina, the youngest of the masters, let a sigh escape.

"Well, that was interesting," Yarina said in her Keffran-tinted Continental accent.

Shevia kept her body straight and her face calm, just as Bhairatonix preferred. Here, in front of his peers, she would continue to play along with the farce. Each of the High Mystics glanced at her on occasion, trying to understand what she was. Some of them harbored curiosity in the secret bay shores behind their eyes, others skepticism. But every one of them hosted a deep fear, of the kind that, if proved to be real, would unravel their view of the world. These were the most powerful Mystics in the world, and she could sense their awareness of the firestorm brewing around her. Shevia didn't like making people uncomfortable, but she was done being a pawn. Sitting Mother had chosen *her*, and empowered her with the Myst—but for what she could not yet say.

High Mystic Willwhite, the one with the beautiful shifting face, turned to Shevia. "Was there more to your vision than what we saw, daughter?"

"No, Master," Shevia lied. She spoke in the Continental language. "But the feeling of pain from the lagharts was very distinctive. They were unprepared for whatever fay came upon them."

There had been more to the vision, but Shevia dared not share it with anyone, especially Bhairatonix. Above the dying lagharts, she'd seen a red banner flutter against a backdrop of thick smoke. On the banner was a twisted serpent, twined around the length of its own body. The meaning had been clear to her. It was a summons.

High Mystic Angelos leaned forward on his cushion. "Your Unveilings are quite remarkable. Before we bring in the next Mystic for assignment, I would like to know how you first came to Unveil the Myst."

Shevia tucked her memory of the banner away safely so that nobody could see it. Outwardly, she displayed herself as a perfectly demure apprentice. "By the grace of my master, I have come to know the Myst."

"We are seeking more specific answers," Yarina said with a bite of impatience.

"Were you not Unveiling the Myst before Master Bhairatonix

apprenticed you?" added Mistress Michaela. It was eerie, looking at her, and then her brother beside her. Their faces were like twin moons hanging in the sky.

"Yes," Shevia said. "But I did not know what it was. I had some guidance from another Mystic, but he only sought profit from my visions. He did not understand how the Unveilings worked."

"And how do they work?" Yarina said.

Shevia looked at Bhairatonix, who nodded in approval. She did so only as a formality, however, knowing that he could hardly require her to keep secrets when the other High Mystics cornered her with direct questions. She had told Bhairatonix many times all she knew of the visions, yet she'd never mentioned Sitting Mother. Through all the intimidation, abuse, and humiliation of her apprenticeship, Sitting Mother was the one secret Shevia clung to, the one aspect of her life she could control and that belonged just to her. If she lost Sitting Mother, she would have nothing. Her bond with Sitting Mother—her only experience of friendship—had evolved from her childhood solitude to become her source of courage and now, at last, her wellspring of power.

"When I was a child I stumbled upon a crack in the ground on my family's estate. Strange fumes rose from that vent. When I breathed them in, I had visions."

"What kind of visions?" asked Yarina.

"When I focused on a particular person, images of their past and future passed in front of me. Although they were not literal representations of what had occurred, when the visions faded I always had a perfectly accurate certainty of what would befall the person."

"It sounds as though you truly experienced oracular Unveilings," said Angelos. "Remarkable indeed. With Crow Tallin upon us, and your presence here in Kelt Apar where the Myst is strong, it is no wonder your abilities shine forth."

"I was a young girl when the Unveilings began," Shevia said. "I still do not fully understand the phenomenon. Since that time, my master has taught me to harness my meager talent. If I do anything today to impress you, it is only because of his grace."

Master Ollfur, the jolly baldheaded High Mystic, leaned forward and pointed at her exposed shoulder. "Tell us about your tattoo."

Before Shevia could reply, Bhairatonix spoke. "The Mystic who *guided*"—he sneered the word—"her before I took her as apprentice believed it would add to her allure if she had a freakish marking upon her."

Shevia kept her expression neutral. Why was Bhairatonix lying? She thought back to that dark memory, to that fateful night three years ago when she entered his secret laboratory. More disturbing than anything else she had seen in the lair had been the snake-image from her skin chalked upon the floor. Had Bhairatonix been studying her? Was she connected to him in a way that she was unaware of? For three years these questions had filled her mind, yet fear had kept her from asking.

Her gaze flickered over to the round, glass sphere sitting on the pedestal on the opposite side of the small room. The moth inside rested at the bottom of the sphere, its wings twitching on occasion. She had seen that, too, in Bhairatonix's laboratory, sketched inside an old tome. More secrets. More lies.

"It is unfortunate," Bhairatonix went on, "that in her youthful exuberance, my apprentice decided to use her skills to expand the design."

Shevia wanted to scream at him, to rip his secrets out, and to expose him as a fraud to his peers. She met his gaze coolly but willed with all her silent might to speak with her eyes, saying, *I fear you no more.*

Yet a part of her wondered if that, too, was a lie.

Instead, she said, "You are very patient with my eccentricities, Master." She hoped he choked on her simpering falsehood.

"I am satisfied. But now we must hurry with our duties," Master Willwhite interjected.

Yarina nodded, and Unveiled a small fay bird, which flew out the window to inform the Green Man that they would see the next Mystic. One by one Mystics came to the upper chamber where Shevia Unveiled visions of people in need. With every Unveiling, Shevia's tattoo tightened a little more, as if it were squeezing her arm.

The High Mystics droned on, sending Mystics across the island. Shevia's mind drifted. She paid attention only when she was needed, summoning the Myst to present her visions before easing back into the privacy of her mind to rest. The day wore on, and soon the room became almost unbearably hot. Sweat poured down the back of her neck beneath her hair. None of the other High Mystics seemed disturbed by the heat, although beads of sweat pebbled Master Ollfur's shaved head.

During one of the endless meetings with Mystics, Shevia heard a tapping sound coming from the glass orb. The moth inside fluttered furiously, throwing itself at the sphere as if trying to break out. Its attempts to escape increased in ferocity. Shevia wondered why nobody else acknowledged it. At the moment,

Yarina was providing instructions to an older woman to attend to a family living remotely on a homestead east of Kelt Apar. The Mystic woman appeared to Shevia to be a walking assortment of twigs and brambles, not much more than a reclusive hex. Many of the Mystics who had gathered at Kelt Apar were so removed from society that it was a wonder they had all once been born into nobility.

But at least they were free, she mused.

Suddenly a cracking sound split the air. Everyone whipped their heads toward the glass orb. Shevia's heart leaped as she saw a small crack, no longer than the tip of her fingernail, running vertically across the glass.

Silence blanketed the chamber. The moth within rested at the bottom of the sphere, slowly pumping its wings.

"You have your instructions, Jollasema," Yarina said to the Mystic woman, but still looking at the moth. "Please travel safely, and in haste."

The hex bowed her head to the floor and departed.

"Our true task becomes more urgent," Michaela said.

Shevia wondered what their "true task" was, and what the moth was.

"Yes," said Ollfur. "But right now, I recommend a brief recess. The heat is stifling."

"Very well," said Yarina. "I'll ask Vivianna to send refreshments to each of your cabins. Let us reconvene in an hour."

"You work your apprentice very hard," Willwhite said.

"She is a fine Mystic," Yarina said. "And will one day make an exceptional High Mystic of Moth, should the Myst choose that as her path. She excels at seeing larger patterns, and few are as gifted at interacting with the fay. I rely on her for a great deal."

One by one the High Mystics left the chamber, leaving only Shevia and Bhairatonix. High Mystic Ehzeeth, the laghart, was the last to file out, but before he left he stopped to peer at the crack in the glass orb. His forked tongue flicked out several times. Shevia could not read his expression to know whether it was concern or another emotion. He had not spoken since her vision of the velten.

With a final glance at her and Bhairatonix, Ehzeeth shambled out. The door shut behind him.

"Your smug lies may fool the others," Bhairatonix said in Qina, "but not me. What else did you see in that first vision? The one you gave to the commoner Mystic girl about the lagharts."

Shevia turned a cool expression on her master. "Are you displeased with me?"

"Do not toy with me, girl! I will—" he said.

"You will nothing," Shevia cut in. Her heart thundered in her chest. This was it, the moment when all pretense broke. A storm of emotions raged within her, but fear of this man was no longer one of them. Sitting Mother was with her. The Myst was her ally. She would not be afraid. "You have no power over me any longer," she said, her voice calm yet forceful.

"Insolent *hetch*," Bhairatonix snarled, using the most vulgar term she had ever been called. "You are nothing without me."

"You broke me once, but now I am beyond you," she said. "My power, *dear master*, exceeds yours."

Bhairatonix surged into the air, lifted by the Myst onto his feet. A storm of rage swirled around him, but still Shevia did not flinch. The knuckles of his visible hand whitened around his staff, while the other remained, as always, in the folds of his robes. Shevia remained on her cushion, looking calmly at him. He bore down over her. "You are *mine*!" he snarled.

"Why did you take me as your apprentice?" she asked. "Did you want to control my visions from the Thornwood? You took me far away to Shenheyna, and isolated me from my family and everyone else. You certainly did not see a worthy successor in me because your shriveled ego cannot imagine a time in which you are dead, nor could you bring yourself to care what happens to Qin when you are gone. You took me as an apprentice because you *feared* me."

Bhairatonix fumed, unable to express his rage. Or perhaps unable to contain his surprise that she was right.

Shevia rose, lithe and graceful, to her feet. "You call me *hetch*, but I am so much more. You denied me a proper staff. You withheld proper instruction from me. And worst of all, you refrained from giving me a proper name. But I do not need you for those things. I am a Mystic, despite you holding me back."

Bhairatonix threw his staff aside and made to grab her throat, but his hand stopped mere inches from Shevia's neck. She did not flinch. Bhairatonix's eyes widened as he looked down at his hand.

"You will never touch me again," Shevia said. The Myst seethed around her, instinctively obeying her commands. A burning pain crawled across her upper arm and shoulder and chest. It was as though Sitting Mother perched there, guarding her from harm. "I will help the High Mystics and the people of Moth until Crow Tallin is over. But when it is done, you will free me from your service, and never seek me out again."

A smile curled across Bhairatonix's face. His hand remained frozen beside her neck. "How long have you planned this moment? Have you lain awake, practicing this encounter? Has it gone as well as you imagined? I hope it satisfies you, girl. For it will not last. The power you so greedily cling to right now is fleeting. You are empowered by something you do not understand. When Crow Tallin ends, and Treorel passes away, you will be snuffed out and left a charred husk. Only through me can you survive."

Shevia thought of the exact time her fear of her master had passed. It had come recently, on a trip to the great city of Yin-Aab. Another memory.

"You will not control me," Shevia said. "I've been used by Mystics for too long. I will never be used again."

Never taking his eyes from her, Bhairatonix slowly moved his other hand, the one he kept hidden away. A shiver crawled over Shevia's skin as five pale and shriveled fingers crawled from the depth of his robes. The entire arm was scarred, burned, and withered. With it, he gripped the neck of his robes and yanked them down. Shevia gasped before she could stop herself. Her eyes dashed back and forth between Bhairatonix and what she saw on his chest.

Woven into his skin was a sinuous black and red serpent tattoo, twisting around and through itself. Two large, bat-like wings protruded from its back. But unlike Shevia's tattoo, the eyes were black and dull, not alive and red like the ones on her skin.

"You've chosen a dangerous game, apprentice," said Bhairatonix. "There is more to power than mastery of the Myst. There is more afoot than you understand. But by all means, continue with your righteous crusade against me. We will see who prevails at the end."

Shevia narrowed her eyes. "Tell me what that symbol is. You owe me that much."

"I owe you nothing!" he snarled. "It is you who should be on your knees, pleading for forgiveness. I *made* you. You think you have power? I will *show* you power." His face contorted in effort, and with a supreme act of will he pulled his frozen hand away from her throat.

"Go," he said, covering himself again with his robes and slinking his wilted hand back into them. "Refresh yourself and return within the hour. There is work to be done."

"I go where I please," she managed, and this time there was a quaver in her voice. Did Bhairatonix know about Sitting Mother? Did he communicate with her, too? Did he have his own, separate companion that communicated to him through the tattoo? A hundred questions arose in her mind, but she needed time to sort them.

"As you say," Bhairatonix said.

Another sound echoed through the chamber. The moth in the glass flung itself against its prison wall repeatedly, filling the room with tiny *tinking* noises. Shevia thought she understood how it felt. She could see freedom. She had hurled herself at the glass, and forced a crack. But despite her efforts, she remained trapped within.

She moved to exit the chamber but stopped at the threshold. The scent of the old wooden door wafted over her. "What is that orb?" Shevia asked.

Bhairatonix used the Myst to lower his large frame on his cushion. "That is the real reason we're here."

Shevia left the chamber without a response. Her only comforting thought was that eventually the orb would break and when it shattered, like the moth, she would be free.

FIFTEEN

THE OUTCAST

Pomella descended the spiral stairs to find Vivianna still sitting in the foyer. Vivianna must've noticed her distracted look because she quirked an eyebrow.

"Was it really that bad?" Vivianna asked.

"I'll dance a jolly when Crow Tallin's over," Pomella said, "But right now, we need to find Vlenar. The High Mystics need us to leave immediately for a laghart velten in the northern Ironlow Mountains."

Vivianna nodded as she stifled a yawn. "I stayed up late organizing the apprentices and servants to prepare rations. You'll find them handing out travel packs on the north side of the tower, by the willow." She glanced at the glowing runes on her forearm.

"You're coming with us," Pomella said.

Vivianna froze before slowly turning her head toward her. "What?"

"Mistress Yarina agreed to let you come with me. There's something big happening with the fay at the velten. I'll need your help."

"What's happening there?" Vivianna asked.

"I don't know," Pomella said. "The fay are hurting the lagharts, somehow. But . . ."

"But what?"

Pomella bit her lip. It was Shevia who occupied her thoughts, along with all the other unanswered questions from the past few days. The unusual fay, the name Lagnaraste, and the moth in the glass orb.

"I'll explain on the road," Pomella said. "Go pack while I find Vlenar. I'll meet you past the wall, on the north road an hour after midday."

Outside the tower, the merciless sun burned overhead as it ascended toward its peak in the sky. A cloud of fay butterflies danced around Pomella as she stepped out. She took a moment to inhale and collect herself.

Across the lawn, Oxillian assisted servants with the disassembly of tents. To her opposite side, a group of Mystics sat in a circle having a discussion. Multiple rings of fay birds flew high above them, looping around like a waterwheel. At any other time, Pomella would've walked over to join the sitting Mystics, but the sense of urgency from Shevia's vision and her other concerns weighed on her. She wondered whether those Mystics would sit as easily once they were assigned a task by the High Mystics.

Pomella's gaze drifted in the direction of Lal's cabin. She

couldn't see it from where she stood, but she knew she should probably go see him again. She needed answers.

"I sssee quessstionsss behind your eyesss," hissed a voice.

Pomella turned. Hizrith stood behind her, near the tower entrance. His Mystic staff was curved, similar to a hunting bow, but twice the thickness. He rested both hands on it as he studied her.

"Yah," Pomella admitted. "Have you met with the High Mystics yet?"

"Sssoon," Hizrith said. "I am hhhere to asssisst Massster Ehzeeth. He isss vvvery old."

"He is very fortunate to have you. Seems like we could all use some assistance during Crow Tallin."

"And whattt asssistancce do you reqqquire?"

Pomella gazed at the tower's upper chamber window. "I need answers to those questions behind my eyes. But I don't think they can be found here."

Hizrith followed her gaze. His tongue flicked out as he thought. "The Hhhigh Myssstics havvve greattt concccerns that afffect usss all."

"Yes, of course," Pomella said. "But it's us that will be out in the island ensuring that everyone's safe."

Hizrith's tongue zipped again. "Theirsss is the greatessst ressssponsssibility. Withhhout them, Crow Tttallin will unleashhh Lagnaraste."

An ice-cold chill rippled through Pomella's body. She slowly turned from the tower's window focus on Hizrith.

"What did you just say?"

Hizrith's eyes widened slightly with surprise, telling Pomella that he hadn't meant to share as much as he had. It vanished in a heartbeat, however. "I sssaid too muchhh. You ssshould asssk your teachhher."

"Nobody will tell me anything," Pomella said, unable to keep the snap from her voice. "Who or what is Lagnaraste, Hizrith?"

"I'm sssorry. I mussst attend my massster. It isss not my placcce to sssay more." He inclined his head in polite farewell, and disappeared into the tower.

"Buggering shite," Pomella mumbled, staring after the laghart, hands on hips. The air of mystery hanging over Kelt Apar and Crow Tallin infuriated her. It was time to get to the bottom of it.

She strode to the willow tree and found a handful of servants working beneath it, just as Vivianna had said. At her request, a virga apprentice hurried to provide her with a travel pack containing food, a blanket, and a large waterskin. Pomella sighed inwardly. More travel. If the rampant fay of Crow Tallin didn't kill her, then fatigue would.

She silently called to her hummingbirds, who swooped out of the morning sky into her palm.

"Hector, go find Vlenar and bring him here. Ena, pass a message to Grandmaster Faywong for me." She paused, considering her message. When she spoke next, she wrapped the Myst around her voice as if to hold and preserve it.

"'Grandmaster,'" she said, looking directly at Ena. "'The High Mystics have me traveling to the Ironlow Mountains to invest—'"

Both hummingbirds suddenly buzzed their wings and lifted off her hand. Pomella stopped and looked around to see what the fuss was all about. Vlenar walked toward her, leading Quercus, who was saddled and carried several travel sacks.

"Well, that was easy," Pomella muttered to herself. Then to the ranger, she said, "You heard?"

Vlenar nodded. "Vvviviannaaa sssent me a messssage."

Pomella loved the ranger's simplicity and ability to quickly adapt. She found herself glad for his company.

After she finished her message to Lal, she and Vlenar followed the river north toward the edge of Kelt Apar. Pomella found herself looking back, wondering about Sim. Perhaps she should find him and say good-bye?

No. She returned her gaze forward. She'd already said good-bye to him enough times in her life. Their brief reunion the previous night had been nice, but she'd have to think of it as nothing more than a momentary assurance that he was alive. She had work to do, and most likely so did he.

She carried her Mystic staff, of course, which over the years she'd come to appreciate as much as a walking aid as she did an implement to focus and Unveil the Myst. Hector and Ena flew high above her, enjoying the bright day.

Vlenar walked at his typical quick pace, his eyes darting everywhere, as if expecting attackers to leap out of the grass to attack them. He wore his leather armor and carried both his sword and an unstrung short bow on his back. Two sheathed belt knives rested on his back beside the natural spikes protruding from his fitted armor.

Pomella increased her pace as they crossed the lawn toward the tree line and the towering hedge wall that now marked the border of Kelt Apar. Seeing it up close for the first time, she frowned. It was built primarily of tightly packed dirt, stone, and grass. It could be climbed, she supposed, but it was too high for large crowds to scale, and too dense to easily topple.

"How do we get through?" Pomella asked.

Vlenar considered the wall and glanced back toward the tower. "Cccall Oxxxillian."

Pomella nodded and tapped the air with a finger. The air rang with the sound of a silver bell as it previously had for Vivianna. A heartbeat later the ground rumbled and broke apart. The Green Man emerged from the cracks and holes that appeared. He towered over Pomella and her horse. His pebbled eyes softened when he saw her. "You called, Mistress?"

"Vlenar and I need passage through the wall."

Oxillian lingered his gaze upon his creation. Perhaps it was her imagination, but Pomella thought she saw a frown touch his face. "Of course," he said.

Another rumble, this one far louder than the previous one, washed over Pomella. A narrow, rectangular passageway, just wide enough for Pomella, Vlenar, and Quercus to pass through, opened in the wall nearby. A handful of people stood on the opposite side, peering into Kelt Apar with wide, surprised eyes. Vlenar's tongue zipped out before he hurried ahead to secure the temporary tunnel.

Pomella studied the Green Man. No matter how many times she saw him, often on a daily basis, she marveled at the intricate details of how he was crafted. He always looked more or less the same, but his eyes, beard, and other features were formed from slightly different rocks or grass or other materials. But always she could see deep thoughts and memories behind those eyes. She thought of what Hizrith had said regarding talking with those who had lived on Moth a long time.

"Ox," she said, "are you familiar with the name Lagnaraste?"

Oxillian considered her. "I'm sorry, Pomella," he rumbled.

"It sounds familiar, but if it involves Crow Tallin, I'm sad to say my knowledge is woefully limited. The closer we come to its peak, the more my mind becomes muddled."

"Why's that?"

"My senses become overstimulated," he said. "It is as though I hear every voice on the island, and feel every hand grasping me at once. I do not understand it, but I somehow lose myself during that time."

A memory from seven years ago trickled into Pomella's mind of Ox, with a body formed of jagged rock, covered in blood and impaling a bandit with his massive fist.

"Are you . . . safe . . . to be around during that time?" she asked.

He smiled down at her. "Yes," he said. "I am told I become withdrawn. I do not remember anything until Treorel passes."

"What do you think of this?" Pomella asked, nodding toward the wall.

"I do as the High Mystic commands," he said.

"I know," Pomella said. "But surely you have an opinion?"

He continued to study her for a long moment. Pomella wondered how much he saw, how much he could sense about her. "Nobody has ever asked me that," he said.

"Really? You've been here nine hundred years and nobody has asked your opinion of what goes on?"

"I'm like the landscape," he said. "Ever present, never changing, as reliable as the rising sun. That is all."

Pomella's heart went out to him. She knew he was capable of complex emotion, having experienced it many times before. But she'd never truly wondered if Ox ever felt *lonely*.

"Well, I want to know what you think," she said.

He looked from Pomella to the wall. "Crow Tallin is a time of great stress, during which everyone, including the High Mystic, is prone to making mistakes. I don't know if this wall is one, but I'm reminded that the only thing that matters in the end is the will of the Myst."

"Now you sound like a Mystic," Pomella said with a grin.

"When you live with them for nine centuries, some ideas stick around," he said, returning the smile.

Pomella reached up to place a hand on his. "Thank you," she said.

"Travel safely," he told her. "Summon me if you require assistance. I know your voice best of all, and even with the muddled confusion of these days, I believe I could find you."

Pomella patted his hand in thanks, then tugged Quercus' reins and led him through the tunnel. Vlenar waited on the opposite side, perhaps five long strides away. The roof of the tunnel loomed above her almost menacingly as she passed beneath. A trickle of dirt tumbled down in front of her.

When she cleared the exit, the wall rumbled to a close, puffing a cloud of dirt. Pomella considered the crowd of people gathered nearby. Most of them appeared to be commoners, but Pomella saw two or three that were well dressed enough that they could've been merchant-scholars. They looked at each other, then back to her. A man in the back of the crowd ran east. Vlenar watched him go until Pomella put a hand on his shoulder to reassure him everything was fine. She didn't want the ranger tackling more people.

The rest of the gathered commoners parted to make room for Vlenar to pass. The laghart ranger commanded his own fearful presence. Pomella wished he wouldn't scowl so often. She knew him to be a quiet, dedicated ranger, one who loved the island. She'd even witnessed him making a joke on occasion. Seeing these people stepping away from him in fear made her sad.

Pomella followed him north. The shade from the trees masked the sun's heat and the familiar scent of evergreen and oak mingled around her. As she entered the Mystwood, the faces in the crowd shifted from Vlenar to her. Their expressions slowly turned from fear and uncertainty to ones of recognition and happiness. Whispers whistled through the people like wind between trees. Somebody spoke a single word, "Hummingbird!"

A hand reached toward her, seeking to brush her cloak. It belonged to a woman old enough to be Pomella's mhathir. Deep grooves cut beneath the Goodness' gray eyes. Pomella wondered what would prompt such a person to leave her home and stand at the edge of Kelt Apar. Had the fay affected her? Or had she come hoping simply to see the High Mystics? Or come to see Pomella?

Pomella lifted her fingertips and touched the woman's hand.

Another hand reached for her, and another. Pomella met each hand. Soon dozens reached in a gentle and unthreatening manner. She drifted through the people, passing from hand to hand. Hardly anybody spoke except to whisper her name or "Hummingbird!" again.

One girl, not much older than Pomella had been when she'd left Oakspring to attend the Trials, held both hands out toward her. "Please, Mistress! Take me as your apprentice!"

Pomella gaped at her in surprise. "I—I'm sorry, I can't," she said, and instantly regretted the disappointment she'd given the young woman.

More hands reached for Pomella, crowding out the girl and her continued pleas to take her as an apprentice.

Hector and Ena flew above everyone's head. Pomella willed them to Unveil themselves, so that everyone gathered could see them. She did that often, hoping that their appearance would show them that the fay were not always to be feared. A couple of people reached toward the birds, but none came close to touching them. The hummingbirds trailed silvery smoke behind them, and a few people let it drift across their fingers.

A flicker of movement in the depths of the crowd caught Pomella's attention. She turned toward it, perhaps expecting to see Berrit, but the face watching her wasn't his. It was a young man in a rough canvas hood and gray cloak sporting a patchy scruff of black fuzz across his face. Pomella's heart leaped with irrational fear. He looked exactly like a younger version of her fathir. But how could that be possible? Her fathir was dead.

Realization washed over her.

"Gabor," Pomella whispered.

Her brother had grown much in the last seven years, but there was no mistaking his darker skin and features that, like her own, stood out so prominently on Moth. He stared at her, eyes narrowed, before turning and vanishing into the crowd.

Pomella wanted to stop and follow him, but he was gone. She wanted to believe it hadn't been her brother. Her gaze lingered in that direction another handful of moments. She made a promise to herself to investigate her brother's whereabouts after Crow Tallin ended. She wondered if he'd even want to talk to her.

Before long, the wall and crowd of people around Kelt Apar faded from view, hidden behind the Mystwood trees, leaving Vlenar and Pomella alone.

"I willl ssscout a shhhort dissstancccce ahhhead," Vlenar said. "Waittt hhhere for Vivvviannna." They had traveled together many times, so the routine was familiar to Pomella. Vlenar did his job well, but she also suspected he enjoyed the isolation of going before everyone else, seeking the safest, most efficient path.

"Wait, Vlenar," she said.

He glanced back at her.

"I need to do something. Alone. Will you wait here for me? Vivianna will meet you here soon."

"Whhhere are you going?"

"I need to meet someone. Can you trust me?"

His slitted eyes narrowed and his tongue zipped out.

"Please," she asked. "I will be back before nightfall."

"We havvve limittted tttime!" he hissed.

"I know," she said seriously. "But this is important."

He glared at her but eventually nodded. "Whiccch directttion?"

"I don't know exactly," she confessed. She glanced skyward and called Hector and Ena. They buzzed down into her palm. Leaning forward, she whispered a name to them.

"Find him," she said. "And lead me there."

A tiny wave of fear rippled from the birds, but they zoomed northeast. Pomella turned to Vlenar again and passed Quercus' reins to him. "I'll leave markers. Look for me before nightfall."

Pomella strode through a Myst-wood she hardly recognized. With Treorel's arrival in the sky, the woods had come to life with fay activity. Hundreds of silver creatures flew above her in the trees or scampered across her path. She walked with a purposeful stride, keeping her eyes on

Hector and Ena, who led her by racing ahead and pausing in order for her to catch up.

Over the years, she'd come to know many parts of the Myst-wood, but no matter how often she explored it, the land presented her with new secret grottos, clearings, and caves. She loved the mysteries it held, and counted herself fortunate to have a life that generally offered her the opportunity to range over its seemingly endless paths.

The deeper into the forest she traveled, the thicker the trees grew until the canopy of limbs above was so thick she could no longer see the sky. Her boots sank into the thick bed of dry leaves and needle fall that possibly hadn't been touched by humans in decades, if not longer. A chill that wasn't entirely born of the air made her tug her cloak tighter around her shoulders.

The hummingbirds led Pomella to a small clearing with a pond that resonated with her memory. The long branches of a gnarled tree bent low over the water's surface. Vines and moss hung like curtains from those branches. Pomella eased toward the water's edge. She searched the tree for the being she'd come to see.

"Mantepis!" she called. "I would speak with you! Come out."

Nothing but shifting shadows moved in the tree's branches. Pomella frowned. "Go find safety," she murmured to Hector and Ena, remembering that the last time they'd come here Mantepis had expressed interest in gobbling up her humming-birds.

The Myst wafted through the clearing like a steady fog. Pomella tapped the end of her staff into the water and stirred it as if it were soup in a cauldron. She slipped her boots off and tiptoed into the lukewarm pond.

"Mantepis!" she called again.

"My master wishes to know what you want," said a voice behind her.

Pomella spun, holding her Mystic staff up. Her eyes widened as a tall man with skin darker than her own emerged from the shadows. Swirling tattoos covered much of his upper body, stretching from his neck, across his bare chest, and down his forearms.

Pomella's pulse raced. "By the Saints," she breathed. "Quentin."

He was a shadow of the dashingly handsome man she'd known doing her apprentice Trials. His shoulder-length braided hair had been shaved, and his once muscular body had thinned to little more than skin-wrapped bones. He studied her with clouded eyes, giving no indication that he recognized her.

Pomella stepped toward him. "What happened to you?" she said, although she thought she knew part of the answer. At the end of the Trials, Yarina had branded him Unclaimed for his role in the conspiracy to murder her.

Her eyes drifted toward the shoulder-height branch he held in his hand. A Mystic staff. She'd never seen an Unclaimed holding one. Her mind raced with questions.

"Why do you wish to speak to my master?" Quentin repeated.

"Your master?" Pomella said as a sense of dread crawled through her gut.

"Master Mantepis is a wise and powerful Mystic," Quentin said in a monotone voice. "I am fortunate to be his student."

"Oh, Quentin," Pomella said. There'd been a time during the Trials where the two of them had encountered the strange fay creature who had tried to entice Pomella with an offer of apprenticeship. Mantepis had accurately predicted that Yarina would choose a noble-born successor over Pomella, and had encouraged her to return to him when the High Mystic rejected her. Pomella had briefly considered his offer in the time between Yarina's selection of Vivianna and when Lal had taken her as his student.

"You apprenticed yourself to him," she murmured.

A flicker of life lit Quentin's face for a moment, but it vanished quickly, leaving the clouded tarnish.

"My master wishes to know—"

Pomella turned her back to him and addressed the tree. "Don't play games with me, Mantepis! You've had your joke, but it's not funny. Show yourself or I will pull you from Fayün by your writhing tail!"

"My master—" Quentin droned on.

"*Mantepis!*" Pomella yelled.

A cloud of swirling silver coalesced in the branches of the tree. Pomella tightened her jaw as the head and body of a snake appeared, nearly as wide around as she was, with four spindly legs that poked out of his scaled hide. His legs gripped the large branch he rested upon, although they likely weren't necessary for him to keep balance. The rest of his bulk wrapped itself around the branch as if squeezing it. Silver fire flicked over the length of his scaled body.

"You've got some jagged nerve," Pomella said, nodding toward Quentin.

Mantepis flicked his forked tongue out. Amusement danced on his face and in his voice. "Pomella AnDone, champion Mystic of the common people!" he hissed. His mouth did not move as he spoke, but a clear voice emerged from him. "I see you like my pupil? He's been quite faithful these past years."

"You've destroyed him," Pomella said.

Mantepis slithered farther down his branch, slinking closer

to her. "Oh, no. Your High Mystic saw to that when she made him Unclaimed. Such a *harsh* punishment for the crime of being loyal to his family."

"Yah, well, he nearly killed me and the High Mystic."

"So you believe he should wither as an Unclaimed rather than become a Mystic under my tutelage? How very . . . *noble* of you, Mistress AnDone."

"He's not a Mystic," Pomella said, trying not to grit her teeth. "He's your slave."

"He doesn't believe that," Mantepis said. "Ask him."

"Master Mantepis is a wise and powerful Mystic," Quentin said with the same expression as before. "I am fortunate to be his student."

Pomella continued to focus on Mantepis, refusing to turn around. "You're vile," she said.

"For a Mystic, you are very quick to judge!" Mantepis hissed. "I'm beginning to regret revealing myself to you. You've learned very little in your time with Faywong. He and the young High Mystic have apparently coddled you."

Pomella stepped forward. "You will speak with respect for my master. Grandmaster is a greater Mystic than you could imagine."

A strange laughter emanated from Mantepis. "He *was* great, once. But he chose a different path, now didn't he?"

"I didn't come here to have you insult my mentor," Pomella said.

Mantepis lowered himself closer to her, unfolding one of his thin legs so that it dipped into the water. "Then why did you come here? Other than to mock *my* apprentice."

"I need to know who or what Lagnaraste is," Pomella said.

Mantepis' tongue flicked in and out repeatedly. His slitted

eyes narrowed. It struck Pomella as a very laghart-like reaction. "Of course you do," he said with some bite. "I'm not surprised the High Mystics tell you nothing. Perhaps they think even less of you than I. Go back to your master and beg for the scraps of his *wisdom*. I have no time for overeager apprentices."

Pomella dissolved the spark of anger before it could ignite a firestorm. Instead, she raised a serene sense of calm, and let that wash over her. Within that mind-set, she pulled on the Myst, letting it flood her with surprising speed and power. Her Mystic staff flashed outward, touching Mantepis, and she spun completely around as if hurling a fishing rod.

The forceful motion surged with the Myst and ripped Mantepis from the tree. His massive body flailed in the air as Pomella slammed him into the pond. The water barely rippled, reacting only to the steps she took. But the snakelike creature thrashed all the same as if she were drowning him.

Pomella called the Myst again, using it to rush the pond water around her legs and lift her high into the air. She loomed above Mantepis, Mystic staff held wide, her hair blowing with unseen winds of Myst.

"I am a Mystic and student of Grandmaster Faywong," Pomella said. "The days of Crow Tallin is upon us and I tire of your antagonism."

Mantepis thrashed beneath her unseen grip. A tingling sensation tickled the back of her neck. She turned just as Quentin rushed her. Without movement, and nearly without thought, Pomella hurled the Myst at him, knocking him back as if he'd been hit by a massive club.

Returning her attention to Mantepis, she saw the fay creature claw his way to his thin legs. He recoiled and hissed at her, "How dare you?"

"No," Pomella stormed. "You reside in the human realm in the domain of the High Mystic of Moth. You've enslaved a man and withheld information I require. Lives are at stake. Give me the information I seek."

"It won't matter," Mantepis said. "You can meddle all you like, but the High Mystics are the ones truly in control."

"Tell me anyway."

Mantepis thrashed in vain against the bonds holding him down. He glared at her with his slitted eyes for a long moment. She remained steady atop her wave, radiating power. Somewhere in the back of her mind she marveled at how easily she Unveiled the Myst.

Finally, Mantepis wilted. "Very well. You are more powerful than I thought," he admitted. "Treorel burns in you. Good. May that fire spark the return of the true Mystics to this land."

"Lagnaraste," Pomella prompted.

"None have asked me of her since Brigid herself, nearly a thousand years ago," Mantepis said. "If it is the queens and barons and sadans of your world who rule the human realm, then it is Lagnaraste who reigns as queen over Fayün. All fay pay homage to her."

"All fay, except you," Pomella said.

A shadow crossed Mantepis' long face. "I reside in Fayün no longer. Lagnaraste saw to that, long ago, when he cast me out."

Pomella frowned. "He? Moments ago you referred to Lagnaraste as queen."

"Your High Mystic Willwhite is not the only being whose

gender changes. Lagnaraste was once the king with a name, but now is queen with another."

"Must you always speak in riddles?" Pomella said.

"I say it as plainly as I can. If you want answers, go to Lagnaraste."

"How can I find her?" Pomella asked.

Mantepis stretched his neck closer to Pomella. "For that, you must go through the veil, where the worlds meet, and enter Fayün itself."

Pomella considered Mantepis a moment longer, then released the Myst. She silently commanded the water to lower her back to the shore and let it retreat to the stillness of being a pond.

Freed of his invisible shackles, Mantepis wobbled to his legs. "You should be careful what you seek. I had an apprentice once, who fled from me and entered Fayün, but became trapped. The fool only took his pet, and nothing else. You would be wise to avoid his fate."

Pomella knew of the veil, of course, the insubstantial barrier separating Fayün and the human world. But she sensed there was more. "How do I get there?"

Mantepis lifted his foreleg to the thick tree branch and climbed back up before entwining himself around the branch. "The passages between worlds change, but you will know it when you see it."

As he came to a comfortable rest, Pomella felt a moment of pity for the creature. It had been so easy to throw him. He appeared far less intimidating than he had before. Pomella suddenly wondered if he lacked the power he so boastfully claimed to have.

"I'm sorry if I hurt you," she said. "I owe you a debt, which I will repay after Crow Tallin."

Mantepis flicked his tongue and considered her. "You owe me nothing," he said. "You remind me of Brigid. She, too, had . . . unconventional . . . methods of seeking information. Interestingly, you share similar goals."

Pomella's mind raced. In the *Toweren*, Saint Brigid had visited a number of powerful beings in her hunt to find her son. One particular creature had proven more challenging than others to tame.

"Corenach," Pomella whispered.

Mantepis slinked back into his tree. "When you live long enough, you gather many names," he said. "I wonder, Pomella AnDone, the Hummingbird, what names will they give you when you take your last breath? Will those names be a praise, or a curse? My last advice to you, given freely, is that you release your hubris. If you fail to do that, you may share Brigid's fate."

Mantepis' eyes shimmered once, then closed, and he was gone.

SIXTEEN

SITTING MOTHER

Four Years Before Crow Tallin

The early-morning sun rose above the mountains of Qin that had become Sim's home. Snow sparkled on the peaks surrounding him, left by late-winter storms that only recently passed. The gentler weather meant that the trails would be open now, giving Sim an opportunity to move on.

But first, he had to burn the remains of an entire village.

For the rest of the world, winter had ended, but here in the highlands, its cold embrace lingered, clutching most of the land as well as Sim's heart. The villagers laid out before him would never feel the warmth of the spring sun again.

Sim fingered the fox orchids he'd found in a patch of sunlight near a spring west of the village. The flowers were the first hope-

ful sign he'd seen in months that the nightmare season was coming to an end. The Qina word Swiko and the rest of the villagers
used for the geyser near their home meant "Mother's Water."
Year round, even in the deepest cold, it emerged from the mountainside, steaming-hot water that would then cool and eventually
freeze. The fox orchids had grown on the banks of the foggy pool.

Look for the unusual petal shapes that resemble a fox's face, Rochella had taught him years ago before they'd come to the village. *They only grow in the Qin highlands, and are one of the few
orchids you can eat. Their seeds, too, can be gathered and consumed,
although if you're less desperate you can powder them and use them as
a seasoning.*

He let Rochella's voice fade into the silence that surrounded
him. He was alone, but the memory of her, and the more recent
memories of Swiko and the other villagers. They'd joined
Dane's voice in the chorus of people he'd lost. Sim didn't think
he'd ever stop hearing those people, nor did he want to.

He stepped forward to place the flowers on the funeral pyre
he'd erected. Swiko had been the first to welcome him into the
village, and the last to die from the plague. In his arrogance Sim
had hoped she and the other villagers wouldn't catch the disease he knew he carried. How he could carry it, and have skin
rashes, but not die was something he still didn't understand.

After only a handful of weeks the skin rashes had begun to
appear on the villagers. Unable to leave because of the snow,
Sim quarantined himself in Bith Yab's old house, but it was too
late. One by one the villagers died the same horrible deaths
that had taken Dane and Pomella's mhathir all those years ago.

Angry challengers had come to the hut, demanding that Sim
be thrown out of the village. But Jal Yab, the old man who'd given

him the onkai staves, insisted that wasn't their way. Sim realized that the elderly man must've known it was too late anyway.

During his time in Bith Yab's home, Sim found a strange parchment letter mixed with the clutter that had resulted from the Mystic's attempted escape from the laghart wivan. The letter was written in Qina, which he couldn't read, but at the top was the same twisted-serpent symbol that he'd seen on the cave where he'd died. He would've asked Swiko to read it to him, but by then she was too far gone.

No tears ran down Sim's face as he laid the flowers across the villagers' bodies. The winter had frozen his heart, locking his emotions in cold ice. He'd come to love Swiko, first for her kindness and affection, and later as her lover and constant companion. Even when the rashes appeared on her body, she continued to care for the others, and came to visit him in his hut on the edge of the village. He brewed cloudcap tea for her every day until his modest stash was gone. There was none more to be found during the winter. The herb slowed the plague, but as soon as it was gone Swiko succumbed. In her final days Sim did what he could to keep her comfortable.

"When spring arrives," she had whispered, "go to Sitting Mother. Look for her on the mountain." At her whispered request, he'd given her an overwhelming dose of silverbane that night, which caused her to drift into a sleep she'd never wake from. She died snuggled into his shoulder.

"Thank you for teaching me," he said to her corpse, speaking in Qina. "May you eat at Sitting Mother's table."

He lit the pyre with a torch, then stood back and let his gaze linger upon her peaceful face one last time. He'd dressed her himself, and placed herbs in her mouth, in accordance with their tradition, so that when she came to Sitting Mother she could contribute to the peh-cha tea that was really the ocean stretching across the world. He'd done the same for all the other villagers, including Jal Yab.

Sim watched the fire consume his lover and her community. The smoke and embers drifted skyward, joining wispy clouds that sailed overhead like ghosts leaving their bodies. And like a ghost himself, Sim gathered his pack and onkai staves and left the village forever.

Months ago, as the winter storms had rolled over the highlands like a fat noble storming a commoner wedding to demand wine, Swiko had told Sim of Sitting Mother, who lived atop the great mountain to the northeast. It was there, at the summit, that Sim's wounds could be healed, his burdens eased, and the way forward revealed. Many people on Qin sought Sitting Mother's wisdom.

Sim didn't know what he would actually find at the summit, if anything. Perhaps Sitting Mother was a reclusive Mystic, or perhaps a Saint. But whoever, or whatever, she was, he felt obligated to find her for Swiko and the other villagers. And maybe for himself, although he didn't really think that Sitting Mother would have anything for him.

Perhaps, he thought to himself as he trudged away from the mountain village, he went because he had nowhere else to go.

We are rangers. We do what we always do. We move, and we survive.

Rochella's ghost, again.

By the time the sun hung directly overhead on his first day

away from the village, Sim's boots were soaked from ice and snow. He adjusted the scarf around his face to keep the cold off. He had no guide, no map, and, if he was being honest with himself, no practical idea of how he'd get to the mountain where Sitting Mother lived. All he could do was walk toward it and hope for the best. He'd learned much about wilderness survival from Rochella, and now it was time to put that knowledge to practical use.

For the first handful of days, he survived on rations he'd brought from the village. When those thinned, he set about tracking animals in the snow, hoping to follow tracks to a den where he could maybe snare a rabbit or fox.

It still snowed some days, but the snowflakes were thin, and melted as soon as they touched anything but existing snow. When Sim descended the side of any mountain, he found less snow, and more signs of springtime. He managed to track and kill a skinny deer with Rochella's bow. Even though the snow was melting in these valleys, winter hung on to the higher slopes. When it was time to ascend a new slope on the far side of whichever valley he'd come to, Sim found less wildlife and more obstacles. When he summited each crest, he looked back across the valley he'd crossed, and looked ahead toward Sitting Mother's mountain.

Keeping warm and dry was his priority. Between his rations, including what he'd preserved from his deer, and what he managed to forage, he had enough to eat for now. More than ever, he was grateful for Rochella's lessons on understanding which plants and roots he could safely consume. His greatest fear was a late-winter storm blowing in and burying him. If he wanted to make it to Sitting Mother, he had to hurry across the many valleys and hard terrain ahead

Rangers roam to the places where there are no trails, Rochella's voice reminded him as he trekked through dense underbrush. *What makes a true ranger is not only the ability to survive, but finding a way through seemingly impossible obstacles.*

At night, Sim set campfires and huddled beneath furs. He slept in hollowed-out trees whenever possible with the fire crackling nearby, letting it go as long as he could in order to discourage hungry mountain animals. On evenings when he was lucky, he managed to find a dry hollow or cave he could sleep in.

He tried his hand at whittling a flute from some elderberry. The branches were hollow, so even his crude attempts at creating an instrument resulted in something that produced sounds when he blew through it.

He also read from *The Book of Songs*. It had been Pomella's book, finely made originally, but now worn and weathered. The book hadn't been crafted to weather long journeys on the road. Over the years it had been thrown into bushes, rained on, dropped, misplaced, and found again. He knew each page by memory now but still thumbed through it every night.

Sim didn't understand the musical notations within the pages, nor had he been taught to read the noble rune language. But he could read the common runes scattered through the book, and he could decipher at least a few of the simpler noble runes using context.

On the tenth night out from the mountain village, under a sleepy crescent moon, the fire crackled as Sim roasted a small rabbit on a spit. He began to sing, surprising himself with his own voice. He used words he'd memorized from *The Book of Songs*:

"Listen Once,
Hear Me thrice.

From stars to shore,
Across paradise.
I cry, I call, I plea.
My lost one,
Come Back to Me.
Come Back to Me."

The tune he used probably wasn't the one the *Book* called for, but there was no other way for him to know. He contended himself with singing what he thought sounded nice.

The next day he came at last to Sitting Mother's mountain. The summit towered above him, lost, for the moment, behind an iron-gray storm cloud. Not wanting to risk being caught out in the open, he decided to set his camp and reserve his strength for a long climb tomorrow.

As he set about looking for shelter, a brief break in the clouds allowed him to see the summit more clearly. He stopped, and his heart raced.

A figure sat at the top of the mountain. The tiny form was hard to distinguish from a distance, forcing Sim to squint against the fading light. It appeared to be a person sitting cross-legged on the ground, peering toward him. Cursing, Sim leaped behind a tree and waited. The hair on his arms stood on end and shivers ran up his spine. He waited as long as he dared before he slunk away and found a safe place to peer at the person.

When he looked again, the clouds blocked his view. His heart raced. Sitting Mother. He was close.

But like a vengeful tyrant, the storm clouds tore into the mountainside, dumping snow. By whatever grace that cared two clips' worth for his life, Sim managed to find a shallow alcove on the lee side of several boulders. Trembling from fear and bone-deep cold, he started his fire and attempted to occupy his attention by carving another flute from his bundle of elderberry.

Thunder and snow rocked the mountain, sending waves of terror through his heart. He clutched his knees hard to his chest, trying to convince himself that it was just a storm. He was a ranger, not a cowardly child. Rochella had never hugged herself and cried in fear. Vlenar didn't cower at what he knew was only some snow and thunder.

Hold a healthy dose of respect for nature, Rochella's voice said from the past, *for it is surely a mighty expression of the Myst.*

More thunder hammered the mountain, and Sim found that he couldn't hold back his tears. He forced himself to play his flute and sang as if it were a peace offering to the storm.

If the storm accepted his offering, it did not say. But the music gave him strength. He let his tears fall but straightened his back. The storm could take his life, but it could not hurt his heart. He'd already lost his closest loved ones. His body was walking death to anyone he met. Perhaps Sitting Mother had seen him or sensed his poisonous presence and had sent the storm to eradicate him.

"I won't be afraid," he said to himself. "The worst has already happened to me."

The winds howled, the skies roared, and within his little shelter Sim waited to die, alone.

It took most of the next day to dig himself out of his cave. In that time he consumed the rest of his food. He preserved his fire as long as he could, using it on makeshift torches to help melt a path out and keep his canteens full.

Exhaustion clawed at him, but he pressed on, seeking escape. He refused the easy seduction of giving up, of lying down and letting the mountain put him to sleep forever in a blanket of snow. He would continue on. Move onward.

Like a ranger.

Eventually, Sim punched a numb fist out of the tunnel he'd dug and exited his snowed-in alcove. Blue skies greeted him. He collapsed to his knees, trying to catch his breath. Weakened from hunger and feeling the effects of high mountain air, Sim forced himself to stand once more.

He gathered his remaining supplies and set off, leaning more heavily than normal on his onkai staves.

There was no food to be found this high up on the mountain. Only icy winds and snow. From this height he could look back across all the valleys and lesser mountains he'd traversed to get here. Down below, Spring stretched forth its hand, bringing warmth and greenery. But here, in the highest steps of the world, winter was ever present and unyielding. Patches of bare rock were rare, and plant life all but extinct.

He was close, though. Sitting Mother waited for him on a high rock outcropping that he could just barely see from his angle.

It took him the better part of the day to find a way to the summit. His body screamed in hunger, but at this point he refused to stop until he found Sitting Mother. She had to have food if she was surviving up here. Even Saints needed nourishment. Sim prayed that she would have food and answers and a cure for the plague he carried.

He stopped.

What if he passed the plague on to Sitting Mother? Enough people had died already. He could never again be near people or civilization so long as he carried the plague like he did now. A Saint like Sitting Mother was his only hope. Surely, if she became sick she would have the means to heal herself. He was hoping, after all, that she would eradicate the disease within him entirely.

He adjusted his packs and continued on. The summit greeted him with fierce winds. He could almost hear voices in the gale. To his surprise, he found a large cluster of bushes at the top. A mountain goat with massive curved horns stood on a nearby rock, staring at him. Sim paid it no attention. He was here, and it was time to find Sitting Mother. He walked toward the southeast edge of the wide summit, looking for her. Rounding a boulder, he found her.

There was no mistaking the figure he'd seen earlier and whom he'd traveled so far to find. Sim set his onkai onto the ground and set his packs down.

Sitting Mother—the Saint he'd traveled so far to see—was a pile of rocks. They'd been stacked carefully on top of one another to resemble the shape of a woman sitting cross-legged. Several bits of torn cloth were pinched together between the top stones to give the semblance of hair. Flecks of faded white paint had been traced across the stones' surfaces, but the runes or drawings had long ago been weathered away.

A tide of emotions surged within Sim, but he remained frozen on the outside. He stared at the pile of rocks for long minutes. Swiko had been wrong. No. She'd *lied*. Sitting Mother wasn't a person. It was probably just a superstition created by a filthy dirt farmer. There was no Saint here, no great Mystic who could cure disease. He'd been such a dunder. During his childhood, even the High Mystic of Moth hadn't been able to cure the plague. The traveling Mystic who'd come to Oakspring had been unable to do anything except let his brother die along with half the village. Why had he believed a crazy story about a Saint living on a cliffside who would solve his problems?

There was nothing left to do. Nowhere left to go. Rochella had been wrong. Some roads truly came to a dead end. He was no ranger. He was just a plague-infested commoner who'd lost everything and could never be around people again.

He screamed. His anguish reverberated off the distant mountains and filled the valley. He screamed again until his lungs gave out, then howled again.

Rage boiled in his veins. He tore one of his onkai blades from its walking sheath and swung it with all his might at the stack of rocks that was supposedly Sitting Mother. The pile shattered. He screamed again. He kicked the rocks, scattering them. He threw some off the cliff. He hurled one at the mountain goat. He cursed and spit, and finally, exhausted, collapsed onto the ground.

His chest heaved like a set of blacksmith's bellows, heating his anger, and boiling away any other emotions.

"Mystics and false Saints," he said through gritted teeth. "I follow my own lead. I reject the Myst."

When the sun crested to its highest point, Sim gathered his possessions and descended the mountain without looking back.

SEVENTEEN

THE OLD WORLD

Faintly glowing leaves from Fayün brushed against Pomella as she emerged from the Mystwood thicket onto the thin path leading north. She slipped past the unusual plants, hardly noting their strangeness anymore as Crow Tallin approached.

The sun had long ago lowered itself toward the horizon, bathing what little of the sky she could see in pink and lavender hues. Finally out on an open trail once more, Pomella paused to stretch her back. She lifted her hair off the back of her neck, trying to cool herself down. Despite the late hour, the sun's furious heat lingered as if it refused to spare the world.

Hector and Ena emerged from the thick tree line behind her. They swirled in a high arc above Pomella's head as if they, too, relished the idea of being in an open space.

"Time to find Vlenar," Pomella said to them, looking north along the trail.

She set out, thankful for her Mystic staff as a walking aid. Her feet were already sore and it was a long way to the velten in the Ironlow Mountains.

A rush of excitement suddenly emanated from her hummingbirds. Pomella's heart leaped as she sensed, through her familiars, a pair of familiar presences. Sim and Vivianna waited on the trail ahead of her. Vivianna sat, legs crossed, serene as ice, on a stool of grass and dirt she'd conjured, while Sim stood a short distance away from her, gazing at Pomella through distant eyes.

"Where's Vlenar?" Pomella asked Vivianna.

"He's up further ahead," Vivianna said. "Not far."

Pomella peered at Sim. As before, a rush of emotions surged through her, but she suppressed them. Now wasn't the time to sort that out. "I wasn't expecting you to come," she said.

Sim shrugged. He carried two straight walking sticks, one in each hand. Each wooden staff had been carved with intricate designs of some kind and had woven beads and feathers hanging from it. Pomella found herself wondering what the staffs were and how he'd come by them. Like the rest of Sim's recent past, they eluded her.

"This is where I need to be," he said simply, and Pomella could tell from his tone that that was all she'd get from him on the matter.

Movement on the opposite side of the path caught Pomella's attention and she found herself once more surprised.

Lal sat on a patch of dry grass twirling his wide-brimmed straw hat in his hand. He smiled when he saw her, and immediately it was as if a weight was lifted from Pomella's shoulders.

He wore his red Crow Tallin robes atop a pair of sandals, which seemed to be his unspoken way of saying he supported her.

Pomella bowed in front of him. "Well, this is a pleasant surprise," she said, before adding, "I'm glad you're here."

"It's been long time since I traveled," Lal said. "Good chance for us to talk. Thought you could use the company."

Pomella glanced at their growing party. "All we need is Broon," she said.

"Broon too lazy," Lal quipped. "He stayed to guard Kelt Apar."

Pomella breathed a silent sigh of relief.

"And look, Pomella," he said, grinning and pointing to some flowers growing beside him. They were wild lilies, ripe in their summer season.

Pomella shook her head in amusement. "You love those little flowers, don't you?"

Lal shrugged. "None grow in Qin. I saw them for first time when I came to Moth, many years ago. I like their simplicity. They sleep in winter. Bloom in summer. Harder the winter, brighter the bloom."

Pomella sighed. Her encounter with Mantepis, and what he'd revealed, rang in her mind. "Grandmaster," she began, "we should talk about—"

"Later, Pomella," Lal said, standing up. "There will be time."

Pomella nodded, letting it go. Somehow, it was easier to do that in Lal's presence. "OK," she said. "Let's find Vlenar. He's probably ready to drag us by the necks to this velten."

They found Vlenar farther up the trail as full night enveloped them. He'd prepared a camp for them and smoothly adapted to the larger-than-expected party size. They set out the next morning and traveled through the Mystwood for three days in relative silence, which suited Pomella just fine. Each of her traveling companions seemed content to keep to themselves for the most part. Vlenar ranged ahead, guiding them up along the foothills of the Ironlow Mountains. Sim lingered behind, keeping close enough to assist if needed, but otherwise out of earshot. At first, Vivianna, Pomella, and Lal took turns riding Quercus, but eventually the younger women let Lal ride him nearly all the time because otherwise they had to stop and let him rest.

Every day, they saw fay animals running across their path, or floating in the air before them, or soaring high overhead. Pomella marveled at them all, especially as the fay they encountered grew larger or more spectacular to behold. Near sunset of the first day on the road, an enormous flock of what must've been tens of thousands of tiny fay birds flew overhead, heading west, toward the ocean. They were too distant for Pomella to make out their features clearly, but each flapped their wings with a steady rhythm. Despite their size and number, they had the steady straight motion of geese flying in formation, only clustered in a massive cloud of silvery fog. As the birds passed overhead, Pomella wondered whether they flew toward lands in the human realm, or Fayün.

In the late afternoon of the second day the forest opened up, revealing Sentry just ahead to the north. Pomella's gaze was drawn beyond the town toward a looming mountain farther ahead. MagBreckan was not as large as the mighty MagDoon, but its jagged summit seemed even more intimidating than its larger cousin to the south. Pomella had grown up gazing at that peak. She'd never walked MagBreckan's slopes, but nonetheless, the mountain seemed like home.

Rather than leading them to Sentry, Vlenar cut to the east, into the foothills. The Ironlow Mountains loomed before them, rising toward the sky and covered in an eternal blanket of evergreen pines and oak and ash.

"What you think of those mountains, Pomella?"

Lal's sudden question surprised Pomella. They'd been hiking in silence the entire day. Vlenar was ahead of them somewhere, out of sight.

"They're beautiful," Pomella said.

"What else?"

Pomella considered the peaks before her. They were a regular part of Moth, and therefore had been ever present in her life.

"They dominate the land," Pomella said. "They're strong, unyielding, and mysterious."

"Ah," Lal said. "You say mountains are just another part of Moth? Dominant part, but still just a feature of land. Think deeper."

Pomella considered it as they walked. Her Mystic staff tapped the ground with each step taken. She took her time pondering Lal's question, knowing he didn't need an immediate answer.

"Mountains are eternal," Pomella said. "Like the Myst, they exist before our lives began, and will live long after us."

Lal nodded. "They live much longer than us, yes, but they not eternal. Mountains change. Grow. Collapse. We cannot see it, but if you live very, very long life—thousands of lives—you see it."

Pomella frowned. How could a person live a thousand lifetimes? She wondered how Lal could know this. And she wondered, too, what he was getting at. If mountains did change over time, then they were like all living things. It was strange to think of them as alive, as if she and Lal were walking upon an actual creature.

"The mountains *are* the land," Pomella said as the answer came to her. "There's no separation between them and the island. Moth is a land of mountains."

Lal smiled. "Yes, Pomella. So, too, is our relationship with the Myst, and with all other things. Every person. Every tree. Every fabric of cloth." He plucked at his shirt for emphasis, then tapped the center of his forehead. "Every thought or feeling. They are all the island. When you see past our separateness, the Deep part of the Myst opens. That is where I teach you to go."

Pomella considered all this. It was difficult to not see herself as separate from the rest of the world. She could grasp the concept that maybe, on some mystical level, she wasn't different from her shoes or the nearby trees, but what about less tangible aspects of her life? How were emotions like affection, love, frustration, and anger one and the same? It was one thing to think about it, and another to grab it with your hand and understand it in a real and solid way.

She thought, too, of the conflicting parts of her life. Lal wanted her to sit in her cabin every day and meditate on the Myst while, at the same time, she felt a need to be out in the world, helping people. There were Unclaimed living in filth, being scooped up into slavery by the Shadefox, as well as commoners requiring assistance to improve their lot in life. How could she ignore those needs when she had the ability to help? Try as she might, she didn't know how to reconcile those separate worlds of her life. They were as opposite from each other as was this world and Fayün.

Pomella opened her mouth to ask Lal about these topics, but Vivianna's voice stopped her short. "Pomella," she said, "you should see this."

Pomella followed Vivianna's gaze and saw a handful of figures walking toward them. She frowned. Apparently, their traveling party was multiplying once more.

Shevia forced herself to express a calm outward appearance as her brothers led her toward the commoner Mystic Pomella and her group. Yarina's student, whose name Shevia had learned was Vivianna, stood beside a brown gelding, clutching her Mystic staff and watching Shevia with an uncertain expression. The ranger Sim stood waiting farther up the road with the laghart.

Tevon glanced at Shevia and shook his head. It had taken some convincing to get him and Typhos to agree to escort her from Kelt Apar. Even Tibron had shown more reluctance than she had expected.

"You are not a petulant child!" Tevon had snapped when she approached him the evening after completing her visions for the High Mystics. "You are a Mystic!"

"Yes," she had said. "And so you will obey me."

"I . . . we"—he gestured to Typos and Tibron—"obey High Mystic Bhairatonix. As do you."

"I will deal with Bhairatonix," Shevia had said. "I am leaving tonight, without his knowledge or consent. You can remain here, and face his wrath in the morning, or come with me and have my protection."

The vision of the twisted-serpent banner fluttering above the dying lagharts still called to her. Sitting Mother wanted her to go there. To learn, to discover the truth, to *find* her.

"You offer *us* protection?" Tevon had sneered. "You are just—"

"Do not make me prove your ignorance, Brother."

Tibron scratched the back of his head. "Are you sure about this, Shay-Shay?" There had been a softness in his voice that managed to pierce Shevia's guards and touch on her affection for him. "I know you may be unhappy in his service, but what you're suggesting would endanger us all, and possibly our family back home."

"The High Mystic scares me no longer. And for the rest, this is why I offer a choice."

Tibron's eyes had searched Shevia's for a long moment before he nodded. "I'll go."

"You are a fool," Tevon had sneered.

"You said it yourself," Tibron had said. "We are a family. Our *sister* requires our help. This is why we left home."

"Your weakness will get us killed," Tevon had said.

"I trust our sister," Tibron had said, and it was settled.

As Shevia approached the party, she saw the one called Grandmaster Faywong standing behind their horse, wearing a wide-brimmed hat. He was from Qin, which intrigued her, but he did not carry a Mystic staff. He watched her with a neutral expression, and Shevia found herself unable to meet his gaze.

"We didn't expect to have more company!" Pomella called. "Did the High Mystics send you?"

Tevon threw Shevia a hard glare.

"We came of our own choice," Shevia said. "Great danger lurks at the velten. I believe you could use my assistance."

Pomella and Vivianna exchanged looks. Shevia knew she did not sound convincing, but she was not about to justify her presence to these Mystics.

"We welcome your assistance," Vivianna said.

They set out, together in name only, with each group keeping to themselves. Faywong rode the gelding, but he kept his eyes closed most of the time. At first Shevia thought he was sleeping, but then she realized he was actually meditating. She tried to discern the Myst around him, but she sensed nothing. Perhaps he was, as Bhairatonix had suggested at the Crow Tallin ceremony, powerless.

That evening, he proved her wrong.

The entire party sat around a campfire that Vlenar had built when a cluster of fay snakes slithered into their camp. They emerged from the darkness, at least twenty of them, each glowing with a silver light. Tevon jumped to his feet, reaching for his sword, but the old man held up a hand to stall him.

The snakes slipped around Shevia's feet and came to rest beside Faywong. They raised their heads and flicked their tongues. Shevia watched with curiosity as Faywong remained at ease. One of the snakes lowered its head as if bowing to him. As it did so, every other snake present bowed its head in unison.

Faywong considered them for a moment, then slipped onto the ground and tilted his ear toward them. The silver snake in front flicked its tongue into his ear. It did so repeatedly until he eased himself back to his sitting position. He reached out and stroked the snake on its head with his finger. If it had been possible, Shevia would've sworn the the snake smiled as it misted away. One by one the snakes came forward, each one licking Faywong's ears in exchange for a touch on the head that sent it away in a dissolution of silvery smoke.

"What was that about?" Pomella asked after the last snake vanished.

"They come for blessing," Faywong said with his familiar Qina accent. "Serpents, reptiles, other similar creatures greatly drawn to the Myst. They more attuned to it than most others."

Shevia itched to pull her traveling cloak tighter around her shoulders to hide her serpent tattoo. She knew some of the others had seen it before, and she felt exposed.

"Other creatures?" Pomella said.

An unexpected tinge of jealousy crept through Shevia. She liked Faywong, and wondered why he'd taken a commoner as his apprentice.

"Likkke lagharttttsss," Vlenar said, reaching over the fire to drizzle a pinch of spice across their meal of assorted vegetables. If there was humor or bitterness in his comment, Shevia couldn't tell.

"Yes," Faywong said. "Lagharts very powerful with Myst. Said to be descended from powerful beings, now long lost."

"Dragonsssss!" Vlenar hissed. The fire hissed as the spices fell upon it, emphasizing the word.

Shevia's spine tingled with energy. She'd never heard that word before but immediately knew what the laghart spoke of. She forced herself to not move, or even breathe, for fear of revealing herself.

"Mystic tradition says dragons once dominated the Old World," Faywong said. "Kings and Queens of Fire. They made war with themselves, tearing world asunder, resulting in creation of human realm and Fayün. That led to their extinction. Humans and lagharts all that left afterward."

Shevia tried to imagine a world ruled by massive dragons, where the fay and humans were inseparable. The serpent tattoo on her shoulder burned with energy.

"What was the Old World like?" Pomella asked.

Faywong stared into the fire and spoke in a low voice. "Very different, yet still familiar. I once saw it in dream, and walked beneath its skies. Beautiful, tranquil, calm. But its time ended, just as this world will someday, and give rise a new."

Shevia wondered at the kind of power Grandmaster must possess to dream of such places and travel there. But she had heard that Faywong had given up his command of the Myst, and wondered when and how he had accomplished such extraordinary feats.

Nobody spoke for a long minute. It was Tevon that broke the silence. "The dragons killed each other off?" He sat closer to the fire than her other two brothers and seemed captivated by the Grandmaster's tale.

"Nobody know for sure," Faywong said. "But dragons are tied to land in deep, profound ways. A dragon *is* the land. The land is the dragon. Destroy world, destroy dragon."

"What did they look like?" Vivianna asked.

"Wings," Shevia said before she could stop herself. "Scales, and fire."

They all looked at her in surprise. Scented smoke from their cook fire obscured the air between her and everyone else. Only Sim watched her with a calm expression. An overwhelming urge to wilt beneath everyone's eyes came over her. But she refused to cower. She was not a little girl suffering her mother's scorn, nor was she Bhairatonix's broken apprentice. She sat tall, and let everyone's judgments roll off her.

"Yes," Faywong said, "all tales agree they were large, like mountains."

They ate in silence after that, but Shevia hardly tasted her spiced food. Her tattoo, with its twisted black and red shape coiled across her shoulder and topped with the head of a snake and the wings of a bat, Bhairatonix's matching tattoo, and the image scrawled on the floor of the High Mystic's laboratory all danced in her mind.

Scales, wings, and fire.

Dragons.

EIGHTEEN

THE VELTEN

Vlenar lead the party north through the Mystwood for another day and a half before arriving at the velten. The ranger often roamed far ahead, leaving markers for the Minam brothers to find. Tibron was usually the one to find these signs, and after some time Pomella began to sense a division among the brothers. Each time Tibron found a small cairn marking Vlenar's route, a dark cloud would gather around Tevon and he'd stomp away.

Sim spent a good deal of his time apart from the group as well, much, Pomella had to admit, to her relief. She needed more time to assess how she felt. A part of her wanted to drag him away and make him tell his story, but life was more complicated now. She was a Mystic, and both Lal and Yarina had made it clear that her focus should continue to be on releasing worldly attachments and connecting to the Myst.

Perhaps Sim sensed some of her hesitation, or perhaps he had his own concerns, but the result was that he rarely spoke to her or anybody else, not even making eye contact. Fortunately, there was plenty to distract Pomella from having to dwell on Sim and his return. She was content to give him space and to focus on the remainder of their journey. Lal's presence was a continuous reminder to remain grounded.

Like Sim, Shevia remained mostly quiet through the journey. Almost immediately after their joining together, Vivianna had made an effort to approach the younger woman and befriend her. From what Pomella could see, Shevia didn't exactly rebuff Vivianna's polite attempts to talk, but she made it clear through her short answers and her body language that she preferred to be on her own. But each night, Pomella heard her and Lal conversing in Qina. Pomella's jaw tightened when she saw Lal more animated than normal when he spoke to Shevia, but she let the emotions go.

These thoughts lingered with Pomella until she sensed a shift in the air as they emerged into the valley they sought. They arrived from the western passage that cut across the northern ridge of the Ironlows. The air weighed heavier on this side of the range. A subtle odor tainted the air. No wind swept across the grassy expanse below them. An eerie silence blanketed everything.

Pomella gazed across the plain, and Lal stepped beside her. "Hmm. Do you feel it, Pomella?" he said.

"Yes," she replied. "What is it?"

Lal scratched his unshaven chin. "Nothing good," he muttered, and gestured for them to continue.

Vlenar went ahead as usual, leading them through overgrown switchbacks that snaked down the mountain. Pomella led Quercus, who had recently begun expressing his frustration with being a pack animal. "I know," she told the gelding as he balked at a sharp turn in the trail. She used a soothing tone, but her frustration with him, and horses in general, tended to be short when he got this way. "I'd also rather be running free right now, but everybody has to help however they can, and that includes you!"

Quercus glared at her but allowed her to lead him down the slope.

As they descended the rest of the mountain, Pomella gazed west across the wide valley. Wild grass stretched as far as she could see, presumably stretching all the way to Enttlelund and the Mothic Sea. The grass was tall and heavy, ungrazed and baked under the season's scorching heat. A handful of barren scrub trees rose above the grass, each appearing like scraggly farmers standing alone in their field.

In the distance, floating as if it were an archipelago of islands in an ocean of grass, was a large assortment of boulders. Hundreds of rocks lay scattered like they were the remains of a shattered fortress. It took Pomella and her party over an hour to walk from the base of the mountains, through the grass and beneath the sun, to the first of the stones. As they approached, a dreadful sense of heaviness fell upon Pomella. Nothing stirred whatsoever. Vivianna appeared cool and expressionless, but Pomella saw her knuckles whiten as they tightened on her Mystic staff. Vlenar and the Qin rangers drew their swords. Sim and Shevia lingered back.

"Is this the velten?" Pomella said, sweeping a sweaty tangle of hair off her forehead.

Vlenar arrived at the first boulder and peered around it. "Yesss!" he hissed.

Pomella looped Quercus' reins around the branch of a nearby scrub tree and followed the rangers. Vivianna walked beside her, as did Lal with a somber expression on his face.

They entered the middle of the rock formations, and Pomella saw that most of the boulders had been hollowed out to act as entrances leading to underground locations. The scattered stones must, she realized, be doorways to laghart dwellings. One particularly large formation was shaped from a cluster of boulders piled together. Atop it stood a carved statue of a human woman with long flowing hair sitting cross-legged with her arms spread and palms facing up. Her downcast eyes, although roughly rendered, were closed in meditative peace.

The statue of whatever Saint that was didn't command Pomella's attention long, but she noticed Sim lingering near it. She lowered her gaze to the base of the monument where a swarm of flies buzzed above three mangled corpses lying in the tall grass. She stifled a gasp. Blood-splattered scales revealed them as lagharts. A weak, dry wind lifted, filling her nose with the rancid odor of death.

Beyond the three bodies, stretching deeper into the velten, more than a hundred other laghart remains lay scattered. Even if Pomella had wanted to count the dead, she wasn't certain she could've because many of the bodies had been torn apart. Blackened, sun-baked bloodstains caked the surrounding grass and rocks as flies buzzed everywhere.

"Sweet Brigid," she whispered.

"Spread out!" Tevon commanded.

The three brothers and Vlenar spread away from Pomella, Vivianna, and Lal while Sim approached Pomella. He had his two strange walking sticks in his hands.

"They're still here," Sim said, dragging his gaze across the massacred community.

Pomella stared at him. Before she could ask him how he knew that, Lal grunted.

"Yes, something stirs," Lal said.

Suddenly Pomella realized what was contributing to her sense of unease. It wasn't the corpses or the lack of sound that made the velten and the valley so eerie.

"Where are the fay?" Pomella said. Since leaving Kelt Apar, they'd encountered the fay almost everywhere. But Pomella had yet to see any in the velten.

Vlenar bent over one of the corpses that had mostly avoided dismemberment. His tongue zipped quickly in and out of his mouth while his slitted eyes narrowed.

Sim was staring again at the monument of the Saint and the particularly large stone entrance below it. "What is it?" she asked.

"In there," he said, not looking at her.

Pomella gazed into the dark entrance, seeing past the roughly hewn threshold. The ground sloped downward on the far side of the doorway, descending into blackness.

Vlenar began descending before Pomella could take a step toward it.

"No," Lal said to the ranger.

Vlenar stopped and glanced back over his shoulder at Lal. His tongue snapped the air. Pomella saw pain in his expression.

"A Mystic go first," Lal said.

Steeling herself, Pomella stepped forward. "I'll go." A part of her screamed that she was being a reckless dunder, but she knew her role. If there was danger ahead, she was not about to allow her master to walk headlong into it first. Instead, like a blathering fool, she would take that risk herself.

Vivianna stepped beside her. Pomella gave her a frail smile.

"Stay here and keep watch," Sim said to the ranger brothers.

"We go where our sister goes," Tibron, the youngest of the triplets, said in his thick accent.

"Sim is right," Shevia said in the same accent. "Guard the entrance."

Tibron frowned but nodded his head. His brother Tevon looked as though he wanted to reply but chose not to. He turned his back to the entrance and assumed an attentive stance. Typhos, the third brother, readied his sword in a single lithe motion.

Pomella stepped past Vlenar. His forked tongue flicked out as he watched her descend into the darkness of the underground laghart dwelling. Pomella saw respect in his slitted eyes.

The tunnel below the monument sloped downward. Pomella summoned the Myst and breathed a smooth ball of light into existence and willed it to float in front of her. Her foot found solid stepping-stones. Vivianna, Lal, and Shevia walked behind her.

Memory came to her of the time she and Sim had explored a similar tunnel on her way to Kelt Apar for the apprentice Trials. They'd found a ruined chamber at the end of that tunnel, along

with an enclave of Unclaimed living in secret. She now suspected that the chamber had been an abandoned laghart velten,
but whatever it had been, she feared that this one would contain
much worse than some terrified people living in squalor.

The tunnel leveled out and came to an intersection. Wide
hallways ran to either side of Pomella, but her attention was on
the door standing slightly ajar in front of her, which had been
attached to the stone wall. Pomella's ball of light shone evenly
across its wooden surface, revealing a smooth surface marred
only by a long gouge that had been torn across it. Beyond the
doorway, silver light flickered and indistinct animal noises could
be heard. Pomella felt the Myst stir.

"Be careful," Vivianna whispered. Behind her, Shevia and
Lal waited with grim expressions.

Pomella steadied her nerves and stepped into the room
beyond.

A feast hall of fay greeted her. Hundreds of strange silver
creatures sat, climbed, or flew around the massive room she entered. Two long tables stretched away from her, laden with both
silver fay food and foul meat from the human realm. A third
table at the far end of the hall ran perpendicular to the others,
connecting them. The creatures appeared to be celebrating,
raising goblets and laughing in a perverse sort of merriment.
Smoky translucent banners and decorations covered the ones the
lagharts had hung in what must've been their central temple or
community center. It appeared to Pomella as if one feast hall
from Fayün had somehow been overlaid on top of the one here in
the laghart's chamber.

A cold chill made Pomella shiver. She'd never seen fay like
the ones before her now. Most of the creatures were shorter

than her but were an odd melding of animal and human. Some had faces that looked like hyenas, and others had those of cats or rodents. Some had tails, and most appeared to walk on hind legs, but a handful hovered and flew in the air with fast-beating wings like her hummingbirds.

"Axthos," Vivianna whispered in awe from behind her. "Wild denizens of Fayün."

"But what are they eat—" Pomella's question died on her lips as she saw the scales on what the creatures feasted on. Chunks of laghart meat were being passed around on platters. Pomella watched as a hyena-like axthos buried its snout into a thick hindquarter.

Before she could gasp or retch, an owl-faced axthos with buzzing wings pointed at her and squawked. The commotion in the hall died.

"Shite," Pomella muttered.

A massive figure near the third table at the far end of the hall rose. At first glance it looked like a brown bear from her world, and indeed it was mostly flesh and blood. But much like the hall itself, something else had been merged on top of it, another presence that augmented it and made it more vicious. The fay within the bear was wolflike, and when it moved the bear's body shifted with it. Silver eyes shone within its sockets. Two rows of sharp teeth snarled at her. The great beast growled something unintelligible.

Pomella pulled a calming breath into her chest. She had faced the fay before, and returned them to Fayün. The ones here might be stranger and greater in number than she'd encountered before, but the concept was probably the same.

She hoped, anyway.

Another figure beside the bear rose. If the giant wolf-bear filled Pomella with fear, this one put a death grip on her heart. It was a laghart, or had been at one point. Gashes and ragged claw marks scarred every portion of its body. Dried blood caked the edges of its many wounds. The laghart lurched as it moved, and Pomella saw it wore shredded robes and carried a Mystic staff. Like the wolf-bear, the laghart had merged with another creature, although Pomella could not quite place what it was. Silver eyes stared out of otherwise-dead sockets. Long, luminous silver hair spilled down its face, looking strange on that non-human face.

The laghart Mystic placed a hand on the wolf-bear to settle it. It hissed, and Pomella realized it must've spoken.

"A wivan," Vivianna breathed.

"That creature is dangerous," Sim said. "It will try to kill us all." He held two long blades in his hand, which Pomella now saw had come from his walking sticks. His face was like stone, chiseled in a way Pomella didn't recognize.

The hall waited.

Pomella planted her staff firmly in the ground. "I am Pomella AnDone, a Mystic of this land. You are not welcome here."

The laghart snarled and spit, snapping at the air as if struggling to form sounds with a physical throat. Gradually the sounds it made became more familiar. Pomella realized it was trying to speak her language.

"Agh. Ahg . . . Ouhrg," the laghart Mystic guzzled.

"It's ensnared," Vivianna said, her eyes wide. "A fay is acting through a laghart." Despite the odd surroundings, Pomella could hear the academic interest in Vivianna's voice.

Pomella summoned the Myst, feeling it quick to rise around

her. She checked her rage and disgust, not letting it overwhelm her, but letting it fuel her words. "These were the chambers of lagharts who lived in peace. How dare you decimate them?"

"Our lahhand," the laghart said.

"This is *not* your land!" Pomella snapped.

The wolf-bear roared and leaped onto the table, scattering silver dishes and a cluster of axthos who'd been stupid enough to roam across the table. Another howl exploded from it, filling the chamber with its rage.

Vlenar leaped to Pomella's side, sword raised and long tongue hissing.

Lal placed a hand on Pomella's shoulder. But before he could speak Shevia stepped forward, back straight, radiating with the Myst and an imperious expression. The younger woman's hair rippled as though an otherwise unseen and unfelt wind swirled around her.

Shevia spoke in Qina, her tone firm and angry. In response, the wolf-bear swiped the air with its claw.

Pomella grabbed Shevia's upper arm. "What are you—*ouch, shite!*"

Pain raced through Pomella's arm and across her entire body. With it came flashing images and sensations. Terror. Anger. Sadness. Pomella saw a cluster of thornbushes build high like a dome over a crack in the ground. It vanished and was replaced by a flurry of other images she didn't understand. A strange outdoor shrine. A magnificent manor filled with shadows. A dank cavern with bookshelves and a large table filled with books and candles.

Quicker than a heartbeat, the images vanished, leaving Pomella with a blistering hand. Silvery light glowed through the twisted-serpent tattoo on Shevia's skin and the clothing covering it. It was the same shape as the one depicted on the walls around the hall.

Pomella snatched her hand back, staring in amazement and horror at Shevia, who glared at her. But before Pomella could open her mouth to ask what that was, the tide of fay rushed to attack like a swollen river bursting across an embankment.

Shevia moved faster than Pomella could believe. She spun once and jabbed her hand outward. Silver fire roared from it, tearing through the nearest axthos.

Pomella had no time to continue watching. Her experience dealing with the slavers across Moth had somewhat helped prepare her for these dangerous situations. She didn't consider herself a warrior by any means, but when someone or something charged at you there was no time to think.

Pomella punched her staff at the nearest hyena creature, forcing it back to Fayün. The axthos vanished in a cloud of silvery smoke. She struck another one as quickly as she could, banishing it as well.

Vlenar ducked and weaved between the fay, slicing them with his sword. The blade swept through the fay as if they were smoke. Realizing the ineffectiveness of his attacks, the laghart dodged and hissed.

"Run!" Pomella called to him. "Take the others!"

Vlenar obeyed without hesitation. He snatched Lal's hand and dragged him out the door and up the tunnel beyond.

After initially recoiling at the sudden violence, Vivianna gathered herself enough to banish several axthos. With a look from Pomella, she followed Vlenar and Lal.

Sim pulled at Pomella's arm. "Come on."

Pomella shook him off as another hyena axthos leaped at

them. She clubbed it with her staff but had to lurch to her side and slam one of the owl-faces swooping toward her. Each time she struck her staff, the fay exploded with light and smoke and vanished.

"Get out of here, Sim! I'll follow!"

On the opposite side of the long table, Shevia shifted from axthos to axthos, incinerating them. Somewhere in Pomella's mind it registered that Shevia was *destroying* the axthos, not simply banishing them back to Fayün. The other woman moved with inhuman grace, dancing through the fay creatures like a wind scattering dandelions.

Pomella wondered where Shevia had learned to move like that. Her movements were as sinuous as a snake gliding across the ground.

At the far table, the strange laghart Mystic waited, its spine straight, and dead face unmoving except for the silvery eyes that darted back and forth in otherwise-scarred sockets.

A deafening roar filled the hall, stunning Pomella down to her bones. Vlenar, Vivianna, and Lal all paused at the exit to stare at the wolf-bear howling atop one of the long tables.

It charged. The already-obliterated feast of laghart flesh flew everywhere as the wolf-bear bore down on her. Pomella narrowed her eyes and punched out a banishment, but it broke harmlessly against the beast like a wave against a mountain cliff.

"Pomella!" Vivianna cried from just beyond the feast hall's entrance.

The wolf-bear snapped at Pomella, but she spun out of the way just in time. A cat-faced axthos hurled itself at her, but she cut through it as it was still in midair.

The wolf-bear rose onto its hind legs and snarled, just an arm length from Pomella. It raised a massive paw to cut her down but suddenly bellowed in pain.

Sim leaned into the creature, one of his blades driven deep into its torso. Nearby, Shevia whipped her head around as the wolf-bear howled. It towered over Sim and swatted a claw toward him, but Sim ducked and somehow managed to yank the blade free.

Pomella ran for the exit, stumbling slightly in her red travel dress. Her hair tumbled in front of her face, but she ignored it as she scrambled away from the assault of fay.

Two hyena-faces tumbled into her path, blocking the exit. Pomella slammed through them with her staff. She stopped for one last look at the dining hall.

Sim still faced the wolf-bear, standing in a wide stance with his blades held aloft. In an instant Shevia was there. She threw her hand forward again, fingers splayed wide, and the wolf-bear burst into flames that surged across its body. The heat from the inferno made Pomella recoil. The wolf-bear rose to its hind legs, stumbled backward, and crashed into the wall. A ruined tapestry ignited immediately. Pomella watched in horror as the flames raced around the walls, and leaped to the feast tables.

"Let it burn," Sim said to her.

Only now, as the wolf-bear collapsed, kicking up a cloud of sparks, and with the fire raging all around the room, did the laghart Mystic move closer to them. Its movements were jerky, as if it didn't know how to control its own body.

"Sssshe comesss," hacked the laghart. "You cccannot ssstop ittt."

"Who?" Pomella demanded, stepping forward. She grimaced as one of the tables collapsed and flared fire beside her. Thick smoke stung her eyes, but she ignored it. "Why did you destroy these people?"

"Blesssssed is she," the laghart said, "ttthe one who bringsss Reunion. What wasss tttorn asssunder will be mennnded."

Flames leaped onto the laghart Mystic, consuming what remained of its robes and flesh. It raised its arms as smoke and fire wrapped around it. Its silver eyes remained visible, however, and stared from Pomella to Shevia.

Sim hustled the others out of the hall and down the entrance hall toward the surface stairway. Pomella followed him reluctantly as smoke burned her eyes.

As she left the hall, a light flashed behind her, and a tentacle of silver smoke lashed out and grabbed her ankle. She grunted as she fell, cracking her chin on the dirt tunnel. The metallic taste of blood filled her mouth.

The tendril of Myst dug into her ankle harder, cutting her skin. Sim was there in a heartbeat, swinging one of his blades, but the metal passed right through the smoke and clanged against the ground underneath.

Pomella tried to stand, but the tentacle pulled her back toward the now fully consumed room of fire. Black smoke poured from the doorway, filling the staircase above. Between the blood in her mouth and thick smoke, Pomella could hardly draw a breath.

"Take her," said a voice. Pomella tried to focus her mind and senses enough to understand who had spoken. Through her confusion and the smoke she saw Lal looming over her. Sim lifted her to her feet and hurried her toward the stairway. Somehow, the tentacle of Myst had been lifted from her foot. She looked back toward the door and saw Lal silhouetted against the light.

"Lal?" Pomella managed through the ringing pain in her head. "Lal, what are you doing?"

"We need to go, Pomella," Sim said insistently.

"But Lal . . ."

Sim had her at the stairs and hurried her up. "He's a grand-master," he said, as if that should satiate her worries.

"You don't understand," Pomella said, turning back once more. "He doesn't have—" She cut off as something inside the large hall—a tapestry perhaps—crashed down.

Sim's blue eyes found hers. "Respect his choice."

The rising fear in Pomella shifted to deep terror. Her heart thundered. "No," she whispered. "No, Lal."

A wave of scorching heat roared from the entrance. Pomella blinked and realized she was on the ground, trying to catch a breath. The world spun around her and for a moment she didn't know where she was.

"Pomella!" said a voice.

Pomella shook her head to clear it. Vivianna bent over her. "Are you OK?"

"Lal," she said as memory rushed back to her.

They were outside now, in the middle of the velten, well away from the entrance to the burning feast hall. Smoke poured from the stone entrance, rising into the sky, and filled the otherwise-clear blue sky.

Tibron offered his arm to her. She accepted it, and steadied herself on her feet. The rest of the group looked at her with concern. The other ranger brothers still had their swords drawn.

"I have to find him," Pomella said.

There was no movement inside the tunnel. She covered

her mouth and nose with her elbow and started toward the entrance again.

"We need to—"

Tibron stopped her. "If you go in," he said, "you'll die."

Vivianna placed her hand on Pomella's shoulder. "He's right."

"Vlenar," Pomella said, looking for somebody to agree with her. Lal was down there, and they needed to help him.

Vlenar's gaze went beyond her to the smoking entrance. "Lookkk," he said.

Hope filled Pomella's heart as she saw a figure emerging from the entrance. It was Lal, but his crimson robes were singed and patches of his tan skin shone with an angry shade of red. She rushed to him as he stumbled, and managed to catch him as he collapsed. Vlenar and Tibron joined her a heartbeat later.

"Lal," Pomella said, looking for severe wounds or burns.

"We ssshould gettt him away from the entranccce," Vlenar said.

"Yes," Pomella said. "Let's—"

Lal lifted his face. Pomella stopped. Silver light shone from Lal's eyes. They looked past her, toward the sky. He began to convulse, his mouth working and biting at air.

"Vivianna!" Pomella called. "I need you!"

Pomella didn't wait for her friend to rush to her side. She drew the Myst to her, and spread it across Lal, trying to find the link that bound Lal to whatever had gripped him.

Suddenly he stopped convulsing and turned his gaze to Pomella. A vicious grin that she'd never seen spread across her master's face.

"Lal?" Pomella said.

He shouted an indecipherable word and once more Pomella

found herself lying on the ground without remembering how she got there. Her whole body ached and this time she could feel a gash dripping blood from her forehead into one of her eyebrows.

Pomella pushed herself to her feet. She wobbled a bit, and had to use her staff for balance. She hadn't been the only one to have been knocked back by whatever Lal had done. Vivianna and Tibron were both struggling to stand, having been thrown a dozen steps from where they'd been standing. Vlenar, too, had been cast aside, but he'd already found his feet and seemed otherwise unaffected.

Lal rose with unhumanly jerky movements. He stretched, arcing his back and looking skyward as if to bask in the sun.

A horrible feeling gripped Pomella's heart. This was no longer her master. In place of his normally kind brown eyes she saw silver eyes that flicked around haphazardly, jumping from one point to the next. It was as if he'd never seen the world before and was getting used to the sense of vision for the first time. A thousand knives stabbed Pomella's heart. "No," she said to herself.

Her master was gone, replaced by a wivan.

Vlenar, approaching Lal, gazed at Vivianna and Tibron lying on the ground. Before Pomella could shout to warn him, Lal leaped toward the ranger and struck with inhuman speed. Vlenar somehow dodged it with his own natural quickness, but Lal came at him again.

Sim and the other rangers swarmed toward Lal. His head whipped around as they approached. He let out what sounded like a choke or a snarl, then backflipped high into the air, his feet rising twice the height of a tall man. He landed on his feet nearly ten steps behind them. With another scream he punched his hands forward, his fingers curled like claws, toward the rangers.

The ground erupted below the rangers' feet, sending them flying into the air. Dirt cascaded down around Pomella. One of the brothers, Tibron, landed hard nearby. She bent over him and saw him clutching his ribs and wincing though clenched teeth.

Shevia stepped through the dust from the attack. "Ahlala," she said, speaking Lal's full name. With her Qina accent, the name sounded more natural, more melodious than when Pomella spoke it.

Lal bent low, twisted with his arms wide, and hissed at Shevia. He punched a hand toward her, and a chest-sized clump of dirt that had been torn up flew at her.

Shevia swung her staff, and despite its skinniness, it smashed through the boulder, scattering dirt in every direction. She spoke again, in Qina, so Pomella could not understand what she was saying, but Pomella clearly heard her repeat Lal's name.

The creature inhabiting Lal snarled and replied in Qina.

"What's he saying?" Pomella called to Shevia. She risked a glance behind her and saw Vivianna helping Vlenar to his feet. Sim was on his hands and knees, shaking his head to clear it. Typhos helped Tevon to his feet while Tibron continued to try to catch his breath.

Shevia ignored Pomella's question and snapped something in return to Lal. She sneered as she spoke, then spun in a full circle and swung her staff in a wide arc parallel to the ground. A sudden gale, tinged with ashes and the smell of sulfur, slammed against Pomella, rippling her hair and robes.

Lal punched a hand out, diverting visible streams of air around him like a rock parting water. He spoke again in a voice that both sounded like Lal yet did not truly come from him. He looked directly at Shevia and said, "Lagnaraste summons you."

The words rippled through Pomella like a curse. The scent of sulfur surged around her again, mixed with a new, unexpected hint of sandalwood.

The blood drained from Shevia's face. Her eyes widened and even from a distance Pomella could see her white-knuckled grip on her staff.

Suddenly Shevia screamed, and ran at Lal, assaulting him with a flurry of blows from her staff. The creature inhabiting Lal dodged every time, ducking or sidestepping her strikes perfectly.

"Don't hurt him!" Pomella screamed, and ran forward.

Shevia either didn't hear or ignored Pomella entirely and continued thrashing her staff. The creature inside Lal cackled, enjoying the game. A heartbeat later the end of Shevia's staff connected, slamming into Lal's ribs. He bent double, and with lightning speed Shevia jammed her staff upward, slamming into his chin and knocking him off his feet and onto his back.

Pomella covered her mouth with her free hand and gasped. Rage and fear boiled in Shevia's eyes as she lifted her staff above her head in order to slam it down onto Lal.

Pomella moved without thought. She was one with the Myst, one with *everything,* and in that moment she became energy itself. All movement around her slowed as though time had decided to pass with the patience of a blossoming rose. In that seemingly endless heartbeat, she shifted herself, as pure force, toward Shevia.

Time raced back to normal, and Shevia flew backward as though punched by a boulder-sized fist. She rolled once and somehow managed to skid to a halt on her feet. Blood leaked from her nose, but wild rage roared in her eyes.

Shevia touched her bloody nose, then looked at her fingers. Her eyes found Pomella. "So we do it this way," she said, then attacked.

Pomella barely had time to raise her staff in defense as Shevia jabbed her own at her. She knew little to nothing of fighting, but she knew enough to keep her staff up in order to not get smashed in the face. She found herself retreating backward as Shevia struck and spun. The woman's movements were surreal in their grace and strength.

Out of the corner of her eye, Pomella saw a figure rushing toward them. She risked a glance that way and saw Sim running toward them. "No, Sim, stay—"

Shevia's staff exploded into Pomella's chest, knocking every breath she ever took out of her body. She tripped backward and hit her head on the ground.

Sim raised his blades as Shevia spun to him. Quick as a luck'n, and once more without thinking, Pomella forced the Myst at both of them, knocking Sim aside and throwing Shevia off-balance.

Pomella gasped for air and scrambled to her feet just as Shevia regained herself. They circled each other four strides apart, staves at the ready. Shevia moved the tip of her staff in a slow arc, mixing Myst and fire.

"I won't let you hurt him," Pomella said.

"Your master is gone!" Shevia snapped. "What is left will kill us both."

"What did he say to you?" Pomella said, keeping both hands firmly gripped on her staff. For once she was glad for the oak's thickness and weight. Her chest burned like fire and breath was hard to find. She needed to keep Shevia distracted. The other woman was faster than her, and probably more powerful with the Myst. She needed to end this quickly.

In reply, Shevia spun in place and hurled a jet of flame from the tip of her staff toward Lal's still-motionless body.

Pomella moved in the same heartbeat and tapped the empty air beside her with her finger. A single silvery chime sounded through the velten.

Before Shevia's flames managed to reach Lal's body, the ground rumbled beside him and tore itself open. Dirt and stone raced upward to form the familiar towering shape of the Green Man. The flames from Shevia's staff blasted into him, but Oxillian shrugged it off like wind. His bearded face bore an expression of anger. Pomella had seen that look only once before, in a cave far away, atop MagDoon when he'd taken a form of hardened stone pulled from the mountain. Now he towered protectively over Lal, his body shaped from dirt that still bore dried blood from the laghart massacre.

"Oxillian," Pomella said, struggling against the pain in her chest for every syllable, "Protect Grandmaster."

Vivianna stepped beside Pomella, staring at Shevia, her staff ready. Sim joined her on Pomella's opposite side.

Two of Shevia's brothers, Tevon and Typhos, placed themselves between Shevia and the Green Man. The leather of Typhos' gloved hands creaked as he tightened his grip on his sword. Tevon held his, too, but turned an angry glare at Pomella.

A silent stalemate lingered in the air. Finally, Tibron sheathed his sword and approached Oxillian.

"Green Man," he said. "Something unnatural controls Grandmaster. Help us constrain him."

"He's hurt, Ox," Pomella added.

"There will be no more blood or fire," Ox said, sweeping his gaze across all of them like a mother scolding her children.

"No, Green Man, you are wrong," Shevia said, her voice suddenly distant and strange. "Crow Tallin is upon us, and none of you understand it. There will be *much* blood and fire to come. This I foresee, as clear as the Mystic Star is bright."

She fixed her lavender eyes on Pomella. "You are at the heart of this, again," Shevia said to her. She retreated two steps, turned, and fled the velten.

NINETEEN

A PATH OF SILVER LIGHT

Four Months Before Crow Tallin

For three days the man known as the Woodsmith—who had lived in the silent highlands of Qin for four years—tried to put the strange events at the ruined slave caravan behind him. In the early morning of the first day he went out to check his traps, which were scattered throughout the forest. He'd caught a hare, which he cleaned and prepared for his meal that night.

He tried to lose himself in his regular day-to-day routine. Familiar habits allowed him to forget, to remain frozen and lost. It was safer there, in the quiet seclusion of mountains, where pain and memory couldn't find him.

The burned face of the Mothic Unclaimed flashed in his mind. The Woodsmith shook it away, banishing it to the deep recesses of his heart where he couldn't see.

The next day, the winter chill gave way to a warm spring morning. The Woodsmith spent the better part of it outside his hut doing chores. He split firewood, cleaned debris off his thatch roof, and cleared the meadow immediately surrounding his house.

With his chores complete, he brought out his onkai blades.

Onkai.

He'd never learned what the word meant. The teacher who'd given him the staves had only shared their names and showed him how to use them. He'd often wondered how a mountain village had come to revere such an unusual object. The villagers were supposedly known throughout the highlands for the unusual and versatile weapon. But those stories, along with the meaning behind their names, had died with the village.

Lifting one of the metal blades, the Woodsmith examined it in the cool daylight. The metal was harder and lighter than iron, something he'd not seen before.

Memories of his past flashed in his mind, but the Woodsmith purged them. The past was gone. Dwelling on it only brought suffering.

He lost himself in the familiar fighting stances he'd been taught. Normally, working up a hard sweat helped him to avoid thinking too much, but today, despite all his efforts to not dwell, the pile of stacked stones he'd seen at the caravan lingered in his mind.

Sitting Mother.

Dangerous memories of his lover, his teachers, and even his long-lost childhood friend bubbled to the surface.

"No!" he snarled to himself, and slammed the onkai into their sheaths.

As the afternoon turned to evening, a light rainstorm dragged itself across the valley. Higher up the slopes there would be snow, but down here the early spring held enough sway to melt the snowfall into rain.

The Woodsmith brought firewood into his cottage and set it into the simple hearth. When he'd first come to the meadow four years ago, he'd been wandering aimlessly. The blue oaks surrounding the open grassland had just felt right to him in a way he couldn't explain. He decided it was as good a place as any to settle for a while.

After nearly a week of building a campfire each night, he'd gathered stones to erect a hearth so that his fire could burn all day and night. The surrounding forest had no shortage of wood to keep it going. Around the hearth he built shelter in order to keep the sun and, later, the rain off him. His shelter grew into a hut and he kept building.

The months turned to years. In time, the Woodsmith found the local trade routes and left goods in exchange for basic tools such as a hammer, cloth, sewing needles, and other scraps of metal. He hauled the stones himself from the nearby river, painstakingly carrying or dragging them the entire way. His hut wasn't big. It was large enough for him to live comfortably.

The peaceful rainstorm pattered outside, and the Woodsmith roasted his hare. The tumble of memories refused to stay away as he slowly turned the rabbit on its skewer over the fire. Its juices hissed on the log, filling the cabin with their smoky scent.

If indeed the Woodsmith was being called by Sitting Mother, what did she want from him? He stared at the back of his hand. Red and purple blisters covered every inch. He had found contentment in being alone. He could never be around people again. Once, he'd allowed himself to hope that Sitting Mother could cure him where no other Mystic could. The Saint had turned out to be false. Yet here she was again, perhaps.

He frowned. No. He had tried that once. Always, throughout his whole life, Mystics had disappointed him. He resolved his will and ate his rabbit.

With his belly full, the Woodsmith brought out his old book. He still looked at it every night even though he'd memorized everything within. It was his one connection to somebody other than himself. He couldn't read all the words, and no matter how he tried to guess or decipher their meanings, the mysteries within remained beyond his grasp. He wondered if, in some strange way, the songs and words in the book were trying to communicate with him. He turned to the page with the lyrics to his favorite song.

The Woodsmith took a small bundle he kept near the hearth and withdrew his newest flute. Like all its predecessors, it had been carved from elderberry. It was as long as his forearm. He'd drilled the holes with careful precision, resulting in an instrument that was his finest yet.

He examined his handiwork before lifting it to his lips. A single note filled the hut. He played more, experimenting with melodies he'd invented, by blowing into the flute and moving his fingers across the various holes until he discerned certain patterns that were pleasant to his ears.

The Woodsmith played for a while trying to get the harmony that he worked on each night. Finally, he found it. He swayed to his own music, a soft melancholy sound that reflected his mood.

With the tune drifting in his hut and his ears, he sang:

> *"Listen Once,*
> *Hear Me thrice.*
> *From stars to shore,*
> *Across paradise.*
> *I cry, I call, I plea.*
> *My lost one,*
> *Come Back to Me.*
> *Come Back to Me."*

He glanced at the book. Checking the words that he'd long ago memorized.

> *Listen now,*
> *Hear me true.*
> *Out of the mountains,*
> *From beyond the sea.*
> *Awake, my Sim.*
> *Come back to me.*
> *Come back to me.*

A chill ran up his spine. He had never seen those words before. The flute drifted away from his lips. He blinked his eyes to clear them and peered at the page again.

They stared back at him, as real as the book they were printed in.

Awake, my Sim.

Firelight cast a warm glow across the angular runes on the page. His heart thundered. What was happening? Was his mind slipping already? Perhaps he'd been too isolated for too long.

"Leave me alone," the Woodsmith growled, his voice barely audible to his own ears. His throat cracked with disuse.

Carefully setting the flute aside, he stood and drew Memory from its sheath. He also grabbed a makeshift torch and lit it from the hearth.

Outside, the rain fell steadily, fat drops that plunked into muddy puddles. The Woodsmith held the torch in one hand and his onkai in the other. The torch sputtered and hissed.

He peered into the gloom, searching every shadow. There was nothing out there, yet why did he feel he wasn't alone? He returned to his hut and placed the torch in his fire.

There on his hearth, impossibly, stood a pile of stones shaped like Sitting Mother.

He waited until the rain passed the next day. The Woodsmith gathered the provisions he'd need for a longer journey than usual. He didn't have much, but over time he'd collected more than he could carry in a sack. He packed food, an assortment of herbs, his two canteens of water, and extra cloth and rope.

As he shouldered his pack and readied his onkai staves he glanced at *The Book of Songs* and wondered whether to bring it. It had been with him all these years, but now he felt as though it had betrayed him. He hadn't revisited its pages since the night before. He itched to open it and see whether the words remained changed, but he was afraid. He hesitated a heartbeat, then left the hut and the book, not knowing if he'd ever return.

It took him three days to find the clearing. It surprised him how easily he found it, even after all these years. It was the same as he'd remembered it, although with far less snow. It was the place he and his teacher had fought the wivan. The place he'd watched his mentor die. There were other details that he noticed now, too, that his younger self hadn't noticed before. The ground was sloped, angled to give the high ground to the laghart. The sky opened directly above him, and the nearby cave sloped deeper into the mountainside than he recalled. The Woodsmith approached the place where he'd buried his teacher. He'd marked it, along with the other grave he'd dug that day, with large rocks. Aside from those stones, nothing differentiated the graves from any other patch of dirt outside the cave.

Setting his onkai blades aside, he knelt and touched his forehead to the ground at the base of the grave.

He missed her.

The hours passed, the afternoon wore on, and the Woodsmith wondered why he'd come here. He knew he needed answers. He needed to understand what was happening with Sitting Mother,

yet a part of him knew that this was only the first place he needed
to visit.

His teacher had always been the one to tell him where to go
next. She'd always known. She'd never hesitated, even when
their destination so clearly led her toward death. He still wondered why and how she'd been so certain of her own death, and
why she'd gone forward with it. Perhaps she'd seen purpose to
her death. Or maybe, he thought with grim reflection, his youth
and inexperience elevated the perception of her confidence and
competency in his mind to be more than she actually possessed.

Even so, the Woodsmith wished she were here now to guide
him. He found himself foolishly hoping for a sign of where to
go next. He wanted assurances that he hadn't lost his mind.
More than anything else though, he wanted to know his purpose. He might be alive, but he drifted through his days like
the shades of his brother and the others that lay at his feet.

Why are you moping? his long-dead brother whispered to him
across time and death. *You know where you need to go next. Get
moving, tyke.*

We are rangers, his teacher said, her voice crisscrossing his
brother's. *We do what we always do. We move, and we survive.*

The Woodsmith growled. "There's—" He coughed, and had
to wet his throat. "There's nowhere left to go," he managed. The
voice that emerged from his throat matched the rocks around
him. "I kill everyone I love."

Out of the mountains, a new voice said in his mind, *from
beyond the sea. Awake, my Sim. Come back to me.*

The strange words he'd seen in *The Book of Songs.*

The Woodsmith's hands trembled as he stood. There was

nothing for him here. He turned his face to the northeast. It was time to return.

He crested the summit of the mountain he'd not climbed for four years and noticed how little it had changed. The same bushes grew nearby; the same mountain goat—or one of its descendants—stared lazily at him with the same curious expression. The same stunning view greeted him.

Time had become a strange concept to the Woodsmith. The seasons seemed longer. The years stretched. And while that meant that stars lingered longer on clear evenings, it also meant that loneliness settled into his bones until it was as familiar to him as his callused fingers. To the Woodsmith, it was a lifetime ago since he'd stood in this same spot.

But not everything was exactly the same on the summit as it had been. The most obvious change was the lesser amounts of snow. At these altitudes, it would be impossible to eliminate it entirely, even in the warmest summer months. But today, only the most stubborn patches remained. Overconfident tufts of grass had sprouted—much to the delight of the goat, the Woodsmith was sure. The mountain had awoken where before it had slept.

He turned his attention to the cliffside where a scattering of stones lay.

He set his onkai staves aside and lifted one of the larger rocks. Small flecks of faded white paint covered its surface. He was surprised to find the stones remained, and hadn't been tumbled down the mountainside by weather or animals.

One by one he piled rocks atop one another. He used both the old white-flecked stones as well as newer ones, forming a vaguely pyramid-shaped pile. Once the base was formed, he made adjustments, giving his creation more definition. At last he set the capstone and stepped back to examine his work.

The stack wasn't exactly the same as the one he'd seen before, but it created the vague impression of a meditating person sitting cross-legged on the ground.

"You called me," he said to the cairn. "So I'm here. What do you want?"

Nothing, save for the wind, answered.

"I'm rotting!" he snarled. "And they're all dead. Everyone!"

The goat bleated nearby. The Woodsmith ignored it.

"Where were you when Bith Yab was dragged from his home? When Rochella's throat was torn out? When Swiko used the last of her energy to touch my face and urge me to see you? Huh? Where were you then?"

Speaking those names aloud for the first time in years tore his heart open. Rage burned in him, a furnace hungering for fuel.

"Last time I came here for them," he went on. "Their ghosts haunt me every day. But today, I'm here to tell you to leave me alone."

He summoned his memories of Dane, of Rochella, and of Swiko, who all smiled at him, filling him with crushing love. It hurt, to think of them so directly, all at once. All of them had died in front of his eyes. Now he had to kill them again.

He collapsed to his knees. The hard stone bit into his flesh. "Good-bye," he said, to all of them, tears welling.

The wind danced across the summit. The Woodsmith inhaled the cold.

"*Sim,*" said a voice, and this time it was very real.

A wave of heat rose up the Woodsmith's spine. He lifted his face toward the direction of the voice and bit back a curse. It was the same cairn as before, but somehow, more than that. A woman's face, ancient and formed of silvery wind, raced across the uppermost stones. Flowing hair blew across her face. She was both young and old all at once. Her face shifted, from that of a young girl, to a beautiful woman, to an old crone, ever changing, but always stunning to behold.

"*Release your burdens,*" she said.

A gentle pressure touched his shoulder, as if weight from a hand. When he glanced, there was nothing.

"*Look within yourself, and find the way.*"

A murky shimmer played across his vision. The Woodsmith turned to it. A path of silvery light stretched before him, down the mountain, across the valley, and vanished into the west, as clear and real as the stones before him. In that moment, he knew, without doubt, that he had to follow it.

The path sang him a voiceless song, one that pulled his true self from the deep shadows of his own fear. The Woodsmith faded and Sim opened his heart for the first time in four years.

Come back to me.

TWENTY

THE MAN WITH NO FUTURE

Two Months Before Crow Tallin

Shevia struggled to stay awake as the hypnotic sway of the carriage lulled her to sleep. She forced her eyes open, hoping Master Bhairatonix had not noticed her momentary lapse in consciousness. She kept her expression blank and hands folded on her lap but dug her nails into her skin. The brief flash of pain was good, mostly because it was all she knew recently. Most days, she just wanted to sleep.

Bhairatonix sat straight backed on the opposite side of the small carriage, his immensely tall frame filling the entire space. He gazed past the orange and black beads shading the window to the city outside. Shevia didn't think he'd noticed her nodding off. It took all of her will not to yawn.

"What do you see out there?" Bhairatonix asked, jolting Shevia to wakefulness. Her eyelids had been getting heavier again until he spoke. Shevia was almost glad for the conversation because it would keep her awake.

Almost.

Bhairatonix nodded to the bead-covered window beside her.

Shevia pulled the beads aside. The first thing she noticed was the brightness. The midday sun revealed the bustling capital of Yin-Aab, with its sloped tile-roofed buildings and clean-swept streets that rose in tiers up the side of Jagacrawn, the Titan Mountain, like ivy crawling up a manor home. Along the road, commoners knelt with their foreheads pressed to the dirt. Bhairatonix had made no secret of his presence in the city. Those who lived here knew exactly who sat within the lacquered carriage.

Some of the prostrated people in the street peeked up as the carriage rumbled past them. One of them was a shirtless, malnourished boy, no older than four years old. The boy's mother, who was perhaps Shevia's age, nineteen, quickly pushed his head back down. It staggered Shevia to see somebody her age as a mother. The very thought of having children was as distant and strange to her as the moon.

Scattered throughout the crowd were other figures that sent a shiver through Shevia. In recent years there'd been an influx of Unclaimed imported from other countries, mostly Moth. Some of the noble houses had apparently overcome the stigma of housing those kinds of people in order to force them into labor. Shevia thought little of it. It didn't concern her.

A familiar figure walked ahead of the carriage, close enough for Shevia to see if she leaned. It was her brother Tibron. Her heart surged with warmth for him. He and her other brothers had been one of the reasons Bhairatonix had come to Yin-Aab. They'd returned from whatever training they'd received to be rangers and were now in the employ of the High Mystic. Shevia had nothing to be grateful or happy about in her life, but being reunited with them—especially Tibron—was as close to joy as she could imagine.

"Well?" Bhairatonix prompted.

The High Mystic's voice crushed whatever tiny seed of happiness had tried to germinate in her heart. "I see the greatest city in Qin," Shevia said.

"Don't conceal your thoughts from me."

Shevia quickly lowered her gaze and then glanced out the window again, hoping to find an answer that would satisfy him. They were in the Shallows, one of the commoner districts, heading toward the outskirts of the city. Soon the buildings and well-maintained roads would fade and give way to the tightly regulated rice-farming district. Behind the nearby buildings, Shevia could discern the Circus and Noble districts rising up the side of Jagacrawn.

"I see wealth and power," Shevia said. "The might of Qin's nobles is impressive and—"

"I will not ask you again for the truth," Bhairatonix said.

"I see freedom!" Shevia blurted in a rush. She hated that her fear of her master overrode her sense of self-preservation. "The commoners groveling in the street may have destitute lives, but they are free to live their lives as they wish."

"Interesting," Bhairatonix said after a moment. "And does the freedom of a rice farmer—a person who is forbidden to leave his homestead for more than a full day, and who will never rise above his station—appeal to you? I believe that same farmer could not even imagine the life you lead as my apprentice. Do you not have gratitude to me for raising you from a merchant-scholar family to where you are now?"

"Yes, Master, of course I do," Shevia said. "You are right. I am beyond fortunate." Her heart thundered, knowing he'd likely see through her insincerity.

"You were the Oracle of Thornwood," Bhairatonix said. "Now you are the apprentice to the High Mystic of Qin. Someday, you may perhaps inherit Shenheyna." His tone almost sounded amused.

"You are beyond generous with your words, Master," Shevia said.

Bhairatonix went on as if he hadn't heard her. "Does the life I've offered you leave you unsatisfied?"

"No, Master," Shevia said quickly, studying their feet.

"Shevia." Bhairatonix pulled her gaze up with his voice. His eyes were softer now, but she knew it was a false safety. "Tell me truthfully. Is there anything I've not given you that you desire?"

A rush of answers hurtled wildly through Shevia's mind like a flock of bats exploding from a cave for their evening hunt. Kindness. Affection. Praise. Useful teachings. Privacy. These and more had been denied to her her whole life. The rice farmer may not have the legal freedoms she enjoyed, but he was never denied those other aspects of life. She needed to answer Bhairatonix, so she settled on the only truthful answer she could voice relatively safely.

"When you feel I am ready, I would like very much to receive my Mystic name."

More silence radiated from her master. Shevia began to wonder if she'd gone too far.

"Why that?" he said at last.

"It has been over six years since you took me as your apprentice. Under your tutelage, I have learned much of the Myst and humbly believe I can satisfy your demands with it." Even in her emotionless shell, she had to repress a scowl. Bhairatonix had taught her nothing. She *could* Unveil the Myst, and do so more powerfully than her master could likely imagine, whenever she wanted. But it had not been Bhairatonix who empowered her. It was Sitting Mother, whose presence lurked within her all the time, a sleeping serpent, coiled and resting until she was needed.

"Then why do you desire another name?"

Shevia swallowed. "It is my understanding that all true Mystics are given a name by their masters."

"Are you not a true Mystic?"

"Only if you say I am, Master."

"I do. As you said, you are quite adept at using the Myst. Your talents far exceed those of most so-called Mystics living in shanties and dirt hovels throughout the mountains. You are not some hedge hex surviving off bugs. You are my apprentice and that raises you above the rest. You have no need of anything beyond that."

"Of course, Master. Thank you."

Bhairatonix nodded, indicating the topic was closed to further discussion. "Is there anything else lacking within your life and education? Is your staff unacceptable?"

The last question dripped with sarcasm, and Shevia had to prevent herself from responding. Yes, her anemic staff was rarely anything but a slight focusing mechanism for her. It suited her needs, she supposed, but she couldn't help but think what it would be like to hold a *real* Mystic staff.

They rode in silence through the capital, and this time Shevia was relieved that she was no longer tired. Bhairatonix pulled the bead curtains back from the window. His faraway, introspective expression was one Shevia was unaccustomed to seeing.

"You may not realize it," he said after some time, "but you and I have much in common. I, too, came from humble origins. I was adopted by a noble family in Qin, and raised in their household. My father and brothers were cruel and hurt me often."

Shevia dared not breathe for fear of interrupting her master's rare moment of vulnerability. Bhairatonix's eyes crinkled as he narrowed them. They were blue, a trait that Shevia had scarcely seen in anybody besides foreign nobles who had visited her at the Thornwood Shrine.

"But I learned much from them," Bhairatonix continued. "They instilled a sense of discipline, and quiet focus. By the time my predecessor, High Mystic Mahnitha, came to take me as an apprentice, I was ready to embrace her harsh lessons and inherit the Myst."

Shevia's pulse raced, but she kept her outward demeanor neutral and attentive. Bhairatonix had never spoken of his master before. She only knew of High Mystic Mahnitha from the few history books she'd been allowed.

Bhairatonix spoke no further, so Shevia returned her attention outside. The tiled roofs, raised wooden walkways outlining the buildings, and seemingly endless line of genuflecting commoners hardly kept her attention. Instead, her mind retreated to that place inside herself where she was safe, where the fear of her master was lessened. It was the place where Sitting Mother dwelt.

The familiar scent of sandalwood and holly filled her nostrils. Her heart slowed. The Myst rose around her. Long ago, it had been the vent within the Thornwood that triggered her visions. But ever since that terrible handful of days when Bhairatonix had gone on his long trip—the last time he'd ever left her alone for more than a few hours—she'd begun to feel Sitting Mother's presence within her at all times. It was as though she carried a piece of her in a secret pocket that Bhairatonix could not see.

The tattoo wrapped around her shoulder and upper arm tingled. The sensation built, like molten iron spreading down through her skin and into the thicker sinews of her arm. Shevia's hand tightened on her thin Mystic staff. When Sitting Mother awoke within her like this, it was a wonder that Bhairatonix did not take notice.

Just as the rising Myst and the pressure in her arm built to a point where she could no longer bear it, the carriage came to an unexpected stop. Shevia glanced at Bhairatonix and saw that his eyes were closed. He opened them a moment later, leaving Shevia to wonder if he'd been asleep or using the opportunity to meditate.

She could hear the carriage driver—an old merchant-scholar Bhairatonix frequently hired to drive him around—shouting at somebody in the road, telling them to move out of the way. The shouting was followed by the sounds of shuffling feet and a cry of agony. Shevia's heart raced. She hoped it wasn't Tibron who'd been hurt.

The High Mystic grunted and irritably rapped his staff on the roof. A moment later, the carriage door opened, revealing Tibron, who bowed. Shevia breathed a silent sigh of relief.

"Your Eminence," her brother said. "Forgive us for stopping, but there is a commoner in the road who refuses to move."

"So move him!" Bhairatonix snapped.

"We tried, Master, but he's armed. He injured Tevon."

Bhairatonix's eyes narrowed. "Are there not three of you? And what of the street full of people who would assist the High Mystic of Qin?"

A flutter of emotion rose within Shevia upon hearing that her brother was hurt, but she dared not express it outwardly. She kept her face smooth and looked to Bhairatonix for direction. The Mystic's eyebrows narrowed before he grunted and stepped out of the carriage.

Tibron immediately leaped to the side and bowed his head as Bhairatonix emerged from the carriage. The High Mystic hadn't indicated to Shevia whether she should follow, but he also hadn't expressly forbidden her from doing so. Taking up her small staff, she slipped out of the carriage. Tibron looked at her with concern, but she ignored him. They were in one of the district's circular intersections. In the center of the plaza stood a cluster of canvas tents housing vegetable merchants. All commerce had apparently come to a halt with the arrival of the High Mystic's carriage. Indeed, all movement of any kind had come to a stop. A sea of people prostrated themselves down every alley and every sidewalk. Shevia estimated that there were several hundred commoners and merchant-scholars gathered.

Bhairatonix ignored everyone, turning his gaze to the lone man standing defiantly in front of the carriage. The only other people standing were Shevia's brothers. Typhos had a sword drawn and was pointing it at the strange man. Tevon stood just behind Typhos clutching his wrist with a snarl.

Shevia studied the man who had caused the ruckus. He was rather tall, if not nearly the height of her master. Long scraggly hair tumbled down his back past his shoulders. A thick beard of reddish-blond hair covered his face. He was wearing animal skins, and in each hand he held a thin blade that jutted from a wooden shaft.

Onkai blades.

Despite their rarity, they were well known in the highlands. Their wielder stood in a defensive stance with his gaze locked on Typhos.

Bhairatonix took two steps forward and raised a finger. Her brother lowered his blade and bowed to the High Mystic. The scraggly man turned to Bhairatonix but kept his guard.

"I would not expect to see a man as disheveled as you carrying onkai," said Bhairatonix.

"I ranger," said the man in broken Qina with a hoarse voice.

Despite his rough accent and tone, Shevia noted that he was a young man, probably less than five years older than she.

"Ranger or not, you are impeding my carriage," said the High Mystic.

The man relaxed his guard and sheathed his onkai with smooth motions. He was familiar with the weapons.

"Forgive," the man said. Shevia wasn't sure if he was asking for forgiveness or demanding it. "I try to hail your driver and ask permission, but I shoved aside. Defended myself."

Tevon's face darkened. Shevia silently warned her brother to keep his noise to himself.

"There are ways to summon me, boy," said Bhairatonix, "and there are other Mystics in this land. Leave off now and I will forget this incident."

The man shook his head. "I come a long way to find you. You are the only one who can help. It is urgent." The man looked at the crowd of prostrating people. "Especially now."

Bhairatonix studied him with a cold expression. "What do you mean?"

The man lifted one of his arms high and slid back his sleeve. Shevia's jaw tightened. Angry red sores covered his forearm. Even from a distance she could see that they festered above purple bruises. It churned her stomach.

The crowd surrounding them muttered, despite the fact that most of them were facedown in the dirt.

"How dare you bring your sickened carcass to this city?" snarled Bhairatonix. He lifted his staff, but at the exact same moment the man withdrew an onkai blade and lifted it over his head.

"I will not be sent away," he said. "The silver path led me here. I carry sickness that will kill everyone here. I know you can cure me. Help me, and in return, I enter your service."

Tibron tensed beside her. Her other two brothers looked from Bhairatonix to the man.

The High Mystic laughed. "Arrogant boy. I will cut you down and burn your corpse. That will just as surely eradicate your plague."

"Is that how High Mystic of Qin tends those in need?" asked the man. "In front of whole city you turn me away? Slaughter me rather than cure? Why not accept the services of a ranger? *Show me* that you are different. Show Yin-Aab you are different."

"Waste my time no further," Bhairatonix said. He tapped his staff and the ranger rose into the air. He clutched his throat, gasping for air.

A tempest storm of Myst built within Shevia. The scent of sandalwood and holly overwhelmed her. Sitting Mother rose within her and the snake tattoo on her shoulder. Pushing her fear away, Shevia stepped closer to Bhairatonix. "Are you certain it is wise to do this, Master? Perhaps you should help him?"

Bhairatonix, who had been about to step back into the carriage, stopped. His eyes tore through her. "That is not your concern, *apprentice*. Get in."

Shevia glanced again at the man kicking his feet in the air, clutching at his throat. Typhos and Tevon circled closer to him.

"With respect, Master," Shevia said, "there are other ways to dispose of this man and his problem without executing him."

Bhairatonix straightened and loomed to his full height. He bore down on Shevia like a mountain over a foothill. A distant corner of her mind screamed at the impending danger. He was going to punish her. He was going to hurt her. Again. He was going to *break* her.

But with the Myst surging within, and Sitting Mother shielding her, Shevia met his gaze.

"Why not heal him?" she said. "Let these people see the might of the High Mystic of Qin."

Bhairatonix's eyes narrowed dangerously and that distant part of Shevia knew she had pushed too far.

He lifted his hand and the man fell to the ground, sucked in air through his lungs. Shevia's brothers stepped toward him.

"Stay back!" Bhairatonix snapped, without taking his gaze from Shevia. A cruel smile curved the corners of his mouth. "I wouldn't want them to get ill. If this plague rat is of concern to you, then I will let you dispose of him."

He waited expectantly. A chill ran up Shevia's spine. She turned and walked toward the man, using every fiber of control she possessed to keep her stride even and her head held high.

The Myst churned around her, spreading across the entire plaza like an invisible wind.

She approached the man and knelt. Startlingly blue eyes were set into a handsome, if somewhat emaciated, face that was covered in those terrible sores.

The man stared at her with no fear. Without moving, Shevia touched the man with the Myst. He sucked in a small breath. As the Myst settled into him, his mind opened before her. It was like putting her nose to a flower and breathing deep. There were no words spoken or exchanged, but somehow Shevia understood this man, sensing his pain and loneliness.

Bhairatonix wanted her to kill him. She reached out and placed a hand around his neck, pressing her thumb into the spot beneath the ball of his throat. Her other hand followed.

The man remained calm as they locked eyes.

Here was a man as broken as she was. What was his story? How did a light-skinned foreigner, who claimed to be a ranger, come to possess onkai? By appearances, it would seem that a diseased man would approach a High Mystic and beg for a cure with desperation. But there was a stillness in his demeanor. Something drove this man, and Shevia suddenly had an overwhelming desire to learn what that was.

Shevia could sense the sickness within him. It had spread throughout his body, yet it had been dulled, like a rusted blade that had lain dormant for too long. Delving deeper, she found a place in his body, near the base of his spine, where the disease was heaviest. It was like an anthill, swarming with the plague. Around it she found something unusual. A broken shell of the Myst surrounded the illness, like a protective sphere that had once safely trapped the disease away. That shell had been fractured somehow, and from that crack, the plague had spread out again.

She inhaled deeply, pulling the Myst from every corner of the plaza, and pushed it into the man.

The plaza melted away as the familiar trance took hold of her. Shevia saw only glimpses of other places, other times racing by in furious succession. A boy with scraggly blond hair, crying beside a creek. The same boy, with a hooded Mystic placing his hand over the child's heart. The same boy, now a handsome young man, taking a vicious sword wound to the chest before being healed by a virga ranger.

Suddenly the man lurched, moving with surprising speed and strength, grabbing her. Despite her height, he was larger than her. But Sitting Mother filled her with strength, turning her bones to iron, and her muscles to granite. She shoved the man back to the ground and straddled him. She pressed harder into him. He clawed at her hands.

The man's neck pulse beat against her fingers. How fragile the human body was, she mused. She could snuff this man's life out in a moment. And perhaps she should, as her master wanted.

Shevia could see Bhairatonix in the corner of her vision. Extending her senses, she could somehow feel his heartbeat, too. A powerful realization swept over her.

She was more powerful than her master. He held her back, but the tide of her power, born of Sitting Mother, could snuff him as easily as the man whose throat she now gripped.

Shevia snarled, feeling the need to express the powerful emotions raging within her. Mystic fire surged through her hands into the man. She sent it forth, commanding it to burn where she sent it. It torched him, making him writhe. Shevia pinned him with her body and hands, as easily as one held a flailing child.

The burning ceased. Only the man's purified body, cleansed in a manner only fire could bring, remained. Shevia released her grip, and the Myst flashed away.

The man bolted upright, shoving her away. Shevia tumbled to the ground beside him. Like her, the man was trying to find his breath.

Her brothers rushed to her, but Shevia thrust a trembling hand up to stop them. She watched the man, who was now on his hands and knees, sucking air. His whole body trembled.

Without taking her gaze from him, Shevia snapped her fingers and pointed to her Mystic staff, which lay nearby. One of her brothers—she didn't notice which—obediently placed it in her hand. Shevia used it to pull herself to her feet. Another brother assisted her.

Most of the gathered crowd no longer had their faces pressed to the ground. They stared with confused or scared expressions. Shevia glanced over her shoulder. Bhairatonix approached. She expected a cloud of rage around him, but instead there was another emotion.

Fear.

It lingered only a moment before he masked it, but Shevia was certain of what she'd seen. Her master looked from her to the man and his eyes widened.

A murmur arose from the crowd. "Look at his skin," somebody said.

The man was trying to rise from his hands and knees. As he moved, the furs around his arms shifted, giving Shevia a glimpse of skin. His clean, unblemished skin.

The man must've heard, because he stared at his hands. If they had been trembling before, they shook even harder now. He rose completely, and yanked back his sleeves revealing perfect, pale-pink skin. He tore layers of fur and cloth off, until he was bare chested. Not a single blemish covered his thin but well-muscled body.

The crowd erupted with talk. Commoners and merchant-scholars stood and pointed. They pushed past one another to see what had happened. Tevon and Typhos looked around, uncertain of whether to secure the crowd or protect their sister.

"Great Mistress!" cried a woman, reaching for Shevia.

A young man with severe burn scars on his face raced forward and dropped to his knees. "Heal me next, Great Mistress!" Tevon clubbed him on the back of the head and tossed him away from Shevia.

Commoners stared and murmured, looking between Shevia and the ranger she'd healed. For two years, as the Oracle of Thornwood, Shevia had been one of the most acclaimed people in Qin, but during that time she had never known what it was like to receive adulation. It had always been a distant knowledge, told to her by other people, rather than through direct experience. Now several hundred pairs of eyes stared at her in amazement.

"Great Mistress," somebody begged, "tell us your name."

Bhairatonix's gaze seared through her. Shevia kept her eyes on the ground. "I am nobody," she said. "My master, the High Mystic, whose name is a song to our ears, has cleansed this man of his plague."

A hundred voices and more erupted at once, surging toward her. Shevia's brothers hurled themselves in vain against the surging crowd of hands.

"Heal me!" said a man.

"Bless my child!" cried a mother.

"Restore my eyes!"

As the crowd came around her, Shevia saw Bhairatonix standing alone, forgotten.

That evening, back at Shenheyna, Shevia slipped into the first-floor washroom near the guest suites. Typhos followed her, carrying a wide basin of water and some towels. Their entrance caused the room's lone candle to flicker, making the shadows dance like a tribe of mountain folk.

The only other person in the room was the man she had healed from Yin-Aab. He sat on a high-backed chair with his back to her. He wore only a pair of ragged pants. His loose, long hair fell down his back.

Shevia motioned for Typhos to set the basin down on a table resting against the wall. As he did so, she placed her Mystic staff against the wall and waited for her brother to leave. The door slid shut behind him, further darkening the room.

The man hadn't bothered to turn around at their entrance. Shevia's gaze slid down his bare arms to the shackles chaining him.

This was Bhairatonix's hospitality.

She had not wanted to see the man again. After what had happened in the plaza, the High Mystic had ordered her brothers to seize him and return to Shenheyna. Aside from that, Bhairatonix had spoken little of the incident other than to insist she "clean the filth from him."

Nervous tension clutched Shevia's stomach. She stilled her nerves and stepped through the dim room to the table. The man looked at her sideways.

"Your name?" he asked with that awkward accent.

"You know more of me than I do of you," Shevia said, not looking at him. "It is better if you speak and fill my ears with truth."

The silence stretched until she was unsure if the man had understood her words.

"Called Sim, am I," he said at last.

With this small detail granted, Shevia allowed herself to study him. "Sim," she echoed. "You are from Moth?"

"Yah."

"I have been instructed to clean you."

The man named Sim rattled his shackles. "In chains?"

Shevia walked behind him, relieved that he could no longer study her with those piercing eyes. It was strangely empowering to stand over a man who had no control over her. Ahg-Mein, Tevon, Bhairatonix. All men who manipulated her with intimidation and fear. But now the tides had shifted.

Shevia reached a finger out and pressed into the back of the seated man's shoulder. Such a small gesture, but it curled her lips in a smile.

Freedom.

No man would ever control her again.

She gently tilted the man's head back so that he was looking at the high ceiling. His long hair tumbled down. Shevia summoned a trickle of the Myst and floated the water basin toward her. It drifted smoothly through the air and hovered near her hands.

She washed his hair in silence, glad that he did not find the need to speak. When his hair was clean, she reached into her silk robe and removed a small velvet pouch. Her heart thundered as she untied strings and withdrew a pair of shears. The blades were as long as her palm, and sharp enough to cut flesh. She snipped his hair away until its length was suitable for a commoner. He claimed to be a ranger, and therefore suited to the merchant-scholar caste, but he did not argue as she clipped it shorter.

Next she trimmed his beard, before separating the shears into separate blades. She lathered his face with soap and shaved him clean. As she did, he opened his eyes.

"Why?" he asked.

Shevia continued to shave him.

"Why?" he said again. "Why heal me?"

"My master is a kind and wise Mystic who—"

"No," he said. "There is no truth in your . . . story," he finished.

No truth in your story. His awkward use of the Qina language resulted in a phrase that resonated with Shevia. His gaze bore straight through her, and she turned away, afraid he'd read her secrets.

"You would have died," she said.

"I nothing to you," he said.

Shevia shifted the blade from his cheek to his neck. Sim stiffened.

"Yah, you are nothing to me," she said fluently in the Continental language. "I hold your life in my hands."

If he was surprised at her mastery of his language, he did not show it. "You won't kill me," he said in his native tongue. "You already had a chance. It would displease your master if you did."

Shevia's eyes narrowed. "You do not know me."

"I see that you were broken," he said.

Her heart thundered. "How do you see that?" she said, but regretted it as soon as the words were out.

"I've been broken, too." He sat forward. "But I've been given a fresh start, in part because of you."

Shevia could not keep her hand from trembling.

"You crave to be free of your master, don't you?" he said. "That's why you defied his order to kill me, and instead chose to heal me."

"You whisper lies in my ears," she said.

"Does he know how powerful you are?"

The scent of sandalwood and holly filled the room. The Myst rose around Shevia. She wanted to burn this man alive, destroy him before he could tear her open further and pull out the secrets she so carefully hid away.

"No," she replied.

The man named Sim nodded. "In the highlands, I came to the mountain where Sitting Mother lives. She revealed the silvery path that leads all true rangers. It led me to the place I could find healing. At first, I thought it led to your master, the High Mystic of Qin. But now I see that it led me to you."

The last words were a whisper, trembling across the dim room. Shevia forced herself to still her breathing. The room suddenly felt stifling.

Sitting Mother.

"My brothers will bring you clothes," she managed. "Tomorrow you will begin your service to my master. In three weeks we leave for the island of Moth for an important gathering of High Mystics. You will accompany us."

This finally caused him to show surprise. Shevia used that

moment to back away from him. She packed the shears into their velvet pouch and summoned her Mystic staff to her hand.

At the door she stopped but dared not look back at him. "You were infected with the plague's seed as a child," she said, telling him the truth of the vision she'd had right before healing him. "But another Mystic came to you. He could not heal you. But he sealed the disease away. It could not hurt you, and so over time your body learned to keep its effects at bay. Then somebody healed you of a great wound. And when she did, the protective shell was shattered."

She waited for a reply, but none came. Shevia had only told him most of the truth from her vision. In every vision she'd ever received, she had witnessed a part of somebody's future. But with this man, the young ranger from the island of Moth, she saw *no* future.

Without glancing back, Shevia left the room, trying to convince herself she was not fleeing.

With her new power and confidence, she would never flee anyone again.

TWENTY-ONE

REBORN IN FLAME

Shevia fled the chaos of the velten.

An ocean of grassland surrounded her, but she hardly noticed. She ran as fast as she could, her lungs heaving like a blacksmith's bellows. Nothing pursued her, yet she kept looking over her shoulder, fearful that something or someone would catch up. Pomella did not scare her. It was the unknown presence in Shevia's life that she ran from. It was the secret she'd never dared to so directly face until now.

It was her friend, who she'd always thought was Sitting Mother. But now Shevia knew her true name, spoken by the laghart wivan. The moment the creature had hissed it, a wave of energy had surged through Shevia's tattoo. It was as though the serpent on her shoulder had heard its name and woken fully, and struggled to rip itself from her skin.

Lagnaraste.

The name roared in Shevia's mind. She tripped over her Mystic staff and crashed into the knee-high grass. Gritting her teeth, she scrambled to her feet but stumbled again.

Ahead of her to the west, rising above the mountains, the Mystic Star shone bright red, burning on her face as hot as the sun.

Shevia clawed at her arms and face. "What are you?" she screamed.

Her friend slowed her writhing and Shevia felt a soothing, calm sensation wash over her. *Do not fear,* the voiceless presence seemed to say.

"Why do you consume me?" Shevia said.

The valley and mountains and sky tore away from reality. Shevia burned as if surrounded by an inferno. The scent of sandalwood and holly mingled with the acrid taste of sulfur. Less than a heartbeat later the pain vanished. Surrounding her now was a world made entirely of silver. In a single moment she saw plants and trees rise and fall, animals grow and die and give way to their descendants. Whole generations cycled through an eternal ecosystem within a location she recognized. The Thornwood. No matter how time shifted, she would recognize those rolling hills anywhere, and would know the forest of bushes that blossomed and died in the same timeless moment.

This was a vision, like the ones she'd had in her time as the Oracle. It was both a dream and the certain truth, layered together in a weave as elaborate as one of her mother's formal gowns.

As Shevia stared at the shifting landscape, a little girl, glowing silver, skipped down the hill toward the thorns. Shevia recognized herself in the girl's face, although her hair and clothes trailed wispy smoke. She watched the apparition slip into the Thornwood and vanish. A chill crossed over her. Her younger self did not emerge. The Thornwood shifted, a girl's scream echoed through the shrubs, and Shevia's heart clenched. She knew what it meant. Like all her visions, the images she witnessed were not literal, but the meaning was always clear. Left alone, without her friend, that little girl would've died in the Thornwood.

The world tore away again and now she was in her parents' banquet hall, watching the silvery form of the fat merchant-lord Obai rise above her silvery body that lay on the table amid scattered dishes. His face was blank like a polished glass, without eyes or mouth or nose. Her faceless mother screamed as Obai drove a knife into Shevia's chest.

Another scream, another inferno of time.

The looming figure of Bhairatonix, face as blank as the others, hurled her across his secret laboratory onto the cold stone lair. Shevia watched as he picked her up by the hair and then shoved her against the far wall like a canvas sack.

Again and again Shevia witnessed her own death, and every time the message came through, wordless and clear: *You live because of me. Alone, you are fragile. Together, we are mighty. I love you, as though you were my own.*

The inferno of imagery flickered out, and with it, the visions vanished. Shevia's whole body shuddered. She wrapped her arms around herself. She understood that she'd come to a crossroads in her life. But the path before her wasn't simple; it seemed more like she'd come to the edge of a cliff, leaving her only with the options to slink back to the safety of land or join the being that ruled her by leaping from the ledge.

The choice was hers. Her whole life, Shevia had done the bidding of others. Her life was not her own. Until now.

Her voice trembled as she voiced the question she'd been too terrified to ask for years. "Why did you choose me?"

The presence soothed her, stroking her mind as gently as a mother cradled a newborn. Anger boiled within Shevia. She pulled at the Myst, commanding it to gather to her like a queen summoning her armies beneath the banner of the Mystic Star.

She lifted her Mystic staff and punched it to the ground. *"Why me?"*

The grass around her erupted in flame. She tightened her grip on the staff and the flame roared higher. She would have her answers or she would incinerate the whole valley. Whether she burned with everything else or not did not concern her. "I will have my answers, *Lagnaraste*!"

Come to me, and you will have them, the voiceless being whispered.

Since childhood Shevia had thought of the presence within her as her friend Sitting Mother and now a being with the name Lagnaraste. What was the truth? Perhaps they were both true.

Regardless of her name, she had never let Shevia down before. Through her power and guidance, Shevia had found the strength to break away from Bhairatonix.

If she rejected Sitting Mother now, everything she'd gained

would vanish. Bhairatonix would hunt her down and break her completely. But by embracing Sitting Mother, Shevia could overcome her master when he inevitably came for her, but at what price?

She set her jaw. Never again would she be powerless.

"So be it," Shevia said.

In response, a crawling sensation crept across Shevia's arm. She held it up and caught her breath. The serpent tattoo *walked* along her skin, stretching as it moved. Scaled foreclaws flexed as though digging into her skin and pulled the rest of its body forward. Shevia rolled her arm and tried to glance at her shoulder as the serpent twisted across her back, chest, and arms. The back and sides of her neck burned as the serpent sought fresh skin.

With every inch that the serpent took, more power flooded into her. Her spine burned as the searing heat of the Myst took over her body. She arched her back and gaped at the sky, arms spread wide. The wind tore at her dress and hair.

The story that Grandmaster Faywong had told her of the ancient dragons resonated within her. It triggered dormant memories Shevia never realized she had. Memories of another time, another world, where the skies and land were united and ruled by great serpents embodying the Myst. Centuries had passed since the last dragons roamed the land. But now, wreathed in a nest of fire, she would at last be reborn.

"Shevia?" came a hesitant voice from nearby.

The trance ripped away from Shevia like old sackcloth. For several heartbeats, the world spun around her. She touched her forehead to steady her vision but couldn't remain upright. She stumbled, still not quite remembering where she was. But rather than hitting the ground, she fell into strong arms that smelled of leather and the dusty road. She opened her eyes and Tibron's blurry face coalesced in front of her. Two other figures—her brothers?—drifted behind them. They were speaking, but she couldn't hear what they were saying.

"Are you well?" Tibron said.

Shevia nodded, and Tibron lifted her easily to her feet.

Tevon strode forward, and in the dim light Shevia could see the rage playing across his face. Memories of her childhood flashed to her mind as she recalled the eldest triplet's temper. Behind him, Typhos watched with intense focus. His hand rested near on his belt, beside his sword.

"Whatever game you play at, Sister, you disgrace yourself and our family," Tevon said.

"Leave her alone," Tibron said. "She's not well."

"By the ancestors, she's not well!" Tevon yelled. "She's not a child any longer. You can't protect her."

Tibron held his ground. "I believe, as a ranger in service to a Mystic, it is my duty to protect her."

"Then you've forgotten your duty to your family!" Tevon snapped.

"I can speak for myself," Shevia said.

"You attacked a grandmaster and another Mystic," Tevon said. "Where is your mind at?"

Shevia's skin warmed from the power still within her. "Keep your questions behind your teeth," she said.

Tevon straightened. "You may be a Mystic, but your actions reflect on us."

"I *am* a Mystic," Shevia said with searing intensity. "I stand above you and your *family*." She spit the last word.

Like lightning from a clear sky his hand struck at her.

Shevia did not flinch or blink. Her brother's intended slap halted mid-swing, inches from her face. Tevon's expression changed from surprise to fear as he tried to retrieve his hand, but it did not move.

"Really, Brother?" Shevia said. "Am I still a little girl you can beat whenever I say something your delicate ears cannot stand? Do my years and power and rank mean nothing to you now? Who disgraces the family now by attempting to strike a Mystic?"

"Sister," Typhos said, his hand now wrapped around the hilt of his sword. He so rarely spoke that it was a surprise to Shevia to hear his voice. He managed to make his single word seem like a plea.

Shevia ignored Typhos and kept her attention focused on Tevon. His palm remained just a breath from her cheek. "How many slaps did I receive by this hand?" she said. "One might wonder where you learned such manners. Perhaps you deserve pity because that's all you learned from Mother and Father."

Her skin warmed as the Myst radiated from her. She could feel it reflected back to her from Tevon's palm. "Poor, poor Tevon. Do you bully your sister because Mother hurt you? Did you become a culk because they were? Is that the family you choose to honor?"

"Sister, I—" Tevon stopped and stared at his hand. "What are you doing? It burns. Shevia—"

"Does it hurt, Brother?" Shevia said, letting her anger press out through her skin. "You wanted to strike me. To touch me. Well, I give you that chance."

She leaned forward until her cheek touched his palm. Tevon screamed as the flesh on his palm burned.

"Shevia!" yelled Tibron. "Stop!"

She kept her gaze on Tevon as he screamed. "Look at me, Brother! Does it hurt like a thousand slaps across a lifetime?"

Typhos stepped forward. Shevia ignored him.

"You will never touch me again!" she screamed. "You are not my brother. I disavow you. I brand you Unclaimed! Begone from my life and this world, traitor to my blood!"

Flames burst across Tevon's arm. He hollered in agony as his fingers disintegrated, followed by his lower arm.

Typhos screamed and drew his sword. Tibron cursed but was slower to draw his. Without hesitation Typhos cut downward, severing Tevon's arm just above the elbow in order to prevent further disintegration. The burning limb ashed away, but the fire continued across Tevon's body. His screams filled the wide valley.

Typhos, the brother who loved Tevon above everyone else, who followed him with blind affection and humility, raised his sword to strike Shevia. Tears filled his eyes. A pang of sadness clutched Shevia's heart as she waited for him to attack her and destroy himself.

But in the infinitesimal moment before he stuck her, another blade sliced through the air. Typhos' sword and the hand grasping it flipped through the air and landed in the blood-splattered grass. Tibron panted hard as he watched Typhos cry out in pain and clutch what remained of his arm.

Tevon's cries cut off as he fell to the ground, the flames consuming his face and upper body.

Clutching what remained of his arm, Typhos stared at the corpse of his brother. Tears coursed down his cheeks. "He did not deserve this." He ran without looking back.

Shevia slowly lifted her hand and pointed at him. Tibron's hand clutched her wrist. She felt him flinch as her skin seared his flesh.

"No, Shay-Shay!" Tibron pleaded through the pain. "Let him go." He tried to mask the agony he felt, and Shevia admired his courage. She let the burning Myst dissolve and lowered her hand. Tibron snatched his hand back. Bloodred burns covered the palm and had already inked their way up his wrist.

"The sister you love is dead, Tibron," Shevia said with a mild voice. "She died as her brother did, burned by the fires lit by the cruelty of her family. But I am reborn now. I pray Tevon will find rebirth in a new, better life. Perhaps Typhos, freed of his shackles, will be reborn now, too. And you, beloved of my brothers, I command you to leave this island. For soon it will be consumed by an inferno. It will become a beacon signaling a new era to the rest of the world. Go, before the fires engulf you, too."

Tibron backed away from her, the shock plain on his face. "Whatever you've become, or whatever speaks to you, I pray it has mercy on you, Shevia." He ran in the opposite direction from Typhos, in the direction he'd come from, still carrying his sword.

Shevia watched him for only a moment more, letting a distant part of herself experience sadness. Then she steeled herself and burned the emotion away with the fires raging within her. She turned to the west and stared at the distant cloud-wreathed peak of MagBreckan.

"And now, dear friend, I come to you."

TWENTY-TWO

A THOUSAND BURNING SUNS

High above the treetops of the Mystwood, Treorel blazed with energy in the night sky, pulling the world toward Crow Tallin. The world around Pomella no longer appeared as it once had. It was as if the encounter with the laghart wivan, the wolf-bear, and other axthos had broken the dam holding the celestial tide back.

As evidence of this, overlaid atop the small clearing where Pomella and the rest of her traveling party rested was a field of wild thistles, silvery and translucent. A swarm of fay bees buzzed through them, pollinating.

Pomella loved the Mystwood, but the near-constant travel of the past several weeks had worn on her. She longed for her cabin, her mattress, and the quiet solitude that life in Kelt Apar generally provided.

She stifled a yawn and glanced at Lal's unconscious form. Now wasn't the time to rest. Vivianna moved around their make-shift camp, seeing to the last of the preparations necessary for the ceremony they were about to perform.

Lal appeared to be sleeping, yet his eyes darted quickly beneath his closed lids. His fingers and legs twitched often, and Pomella wondered what he saw in his dreams. She refused to acknowledge the possibility that he was consumed by a fay and no longer present in his body.

"Hold on, Master," Pomella whispered. "I'm coming for you."

Lal's body lurched in reply. His mouth opened in a silent scream, before he collapsed again, not moving except for his hidden eyes.

"Hurry, Vivianna," Pomella said. "Please."

"Almost ready," Vivianna said as she moved around their makeshift camp, tending the fire. An uneaten pile of mushrooms and wild blackberries that Sim had found sat beside Pomella.

As focused as she was on the upcoming ceremony, Pomella couldn't help admire how calm Vivianna appeared. Her commitment to the solitary life of a Mystic impressed Pomella deeply. Someday, Vivianna would inherit the responsibility of Kelt Apar, and become the High Mystic of Moth. As much as the two of them shared, including living on the same grounds, it was becoming more and more obvious to Pomella just how different their paths were. Vivianna walked a well-trod path that had been carved by the feet of a thousand noble-born Mystics before her. Pomella, in turn, walked through a life that was as lonely and unfathomable as the deep groves of the Mystwood.

Vivianna momentarily shifted away from the fire, and Pomella caught Sim watching them from the nearby shadows, silently whittling a branch of elderberry. He'd taken over Vlenar's role as guide on the return journey. Despite being gone so many years, he had led them quickly back across the Ironlow Mountains for the past day, and in some ways he'd done so more efficiently than Vlenar.

Sim hardly spoke, though, and he slept apart from everyone else. Pomella yearned to approach him and try to bridge the divide between them, but there was no time. Whatever connection was possible with Sim would have to wait.

Vlenar, for his part, had stayed behind to tend to the dead lagharts. *I know thhheir ritesss,* he'd said. *I shhhall sssend them on to the Eternal Skies.*

His words made Pomella think of her conversation with Hizrith, and what he'd said to her about the laghart city of Lavantath, and the great palace called Indoltruna at its heart. Did Vlenar believe in the Golden Ones? Were they as real as the Saints, like Brigid and the others?

She didn't know, but the man whom she would normally ask lay dying before her. Right now, Lal was the only thing that mattered. Even Pomella's worries about Shevia would have to wait. The three brothers had gone after their sister and not returned, but Pomella couldn't bring herself to have anything more than fleeting concern for their fate, and Shevia's, right now.

Vivianna settled herself on the opposite side of the fire from Pomella. "Are you ready?"

Pomella nodded.

Nearby, Oxillian stood as a silent sentinel. He'd carried Lal the entire way from the velten into the Mystwood where they now were. Pomella had wanted to perform this ceremony right after Lal had collapsed and Shevia fled, but Vivianna had urged her to take him into the Mystwood first. The Myst was stronger there, closer to Kelt Apar. Even with Treorel, it was essential that they have every advantage possible to try to separate Lal from the creature within him.

"Grandmaster's body has been overtaken," Vivianna said, looking directly at Pomella. "A fay creature—who I believe may also be a Mystic—ensnares him. Without intervention, Lal will almost certainly die. In order to purge the wivan from his body, you will need to descend into his mind, and banish the creature. While you are within him, you will be vulnerable. You must return to your own body, or you risk dying as well. I will wait for you in between, and give you a beacon by which to guide you back. Sim and Oxillian will ensure we are not disturbed. Do you understand all of this?"

Pomella nodded. "Yes."

"Are you certain you cannot wait until we return to Kelt Apar, where the High Mystics can conduct this ceremony?" Oxillian asked.

"There's no time, Ox," Pomella said. "We may have already delayed too long. Besides, I'm his current student. It should be me."

Light from the campfire flickered across Vivianna's face. "Let us begin," she said. "Go with the Myst. Bring him back."

As one, Pomella and Vivianna closed their eyes and straightened their backs in matching cross-legged positions. They rested their palms faceup in their laps above their Mystic staves. A warm evening wind drifted through the Mystwood, dragging the scent of a nearby sage bush to Pomella's nose. The familiar smell reminded her of Lal's cabin, and that in turn steeled her resolve.

They drew upon the Myst. Its current was like the Creekwaters, swollen with rain, surging around her. She guided that Myst with her breath and mind, gently easing it toward Vivianna. Vivianna received it, and mixed the flow with her own. They had decided earlier that Vivianna would lead the ceremony. Her affinity for the fay would be a boon to their efforts.

Pomella felt, rather than saw, the Myst build between herself, Vivianna, and Lal. The hair on her arms stood upright. Her spine tingled. With this much power, what wonders could she achieve? She could single-handedly stand against the barons of Moth and force them to accept the Unclaimed, or to allow every commoner the opportunity to become a Mystic apprentice if they chose. With the Myst at her command, she could become a baroness herself. A queen. The Mystic Queen of Moth.

She let the surge settle, and breathed out the breath she now realized she'd been holding too long. It was normal for such stray thoughts to arise. The mind worked in strange ways. It was impossible to fight against its slippery nature. Instead, she'd been taught to separate herself from it. To be aware that it was running away on wild adventures. The Myst and its energies were bound to one's heart, not to the mind.

Taking one more calm, steadying breath, Pomella let those thoughts slip away so she could save the man who'd taught her those lessons. She sought the Crossroads, the place where her world blended into Fayün. It rushed to her, as easily as blinking. The sensation of her world faded around her until she floated alone in darkness. In the dim Crossroads she imagined a single point of light in that darkness, a pinprick of energy like a star.

The light flared, and even more of the Myst rushed her. Pomella inhaled sharply, forcing herself to not be drowned in the tide of energy. Suddenly the surge steadied itself and became a smooth flow. Rather than being drowned by it, Pomella now floated atop an ocean of Myst. A warm presence she recognized as Vivianna shone over her. There was nothing to see or use to otherwise identify the warmth as her friend. But it resonated in a way that unmistakably identified her.

"*Bayyy-lew!*" Vivianna chanted. Pomella didn't recognize the specific word but knew it was the anchor she could hold on to as she descended into Lal's mind.

Over and over Vivianna chanted "*Bayyy-lew!*" until the Myst surrounding them both vibrated in time to her words. Pomella had full control of the Myst surrounding them now, conducting its flow like a skilled musician played an instrument.

Another resonance of energy arose within the Crossroads with her. With every chant Vivianna intoned, it grew and became more solid. Pomella recognized it immediately.

Lal.

Over the course of seven years and countless sessions of sitting in his hut, going through these meditative exercises, Pomella had come to recognize the resonance that represented her master more easily than anything else. His light was her sun, the star around which she circled. In the human world, he was an old man, devoid of obvious power, filled with charm and a ridiculous sense of humor. But here, in the Crossroads, and when she'd sat with him before, he blazed brighter than anybody else she'd ever met.

Today, though, he was diminished. The normally vibrant energy that represented her master shone only a fraction of what it normally did. Pomella kept her emotional reaction to this at a safe distance.

Another presence grew around her, one she did not recognize. It was a second vibration of energy, shining with its own light, seeking to drown Lal's out.

The wivan.

"*Bayyy-lew!*" Vivianna chanted.

Pomella surged the Myst. "*Show yourself!*"

The light that entangled Lal responded by lashing out, slicing at them with the Myst. Pomella reacted faster than Vivianna. With a single thought, she whipped the Myst out, using it as a shield to deflect the attack. Outwardly, sitting beside Vivianna, Pomella did not move except for a slight eyebrow twitch.

Lal's light flickered. They were losing him. The wivan's grip strangled him. Whether the creature realized it or not, the wivan's possession of Lal only dragged them both deeper toward destruction.

Pomella focused on Lal's star and faded everything else away from her awareness. She *moved* toward him, willing her consciousness to shift such that soon she was on his star's threshold.

The wivan's fiery presence loomed over her, sinking his claws deeper into Lal's rapidly diminishing light. His formless eyes watched her, waiting. Pomella found it strange that he didn't attack her. It was as though he was waiting for something.

The answer came to her immediately. The wivan wanted to survive. He knew Lal was dying, and if he did so, the wivan would perish with him. The only way for the creature to survive was to find a new host to ensnare. If she went too far into Lal's consciousness, Pomella's body would end up providing a perfect host.

Pomella plunged toward Lal. Her instinct told her that hesitation would only hurt her at this point. With her formless body she rushed through the Crossroads. The pinprick that was Lal's light grew until it was a mountain, making her feel as though she were an ant beside MagDoon.

Like water tumbling over a cliff, there was a final rush as she raced toward Lal's light. Her mind burned away and she wanted to scream with a formless voice. The world shuddered. The world exploded in light.

She stood in a small, strange valley between rolling hills that she didn't recognize. White-gray boulders dotted grasslands while overgrown thorn hedges filled most of the valley floor. Thick gray clouds roiled overhead. Pomella breathed deep and the scent of pending rain filled her nostrils. Where was she? She peered down at herself and gasped. Her entire body, along with her Mystic staff, was formed of translucent, silvery light, as if she were a fay creature herself. Smoke gently wafted off her like fog above a pond on a cool morning.

Two ripples of motion tickled her ears. Pomella couldn't help but grin as Hector and Ena flew past her and swirled in the air. They zoomed around her, exploring the nearby boulders and thornbushes. Their enthusiasm and youth rolled over her.

She held out her palm for Hector to alight on. His body and her hand merged as easily as two shadows coming together. When they did so, she suddenly became *aware* of him in a way that went far beyond their normal bond. Every pulse of Hector's tiny heart trembled through her body. His thoughts skittered through her, leaping from place to place so quickly that she couldn't keep up. But mostly, overwhelming everything else, she felt

Hector's deep love for her. It was like a little match that lit her own heart.

Hector buzzed away from her hand and their connection broke. But a lingering affection remained with her. Pomella marveled at the experience, and at the little bird. She couldn't wait to tell Vivianna about it.

As she thought of Vivianna, a distant memory returned to her. Of where she was. And what she needed to do. Overhead, the rolling storm clouds pulled together. Lightning suddenly leaped through them, briefly illuminating their interior. A heartbeat later thunder shuddered the whole world. The sound shifted and vibrated, and it sounded to Pomella as though the thunder carried another sound with it, like it was delivering a message.

"Bayyyy-lew!"

Pomella had to steady herself. The whole world shook with Vivianna's warning, her reminder.

Another sensation tickled the back of Pomella's head. She turned in the direction of her hummingbirds and felt her stomach leap in surprise. A young boy, perhaps nine years old, stood on a nearby boulder. He had light-brown skin and wore a fine coat and shoes. A long braid of hair hung below his shoulders, marking him, along with his wealthy clothes, as a noble. In the distance behind the boy, upon what she guessed was the highest hill for some distance, stood a fine manor house. A ridiculous urge to bow to the boy came over Pomella, but she managed to ignore it.

The boy looked directly at her, clearly aware of her. She knew him, even though she'd never seen him like this. There was no mistaking his face. "Lal," she said, and this time she bowed.

Not because he was a young nobleman, but because, even as a little boy, he was forever her master.

The boy spoke in Qina and pointed.

Pomella looked over her shoulder but only saw more rocks and thornbushes. "I don't understand," she said to the boy.

Hector and Ena returned to her, and buzzed in an agitated manner. The boy pointed again, and this time he yelled.

Pomella looked again at where he was pointing. "What are you—?" She cut off as she saw it.

A short distance away, a thin column of smoke rose from what seemed to be the very center of a cluster of thornbushes. The smoke grew thicker as it rose. More thunder shook the ground.

"Ssshhhe comesss!"

Pomella spun back toward young Lal and saw him staring at the sky. Above him, the clouds had shifted again, this time to form the shape of a laghart's scaled face.

Lal yelled a Qina word, "*Gee!*," and ran back toward the manor house.

Flames erupted behind her, shooting upward from the thornbushes. Hector buzzed wildly above Pomella's head while Ena poked her free hand several times as if dipping for nectar from a flower.

The world began to blur and spin. Pomella had the distinct impression that wherever she was—Lal's memory most likely— it was fading, or ending. Hector zoomed away, following Lal, and Ena tapped her hand again. Pomella realized she was trying to get her to do something. Following instinct, she reached out and wrapped her hand around Ena.

Her wispy, silver body dissolved into light just as the

memory-world collapsed. She merged with Ena, and together they sped deeper into Lal's memories. She had no idea where she was going or how she was being guided. She held tight to her little hummingbird and trusted she would lead her true. The world rushed and exploded with light once more.

This time, she found herself standing just inside the doorway of a familiar room. Floating orbs of light drifted near the ceiling of the library in Kelt Apar's central tower.

Pomella opened her still-silver and translucent hand and released Ena. A heartbeat later Hector was there, too, dashing from nowhere to join her near the window on the far side of the library. Beside Pomella, on the other side of the doorway, stood a short Qina woman holding a Mystic staff. A thick head of curly braided hair plummeted down her back well past her hips. The woman, who was perhaps in her mid- to late thirties, wore a dress colored red for Crow Tallin. Her upper arms were bare, revealing a multitude of intricate tattoos. She gave no indication that she could see Pomella. Her attention was focused on the gathering of four other people in the library.

Two Mystics sat up on cushions at the far end of the room with their staves resting nearby.

One of them, who Pomella realized must be a High Mystic, was a man who also bore Qina heritage and wore dark-red robes. All of his gray hair was pulled into a bun above his head. Beside him sat a plump, kindly looking woman with light skin and short-cropped hair that was just beginning to fade from auburn to gray. Like the others, she wore a red dress, and this one had full-length sleeves with elaborate embroidery along its seams.

A sense of familiarity tickled Pomella's mind. She looked

around the library, trying to place it. A ring of paintings decorated the room, some resting between books on shelves and others mounted directly to the tower's stone walls. Pomella recognized most of these images, as they were portraits of former High Mystics who had presided over Kelt Apar. But several paintings that Pomella was familiar with were missing. One was Lal's portrait, and the others were of the masters before him, including the woman now seated in front of her.

"Ghaina," Pomella whispered. Indeed, it was her, a woman Pomella had only seen before in a painting. In awe of the being in her presence, Pomella stared at Great-Grandmistress Ghaina. She had been the High Mystic of Moth two generations before Lal's tenure. One of her students, Mistress Joycean, had become Lal's teacher.

Lal rarely spoke of either person, except to say that they had been the kindest people he'd ever met. Looking at Ghaina now, Pomella was stunned at how beautiful her blue eyes were. They were like bottomless pools of a clear, eternal ocean. According to the lore Pomella was familiar with, Ghaina had been taught by Saint Serrabeth, one of the legendary Mystics of Moth, whose portrait rested on a shelf just an arm's length away from where she stood. It filled Pomella with both joy and intimidation to know that she was now connected to that lineage.

The final two occupants of the room were young men who stood facing the High Mystics. Pomella could only see their backs but immediately recognized the first. It was Lal, now older, perhaps seventeen or eighteen, with his hair still long. Pomella's attention leaped to the oak staff he held that was about his height and slightly curved.

Realizing she was in the presence of not just one but two past masters of her lineage, Pomella bowed.

When she rose, she looked at the last person in the room, a boy no more than five or six years old. He seemed tall for his age, pale and skinny. From her angle, Pomella could see only his thin legs and bare feet poking out from a rough woolen blanket that was draped over his shoulders but kept slipping off. The boy, who had a shock of red hair, sniffed pathetically from time to time and appeared to struggle to keep the blanket on.

"Where in Mystwood did you find him?" asked the High Mystic with the gray hair bun in a thick Qina accent.

"I see him, naked lying under stone by north-most border, Master," said teenage Lal. "Mystic staff was near him. Downstairs now." His voice sounded less weathered to Pomella, and full of strength, although she could tell he was just beginning to learn the Continental language. He stood tall with his staff, full of pride and confidence. It was interesting to her how he'd changed in the sixty years between this Crow Tallin she was witnessing and the one she was alive for. What lessons did the young man before her have yet to learn? What experiences would he go through that would ultimately lead this enthusiastic youth to become her kindly and thoughtful master who had decided to retire from the world and give up his possessions, his title, and his power in order to seek something more profound?

Probably, she realized, the same lessons she herself had to learn.

"Do not be afraid, young man," said Great-Grandmistress Ghaina to the shivering boy. Her voice sounded like bell chimes. "Do you have a name?"

The skinny boy with red hair sniffed again but said nothing. He stared straight ahead, lost in his own mind, not seeing anything. The blanket slipped off his shoulder, exposing his naked backside. A bony spine stuck out on his emaciated back.

Lal bent down to retrieve the blanket and fixed it back around him. As Lal placed it near the boy's shoulder, the boy lazily lifted his hand to hold it in place. Pomella heart raced. The boy's hand was burned and mangled.

"Bayyy-lew!"

Vivianna's chant resonated across time and the tower, vibrating Pomella.

Nobody reacted to this except Ghaina, who blinked and looked around the room. She turned to peer at the nearby window where Hector and Ena had perched on the sill. A faint smile appeared on Ghana's face before she turned back. For a moment, the High Mystic's eyes slipped past Lal and the boy to settle on Pomella. Immediately Pomella's entire body tingled with energy. Her spine grew warm, from the base of her tailbone to the back of her neck. For a fraction of a second their eyes met, and Pomella found herself lost in the depths of her great-grandmistress' wisdom.

Then, quicker than a heartbeat, the moment passed and Ghaina looked again at the boy in front of her. She leaned forward in a kindly and conspiratorial manner.

"You can see the little hummingbirds, can't you?" Ghaina said to the boy.

Pomella felt as though her heart might pop out of her translucent chest.

At first the boy did not move, and she wondered if he understood their language. But slowly he turned and faced the far window where Hector and Ena were. Then his gaze dropped to the floor again and he did not move.

"The Myst resonates with him," said the other High Mystic. "There are curious and concerning circumstances about his arrival that I wish to explore."

Ghaina leaned back to an upright position on her cushion. "Yes," she said. "You were wise to bring him to us, Lal. But first, Master Challando, he must be cared for. He is just a boy, and needs love and attention. In time, we will learn his story."

"Crow Tallin is over," said High Mystic Challando. "You done much for all us, Mistress Ghaina. I will see boy raised in suitable house, and taught of the Myst."

"But is from Moth," said Lal, and Pomella couldn't help but raise an eyebrow at the way he interjected himself into the discussion between two High Mystics. Even with him standing right there, it was difficult for her to see that he was not much more than an eager apprentice.

"Perhaps," said Ghaina. "But there is more to his story. His mind wanders. I think he has seen other skies besides our own."

"Please," said Challando, "let me honor your Crow Tallin leadership. I will ensure this boy is brought up to become a Mystic. My apprentice, Mahnitha"—he gestured to the tattooed woman standing beside Pomella—"will take him to a good home and train him when he is old enough."

The woman beside Pomella stiffened slightly but bowed obediently.

"Bayyy-lew!"

The library rumbled all around Pomella as she realized the

memory was collapsing like the previous one had. Hector and
Ena leaped from the windowsill, returning to her.

"Very well, thank you," said Ghaina. She turned to the boy.
"You will be safe, young man. The High Mystic of Qin will see
that you are educated. Come back to us when your memory
returns."

Lal bowed to the High Mystics and gently guided the little
boy out of the library. As they left with Mahnitha, the boy peeked
briefly at Pomella. Familiarity raced over her.

Bhairatonix.

He was sixty years younger than the old High Mystic she
knew, but there was no mistaking his face and lanky frame. It
was strange to see his tumble of red hair rather than the long
gray beard she was accustomed to.

There was a vacancy to the boy's eyes, and she wondered
at the horrors or mysteries he'd witnessed. How did this crippled orphan become the High Mystic of Qin? She shivered, and
reached out to Ena as the memory-world vanished.

Pomella and Ena flashed through Lal's memories and landed
on Kelt Apar's lush green lawn. She stood near the southern
edge of the Mystwood, where Lal's cabin was. Only, in this
memory, the place where his cabin ought to have been was an
open patch of grass. The central tower stood where it always had,
although there were fewer cottages on its far side. Above her, the
same dark clouds she'd seen earlier roiled with pending rage.

Ena flew from her hand and joined Hector. As the hummingbirds buzzed across the open lawn, they passed two men
strolling toward her. Lal and Bhairatonix, both carrying Mystic
staves, were more familiar to Pomella in that they were much
closer to the ages she knew them as. Lal's long hair and serene

face marked him as the High Mystic of Moth, before his retirement.

The two masters walked right past Pomella with an easy manner. As usual, Bhairatonix kept his left hand tucked into his layered robes. Pomella knew now why he kept it that way. Neither gave any indication that he could see Pomella. She walked slightly behind them, listening carefully.

"I'm sorry to hear of the devastation the plague has brought your island," Bhairatonix said in Continental. "Is it as widespread as they say?"

Lal sighed. "It is worse."

"That is unfortunate," Bhairatonix said.

"Will you help us?" Lal said, and Pomella could hear an uncharacteristic desperation in his voice. The lines on his face, along with the circles under his eyes, told a story of stress and little rest.

Bhairatonix did not respond, his expression suddenly distant.

"Please, friend," said Lal, "thousands suffer. Whole communities decimated. You are the greatest healer among the High Mystics. Is it true you cured a man with the plague in Qin?"

The desperation in Lal's voice broke Pomella's heart. She remembered from her childhood when the Coughing Plague had torn through Moth, claiming her mhathir's life, along with the lives of so many others in her village. At the time, people like her fathir, and others who had survived only to lose their families, had bitterly cursed Lal for his lack of assistance. They believed he turned a blind eye to dying commoners, but Pomella could see in Lal's face just how desperately he sought a way of helping.

Bhairatonix remained silent for a while as they circled the outer edge of Kelt Apar. Finally, he spoke, but his eyes did not turn to Lal. "The Mystic Star will return in a decade and a half," he said. "It will bring with it, of course, Crow Tallin."

Lal eyed Bhairatonix suspiciously. "Yes?"

"For centuries we High Mystics have gathered here to secretly prevent a certain event from happening. In these desperate times, perhaps our thinking should change."

"What do you mean?" Lal asked with a hesitant edge to his voice.

Bhairatonix finally turned his gaze on to Lal, and Pomella could see a fiery excitement dancing in his eyes. "I speak, of course, of the Reunion."

Lal frowned. "I do not understand. How—"

"Think on it, Ahlala!" Bhairatonix snapped. "Think! Kelt Apar is the most powerful location in this world because it is closest to Fayün. During Crow Tallin, the worlds merge. What if we allowed the Reunion to take place? What if we let the worlds *stay* united?"

Lal stared at the other High Mystic with a wide-eyed expression of shock. "I asked your help because you are the only one who can cure plague. In response, you speak of what is forbidden. You suggest we break our most sacred duty."

"I suggest we harness the power of a new world and eliminate all suffering! Look beyond dogma and consider what wonders we could achieve."

"It will destroy us all," Lal said. "The fire and blood . . ."

Bhairatonix stopped and loomed over Lal. "Your island is already burning with the flames of a disease you cannot control."

Thunder rumbled through the memory.

"Bayyy-lew!"

Vivianna's chant sounded across Kelt Apar. A shadow crossed the compound, and Pomella saw another figure hovering above the path in front of them. He had a vaguely laghart-like appearance, with sharp spikes emerging from his arms and legs and spine. Bat-like wings protruded from his back. The wings flapped hard, keeping the creature aloft. Like Pomella, he was made from silver smoke that blew in an otherwise-unseen wind.

The wivan reached behind his back and withdrew a long, serpentine-shaped knife. The wivan's eyes found hers, then latched on to Lal with menacing force.

"Lal!" Pomella shouted as the wivan swooped down to attack.

A surprised expression crossed Lal's face. He looked toward Pomella but seemed to stare straight through her.

The wivan closed the distance between them with lightning speed, his knife poised to strike.

With instinctive force, Pomella summoned her hummingbirds. Hector crashed into the smoky creature's face. The wivan spun and waved him off, refusing to let the little bird slow him down. Lal and Bhairatonix continued to walk, seemingly unaware of the pending attack.

"What you suggest is madness," Lal said to Bhairatonix. "For nine hundred years we guard against the true threat of Crow Tallin. The Reunion will not bring power like you think. It only brings death."

"I am disappointed in you," said Bhairatonix. "You are the First among us, yet you do not have the wisdom to see the truth. Perhaps you are no longer qualified to preside over this island."

Pomella watched as Bhairatonix looked directly at the wivan and took a step back to give him room.

The wivan leaped again, and this time Pomella had no choice. She leaped in front of Lal just as the creature stabbed. She managed to knock aside the knife, but the wivan retaliated with a claw toward her throat. She felt the creature wrap himself around her, trying to choke her life away.

The memory-world tore itself apart like thin canvas, and she found herself spinning in a world of utter darkness. The only light she could see shone from herself and the wivan trying to destroy her.

"Bayyy-lew!"

Vivianna's voice pulsed through Pomella, giving her strength. Connected as she was to the wivan, she expected to feel cold rage coming off him. Instead, the creature expressed only grim determination.

"The Reunion comesss. Lagnaraste will be ffffree," breathed the wivan with deadly calm.

Pomella filled herself with the Myst and, bolstered by Vivianna's chant, rallied her own assault on the wivan.

They tumbled through an eternal darkness, into the depths of a place she could not fathom or describe. Pinpricks of light illuminated all around her.

"Bayyy-lew!"

The chant was fainter this time, more distant. More stars emerged in the blackness as they fell, seemingly brought to life by their passing presence, each giving her a mote of strength.

Pomella knew that she struggled not only for her life but for Lal's as well. If she failed, the wivan would consume both of them.

The creature clawed at her neck, although now their translucent bodies had twisted together such she could no longer sense where hers ended and his began. The wivan's cold resolve filled her, and a corner of her mind wondered if he felt her panic and fear, and used those emotions as kindling.

"You will not take my master from this world!" she snarled.

The wivan responded with another assault. By now Pomella no longer sensed a body surrounding her. There was only conscious *space*, and the glowing lights of eternity. The wivan swelled around her, and she sensed herself dim.

"*Bayyy-lew.*" The chant was a far distant whimper.

Pomella could struggle no more. The wivan was too powerful. She had nothing left to throw at him, no means of fighting. This was how it would end. Sitting in stillness, trapped within an endless fall through the unfamiliar void beyond the Crossroads.

Pomella. Huzzo.

One of the pinpricks of light pulsed with the word. Her name. Her Mystic name. It came from Lal's voice, warm and affectionate.

Huzzo.

The name echoed from another direction, from another star in the endless sky. It was a woman's voice, one she did not recognize.

Huzzo. From another direction, another star, another woman. This voice she did recognize from the memory she'd just earlier witnessed. It was the silvery chiming voice of High Mystic Ghaina.

One by one her name rang out through the endless stars, voiced by the past masters of untold generations. The lineage of her Mystical past blazed around her.

"Help me!" she called to the masters. "Let this lineage not die."

Like the dawn arriving after a long winter night, strength, warmth, and the Myst bloomed within Pomella.

It was as though a thousand burning suns rested in her heart, giving her their strength. She inhaled deeply, filling herself with the Myst. The wivan became distinct from her, and confused. He scrabbled to keep hold of her, but Pomella felt herself growing in the void, becoming larger and larger until the wivan was little more than an insect trying to cling to her.

She exhaled a word, "Huzzo," and she exploded with the Myst. The wivan vanished in an instant, incinerated by her light. She pulled the energy of a thousand past masters, seeing their lives and faces in one instantaneous moment. Each one had a star now, and each connected to her with a beam of silver so that she shone with infinite rays coming off her.

As she exhaled again, the beams vanished, leaving only the drifting stars around her. The memory of endless lives died with it, but their echo remained.

Far above her, she heard Vivianna call, "*Bayyy-lew!*"

The entire void, and the Crossroads beyond, began to tremble. She was still within Lal, and he was dying.

Pomella radiated a pulse of thanks and love to her past masters, acknowledging their ever-present desire to guide her.

She peered upward through the void, and *lifted* herself toward Vivianna. The stars roared past her; the place she was in began to collapse, just as the memories had. She fled faster, knowing she had to get out.

"*Bayyy-lew!*"

The chant sounded stronger now, but more desperate, telling her Vivianna knew what was happening.

Pomella let go of her worries. She let her anxieties and fears drop away like weights that only served to hold her back. She remastered the sense of calm that Lal had shown her, and let herself soar to Vivianna's voice with the speed of a sunbeam.

She opened her eyes to the human world, and found Vivianna sitting beside her. They looked at each other for a moment, then smiled at the same time. A tear traced down Vivianna's cheek, and Pomella felt one on her own.

"Thank you," Pomella whispered.

Vivianna took her hand and squeezed.

They turned to Lal. His face was gray yet calm. No more tension lined his face. His eyes were closed, yet his lips moved.

Free of the fears she'd been carrying, Pomella slipped beside her dying master and took his hand. She leaned in and kissed his forehead.

"The oracle," Lal whispered, and Pomella had to place her ear by his lips to hear. "She carry . . . danger. Find her. Find . . . Lagnaraste."

He drifted, and his eyes grew distant.

"Lal," Pomella said, stroking his head. "I'm here. Stay."

"I join the masters," Lal breathed, "to dwell in the Deep, so tranquil, so calm. Go there to find me. Find . . . everything, my Huzzo."

His last breath touched Pomella's cheek, and he died. His body relaxed, then dissolved into a silvery light that wafted around her once, twice, and was gone.

TWENTY-THREE

SAINT BRIGID'S TEARS

Moonlight shivered on the surface of the lake, creating a wobbling twin of the near-full orb hanging in the sky. Silence filled the clear night as if nature itself respected the solemnity of what was occurring at the shore. Pomella stood beside Vivianna with her head bowed and both hands holding her Mystic staff.

Sim had been the one to find this lake, a quiet oasis surrounded by poplar, oak, and peach trees located a quarter hour's walk east of their campsite. He waited nearby, standing beneath a peach tree whose branches rustled in the wind.

Vlenar, who'd returned from the velten at sunrise, approached the lake's edge, carrying Lal's folded robes. The garments were the only things resembling his remains. Pomella's hands still tingled from the cool sensation of his body dissolving into light when he'd died. Even now, it was hard to believe he'd actually been there, with her, in her arms less than a day ago. It was as though he'd never existed. Her mind refused to bring forth a clear image of his face. It was like trying to remember a face from a dream.

Conflicting emotions of sadness and joy for her master's ascension into the Myst wrestled within her. Her instinct as a human was to only see the end of his life, and the hole his absence left in her heart. But another part of her, the trained Mystic within her, who had direct, firsthand experience with the Myst, knew that Lal's reality was just another transition. *Just as rain is pulled from the sea and returned through rivers,* Lal had once said, *so life arises and returns to the Myst.*

Still, Pomella could not stop tears from welling beneath her eyes as Vlenar placed Lal's bundled clothing onto the edge of the shore. Sim had offered to weave a basket, but Pomella had said there'd be no need.

Pomella let a moment of silence pass over the gathering after Vlenar stepped away. High above, shining nearly as brightly as the moon, was the red Mystic Star. Pomella lifted her chin and swirled the Myst. It flooded her in a massive tide, threatening to sweep her away. Without moving, she tapped the Myst and sounded a silver bell.

"Oxillian," she called, "it is time!"

The ground rumbled and the Green Man emerged from the ground. Heavy branches lifted amid piles of dirt to build the bones of his familiar form. Overripe peaches dotted his body and formed his eyes along with exposed seeds that acted as pupils.

The wind rose from the southwest—a different direction from the normal eastern winds—carrying the sound and feeling of a rushing tide. Streaks of silver light sailed over the landscape toward Pomella, across the mountains and grassland, before suddenly resolving into the likenesses of Yarina and the other High Mystics. Their silver apparitions glowed like candles.

Pomella bowed to the fay-like images. "Welcome, High Mystics."

"Hello, Pomella," said Yarina. "We come at great expense, riding the surging tides of Treorel. Our time is short."

"Yes, Mistress," Pomella said. "Do you have words to share?"

"Many," said Yarina. "But most will have to wait. Given the circumstances of our time, and in deference to our master's love of simplicity, I will say only that his passing strengthens us in our most needed hour. Just as he once took the oaths of an apprentice, and received his Anointment to become a master, now he once more paves a path for us all to follow. I owe him everything, and reaffirm my love and commitment to his vision."

The other High Mystics remained silent, with their heads bowed. Silver smoke rolled off each of them, wafting across the lakeside grass. The twin masters, Angelos and Michaela, stood as still as the moon.

It was Master Willwhite who caught Pomella's attention, however. His face, which had always been delicate, had shifted in subtle ways, and was now definitely female. The High Mystic's majestic beauty shone like a star, filling Pomella with an unspoken reminder that everything in life changed.

Heavy tears covered Master Ollfur's face, but so did a smile that stretched to his eyes. Pomella imagined he was thinking of a joke he'd shared with Lal. She appreciated his tears. It lightened her, knowing she wasn't alone in her grief.

She noted, too, the absence of Bhairatonix and Ehzeeth but

did not dwell on it. Whatever their reasons for not coming, they were not her concern. This ceremony was not about them.

Pomella waved her hand, extending the Myst beyond her, and one by one shimmering white lily petals unfolded on the water's surface, revealing a flower with a golden center. Hundreds appeared, until they covered all of the visible lake.

With another wave of her hand, this time the opposite way, Pomella deftly formed a silver boat beneath the bundle of robes resting on the lakeshore. She'd only planned to craft a simple raft, but the Myst extended itself as if of its own will, elongating what she created until it formed the shape of a sinuous creature, with a long neck and serpentlike head framed by a great mane of flowing hair. The stern extended upward in a long tail and curled at the end, acting as a hook for a globe of light that shone bright and blue. Collectively, the boat had become a scaled serpent radiating power and majesty.

A dragon.

"And thus the Myst pays tribute to a grandmaster," said Willwhite. "Remarkable."

The boat sat in stillness above the lake's lily-covered surface, rippling small wakes of silvery smoke at its waterline. Pomella thought of Lal's campfire story, and how dragons were one with the land, supposedly bringing harmony to the world and its inhabitants. Lal's life was marked with notable struggle, none more apparent perhaps than his tenure during the years of the Coughing Plague, but she had been blessed to see his more experienced, self-aware self.

Harder the winter, brighter the bloom. Lal's recent words echoed in her mind.

He'd given up all labels and even his Mystic staff in order

to experience the true essence of what it meant to be a Mystic. By shedding himself of distractions, he'd allowed himself to further the agenda of the Deep Myst. Pomella did not fully understand it yet, but she silently vowed to dedicate her life to it, just as he had. If she, or any of them, survived past Crow Tallin.

As it often did, a song welled within Pomella's heart. It longed to be freed by the winds of her breath, a tribute to carry Grandmaster's funeral boat into the sky.

But like her time at her fathir's graveside at Reyman's Hey outside Oakspring, she couldn't bring herself to sing. With her fathir, it had been because none of the songs fit their strained relationship. Now, with Lal, who valued simplicity and privacy, she thought she'd save it for another time, when she was alone and unburdened by stress.

Pomella lifted her palm skyward and held it just moments before snapping it down. The boat, the lilies, and Lal's clothes burst into flame, making it appear as if the lake were on fire. The scattering ashes rose to the stars. The mixture of red, orange, and silver fire reflected off the water before it all merged into a single blue color that somehow spoke to Pomella of Lal.

One by one the High Mystics faded away. Yarina was the last to leave. Pomella saw tears upon her silver cheeks. They met eyes, and for a moment they were not student and master, but rather equal peers sharing a moment of sorrow for the teacher they had in common. With a smile, Yarina faded.

Oxillian smiled at Pomella, then rolled himself back into the ground, leaving his branches and peaches in the muddy soil.

Out on the lake, the blue flames extinguished themselves, leaving the water tranquil.

Vivianna, who had remained silent throughout the brief ceremony, said, "I will set up our cots for tonight. We should be walking by sunrise."

"Return without me," Pomella said, her eyes still on the place where the boat had vanished. Nothing disturbed the water in that spot. It was as if nothing had passed over it.

She turned to Vivianna, who had a surprised expression on her face. "Take Vlenar and hurry for Kelt Apar."

"But where—?" Vivianna began.

"I have to find Shevia. She's somehow important to something happening with the fay, and maybe all of Crow Tallin."

"I will go, too."

It was Sim who spoke, and Pomella found herself grateful for his offer.

"Can you track her?" she asked, knowing the answer before he replied.

He nodded, but it was little more than a dip of the chin.

"I believe Shevia is ensnared by a powerful fay creature," Pomella said, voicing her suspicions. "In some way, she's become, or is in the process of becoming, a wivan."

Vivianna's eyes went wide. "By the Saints," she said. It was the first time in all these years together Pomella had heard her Continental-born friend use the Mothic expression. "What will you do when you find her?"

Pomella eyed both of them. "Whatever I must."

Shevia stood at a crossroads. Dirt caked her dress, hair, and feet. She'd traveled for at least a day or two, although her mind was so lost within itself that she no longer cared to keep track. Her stomach rumbled.

The path behind her led back toward the Ironlow Mountains. Up ahead, an intersection offered a road going north–south with a sign indicating Oakspring and Sentry. She brushed her disheveled hair from her face. Directly to the west, Mag-Breckan loomed above the northern edge of the Mystwood.

An oxcart plodded south along the main road. A farmer and a younger man—probably his son, about Shevia's age—walked beside it while a short-haired woman clutching a sleeping baby rode on top of the cart. The farmer eyed Shevia suspiciously before an expression of shock bloomed on his face when he saw her Mystic staff. He snapped something to his family and they pulled the oxcart to a stop.

Moments later, the men prostrated themselves on the ground in front of her, while the woman bowed as low as she could from her seat. "Greet'ns, Mistress," said the farmer into the dirt. "We're on our way to the Mystwood. They-a says the High Mystic is protecting anybody who stays close to Kelt Apar."

Shevia licked her parched lips. "Do you have water?" she said in their language.

The farmer exchanged looks with his son before the younger one rose and brought Shevia a hide flask from the cart.

It was all Shevia could do to not snatch the flask from his hands. The farmer's son bowed awkwardly as she guzzled the water until she coughed. Catching her breath, Shevia forced herself to bring focus to her present environment. She opened her mouth to thank the farmer but then stopped.

Behind the family, on the far side of the road, stood the ghostly silver image of a young boy. He was naked and disheveled, with his arms wrapped around his body. He shivered, with his knees touching, and kept his eyes on the ground. Sorrow and fear radiated from him like heat from a fire.

"Ah, Mistress," said the farmer, "begg'n pardon, but are you well? Can we assist you in any way?"

There was something terribly familiar about the boy. A wind that Shevia could not feel tugged at his hair. He raised his face and looked directly at Shevia.

A snarl curled at the corner of Shevia's face. The boy turned and ran west, into the wilderness, toward MagBreckan.

"Mistress?" the farmer repeated, concern and fear rising in his voice.

"Food," Shevia said at last. "As much as you can spare. Quickly!"

The baby cradled in the woman's arms began to cry. The farmer and son hurried to the cart, and quickly sorted through their stores to fill a canvas sack for her. Shevia waited with as much patience as she could muster. The silver apparition of the little boy dwindled into the trees on the far side of the road.

The farmer handed Shevia the sack of food, which she accepted without comment. They bowed to her and she strode after the silver boy.

As she passed the woman and the crying child she stopped. Looking down at them, she saw a fist-sized fay creature perched upon the baby boy's head. The child's family obviously couldn't see it. The fay appeared to be some kind of insect with six pairs of wings and multifaceted eyes. Its snout sucked upon the baby while its abdomen swelled with whatever it was it drew from the child.

Shevia reached her hand toward the fay. Presumably thinking Shevia was directing the gesture toward her, the mother
bowed her head and said, "Please, great mistress, we are your
humble servants."

Shevia closed her fist and the fay insect burst into flames. It
squealed once and popped into a cloud of incinerated ash.

Shevia touched the child's head and felt it burning from fever. She took a deep breath, and drew the heat from the boy into
her own body. He quieted immediately. His bright eyes lingered
on her a moment before closing as he drifted off to sleep.

"Your child will not suffer from fever anymore," Shevia told
the woman.

The mother's eyes widened. The woman placed her hand on
the child's forehead and began to tremble. Shevia saw the mother
wore a cord of intricately twisted ropes around her wrist, which
she understood to be a local custom. "Than-thank you, great
mistress," the woman said. "You are beyond kind."

"Do not go to Kelt Apar," Shevia said. "The world is about to
change. Go east. Go to Enttlelund." She stumbled over the
awkward name with her accent. "Go to the Continent."

"As you command, Mistress," said the woman. "But we cannot pay for passage."

Shevia reached down and pulled the woven cord from the
woman's trembling wrist. Wrapping the Myst around the cord,
she *shifted* the bracelet's nature, and rewove it as a cord of gold.
She dropped it into the woman's hand.

"Go. Give thanks to Sitting Mother."

The woman's mouth fell open, but she could not find words.
Shevia swept away from the family and did not look back. As

she approached the tree line where the boy had vanished, she began to run.

Evening descended as she finally caught up to the boy. For most of the day, Shevia had trudged through untamed wilderness by scrambling over rocks and crossing jagged streams. More than once, Shevia was glad she had her Mystic staff to help her navigate the various obstacles she encountered. Because this was the edge of the Mystwood, and Treorel shone brighter than ever in the sky, denizens of Fayün crawled all around her. She shooed them away, and on one occasion had to incinerate an overeager axthos who leaped at her from a tree.

She found the ghostly boy standing on the edge of a wide pool that was fed by a towering waterfall. Silver smoke rolled off the boy's naked body and mixed with the similarly colored mist rising from the waterfall's base. He was tall and lanky for his age, with a knobby backbone. He faced away from her, his gaze directed into the water.

Shevia steeled herself. "Show yourself."

The boy looked over his shoulder. Tears streaked his dirty face. Her earlier suspicions had been correct. Her teeth clenched.

"You," she sneered. Many of Bhairatonix's features were the same as a child that he had as an adult. It was strange to see him this way, a weak, crippled little child compared to the towering master she had once feared. Her mind raced as she wondered why and how she was seeing him.

"Why are you here?" Shevia snarled.

The boy sniffed once, soundlessly, and fell into the pool.

Shevia approached the water's edge and peered in. It looked like a normal pool of water to her, but as she gazed into it she beheld a shimmering light deep within its depths. That light called to her, like a shiny coin at the bottom of a fountain.

"Shevia," came a voice from nearby.

Instinct took over. Shevia *uncoiled* and hurled a globe of fire at the speaker. Too late, she realized who it was.

The fireball roared across the twenty steps between her and Sim, but he was ready. He lifted his onkai blades and crossed them in front of himself. The fireball crashed into the blades and exploded in a shower of sparks and ash.

Shevia's head spun as reality crashed back to her. Her body relaxed, leaving her trembling. Her heart pounded as she caught her breath.

For several thundering heartbeats, nothing moved except a scorching ring of fire surrounding Sim. Shevia took a deep breath, and wafted the Myst away from her, extinguishing the flames. The inferno groaned as it snuffed out.

Sim lowered his onkai. The flames Shevia had thrown at him had only singed some hair on his arms but, beyond that, had not affected him. He studied her.

She had a wild look about her eyes. She still wore the same dress she'd had on at the velten, but now it had holes that revealed bloody scrapes beneath. Smoke and ash swirled in the space between them.

He sheathed his onkai. "You could've burned the forest," he said in Continental.

Her eyes narrowed. "Why did you follow me?"

From the moment she'd fled the velten, the silver path had illuminated in his sight, drawing him westward, in the direction she'd gone. Whenever he let his gaze linger for more than a minute in one place, it emerged from the ground and lit a path. He didn't always know where the path would lead, but this time he'd known from the start that it would lead to her.

Traveling with Pomella had been more awkward than he'd anticipated. They'd had two days and a night alone on the road, mostly traversed in silence. He'd led the way, feeling her eyes on the back of his head the whole time. So much had changed in their years apart.

Pushing those thoughts aside, he approached Shevia. The tattoo on her shoulder had grown, and now encompassed most of her exposed skin. The serpent's scales were more defined, more textured, as if they were truly a part of her flesh rather than inked illustrations. As Shevia moved, the serpent itself seemed to shift separately from her.

"Your skin," he said.

She narrowed her eyes. "I will never be powerless again."

He nodded. He didn't fully understand, but it was clear she was drawing power from a connection to something related to the tattoo. "Yah. You have power. But you crave freedom."

Silence stretched between them. Finally, he scratched his head. "My fathir's a blacksmith back home," he said, reluctantly bringing up his own past. "Tried to impress him once. I over-forged a scythe commissioned by Ilise AnCutler's sons. I wanted to make the metal as hard as I could, figuring it'd be better. *Stronger.* But all it did was shatter."

He noted her hands shaking, and whether that was from the Myst coursing through her, or nerves, Sim couldn't tell.

"I've been reforged," Shevia said in a low voice.

"Yah, but by whom?" he said. "And for what purpose?"

She looked at him, visibly surprised.

He pressed on. "Do you remember telling me we are alike? Both broken by what we've lost. We can be found. When Crow Tallin is over, we can return to Qin."

He wanted to go back to the highlands, away from Moth. He could take Shevia home, and from there they would part.

"You cannot repair me," Shevia said. "Only Sitting Mother can."

The name rang through Sim like an iron bell. Memories flashed in his mind: Swiko, the rag doll, the stones at the summit of the mountain, the little cairns he'd seen around the slaver wagon and later his cabin.

"What did you say?" he whispered.

"Sitting Mother," she repeated, but this time in Qina. It sounded to him exactly how Swiko had spoken the name.

Sim couldn't meet her eyes anymore. Even here, on the other side of the world from the highlands, Sitting Mother haunted Sim. He half-expected to turn around and see a cairn of stones piled beside the pond shore.

"She has guided you, too, hasn't she?" Shevia said with a slight tone of wonder to her voice. She'd switched to speaking Continental again. She leaned closer to him. "Then it is no wonder she brings us together."

Slowly, as if afraid he would burn her, Shevia reached toward his face in exactly the same way that Swiko had done the day she'd convinced him to stay in the highland village for the winter. He recalled those quiet winter evenings spent with her, and how bittersweet they'd been in the end. Gently, he leaned away from Shevia, not letting her touch him.

She stepped closer to him. "Come with me," she whispered. "To Fayün, where we can meet Sitting Mother face-to-face together."

Sim held her eyes and for a moment saw deep into her, past the pain, past the confusion, to find a shy, vulnerable woman seeking freedom.

"I'm sorry," he said.

In one swift motion he placed a shiverbane-soaked cloth over her nose and mouth. Shevia's eyes widened, then rolled back in her head. Sim caught her as the potent herb dragged her to unconsciousness.

Pomella emerged from the Mystwood trees. All around her in the trees and grass, small woodland denizens of Fayün peered at her, perhaps not realizing they'd drifted into the human world, wondering what she was doing near their homes. She walked quietly, her Mystic staff pressing into the forest floor.

Sim stood near the edge of a wide pond that fed a stream leading south. He'd told her that the creek met others before eventually terminating at Loch Bracken. The waterfall, known to the locals as Toormabridga Fallah, poured into the pond, having been fed year-round by the rain and snow running off Mag-Breckan.

Toormabridga Fallah. The Falls of Saint Brigid's Tears. Pomella had grown up less than twelve miles from this location, as the crow flew. She'd heard of this location but, along with everything else on MagBreckan, had never ventured out to see it. Standing near the swirling mist wafting off the falls, she felt her world and Fayün blending more tightly than ever.

She lowered her hood and gazed skyward. Treorel would sail behind the moon in two days, marking the peak of Crow Tallin.

Hundreds of silver lotus flowers sprouted around the shore. They were made entirely of translucent light, but within their cores were tiny motes of blue fire. Yes, Pomella thought, this location was different from other places in the Mystwood. There was a sense of permanence here.

She turned her attention back to Sim. He was folding a handkerchief and carefully placing it in his pocket. Shevia lay at his feet, eyes closed, leaning against his leg. Her Mystic staff lay beside her.

"I don't know how long she'll be out," Sim said.

Pomella bent to look more closely at Shevia's tattoo. It had grown since Pomella last saw her, confirming what she'd suspected all along, that it wasn't a simple application of ink beneath the skin. The serpent's—no, the *dragon's*—scales were textured and recessed into her skin. Pomella considered touching them but thought better of it.

"Take her to Kelt Apar with me," Pomella said. "There's somebody I have to speak to."

Sim studied her for a moment, giving away no other outward reaction. "Why?" he finally asked.

"Because there's something going on with this Lagnaraste that I need to know about," she said. "If Shevia was ensnared by a powerful wivan, and it wants to break free, then Crow Tallin is likely the time it wants to do so."

Sim nodded, which was not the reaction she'd expected him to have. "Is this the entrance?" he said.

"Yah, to Fayün," she said. "This is what she was seeking. I never knew a place like this existed, but I feel like this entrance has always been here."

"What do you expect to find there?" Sim said.

Pomella sighed and held out her hand for him to take. "Answers, Sim. With Lal gone, I'm alone on this path. Something bigger than we know is happening with Crow Tallin. It's going to affect us all, and I need to be prepared."

"The High Mystics expect you back," Sim said.

"Yes, but what help will I be when Crow Tallin arrives?" She peered into the depths of the waterfall. "Here I can make a difference."

He considered her with those blue eyes she knew so well. She longed to know the story of his last seven years. "I wonder," she said, "will we always circle around one another like this, like the Mystic Star passing by our world, never to linger, but only to be seen at a distance?"

His unspoken reply hid behind whatever memories he carried.

The Myst stirred within Pomella, reminding her of the urgency. She backed away into the pond until her ankles were wet.

Hector and Ena swooped down from the trees, dancing with the other fay birds chirping and leaping from branch to branch.

Without words, she pushed the Myst toward Shevia, creating a shimmering sphere, which shrank and reshaped itself to fit her exact shape. Pomella marveled at how easily she manipulated the Myst now. By instinct alone she found she had the knowledge and skill to manifest whatever she needed. Under Treorel's power, using the Myst had become as easy as singing.

"That will keep her asleep for a while," Pomella said.

She turned and waded into the water, using her staff to steady herself. Hector and Ena buzzed excitedly, urging her on. "Show me the way to your realm, little ones," she said.

They spun once and darted straight into the waterfall, vanishing behind its misty downpour. Pomella paused at its edge, soaked now completely, and standing in water up to her waist.

"Pomella!" Sim called.

She looked back at him over her shoulder.

He spoke, and she could barely discern what he said.

"Come back to me."

The words haunted Pomella as she turned toward the cascade, and stepped through.

TWENTY-FOUR

THE TOWER OF ETERNAL STARLIGHT

Pomella plunged through a firmament of worlds and stars. The water surrounding her became rain, then mist, and then sunshine. She began falling down, only to feel her stomach flip as she realized she was now falling *up*. The colors of the Mystwood—the greens and browns of the trees and ground—slipped into uniform shades of silver.

She didn't crash to her feet but rather found herself already standing knee-deep in the center of a waterfall-fed pond resting in the forest of a silver world. The spinning feeling settled, and Pomella looked around.

Fayün. The realm that existed on the other side of the human world, like the opposite side of a coin. Trees that moments before had not been visible to her now towered above her, stretching impossibly high toward a gray evening sky. The flowers she'd observed on the shores of the pond beside Sim and Shevia were there with their tiny azure flames trembling within their cores. Familiar fresh scents filled her nose, like the clean air after a rainstorm.

Looking down, she found she was naked, yet she still held her Mystic staff. A rush of self-consciousness washed over her, but she shook it off. She was a Mystic, a traveler between worlds, and she had nothing to be embarrassed about. Still, though, she preferred not to go uncovered. She swept her staff around her head with two hands and pulled flowers and water and grass around herself. They wove themselves together under her instinctive command, forming a graceful yet simple dress dotted with lily petals. Her feet remained bare, just as she liked.

She smiled, satisfied with herself. Vivianna would be proud, too, she knew, although she wished her friend could share this experience of being in Fayün with her.

Setting aside thoughts of Vivianna, Pomella strode out of the pond to stand at its shore. No water clung to her. She found she was perfectly dry, as though she'd emerged from a bath and already toweled herself off. Her sturdy dress of flowers and grass slipped across her body as she moved, feeling like silk. She peered closely at the fabric and could see water coursing through it in rivulets.

A shimmer of gold caught her eye. In this land of a single color, the golden light shone like a bonfire. It came from the branch of a tree, and Pomella saw that it was a squirrel. Golden smoke wafted from it, just like with a fay creature back in the human realm. The squirrel scampered along the branch and leaped to another tree and, mid-jump, faded back to the human realm.

As she watched the squirrel vanish, more golden creatures and plants appeared along the quiet glade she stood within. "Well, would you look at that," she muttered to herself.

Here in Fayün, just as in the human realm, the worlds were merging. She glanced upward, past the massive treetops, and there, shining as expected, was the bloodred Mystic Star. Its power shone down on her, filling her with an abundance of the Myst.

For a brief moment, she saw a large golden shape appear beside her at the water's edge. It was Sim, formed entirely of misty golden light. He stared past her at the waterfall.

She reached out to touch his arm. Her hand tingled as she did so, but he did not stir. Most people, even rangers, could generally not feel or sense occupants of Fayün. "Go to Kelt Apar," she whispered, dropping her hand. "I'll return soon."

Pomella mentally reached out to Hector and Ena. They flew to her immediately, appearing just as they normally did. She held her hand out for them. "Can you show me where to go?" she asked.

The little birds looked at each other, as if each was wondering if the other sibling had the answer. Pomella frowned.

A bubbling noise sounded behind her. Pomella turned as a wide, slightly curved stone lifted out of the water. As it rose, more and more of it became visible until it filled nearly the entire diameter of the pond.

Pomella's eyes widened as a massive scaled head emerged from the water as well. This wasn't a stone, she realized. It was a shell.

A tortoise, made entirely of shimmering silver light, of course, rose before her and moved his head in her direction. Water and smoky mist dripped off him. He angled his head so one of his eyes focused on her.

Pomella waited for him to speak, but after a long moment of silence she determined that he either couldn't or was choosing not to talk. She marveled at the creature, having never seen a fay of his size.

She curtsied. "I am Pomella AnDone," she said, "a Mystic from the island of Moth, and student of Grandmaster Faywong. I seek a guide to take me to Lagnaraste."

The name echoed in the air like a living thing, shivering the trees, rippling the pond, and warming the air. Fay creatures throughout the nearby trees squeaked and scampered to new locations. The tortoise lifted his head slowly, still considering her. Then he looked away from Pomella, toward the horizon. Pomella didn't know if normal compass directions were the same here, but if this had been the human realm she would've guessed that he peered north. The pond fed a narrow stream leading in that direction.

"Please," Pomella said, "if you understand me, I need to find her."

"She's a-tricky t'find," said a nearby voice. Pomella spun and found a man with a bushy red beard watching her from up in a tree.

Red, not silver.

Pomella felt an unexpected surge of fear at seeing that he appeared as she did, with normal colors. He had pale, freckled skin, common for those on Moth, along with short, neatly groomed hair that matched his beard. He was shirtless, and appeared to be in his mid- to late thirties, although it was difficult to tell because of his stooped stature, the bags under his eyes, and his gnarled hands. One of those hands clutched a short, lumpy stick that had bundles of silver fruit tied to it. Pomella counted four bananas, two oranges, and a bundle of grapes. He wore loose pants that shimmered with silver light.

"Hello, can you help me?" said Pomella, wondering who this man was.

He shrugged. "Maybe, eh? I see yeh figured how t' dress yeh-self," he said, and Pomella noticed his clear, if archaic, Mothic accent. "Took m' weeks t' puzzle that out."

"Who are you?" Pomella asked. "And why are you . . . ?"

"Why'm I not silver a-like everythin' else?" he offered.

"Yah."

The man plucked a grape from the top of his stick. "M' name's Rostrick," he said, and he popped a silver grape into his mouth. "I'm a Mystic, a-like you. And a-like you, I came here from tha' falla." He gestured to the waterfall tumbling on top of the giant tortoiseshell.

"And you've been here weeks?" Pomella said.

"Maybe a mite longer. Time's a-different here from there, as yeh'll see. The longer yeh stay, the stranger 'tis."

"Why are you in Fayün?"

"We're a-Mystics, no?" he said, grinning. "Studyin' Fayün, 'tis what we do."

"I've never met you before. Do you live on Moth?"

"I live here, as yeh can see."

Pomella frowned. This man, Rostrick, seemed polite enough, but he seemed out of place, and she didn't trust him. His dated accent somehow made him sound even more suspicious. She had to start somewhere, however.

"I've come here to learn about Lagnaraste. What do you

know about . . . her?" Pomella asked, rembering the discussion she'd had with Mantepis about Lagnaraste's undefined gender.

At mention of Lagnaraste's name, the same warm wind from earlier raced through the clearing, stirring the plants and fay creatures.

"She's a-name yeh don't use lightly round here," said Rostrick. "But eventually, all roads lead t' the tower."

"Tower? Look, Master Rostrick," Pomella said, stepping toward his tree. "I have very little time, so if—"

"Time?" The voice came from another tree behind Pomella. She whirled around and found Rostrick in that tree as well. Looking back at the place he'd just been, she saw he was gone.

"Oh, precious shadow flower," Rostrick said from his new location, "in Fayün, there's always *time*."

"I need to find Lagnaraste," Pomella demanded, dropping all pretense. Again, the hot wind shuddered through the clearing. "If she claims to be the queen of this domain, I would speak to her."

Rostrick considered her as he ate another grape. "Aye, I can take yeh," he said. He plucked and peeled a banana from his Mystic staff. "Yeh a-came at t' right time."

"Is she far?"

"She's just a-down the river," he said, and this time he spoke from a nearby rock, still eating his banana.

Pomella never quite saw him move. It seemed he shifted during the fraction of a second it took her to blink. Her jaw clenched. She tired of his game. "Then let's be on our way." She strode along the riverbank, intending to follow wherever it led. Hector and Ena followed behind her.

"*I-I-I* wouldn't a-suggest walking," Rostrick said. He drew

out the first word, making it last several seconds. "Crow Tallin 'tis upon us, yeh know, and the Towerway isn't a-very safe.
The luck'ns n' axthos be out n' such."

Luck'ns? Weren't those just legends? She decided not to voice
this thought, however. She was in Fayün, so nothing should
surprise her. "Then how will we go?"

"We'll a-ride Tuppleton," Rostrick said. He indicated the
giant tortoise with his banana peel. "He's a-bite faster than
yeh may think. More important, his shell'll protect yeh."

As if to demonstrate his strength, the massive tortoise lifted
one of his forelegs and splashed it down into the water with
mighty force. He snorted, and a jet of cool air wafted across
Pomella.

Pomella tried to ignore the possibility that a fay tortoise had
just puffed snot over her. "What do you think?" she said to her
hummingbirds. Ena hovered hesitantly beside her head, but
Hector didn't wait even a moment. He zoomed toward the tortoise's head and spun around it. Tuppleton tried to follow his
movements, but it was like watching a tree trying to chase a
rabbit. Hector alighted onto the crown of the creature's head
and waited.

"I guess that settles it then," Pomella said. "Very well, Rostrick, I will take your offer."

Rostrick bowed slightly and gestured her forward.

Tuppleton lowered his head for Pomella to climb up, but instead of trying to scramble up his scales, she reached out her
hand and held on to Ena, just as she had done when she traveled
through Lal's memories. The hummingbird took her aloft and
she floated through the air, like a mote of dust caught in the
wind. Ena set her onto Tuppleton's mostly smooth shell.

Rostrick already stood atop the tortoise. He winked at Pomella. "Tuppleton awaits yer command, Mistress," he said with a polite bow.

With her hummingbirds swirling around her, and a cloak woven from the water and grass of Fayün, Pomella raised her staff and pointed downriver. "Take us to Lagnaraste," she said.

The warm wind surged as Tuppleton's leg lifted and plunged downward, taking the first step down the river. Pomella wavered with the motion but managed to keep her balance. Rostrick sat cross-legged atop the shell with his stick across his lap. He closed his eyes and Pomella saw a faint smile of contentment appear on his face. She didn't share his ease.

Free of the clearing, and once he found his stride, Tuppleton moved with surprising speed. He walked above the river, following its course like a trail through the forest. The river surged against his feet. An endless world of strange silver trees, shadows, and floating points of light passed them. Curious eyes peered at Pomella from within hidden branches in the treetops. Far below on the ground, small fay critters scattered as Tuppleton stomped past.

Some of the trees were of a kind Pomella had never seen before, and many didn't even resemble trees at all but rather looked like massive flowers, mushrooms, and even faces. Motes of light drifted everywhere like fireflies, but whenever Pomella tried to look at one up close it faded away.

A thick fog lay up ahead, limiting how far down their path she could see. But everything before that appeared clear, and from what she could see, the river ran fairly straight.

It was difficult for Pomella to tell how much time passed on their journey. The stars overhead were frozen in place, and she could not see the moon. To her surprise, she recognized all the same constellations as the ones in the human realm. Treorel blazed bright, dominating the heavens and casting a pinkish glow across the crystalline-like landscape. If she shifted her mind, Pomella imagined the Fayün landscape was like a wilderness covered in eternal ice and snow.

Hours passed, and Pomella grew hungry. Rostrick had fallen asleep on his back. She watched him as he snored, trying to understand why a human would come to live in Fayün. As she pondered this, she heard a commotion in the treetops. Turning in that direction, she saw a fay creature about the size of a watermelon with long, spindly arms and a prehensile tail swinging beside them, keeping up at a steady pace. At first she thought he was a monkey, but when he turned his face toward her she saw he was far more human, with a wide, squashed nose and scraggly facial hair. When he saw Pomella watching him, he stopped on an outstretched tree branch up ahead and held his arm out toward Pomella, clearly inviting her to touch it when she passed.

Pomella gave him her fingertips, curious to see what he would feel like.

The monkey creature let out a piercing cry. His lips pulled back in a sneer and he yanked Pomella hard, nearly tumbling her off Tuppleton.

Rostrick was there in a hearbeat. He smacked the creature and scolded it with some words Pomella didn't quite catch or understand. The creature vanished into the trees, throwing one last annoyed expression back at them.

"That's Raball," said Rostrick, not showing any sign of having been asleep moments before. His sudden springing to alertness sent chillybumps across Pomella's skin. "He won't a-hurt yeh as long as yeh stay on the shell. Careful t' a-keep yeh hands t' yehself."

Pomella rubbed her sore hand as she frowned at the other eyes peering at her from the trees.

Later, as Pomella was trying to estimate how much time had passed—an hour? A day?—they emerged from the fog line and Pomella couldn't help but gasp. A steep valley opened up below them, shaped like an arrowhead with the farthest tip culminating across from them at the base of an angular mountain. Silver eagles soared in the sky circling the river that bisected the valley. It was like looking over the Mystwood, only one made of glass-like silver.

Overlaid across the valley was a sprinkling of golden trees. Two birds, shining yellow like the sun she was familiar with, fluttered across the treetops as Pomella watched.

Rising over the entire valley, at the very summit of the distant mountain, was a towering monolith. From Pomella's vantage, a constellation of twenty stars formed a perfect circle around the structure, like a celestial crown. The hair on her arms rose. Memories she barely recognized flooded her mind. It was like suddenly remembering a dream from long ago that she'd forgotten.

"The Tower of Eternal Starlight," said Rostrick. He was eating an apple now. Pomella wondered where he'd gotten it, as she hadn't seen it attached to his stick before.

"T' only appears near Crow Tallin," he continued. "If it comes a'tall."

Tuppleton deftly carried them down the hillside, still following the river, which cut a narrow gorge into the valley floor. The gorge fed the river to a wide fissure that stretched as far as Pomella could see in either direction. Several rolling hills stood between them and the slopes of the mountain. They would have to somehow cross the gap, as well as the hills, to reach the tower.

Tuppleton led them to a relatively calm pool that rested safely beside the waterfall. This close to the edge, Pomella could see the river plummeting over the edge in a raging torrent of sound and chaos. She shuddered, not wanting to look over the edge into the fissure's depths.

"Ye'll need ta go on yer own now," Rostrick said. "I'll wait 'ere for yeh. 'Tis a long walk to the top, though."

Tuppleton eased himself into the water as if relaxing for a bath. Pomella spun the Myst around her like a vortex and leaped from the tortoise's back without thought, landing softly on the Fayün soil.

"If yeh see any peaches up a-there," Rostrick called, "bring 'em back down, m'kay? Tuppleton loves ta eat 'em."

Pomella looked up the mountain. "How do I cross the fissure?"

"Yeh cross the bridge, a-course."

Rostrick waved his hand, and a thin bridge, no wider than a windowpane, shimmered into existence. The bridge began near the waterfall and arced its way up and across the gap before settling itself on one of the opposite hills.

"Go with-a the Myst," Rostrick said with a wink.

Pomella approached the base of the mostly translucent bridge. There were no hand rails; it was simply a narrow pathway. She took a steadying breath and stepped out onto it, silently praying it wouldn't crack beneath her weight.

The bridge held, and she crossed. Warm winds howled from below, billowing her dress and hair. Hector and Ena stayed close, but they, too, struggled against the wind. When

Pomella reached the midway point, she couldn't help but peer downward, into the depths of the fissure. It was hard to discern details, because of the uniform silver and dancing motes of light everywhere, but narrowing her eyes she could see lights *pulsing* far below, like bellows breathing life into a forge.

Pomella shuddered, then hurried across the rest of the bridge. When she reached the safety of the hills, she located a trail leading upward and followed it. Fay creatures watched her pass, including the strange monkey fay Rostrick had referred to as Raball. He screeched at her from a nearby tree. She ignored him and carried on.

When she reached the crest of the hill, she wiped her brow. Ena hovered in front of her. "OK, let's try something different," Pomella said, and merged herself with the Myst and the hummingbird. Her weight dropped away and she felt the familiar tug at her arm as Ena lifted her skyward. She alighted back to her normal self on a rocky ledge a hundred or more steps up the mountain.

"Further," she said, and ascended again on Ena's wings. She leaped higher and faster this time before landing. With each leap, more of herself dropped away, until with her last leap she seemed on the verge of becoming little more than vapor. Her feet touched down at the summit of the mountain, and Pomella had to steady herself as weight and mass returned to her. Her hummingbirds hovered beside her as she studied the massive silver monolith rising in front of her.

There was no visible entrance to the Tower of Eternal Starlight except for a single window high up near its top. It dwarfed Kelt Apar's central tower, yet it resonated with the same energy that Pomella sensed while standing near it. She traced her fingers across the stone and noticed carved writing from an unknown language cut into nearly every inch of the surface. Her spine tingled as the Myst churned around her.

"Lagnaraste!" she called, and the word echoed off the tower walls. "I am Pomella AnDone. I would speak with you."

At the sound of Lagnaraste's name, a surge of scuttling noises sounded all around the tower. The ground burst open as snout-faced axthos tunneled out of it. Some wore loincloths of twine and mud and leaves while others were outright naked. Most carried primitive weapons made of what appeared to be bone or stone tied to heavy wooden handles. They screeched and squawked, and a few tried in vain to snatch her hummingbirds, but none dared come closer than just beyond the reach of her Mystic staff.

"I seek your queen," Pomella stated, letting her impatience temper the iron in her voice.

"I am she," came a gentle voice from the tower.

Pomella turned and gazed at the monolith. The carved words in the stone shifted and flowed until they formed a distinct shape. Thousands of runes twisted around one another, overlapping and rolling until they collectively illustrated the figure of a woman.

The image resolved to reveal an imposing figure with high cheekbones and other strong features that were accented by shaded eyes and full lips. She was nearly a hand length taller than Pomella, but her hair was cropped short. Her clothes appeared to be a mixture of leather and fur encircled with a wide belt. She wore boots that reached to her knees, covering tight-fitting breeches. The illustration of the woman moved in a life-like manner, perfectly mimicking her expressions and natural gestures.

The woman spoke and words echoed out of the tower wall. "I had not expected it to be you who came to me, but the other one."

"Who are you?" Pomella asked.

"I have many names," the woman said. "The few who come to this tower all bring new ones for me. Please, sit, be at ease."

A handful of axthos stumbled forward, rolling a large rock for Pomella to sit on. Pomella ignored the makeshift seat. "Tell me your name," she demanded.

"You don't know me, Pomella AnDone?" the woman said, pacing along the wall like a drawing brought to life. "You sing of me every springrise upon your village green. As a girl you dressed in my cloak and dreamed of having hair o' flame like mine." The woman looked directly into Pomella's eyes, piercing her like an arrow. "They called me the Red Huntress. The First Mystic of Moth. She Who Tamed the Corenach. I am Brigid, Daughter of None but the Woods."

Pomella's heart thundered in her chest.

The woman relaxed her posture. "And I, alas, am Lagnaraste."

A thousands questions tumbled into Pomella's mind. How was this possible? Nobody denied that Brigid had been a historical figure, but she was mostly legend, perhaps even a combination of centuries' worth of stories passed down through the villages on Moth. Pomella had prepared herself for the unexpected, but this unhinged her. "How?" was all she managed to say.

"Oh, you know the story, Pomella," said Brigid. "The tales get a surprising portion of it right. The high points, anyway."

"Your adventures. Your conquests. Weren't they all to save your son?" Pomella said, thinking fast. "He was stolen."

Brigid's eyes narrowed. "So I believed, and so the legends say. We were colonists from a land you now call the Continent. Our newly crowned *shalla* sent ships to a newly discovered island off the west coast. It was home only to a small population of lizard-men. My husband had died the previous winter, and so I went seeking a new life with our child, Janid, who was just a boy. The fresh land we discovered sang to us of possibility. The rains that fell from its sky washed the wounds of my heart."

The eyes of the illustrated Brigid grew distant, becoming lost in a time long past.

"My child wandered to the very same waterfall you came through," Brigid continued, "although I did not know it at the time. To me, he'd simply vanished. I searched for him for days, refusing to believe he was dead. And then I found one of the fay, a wretched-looking thing not unlike my friends that stir around you now. He told me I had the same eyes as the newcomer to his land. And so I learned of Fayün and began my hunt. For six years I searched. For *six years* I endured and killed and conquered forces that even the great kings dared not face. My own people rejected me. Only the lagharts offered assistance in my quest. With their help, I came at last to a cave at the top of a great mountain where I met a Nameless Saint. I offered her my Fire Branch, my cloak from the lucklesslings, and even Dauntless, the bow I had won from the hundred-eyed beast living in the deep heart of the mountains. But the Saint ignored it all, and challenged me to revoke my claim to those trinkets and everything else that held me back. She *unmade* me with a glance, and prepared me for my time with the *Zurntas*. Eventually, after humbling myself to them, the laghart masters deemed me ready to learn of the Myst—the first human they'd ever taught—and so I became a Mystic.

"During Crow Tallin, nearly a thousand years before you drew your first breath, in the place where your forebears later built the stone tower of Kelt Apar, the *Zurntas* and I summoned Lagnaraste, the King of the Fay. The last of the dragons, and the force that had split the united world into Fayün and the human realm. The *Zurntas* sought only peace, and I sought my son. But the king was a hateful beast that mocked my request. He accused the *Zurntas* of meddling with the world he'd created and burned them alive. He dragged me to this realm and imprisoned me within the same tower where my son had been kept. Same tower, but different rooms. For ages beyond knowing I could hear Janid crying for me. You are not a mother yet, Pomella, but I assure you, there is no greater agony than listening to your child scream your name while you can do nothing."

Brigid's expression hardened and she looked upward along the very wall her image was rendered upon. "I was locked in the highest chamber, in the only room with a window. I believe he provided that window to give me hope, so that he could better enjoy my torment. I despaired and nearly lost my mind until one day—a single day among the seven lifetimes I existed there—I saw the Mystic Star. Its light empowered me. I tilled the foundations of my heart and mind and at last arrived within the Deep, that place where the true nature of the Myst resides, where every name is revealed. Empowered by the Mystic Star, I confronted Lagnaraste, and we battled through the endless halls of the tower. In the end I freed Janid, who escaped to the human world, and I was left to confront Lagnaraste. I had achieved my goal of freeing my son, and I had risen to a level of power I could not have previously comprehended. I enslaved the dragon's mind. I claimed his power and incinerated his carcass. But despite my tremendous power, I remained locked in the tower, unable to break the walls that were forged by the First Masters from the iron of the world's core."

She paused, breathing deeply, as though she had just lived the experience again.

"Why are you telling me this?" Pomella asked.

"Because I need your help, Pomella. I need to be free. I need to join my son at last."

Memory of the wivan's voice rang in Pomella's mind. "The Reunion," she breathed.

Brigid's lips curled into a smile that sent a chill through Pomella. "Yes. The fay have taken a liking to the term. They are as eager for it as I."

"Does . . . Janid still live?" Pomella asked.

"Yes," Brigid said. "After he escaped the tower, I knew I had to wait until the next Crow Tallin, when the worlds temporarily merged again. Only then would I have a chance to return to him. There are two places in the human world where the distance between worlds is exceedingly thin. One is Kelt Apar, in the heart of your Mystwood, which we called simply the Great Forest in my time. The other is on the far side of the world, in mountain country, amid some rolling hills where a large thorn patch once grew. Within the Deep, nothing happens without reason, so it was only a matter of time before a little girl stumbled upon me. She was afraid and nearly broken, so I breathed power into her. I showed her visions of the future, and slowly, by the measure of her time, she came to love me. And so that is why

I am surprised you came to me, and not her. The Myst, and the Deep, work in ways none of us can know."

"Shevia," Pomella said.

"Yes," said Brigid. "Between the Mystic Star and the gifts I've given her, she has the power to free me and bring about the Reunion."

"How do you need to be freed?"

Brigid lifted her palm and above it more carved words moved to form the sketch of a glass sphere. "After Lagnaraste destroyed the *Zurntas,* their velten in the heart of the Great Forest lay in ruins. The fay dragon lingered on the island, but as Crow Tallin ended, his power in the human realm faded. He receded in size and power until at last he was little more than a tiny moth fluttering through the forest. Some human settlers followed it to the place you now call Kelt Apar and found the dead lagharts. The human Mystics among them—my first apprentices before I was taken—divined what had occurred. They feared what would occur should Lagnaraste return, so they encased him in a glass sphere, and brought forth a tower and a guardian from the soil to protect it. As long as the moth is encased in that glass, I—who inherited Lagnaraste's essence—cannot leave the tower or enter the human realm."

Pomella saw in her mind the glass sphere kept in the upper chamber of Kelt Apar's tower and the moth within it that continuously threw itself against the inside of the glass, trying to break free.

"That's why the High Mystics gather in Kelt Apar during Crow Tallin," Pomella said, suddenly understanding. "They're preventing the sphere from breaking open."

"Yes," said Brigid. "Since the founding of Kelt Apar, they

understood that only during Crow Tallin could Lagnaraste break free. So on every occurrence of the Mystic Star's arrival they pool their powers to strengthen those walls. What reason did they tell *you*, Pomella? Did they say they gathered to help the poor citizens of the island? Do you see their lies?"

Pomella's hand tightened on her Mystic staff. She evened her breathing as her mind raced, trying to take in all that she'd just learned. Whatever she'd come to expect from this journey to Fayün, this did not resemble it. She looked upward along the length of the tower again, and saw, far above, the single window opening near the top. Somewhere in the room beyond was the heroic woman from her childhood stories. But everything had changed now. Pomella didn't know whether to trust the rendering of the woman before her.

Brigid watched her with those strange, shifting eyes. "I know this must be overwhelming. I do not imply that your masters wrongly deceived you. They do not know the full truth I've shared with you. They continue a tradition that's been passed to them for nearly a thousand years. The creature they've held at bay—the fay dragon Lagnaraste, who broke the world—was destroyed. I hold his power now, and I carry no vengeance in my heart. I swear to you, on my Mystic name, that I wish only to be reunited with my boy, who still walks your world. Free me, and I will find him at last. Free me, so that I can live in quiet peace."

"I—"

"Please, Pomella. It is only during Crow Tallin that the glass sphere can be broken. Do this for me, and I will teach you of the Deep. I will take you into the Mystic Skies where you will discover the true nature of the Myst. I will complete what your master began, and we will honor him together. He alone,

above all the other masters, understood that the supposed purpose of Crow Tallin was false. It's why he retired when he did.
He did not want to be a part of Crow Tallin, so he passed the
Mothic lineage to his successor earlier than anticipated. The
culmination of his life's efforts is now in your hands. You have
the ability to fulfill not only my dream, but his."

"I need to return and speak to the High Mystics," Pomella
said, taking a step back. "They need to know all of this."

Brigid stared at Pomella with the piercing eyes of a legendary hero. "Go with my blessing," she said. "As a token of my trust,
and to strengthen your belief in all that I've said, I offer you a
gift. Touch your staff to the tower walls and I will imbue it with
my symbol. Listen to it speak, and it will whisper the future, or
the Mystic name of anything you choose. By all the Saints that
live and ever will, and on the memory of your grandmhathir,
fathir, and Grandmaster Faywong, I swear to you that I do not
deceive you."

Pomella closed her eyes and took a deep breath. Everything
Brigid had told her resonated with truth. She wished she could
speak to Lal, to ask him the multitude of questions now tumbling through her mind.

She sat on the ground and rested her Mystic staff upright
against her shoulder. She retreated into herself. Her mind raged
with a thousand questions. At times like this, she knew she had
to depend on her training. Her mind was like the fay monkey
Raball, swinging from thought to thought. It was too elusive,
too quick, to try to capture. In order to make sense of anything,
to know the truth, she had to move past the mind and go to her
heart. Such was the way Lal had shown her.

Pushing aside her normal senses, she concentrated on her

breath, counting each one, bringing her attention to the flow of air into her lungs, and then to her exhale. Fayün, the axthos, and everything else around her faded away until at last she dwelt in the Crossroads. She came to it more easily than ever. It was like walking in your home at night, knowing the way without seeing.

For long moments Pomella drifted in a peaceful sky of Myst. It swirled around her like thin clouds, pulsing to the rhythm of her heart. Below her swirled a vortex plunging into an abyss, a place that called to her in a voice that was her own.

Please, she prayed silently to the Saints and to Lal and anybody else who had come before her in her long line of past masters, *guide me. Help me to know the path I must take.*

The vortex below her swirled, but she stayed aloft in the sky, fearing what lay below. She pulled the Myst tighter around her, sending out her request for help as far as she could shout within this timeless place. Why did the masters not rush to her to help?

Something clunked beside her.

Pomella's eyes popped open and she saw that her staff had slipped from her shoulder to topple against the tower. She stared at it, then smiled. Maybe it had to do with the Myst or the past masters, or maybe not. But one way or another, she had made her decision. She wrapped both hands around her Mystic staff, keeping it pressed against the side of the tower.

She stood. "Very well, Saint Brigid, I accept your gift. I will return to Kelt Apar and discuss this with the High Mystics before Crow Tallin ends, if it is not already too late."

As if in response, the oak staff grew warm. The base of it

swelled, then split as a new tendril of wood emerged and wrapped itself around the existing staff. Up it rose, circling in a long, slow spiral, changing from a warm polished brown color to white. As the new wood neared the top of the staff, carved scales revealed themselves, and the leading edge reshaped itself to that of a snake's head. The serpent's face was diamond shaped and rested directly against the staff.

Slowly, Pomella removed the staff with its carved snake twisted around it from the side of the tower. As she held it vertically beside her, Pomella saw the snake's head was level with her own.

Pomella gave the tower one final glance then swept down the mountainside. The axthos leaped out her way, scrambling over each other in an effort not to get too close.

"Ena!" she commanded, and reached out as the little hummingbird zoomed to her hand. In a single leap she descended the mountain, moving as swiftly and gently as a sunbeam. She alighted beside the glass bridge and released Ena, then hurried across to the pond where Tuppleton rested. Her hummingbirds followed, as eager as her to return.

Rostrick looked up at her from Tuppleton's shell where he'd been lying on his back with one leg crossed over the other and hands behind his head.

"I need to return to the waterfall we came from," Pomella told him. She briefly considered using Ena to *skip* back there, but she wasn't sure she could leap that far without seeing her destination. That, and Rostrick had told her that Tuppleton's shell would protect her in Fayün.

Rostrick studied her with new interest. His eyes flicked to

her staff, and Pomella could see the questions burning in his eyes. "Aye, come a-tup 'ere and we'll get you a-back quick as a luck'n." He winked at her.

As they rode Tuppleton upriver out of the valley, Pomella looked back at the Tower of Eternal Starlight and the constellation ring encircling it. Near the very top she could make out its one lone window—an empty black square set against the infinite shades of silver—and thought she saw a flash of movement.

Never in all her life, even in her most fanciful dreams, had Pomella ever imagined she would encounter Saint Brigid herself. All of her preconceived notions of Lagnaraste and Crow Tallin had been shattered like fine glass. She thought of Brigid's request to free her from her prison. If the Saint's story was entirely true—and despite some nagging doubts, Pomella believed it was—then there was no reason to not help her. Lagnaraste had already been defeated and his power transferred to Brigid. Pomella found herself excited by the possibility of helping the Saint complete her tale. Perhaps, when it was all over, she'd have the opportunity to compose a new stanza for the *Toweren*.

But more than that, she was excited for the possibility of learning from Brigid. Between the Saint's adventures across Moth, her apprenticeship to the *Zurntas,* and her time in Fayün, Brigid likely had an unequaled mastery of the Myst. Lal would forever be her teacher, but in his absence Pomella could learn from Brigid all the secrets he never had the opportunity to tell her.

She yawned. Time might be strange in Fayün, but for her, she hadn't slept in what felt like the life of the stars.

"Would yeh like a wee bit o' nosha?" Rostrick asked. He sat

at the front of Tuppleton's shell, facing backward toward her. He held out a silver piece of fruit for her.

Pomella didn't know what nosha was, but it sure looked like an apple to her. "Thank you, but I think I'll just rest a bit instead."

"You're a-tired, and travel'n 'tween worlds besides. Do yeh expect a feast when yeh come a-back ta the Mystwood? Eat." He tossed the apple to Pomella, who barely caught it before it clunked into her head. Rostrick grinned at her, but not in an unfriendly way.

"Oh buggerish," Pomella said. The apple seemed like any other fruit except for its silver gleam. She watched as Rostrick took a bite of one of his own. Hesitantly, Pomella took a bite. It was sweeter than she expected, full of flavor. She took a second and a third and quick as a luck'n she munched it down to its core.

"Not'sa bad, eh?" Rostrick said. "Another?"

"No th—" Pomella yawned again. "Thank you. I'm OK." Her eyelids grew heavy, but she didn't like the idea of sleeping. Not until she returned to the human realm anyway. She caught herself nodding off, so she asked Rostrick something that she'd been wondering about. "Who was your master, Rostrick? Are they still on Moth?"

Rostrick studied her for a long moment, then looked off into the passing trees. "Me masta' and me had ta bit of a fall'n out, yeh could say. 'Twas a hard culk in the end."

A massive yawn consumed Pomella for a moment. Unbearable fatigue rolled over her. Even as he spoke, she felt herself falling asleep. Only the shock of how harshly Rostrick thought of his master kept her awake in that moment.

"I 'twas less an apprentice and more a slave," Rostrick continued. "Me masta' was wise, yeh, but merciless. Came from an ancient line o' Mystics."

Something was wrong. Sleep pressed down on her like a pillow across her face. She tried to sit up straighter, but instead her body eased itself down gently on Tuppleton's shell.

The last thing Pomella saw as she drifted asleep was Rostrick standing over her. He eyed her curiously, then threw his stick of fruit branch off the shell into the woods. "I escaped me ol' masta', Mantepis, but not b'fore he broke my Mystic staff. I came 'ere, to Fayün, and ate its food and have been trapped 'ere ever since. Yeh need a staff to a-come'n go, yeh see. It anchors yeh 'tween worlds. So I thank yeh now for a-helping me t' escape'n all."

Where fear should've gripped Pomella, sleep snared her instead.

She had no idea how long she'd been out for, but it must've been only moments or minutes. A sharp *poking* sensation pierced her forehead. Pomella's eyes fluttered as she struggled to lift her head. A cloud of smoky silver blurred in her vision. It shifted, and the pain blossomed again on her forehead.

"Hector?" she managed. The hummingbird pecked her again. She looked past him and saw Rostrick still astride Tuppleton's back, holding her Mystic staff. He was spitting curses at Ena, who spun and dove toward his face.

Pomella tried to stand but wobbled. Fayün spun around her, and she fell back onto the shell. Hector buzzed in front of her, urgently.

"Get 'em off me!" Rostrick yelled. "Luck'n's, to me!"

The nearby trees burst open as a swarm of melon-sized fay

monkeys swung out and landed on Tuppleton's shell. They scrambled over one another toward Rostrick, climbing his back and charging across his outstretched arm to launch themselves into the air toward Ena. But the little hummingbird wove and spun and easily avoided their grip.

A pair of monkeys—luck'ns, Pomella now realized—scrambled across the shell toward her. Their faces contorted, revealing fierce teeth in their gums.

Pomella reached a trembling hand toward Hector, and grabbed hold of him, just like she'd done before when she skipped with Ena. Strength and shocking energy surged through her. The two luck'ns leaped at her with their grubby hands outstretched. She punched them with her free hand, sending them hurtling off Tuppleton's side. Pomella marveled at the power surging through her fist. More luck'ns swung in from the trees and charged her, but she pounded them off the shell as easily as the first.

On the far side of the shell, Rostrick swung Pomella's staff at Ena, snarling as the little bird continued to evade the blows.

Tuppleton came to an abrupt stop, and Pomella had to catch her balance. She whipped around and saw they'd arrived back at the glowing waterfall where she'd first arrived from the human world. Rostrick saw it, too. He narrowed his eyes and ran along the edge of the shell.

"Stop him!" she yelled to her hummingbirds. Ena darted toward Rostrick, who swatted at her. Ena spiraled around his forearm, slicing a long cut along it before flying away in a wide arc, trailing silver dust behind her. She circled back, readying for another assault.

Suffused with enough strength and wakefulness for the

moment, Pomella released Hector, who barreled for Rostrick. A luck'n leaped into the hummingbird's path, acting as a shield, but Hector slammed into it, knocking it aside.

Ena dove at Rostrick again, and tore through the hand that held Pomella's staff. He cried out in pain as the staff fell onto Tuppleton's shell, rolled to the edge, and toppled off the side.

Pomella ran for the edge and leaped into the pool of water. She splashed into it, and the icy shock of cold shot through her. Another splash sounded as Rostrick plunged into the water behind her. Pomella flung her soaking hair away from her face and saw her staff floating on the water's surface, drifting slowly toward the waterfall.

She and Rostrick splashed through the water, converging from different angles toward the staff. Behind them, more luck'ns dove into the water. Pomella was a half a hand length closer to the staff than Rostrick, but his desperate ferocity to escape his prison gave him strength.

"Ena!" Pomella cried. "I need you!"

The hummingbird zoomed low across the surface, kicking up a trail of water behind her. Pomella reached out a hand and caught Ena as she flew by. Her body lightened and she felt herself speeding along the water. She reached out with her free hand and snatched her Mystic staff.

"Ah ha!" The cry burst forth from her as Rostrick snarled and leaped. Just as Pomella reached the plummeting waterfall, Rostrick snatched a fistful of her hair.

"'Tis *my* time!" he yelled. "I won't a-stay here any longer!"

Pomella struggled against his grip, grinding her jaw with the effort. She still gripped Ena, who pulled her in the opposite direction.

Suddenly Hector dove and slammed into Rostrick. He snarled and lost his grip on Pomella. Ena carried her forward and they plunged into the waterfall.

But in the fleeting moments as Pomella shifted between worlds, a luck'n snatched Hector out of the air. Pomella's chest tightened as its grip squeezed her hummingbird. She watched in horror as Rostrick snatched the bird from the creature and with a sickening twist wrenched his neck.

Pomella screamed in pain as the hummingbird died and the worlds shifted and she fell through the veil.

TWENTY-FIVE

MASTER OF FIRE

Shevia awoke to a clear, star-filled evening. She could feel, rather than see from her angle, the Mystic Star hanging above her. It was like a bonfire burning with power. With it came memories of Sim and the waterfall.

Shevia bolted upright, gasping for air. Anger boiled within her, but she forced herself to regain her composure. The sadness, hopelessness, and feelings of powerlessness had long ago given way to her new reality. She would not let anger control her anymore.

Instead, she *was* anger; she was fire.

She realized her hands were bound with rope, which almost made her laugh, but a foul taste coated her mouth. She spit it out.

"Your head will be sore until sunrise," Sim said from nearby. Shevia found him and regarded him with a neutral expression. They were on opposite sides of a campfire over which a small skinned animal cooked, its juices just beginning to hiss across the coals. She caught fleeting glimpses of fay animals dancing in the smoke between them. Just beyond the fire's edge she saw silver-colored streaks as other fay ran between worlds. Pomella's brown gelding was tied to a nearby tree, nibbling grass.

The fires within Shevia raged to an inferno. Her serpent tattoo itched. She could destroy him right now.

"Shiverbane works instantly and lasts anywhere from a few hours to several days depending on the dosage and the person taking it," Sim added as he poked the fire with a stick. His onkai blades sat beside him, within easy reach. He flicked a glance at her but looked away as soon as their eyes met.

"Why?" Shevia demanded in Continental. Before he died, she had to know.

"Because it would've been a mistake for you to go to Fayün."

Her eyes narrowed and the fire within her flared. "A mistake? You presume to know what is best for me?"

"Lagnaraste," Sim said, ignoring her question.

Perhaps it was Shevia's imagination, but it seemed as though the campfire momentarily had flared higher when Sim had spoken the name out loud. "What do you know of her?" she said.

"So it's a she," Sim said, nodding. "I've heard that name before. In Qin."

Shevia waited for him to continue. The silence yawned between them like the distance between stars. In this silence she decided his next words would determine if she would kill him or not.

"Five years ago," Sim said, "I came with my mentor to a remote village in the highlands. We sought a Mystic who could cure the plague I carried. Upon our arrival we learned he'd been kidnapped by a wivan. We tracked the creature to his lair and destroyed him, but not before he killed my teacher." The fire's reflection crackled in his black pupils. "Before he died, I heard him speak Lagnaraste's name. And I saw an illustration that he had drawn in his lair. That." He pointed to Shevia's shoulder and the twisted-dragon tattoo upon it.

"I also found this," Sim continued, and removed a handful of folded papers, which he handed to Shevia. "I cannot read Qina, but the symbol matched one I found in the wivan's lair."

Shevia lifted her tied hands and took the papers from him. Her chest tightened when she immediately recognized the handwriting.

To my esteemed colleague and friend, Bith Yab,

By the grace and vision of the Myst, it has come to my attention that you have undertaken research into the nature of the master of Fayün and the Reunion. Because such topics are the domain of the High Mystics, and of personal interest to me, I hereby command you to cease your explorations. Furthermore, you will immediately come to call on me at Shenheyna and bring this letter. Come alone, and tell no one of this correspondence. I expect your presence before the third new moon of the year. If you decline my invitation, I will see to it that your studies are concluded by other means.

Under the light, and from within the Myst,

I remain,
The High Mystic of Qin,
Bhairatonix Chanjoll

Below her master's signature rested a black-ink rendering of the twisting serpent that adorned Shevia's upper body. Her skin began to burn as the inferno of hatred for Bhairatonix raging within her threatened. She could feel Sim watching her, obviously curious as to the contents of the letter. Carefully, and with controlled breaths, she subdued her anger. The time could come soon.

"I hope you honored this Bith Yab," Shevia said.

"As best I could."

Shevia stared into the fire. What sort of "personal interest" did Bhairatonix have in Lagnaraste and the Reunion? She thought of the dragon tattoo spreading across his chest.

"My master is among those who seek to bring Lagnaraste into this world," she said. "I believe he secretly opposes the High Mystics in this regard."

"And what do you want?" Sim said.

"To be free," Shevia said immediately. "To tear down the walls that imprison me within this world of servitude to my master and other Mystics."

The flickering fire danced in his eyes as he considered her. "I know what it's like to want to be free of Mystics," Sim said. "And I, too, have heard Sitting Mother's call."

The fire within Shevia coiled tight, ready to strike. "You've said that before. What do you mean?" she said.

"She drew me to herself in the highlands," Sim said. "I denied it for a long time, but at last, I came to her mountain and found her."

Shevia's heart raced, but she forced herself to remain calm as he continued. She wondered if he'd truly seen her.

"It was she who revealed the silver path to me," Sim said. "Since that time, it has led me true."

"Where does this path lead you now?"

"First to you, and now, back to Kelt Apar."

"Why?" she said.

"I don't know."

"How far from Kelt Apar are we?"

"About a day."

Shevia held up her bound wrists. Sim nodded and reached for a belt knife. Without thinking, Shevia incinerated the ropes and let the embers fall away.

Sim watched them fall, then put his knife away.

"Nobody will ever bind me again," Shevia said.

"Then where will you go next?" Sim asked.

"Crow Tallin arrives tomorrow. I will see Sitting Mother. Fulfill your duty, ranger. Follow your path, and take me to Kelt Apar."

They arrived with the late-afternoon sun, which still burned with the ferocity of deep summer. A massive gathering crowded the wall that the Green Man had raised. Shevia wove a hooded cloak of silvery Myst and receded into its depths. Sim strode ahead of her, leading Pomella's horse. At the first signs of the gathered commoners, he'd shifted one of his onkai from a walking stick to a readied weapon. Shevia doubted he would actually lift it against them. He had risen from their caste, after all.

He and Shevia moved without speaking, just as they had since finishing their campfire talk the previous night.

Sim led her across the river to the northwest side of Kelt Apar where the crowd was thinnest. There he struck through some dense underbrush, lifting branches for her to walk beneath. Walking through the foliage reminded Shevia of traversing the Thornwood. The hidden path snaked its way through the thicket until it terminated against the hedge wall.

Sim placed a hand on the wall and said, "Oxillian." A heartbeat later the leaves and branches twisted beneath his palm, then pulled away, revealing a passageway through. Shevia went first, leading Sim. As soon as she stepped foot onto the dry grass beyond, another surge of power rolled through her.

The ground rumbled and the Green Man emerged from the soil. His eyes of stone narrowed upon seeing Shevia.

"You should not be here," Oxillian said.

"She's under my protection," Sim said.

"Where is Mistress Pomella?" the Green Man asked.

"She is safe," Sim said. "She chose another path. We seek the High Mystics."

The Green Man shook his massive head. "The High Mystics are gathered in the tower, but command that they are not to be disturbed during Crow Tallin."

Shevia strode past the Green Man, not bothering to reply. He moved to stop her, but Shevia's look radiated such power that even the Green Man hesitated.

Satisfied she would not be hindered, with her Myst-cloak billowing behind her, Shevia strode toward the central tower and its green conical top and windows spiraling up the side. It struck her how deceptive the whole structure was. A little wobbly tower located in a peaceful pasture marked the heart of the world's most powerful location. By rights it should've outshone Shenheyna. As she crossed the lawn, she wondered what the dwellings of the other High Mystics were like. It was just another bit of knowledge that Bhairatonix had denied her.

A circle of foreign Mystics and their apprentices sat in a circle near the tower. One of them—a Rardarian—eyed her and Sim as they entered the central tower.

Vivianna and Hizrith, the laghart Mystic, stood outside the tower's main entrance, conversing in low tones. Vivianna's expression darkened when she saw Shevia. "What are you doing here! Stay out of—"

Shevia didn't twitch a single muscle as she threw both Vivianna and Hizrith against the tower's outer walls, pinning them against the stone. Vivianna cried out in pain while Hizrith clutched his throat. His serpent tongue whipped out and lashed the air.

Sim's hand landed on her cloaked shoulder. "This isn't the way," he said.

For him, she stopped. For him, and only for him this once, she turned and said, "For what we've shared and discussed, I will spare you. But if you ever touch me again, I will kill you."

She flared the fires within her, and her cloak erupted into flame. The fire did not burn her, for she was born of fire now. Sim snatched his hand away. Shevia entered the tower.

She strode up the stairs, carrying a firestorm within and around her. With every step, her righteous anger grew. Now was her time. Crow Tallin was upon them. Her old friend Sitting Mother, Lagnaraste, the Queen of Fayün, the fay dragon, graced her with fires and power no human had ever possessed. This was *her tower* now.

Her world.

She blasted the door to the uppermost chamber off its hinges. It flew less than halfway across the circular room before incinerating into ash. She stepped through the ruined doorway wreathed in fire.

The High Mystics sat in a ring on their cushions, all facing the pedestal holding the glass sphere encasing the moth. The little fay creature within the glass rested at the bottom, its wings drooped to its sides.

As Shevia had expected, it was Yarina who rose to her feet, burning with outrage.

"How *dare* you?" the High Mystic demanded.

"Get out," Shevia said in a deadly quiet voice.

"Crow Tallin is upon us and the critical moments approach," said High Mystic Ollfur. Shock and fear clouded his normally cheerful face. "Please, there are essential tasks we must accomp—"

Shevia roared fire across him. He fell back, writhing for mere seconds before crumbling to ash.

"Who else stands against me?" Shevia screamed.

"You have no idea what you're doing!" Yarina yelled, her hair coming undone from its intricate knot above her head.

"Get out!" Shevia screamed, and a ring of fire encircled the room. A wave of the Myst assaulted her, likely thrown in a pathetic attempt by one of the masters to harm or stop her. The attack would've overwhelmed any other Mystic on any other day, but now, beneath Treorel's glow, nothing could pierce her. She shrugged it off like water splashing against rock.

Most of the remaining High Mystics rose as one. Master Ehzeeth struggled but managed to find his feet.

Master Willwhite, now appearing fully as a woman, gaped at her. "What have you become, child?" Her face shifted with silvery light, as soft and gentle as the moon.

"I am the Mystic Dragon," Shevia said, and roared more fire.

The High Mystics hurried for the doorway. Cowards, Shevia thought. In the end, they were all cowards. "Not you," she said, pointing to Bhairatonix. He still sat, seemingly unconcerned or unsurprised by the atrocities occurring before him.

To her surprise, a tiny smile played at the corners of his mouth.

"You cannot do this," Master Angelos said from the doorway.

"Lagnaraste, the fay dragon, will destroy the world," his sister, Mistress Michaela, added. "You cannot stand against it."

"I have no time for you," Shevia said, and obliterated them. The twin High Mystics screamed and fell to their knees. As they died, their hands reached for each other but fell short before incinerating.

"Sitting Mother has called to me, and I will be free," Shevia said to the remaining High Mystics. "Leave, or I will burn you all."

Smoke choked the room, venting out the small window. Yarina's eyes narrowed in determination. The High Mystic reached for the glass sphere, but Shevia jabbed her staff at her hand, knocking it away. "Leave it!" Shevia snarled.

"We must protect it," Yarina intoned.

"Your knowledge and traditions mean nothing anymore. The Reunion is upon us," Shevia said. "I do not wish to destroy another High Mystic."

Yarina stood tall. "This is my duty and my tower. I will not abandon either."

Shevia sighed. "So be it, Mistress," she said, then screamed fire at Yarina.

The High Mystic was ready, however, and threw her hands and Mystic staff up. An arc of silver light circled upward to protect her, but the concussion of the attack blasted her backward and through the tower wall. Stone exploded outward along with Yarina. She hung there in midair for a moment before plunging downward and out of sight.

Shevia reached out her hand and the glass sphere flew to her. The Myst stormed around her, billowing her robes and hair. Her dragon tattoo burned like hot coals on her skin, but rather than harming her, it invigorated her.

Bhairatonix stared at her calmly from his cross-legged sitting position. "Well done, apprentice. You are fulfilling everything I planned for you."

Shevia ignored him and gazed into the sphere in her hand. The moth within stirred its wings feebly. It gave no indication that it saw her. "Such a small thing, so feeble," she mused. "But small things have a way of becoming powerful when they are set free." She held out her arm as if to drop the glass.

Bhairatonix's smile grew. "Do it. Break the glass and discover your purpose!" Bhairatonix snarled. "You see me as a tyrant. You believe yourself broken under my cruel malevolence. But do you not see, Shevia? In my wake you've become one of the most powerful Mystics to ever live. Through my mastery of the Deep I've guided you here to this moment to fulfill plans made nearly a thousand years ago by grandmasters who are alive in the Myst and watching you this very moment. Embrace the gift I've given you! Fulfill your destiny. Destroy the glass!"

"You've given me nothing!" Shevia snarled. "You claim to have mastered the Deep, yet I see through your obvious lies. You've denied me a Mystic name and a proper Mystic staff. Your own powers wither while mine grow. *I* healed the ranger Simkon AnClure from the plague that you could not touch. I conquered the other High Mystics. You are nothing. I am the master now."

"You have strength, but that is nothing compared to the will of the Deep."

Myst and fire pooled in Shevia's hands. Her heart thundered in her chest. "Then it is time for you to join your predecessors in the so-called Deep."

She roared fire over him. It surged from her hands, shifting from red-orange to a shining blue. The stone in the tower glowed red and wavered as it turned molten. The roof above them burst into flames, but Shevia ignored the falling embers.

When the fires in her hands vanished, Shevia stared at the devastation she'd wrought. Bhairatonix sat, completely unharmed amid the still-molten stone. His robes were incinerated, leaving him naked. His black tattoo seemed to mock her. Another portion of the tower wall behind him had fallen, exposing the open air. He lifted his gaze and Shevia actually felt a trickle of fear. Bhairatonix stood, unfolding his long body. He gathered his mangled left hand to his chest. Shevia had to force herself not to step away.

"There is no power you possess that will harm me. As my apprentice, you are bound to me, and prevented from harming even a hair upon me."

An old and familiar panic welled in Shevia. He was going to punish her again. She screamed and breathed more fire across him, but when she ran out of breath he still stood there, untouched. He strode toward her, and she saw death in his eyes.

"Do not touch me!" she screamed, and swung her staff at him. He caught it mid-swing. The staff trembled between their grips, then suddenly shattered. Shevia screamed, and Bhairatonix threw the useless shards onto the ground.

"I, Bhairatonix, First among the High Mystics of this world, do hereby, in the name of the dragon masters of old, command you to break that sphere."

He seized her throat. Shevia gripped his hand with her free one, still holding the sphere in the other. His grip was like iron. She scrabbled at it. She reached for the Myst and called to Sitting Mother, but her powers melted as she tried to pry him off her.

"For nearly a thousand years the High Mystics have guarded this sphere during Crow Tallin, pooling their powers in order to keep it intact. But they don't realize how *wrong* they are. The dragon Lagnaraste must be let loose. The Reunion she brings will change the world forever. You do not see it, but our world is broken. By reuniting with Fayün, we will bring a new era of glory in which Mystics are properly revered by all, human, laghart, and fay."

The corners of Shevia's vision darkened. The Myst melted away from her, and as it fled she felt her body breaking. She squeezed her eyes shut against the tears that she couldn't help from forming. She couldn't let it end like this. Not after how far she'd come. She would gladly accept a thousand other deaths, but not like this. Not at the hands of *this* man, of all people. She called again to Sitting Mother but heard nothing. Why did she not answer?

"Shevia!" called a voice.

Shevia managed to crane her neck to see Tibron standing in the doorway, his hand covering his mouth from the smoke. She tried to scream at him to flee, but she could not make a sound. She had no idea how or why he'd returned to Kelt Apar, but she didn't want him to die.

Or to see her die in Bhairatonix's grip.

Tibron drew his sword and rushed toward Bhairatonix. "Release her!"

The High Mystic dropped Shevia and used the Myst to throw Tibron toward the gaping hole in the tower. Tibron screamed but managed to catch the ledge to prevent himself from falling.

"I release you from my service," Bhairatonix sneered at Tibron. "You and your brothers were useless anyway."

Shevia coughed as she tried to catch her breath, but the thick smoke made it difficult. She still held the glass sphere in her hand. Her broken staff lay nearby. Only now, as it lay broken in front of her, did she realize how attached she'd become to it. Like her, the former broom handle had gone from a feeble object to a mighty artifact that made towers and High Mystics tremble. And now, like her, Bhairatonix had broken it.

Freedom.

The word whispered across her mind. Whether it came from herself, Sitting Mother, or somewhere else, Shevia did not know. But in that moment, her eyes widened as realization dawned on her.

She pushed herself to stand on trembling feet. "You are not my master," Shevia managed.

Bhairatonix left her brother hanging on the broken tower's

ledge. His tall, naked body strode through smoke and wreckage. "Rage all you like, you are mine."

"No," she said. "I am free from your lineage. I reject your tyranny. I am a Mystic, despite you."

"That's impossible—" Bhairatonix began.

A loud cracking noise sounded above. Shevia glanced up in time to see the roof collapse. Without thought, she threw a wall of blue fire above them. The wooden beams incinerated as they passed though, falling harmlessly as ash afterward. Beyond the broken roof, the full moon blazed in the calm night sky. Treorel shone on its very edge as it prepared to pass behind.

Shevia surged the Myst and flexed her back. Silver wings, twice her height and shaped like the wings on her tattoo, erupted from her back. She felt like a moth crawling from its cocoon and spreading wide under the sun for the first time. She took the glass sphere in one hand, grabbed Bhairatonix with the other, and leaped into the air, smashing through the remains of the tower roof. For a moment they hovered in midair, high above Kelt Apar, bathing in the Mystic Star.

And at that moment, Treorel passed behind the full moon, and Crow Tallin came upon the land.

A slow, creeping sense of cold crawled across Shevia. All around her, a red shadow crossed over Kelt Apar, bathing everything in the color of blood and fire. The moon's surface tinted to an angry red.

The Myst churned as though it had been heated to a boil. The air around her rippled like a curtain, and as it shifted Shevia could see beyond to a realm of endless silver. Everywhere across Kelt Apar, the veil between worlds fell away.

Shevia's spine burned with power. Untold waves of the Myst raced through her veins, filling every fiber of her being.

She crashed her feet hard into the ground. The soil around her erupted and a shock wave of fire rippled outward.

A scream sounded from the tower as Tibron fell. She caught him with a cushion of Myst, easing him to the ground.

A gathering of nearby Mystics backed away. Vivianna ran toward her from the tower, but she was too far and too insignificant to stop what was about to happen. The Green Man, who held Yarina's broken body in his arms, turned his fierce gaze upon her.

Shevia ignored them all. Bhairatonix squirmed beneath her grip, clawing at her hands. She could feel him throwing the Myst at her, but it did not harm her. "How?" he snarled.

"By shattering my staff, you violated your end of our connection. I am the master of my own fate now. You have no power over me."

She felt the Myst surge in her old master's body as he prepared yet another assault on her. "You denied me a proper Mystic staff," Shevia said. "You broke the twig you deemed to give me. Now I claim a new staff."

Bhairatonix's eyes widened. "No—"

Shevia wretched his neck, snapping it. She flared the Myst and fire erupted across his naked body. She yanked her arm up and tore his spine out. It came out cleanly, like a sword being drawn from its sheath. The meat from his body slid free and his head thumped to the ground. The Myst and fire purified the long line of bone in her hand, hardening it. Power surged through it, focusing her. The dragon within her raged. The moth in the glass flew wildly within its prison.

Near the tower, the remaining Mystics stared at her in horror. Vivianna skidded to a halt, covering her mouth as if trying not to vomit.

"I call upon Sitting Mother," Shevia said. "I summon Lagnaraste."

She let the glass sphere fall from her hand.

TWENTY-SIX

THE FALL OF THE CROSSROADS

Pomella lay on the banks of the pool beside the waterfall with sand and mud caking her lips. Her vision cleared, bringing silver fay into focus. For a panicked moment, she feared she was still in Fayün. Then she saw the brown and gray of the ground. She sighed with relief into the dirt.

She pushed herself up and marveled at her surroundings. It was hard to tell where the fay realm began and the human world ended. Trees from both worlds occupied the same place, inter-mixing their branches. Familiar, human-realm animals chased fay creatures across the ground. Behind her, twin waterfalls roared into the silver and blue water.

A deep feeling of sadness and loneliness washed over Pomella. Her mind raced to make sense of it, tried to remember what had just happened. A warning in her heart tried to stop those memories from crashing home, but it was too late. In a heartbeat, she remembered everything.

Hector.

A scream ripped out of Pomella's throat. She scrambled to her feet and spun around. "Hector!" she called, and summoned him with the Myst. She pulsed the command again, calling to him as she had a thousand times.

"*HECTOR!*"

A hummingbird spun into view, but it was only Ena.

Tears poured from Pomella's eyes. Her chin and hand shook as she reached for her remaining familiar. "E-Ena," she sobbed, "Where is Hector? Tell me he's not really . . ."

Ena alighted onto her palm, and Pomella sensed the overwhelming sadness and loss echoing from the little bird's tiny heart. Hector was gone. Ripped apart by—

No. No. *No!*

It was all too much. First Lal, now Hector. They were equal losses in her mind. She refused to think of one as greater than the other. In losing Lal she lost her teacher, mentor, and friend. But in losing Hector she lost a part of herself. Her heart might still be beating, and her lungs might still draw breath, but without a doubt a small part of her had just died.

She placed her face against Ena, trying to somehow feel Hector through his sister. Hector, who had died allowing her to escape. Hector, who gave her the strength of a hundred people.

"I'm so sorry, Ena," she said. "I'm sorry I wasn't fast enough, and that he needed to sacrifice himself."

Ena flew from her hand and darted for Pomella's Mystic

staff lying on the ground. It appeared as it had in Fayün, with intertwined trunks of polished brown and silver oak, topped with a snake's head. Ena landed on the staff's uppermost portion and quirked an expression at Pomella. The message was clear to her. *Pick up your staff and give meaning to his sacrifice.*

Pomella took a deep breath. She looked skyward and saw Treorel nearly in line with the moon. Once it slipped behind, the human and fay worlds would be completely overlapped. There was well under an hour before that occurred—but she was a full two days' journey from Kelt Apar.

"You're right," Pomella said. "We have work to do." She held her hand out and her Mystic staff leaped to her. Ena alighted from the staff and circled upward. At Pomella's command, the Myst circled around like a vortex. "Take us to Kelt Apar," she said to Ena. She wrapped her hand around the hummingbird and willed her to lift them skyward.

The Mystwood and the rest of the world fell away as they rose together as a glowing streak of light. Under the light of Treorel, such feats came as easy as walking. They circled Mag-Breckan, twisting close to its summit as if to whisper a secret.

Ena spun them once in a circle to gain momentum, then zoomed across the landscape like a shooting star. Below them, in the space of a heartbeat, Pomella saw the Mystwood reveal itself. Fayün lay atop the trees like a perfectly fitted blanket. To the west, the surface of the ocean rose and fell, rolling gently as it breathed. Pomella focused attention on her destination. MagDoon loomed ahead, dominating the Ironlow Mountains. The familiarity of home washed over Pomella as they approached Kelt Apar.

Ena set her down outside the grounds, within sight of the hedge wall. Weight and substance returned to her as she took in her surroundings. She released Ena from her grip. The hummingbird circled her once, then hovered nearby.

"Why'd we stop here?" she asked the hummingbird.

Ena didn't reply, but Pomella thought she knew the answer anyway. She couldn't see it, but some sort of barrier surrounded Kelt Apar. Perhaps it was related to Oxillian's wall, or perhaps it was tied to the land's nature; Kelt Apar could not be easily found within the Mystwood. Regardless of the reason, this was close enough. She'd have to get through the wall on her own.

Pomella looked toward the towering hedge surrounding the grounds. Even from outside, she could see that Kelt Apar was on fire. Heavy black smoke rose from inside, lifting toward the night sky, obscuring Treorel and the moon.

Between Pomella and the wall was a sea of rioting people. Hundreds of men and women ran between the trees carrying torches or weapons or both. Parents stood outside the tents they'd lived in for weeks, trying to keep their children safe from panicked individuals or roving bands of marauders.

Adding to the chaos were the fay creatures. Most of them ran in panicked fear, not realizing or understanding that Crow Tallin had dragged them into the human realm. But Pomella also saw silver axthos running among the humans, swinging crude clubs or launching barbed arrows.

A man ran straight at her, his eyes wide with panic. Before Pomella could react, he vanished, drifting momentarily into Fayün. Moments later, he appeared again, on her opposite side, still running.

"Please, Mistress," came a nearby voice. Pomella spun around as a cluster of disheveled men and women approached. The one who'd spoken was a woman, younger than herself, who clutched a child to her chest. "Help us. How long will this go on for?"

"My boy was bitten by a fay spider," said one of the men. A bloody gash shone on his chin. "Help him, please."

"Please, Hummingbird, what do we do?" said a second man.

Hands reached for her. "I—" Pomella backed away. Now wasn't the time. She wanted to help these people, and knew they were afraid.

"This will pass," Pomella assured them, trying to sound convincing. "Crow Tallin will be here momentarily. More fay will come before the end. Expect more strange occurrences. Find shelter if you can and trust in the Myst and all will be well."

Her words sounded hollow to her, but she saw tension drain from some of the grubby faces around her. She glanced back toward the wall, and the smoke beyond.

The crowd around her grew. A couple holding an infant stepped directly in her path. "Hummingbird," the mhathir said, her face gaunt and filled with tears. "My child, she's, she's—"

Before Pomella could gently move the couple aside to open the path, the mhathir held her baby up for her to see. Pomella barely contained a gasp.

The child, no more than a day or two old, was half fay. Overlaid atop her human face was that of what appeared to be a rabbit. The child snoozed soundly, her human and rabbit ears rising up and down with her breaths.

"Our Niella, she's—she's—"

Pomella touched the mhathir's cheek to reassure her, and then reached down to the child to wrap the Myst around her like a blanket, using it to find a seam between the child and fay. It was as if the two had been fused together somehow at birth. She found herself wondering how many children born during Crow Tallin would be like this.

Carefully, Pomella tried to slip the Myst between the child and fay to separate them. The child's strange face scrunched and she made a little cry in her sleep. Pomella pressed harder, but the bond between fay and child held tight, refusing to let her divide it. The child began to cry.

"I'm sorry," Pomella said. "I cannot do more right now. I must return to Kelt Apar."

The mhathir's face crumbled with sadness. "No, Mistress. Please!"

"I'm sorry," Pomella said again, her heart wrenching, and tried to step past the couple.

The woman's husband put a heavy hand on her shoulder. "You've gotta do something," he said. "Our tyke's not well!"

Pomella pulled away from his touch. More commoners pressed in toward her. "I—"

"Mystic!" another person yelled. "Why's this happening?"

"We're cursed!" yelled another.

"Sing to the baby! Save her!"

"My son's taken by the fay!"

Their pleas washed over her. More hands reached for her. The path to the wall was now completely obscured.

"The Mystics are bringing this upon us!"

"No," Pomella said, responding to the last. "No, we are not. Crow Tallin is—"

"Why are the Mystics punishing us? Aren't our lives already hard enough?"

"Heal the child!"

"I can't," Pomella said, turning about, trying to focus on one face at a time. The surge of hands and voices overwhelmed her. A hand grasped her Mystic staff. She yanked the heavy branch back but more hands reached for it.

The Myst rose around her again. All she had to do was flash it outward to give herself some room. Too many hands reaching. Too many voices. She needed—

Thundering horse hooves pounded through the trees. Pomella turned and saw a rider pushing the crowd back. "Get away from her! She's not hurting you!"

It was Berrit.

He wore his ridiculous-yet-charming hat and had a case with his musical instrument on his back. He held a thin baton in his hand, which he swung harmlessly in the crowd's direction to discourage them from approaching.

"Are you OK?" he called to her.

"Yes," Pomella replied. "I need to get to the tower."

"Go," he said. "I've got these people."

There was no time to waste. Pomella ran for the wall. With the Myst surrounding her like a cloak, she focused on radiating serenity toward everyone. But trying to calm the riot was like trying to extinguish a forest fire with a single bucket of water. Ena raced in blinding circles around her, trailing silvery smoke, which collectively formed a sort of ringed barrier around her.

As she raced toward the wall, more people noticed her. Hundreds of faces turned to look in her direction. But rather than rushing toward her, they backed away, wide-eyed.

Screams assaulted her from all sides. "The Mystics are abandoning us!"

"Open the wall, Hummingbird!"

"Tear it down!"

"Burn it!"

The crowds stormed around her, even more fiercely than before, but this time nobody came closer than the protective ring Ena formed.

"*You've* abandoned us!" cried a voice, and a stone flew in her direction, but Ena intercepted it and shattered it into dust.

Just as Pomella arrived at the wall, screams sounded behind her. She looked back and stopped short. At least twenty mounted horsemen charged through the crowd. They ran toward the place she had just been standing. From this distance, she could still see Berrit, sitting astride his gelding, turning toward them.

A whistling sound tore through the forest, followed by a sickening thud, and an arrow blasted into Berrit's chest, splashing blood across a gathering of commoners standing near him. His horse whinnied, and Berrit's lifeless body slipped to the ground, followed by his hat.

"No!" Pomella cried, taking a step toward him. She stared in wide-eyed shock, unable to process what had just happened.

The horsemen surrounded the gathered commoners who were trying to run. The mounted men kicked them back, or used looped nets attached to long poles.

Slavers.

The last horseman to arrive wore a gray mask with strange red markings on it. The figure strode past his men, who rounded up the panicked commoners. He stared straight at Pomella.

Her heart raced as recognition came over her. She'd never seen him in person, but this had to be the Shadefox, the leader of the slavers.

More screams came to Pomella, but this time they came from the opposite side of the wall. She looked skyward and saw Treorel on the very edge of the moon. Crow Tallin was moments away from beginning.

Pomella lifted her staff to Unveil an attack on the Shadefox in order to maim or disable him quickly. But as she did so, the Shadefox lifted his hand and removed his mask.

Pomella froze.

It was her brother, Gabor. He was only a teenager, barely old enough to shave, but somehow, impossibly, he stood there, at the head of a highly organized band of slavers.

The recognition and hate radiating from him was as bright as the full moon. He slipped his mask back on, turned his horse, and shouted commands to his men.

At that moment, Treorel passed behind the moon, and Crow Tallin painted the land in red shadows. Overcome by emotion, Pomella fled. She ran to the wall and pressed her forehead against it. Tears ran down her cheeks.

Flickering torchlight lit the night. All along the wall's length people threw rocks, branches, or whatever else they could find at it, trying to breach the barrier. It was only a matter of time before they succeeded.

"Ox," Pomella said through her tears. "It's me."

In response, a narrow tunnel opened, and she squeezed through. The tunnel closed behind her as she pushed, urging her along quickly. The torrential sounds of thousands of rioting people suddenly became muffled, although the crackling of the burning wall became louder and more clear.

Pomella stopped as she stepped out onto the grass. "No," she whispered. She didn't know how much more she could take.

The central tower was on fire. Most of its roof along with the walls of the upper chamber were shattered. Smoke and flames rose from that room, seeming to signal the end of yet another important part of her life. For a moment, Pomella lost track of where she was. Half of what she saw was the Kelt Apar she knew, and the other half was a rocky landscape.

And standing in the same place as the broken central tower, a huge silver spire, covered in carved writing, rose into the sky.

The Tower of Eternal Starlight.

A nearby rushing sound startled her as an arrow lodged itself into the grass. It was well out of reach from her, but it had come from outside the wall. Another arrow fell from the night, and another. More than a few of those arrows had flames on their tips.

Pomella ran toward the central tower where a cluster of people were gathered. Pomella recognized some of the Mystics, including Vivianna.

Oxillian lumbered forward, looking uncharacteristically dazed and frightened. He stumbled like a drunkard, falling at times halfway into the ground before climbing out and tumbling forward. Mistress Yarina limped beside him. Her normally immaculate hair was tossed in disarray, and her red gown was torn. Blood covered one side of her face, and she cradled what appeared to be a broken arm.

A roar sounded behind Pomella as a flaming section of the

eastern wall toppled inward. A storm of rioters rushed onto the Kelt Apar grounds. More than one caught fire as they scrambled across the still-burning remains of the wall.

Suddenly the ground erupted upward as Oxillian rammed pillars of soil toward the sky. "You cannot invade this domain!" he cried.

"Don't hurt them, Ox!" Pomella cried, looking quickly over her shoulder as the Green Man continued to pound rock and dirt toward the rioters.

This was all wrong. Pomella thought of Brigid, and the peaceful demeanor the Saint had demonstrated in Fayün. She thought of Lal, and his smiling face as he had so often swept leaves across these grounds. How could everything have come to this?

Shevia.

Pomella rounded the far side of the tower and saw her, wearing an actual cloak of fire across her shoulders. The young woman carried a strange Mystic staff. Pomella's stomach lurched when she saw that it was made of bone and there was a severed head and pile of flesh near the woman's feet.

In her other hand Shevia held the glass sphere. The moth within it—Lagnaraste, Saint Brigid—frantically bounced against its prison. Shevia held her arm out wide, spoke some words Pomella could not hear, and let the orb roll from her fingers toward the ground.

"No!" Yarina yelled, and stretched out her hand.

Pomella watched it fall. Ena could catch it. All she had to do was command her to streak across the grass with the speed of a shooting star and bring it to her. The hummingbird hovered beside her, poised and ready.

If the glass broke, everything that the High Mystics had

worked for would be undone. For nearly a thousand years, hundreds of the world's greatest masters had dedicated their lives to ensuring it remained intact. Kelt Apar's central tower and Oxillian had been raised up to protect it.

Unbidden, something Brigid had told her about Lal came to Pomella's mind. *It's why he retired when he did. He did not want to be a part of Crow Tallin.* Perhaps, Pomella thought, he'd come to understand what she had, that the old Lagnaraste—the last of the dragons who tore the world apart—had been defeated long ago by Brigid and that the High Mystics' purpose for holding her back no longer applied. This Crow Tallin marked the end of an older way of thinking.

The world needed to move forward. Moth needed to embrace a new tradition, a new way of thinking. It could begin, right now, with her, by freeing the Saint who had inspired untold lives over the centuries.

This was the moment to set Brigid free.

With a silent command, Pomella summoned Ena to her palm, withholding her from catching the sphere.

The glass sphere smashed into the ground. Its shards blew outward with a tremendous rush of wind and energy. Yarina fell to her knees and screamed. Oxillian stumbled to his knees. Half of his body sank back into the ground. He seemed to be fighting against the soil, trying to remain upright.

Oblivious to the carnage, Shevia knelt beside the glass shards. She held out her palm, which, even from this distance, Pomella could see was trembling. The silver fay moth stood calmly among the shards. Wispy smoke wafted off its wings as it pumped them slowly. It crept forward onto Shevia's outstretched finger.

Yarina stared in openmouthed horror. The High Mystic shifted her attention from the shattered orb to Pomella. The sadness on her face broke Pomella's heart. *She knows*, Pomella thought. Somehow, the High Mystic knew Pomella could have stopped the glass from breaking.

Shevia stood upright and lifted the little moth to her eye level. Her cloak of fire rippled around her, yet did not burn her.

Pomella strode forward. But before she could say anything, a multihued beam of light descended from the sky. It looked like a rainbow, only perfectly straight, or perhaps still curved, but stretching so far away into the stars that its arc could not be seen. A powerful sense of harmony radiated from it as it fell, as slow as a snowflake toward Shevia's finger. The beam began at the moon, and tapered downward until it shone on the moth.

The fighting around Kelt Apar slowed and stopped as the rioters turned stunned expressions toward the light.

Pomella's heart thundered. Vivianna, Yarina, and the other gathered Mystics stared with mixed expressions of surprise and horror. Those expressions softened as the rainbow light shone peace across the lawn and burning tower.

The tiny moth that had been contained within the glass fluttered off Shevia's finger and dissolved into the rainbow. Shevia closed her eyes. Her body tensed and she rolled back her head.

Suddenly her eyes and mouth flared open. She fell to her knees, screaming silently before falling forward and placing both hands flat on the ground. Her chest heaved.

A lurking fear rose in Pomella's chest. Shevia rose, but Pomella could immediately see that it was another person who moved her body. She had the bearing of a queen, and the serenity of a High Mystic. Pomella could feel the Myst thundering around her like a firestorm barely held in check.

"Saint Brigid," she whispered.

Sim stood in the center of Kelt Apar as Crow Tallin engulfed the land. Shevia had entered the central tower as soon as they'd arrived, but he knew that was a fight he couldn't get tangled up with. He would leave the Mystics to their arguments.

Not a cloud hung in the sky, but Sim knew when a storm was brewing. If the highlands of Qin had once whispered silent warnings to him, Kelt Apar now screamed.

He walked slowly through the grounds, watching Mystics cluster together nervously. The ones who saw him looked away, not concerned with what a single ranger was up to. The fay ran and flew everywhere. An axthos materialized in front of him for a moment, and screamed. Sim waited calmly for the creature to charge him. His onkai were secured on his back, but always within reach.

The axthos must've seen something in his expression or otherwise changed its mind. It skittered away, looking back over its shoulder at Sim before dissolving back to Fayün.

Soon enough, Sim mused, there would be no distance between this world and the fay realm. He continued his patrol of Kelt Apar, circling south past the cabins, which appeared empty, and crossed the last bridge spanning the river.

An explosion erupted from the central tower. Faster than

thought, Memory and Remorse were in his hands, their blades reflecting orange and red flames that roared from the tower's roof.

A body fell from the upper chamber, and another hung from a ledge. A figure, Shevia, *flew* skyward, carried by silver, bat-like wings that emerged from her back. As she crested, a thick red shadow crossed over the land. Sim looked toward the moon and saw the Mystic Star's red light vanish behind it.

Crow Tallin had begun, and with it came the fay. Hundreds of them, ranging from seemingly regular creatures to shambling axthos, all appeared at once. Within moments, a portion of the eastern wall collapsed, and a crowd of rioters stormed onto the grounds.

But despite all the chaos, Sim drew his attention to the most impressive sight before him. A massive spire of silver stone appeared, overlaid exactly on top of the smaller, broken stone tower in the center of Kelt Apar. It rose to the heavens, perhaps a thousand steps tall. The entire tower was covered in runes he could not discern from a distance. At the top, backlit by the blood moon and a constellation of stars, stood a single window.

As he stared at the spire the silver path, shining as vibrant as ever, shimmered into existence at his feet and wound its way across the grass to the base of the tower.

Calling him.

Pomella watched as a legendary Saint walked across Kelt Apar's lawn in Shevia's body. It had to be her. Only a woman such as Brigid, who had accomplished so much in her life, could command such a presence. She moved in the same graceful, flowing manner as Brigid's moving illustration had on the wall of the Tower of Eternal Starlight.

Brigid—through Shevia—looked at her. "Greetings again, Pomella AnDone."

Yarina, Vivianna, and a woman Pomella recognized as High Mystic Willwhite, gathered around the Saint who'd ensnared Shevia's body. Master Willwhite actually shook with emotion and, unable to remain standing, fell to her knees.

Master Ehzeeth, the laghart High Mystic, was the last to shuffle forward, assisted by Hizrith. Both of their tails swished with excitement. Ehzeeth's tongue zipped in and out repeatedly.

"By evvvvery ssstar and zzzurtttna," Ehzeeth hissed, "my ladyyy, the lagharttt People are yoursss!"

Brigid approached him and placed both her hands upon his scaled face. As she moved, her body *rippled*. Shevia's tan skin wavered, fading to a paler tone before cycling back. Her dark hair shifted toward red but returned a moment later.

"Listen Once, hear Me thrice," Brigid told the lagharts. "From stars to shore, across paradise. I cry, I call, I plea. My lost friends, tell them, tell them, Come Back to Me. Come Back to Me."

Ehzeeth stiffened at her gentle touch and her words. When she finished speaking, his eyes widened with rhapsody, and he slumped to the ground, dead. Hizrith fell to his side, his tongue zipping in and out.

Compassion shone on Brigid's face. It was a strange expression to see on Shevia's normally withdrawn, bitter one. "He will carry my call to the *kanta*," Brigid said, "whose eyes will open and see the Golden Ones and the People of the Sky for what they truly are. Go forth, Hizrith, High Mystic of Lavantath, and bring our people home."

Hizrith closed his dead master's eyes and then prostrated himself at Brigid's feet.

Brigid turned to the other High Mystics. "Sons and Daughters. I am Brigid the Red, Daughter of None but the Woods. For nearly a thousand years you guarded the sphere that kept me locked in the Tower of Eternal Starlight. You sought the will of the Deep, as your predecessors have done. I commend you for your dedication to the tradition during Crow Tallin." Her face darkened. "But for every year that passed, you ignored my calls to set me free. Only these women"—she gestured to herself and then to Pomella—"mere adepts in comparison to your might and experience, braved hardship and danger to free me. They will be elevated."

Yarina stepped forward, and for a moment Pomella could see her regain some of the composure and grace that she normally showed. "Saint Brigid," she said, her voice only slightly trembling, "I am Yarina Sineese, the High Mystic of Moth. Your coming is . . . overwhelming. Please understand that—"

"We will speak later, daughter," Brigid said, and Pomella could not ignore the reproach in her voice. "Where is my son? I have waited long enough for him. Where is Janid?"

Smoke, embers, and ash, carried by a light evening wind, were the only answer. Shouts and other mutterings sounded throughout Kelt Apar as people watching spread the word of what they saw. Brigid looked across the faces of those gathered. She stopped when she came to Pomella.

"My son," she repeated.

"We don't know him, Mistress," Pomella said. "Please. We must calm the riots. When Crow Tallin is over we will help—"

"Crow Tallin will never be over," Brigid said. "The Reunion is upon us, and I will have my son."

"I don't understand, Mistress," Pomella said. Fear rippled through her.

"I have sensed him in your world. He was here, at this tower! *Where is he?*"

Before Pomella could speak again and try to reason with her, Brigid's eyes fell upon an exceptionally long Mystic staff lying nearby. She held out her hand and it flew to her. Her eyes danced with excitement. "My old staff. He is here! I gave this to him, so he could escape Fayün. Janid! Where are you? Come back to me! Janid!"

She stopped as she found a mangled body that had been near the discarded staff.

Bhairatonix.

The Saint's eyes widened and the blood drained from her face. With a scream that tore across all of Kelt Apar, Brigid rushed to the High Mystic's bloody remains. Another harrowing cry ripped from her, slapping the air like thunder.

Pomella's mind raced as she tried to make sense of what was happening. From Lal's memories, Pomella knew that Bhairatonix had been found as a child in the Mystwood by Lal shortly after the most recent Crow Tallin sixty years ago. *In the end I freed Janid, who escaped to the human world,* Brigid had told her back in Fayün. *"After he escaped the tower, I knew I had to wait until the next Crow Tallin, when the worlds temporarily merged again. Only then would I have a chance to return to him.*

"Vivianna," Pomella said quietly, feeling a sudden dread rise in her chest, "find Oxillian and the rangers. Get everyone out of Kelt Apar *now*."

Brigid turned her expression on to Pomella, and the motion was like a blade being drawn from its sheath. "You," she breathed. "You wretched, ungrateful *chyat*!"

"Pomella did not kill him!" Yarina intoned. Her serenity had returned, and her voice did not lack for strength. "He was killed by the girl whose body you control."

The bloodcurdling scream that tore out of Brigid was the sound only a mother could make at finding her son dead after waiting nine hundred years for him. Brigid surged to her feet and screamed fire from her mouth. She held a Mystic staff in each hand, including Bhairatonix's spine.

Hard winds carrying ash and fire from the burning wall suddenly raced through Kelt Apar, surging toward Brigid. The twisted-dragon tattoo on her upper body writhed and began to shine with silver light. The dragon clawed its way across her skin, and then *crawled* off her body.

Pomella took a step back. The dragon grew as it separated from Brigid. One of its claws touched the ground, followed by another. The long, twisting body, reminiscent of a huge snake, uncoiled itself as it peeled itself off Brigid's skin. It continued to swell, growing in size until it dwarfed Oxillian. The creature resembled Mantepis but was far more massive, with huge legs that held it aloft. Massive, bat-like wings unfolded themselves and flexed wide. Silver smoke rolled off its entire body.

The dragon reared its head and roared. The sound thundered across Kelt Apar. Most of the rioters screamed and ran, although some lifted their weapons against the creature that now stood as tall as the broken central tower. Arrows flew toward it, but they bounced harmlessly off its thick hide. It was strange, even to Pomella, to see a fay creature so *real* within the human world.

The dragon loomed high above Brigid. The Saint's rage and grief contorted Shevia's face. "Janid!" she screamed, and raised both staves upward into the air. The fay dragon leaped into the air, pumping its wings once, twice, before arcing high into the sky. More shouts and cries from beyond the wall assaulted Pomella's ears.

Brigid spun Shevia's body in a full circle, punching both staves horizontally toward the wall. The fay dragon looped once in the air, tucked its wings, and stormed down in the direction she pointed as if it were a puppet on sticks. It spiraled as it flew, and screamed.

Blazing fire erupted from its mouth, melting anything it touched. Pomella grabbed hold of Ena and shifted to a safe distance, but her heart thundered as she looked back toward the tower. Vivianna knocked Yarina aside, but their proximity to the dragon's inferno ignited their clothes.

Vivianna kept her head, and scrambled to her feet. With a wave of her staff, a rushing wind swept over her and the High Mystic, extinguishing the fire. Vivianna pulled Yarina to her feet and led her to the far side of the tower.

The dragon blasted through Oxillian's wall, then arced high into the sky. Brigid swung her staves down in parallel motions from her shoulder to hip, and the dragon responded with another pass.

"Take me to her, Ena," Pomella said, and felt the world rush as the hummingbird zoomed her to a patch of ground in front of the Saint. A grass fire licked at her robes, but she extinguished it with barely more than a thought.

"Is this your legacy, Brigid?" Pomella called. Ash and smoke billowed across her. "I know you are hurting, but this is not the way of the Myst."

"You know *nothing* of my hurt," Brigid raged. "I exist in the Deep. Every action I take is informed by a grander vision for the universe that you cannot comprehend."

"How can death and fire, born of revenge, come from a place of peace and wisdom and grace?" Pomella replied.

"You are not a mother," Brigid said. "You can never understand."

She jerked her body again, spinning her staves in a graceful blur of motion, commanding the dragon to attack from another direction. Pomella tried to make sense of what was happening. Shevia had become a wivan, completely ensnared by Brigid. Shevia, like Lal, was lost somewhere in her own mind and body, held prisoner by a captor.

And like Lal, she had only one place to go.

"Then help me understand," Pomella said. She commanded Ena to surge ahead, and a heartbeat later she stood directly beside Brigid. Pomella jabbed her hand out, placing her palm on the other woman's forehead. She closed her eyes and, with a supreme act of focus, entered the Crossroads, and Shevia's mind.

The central tower loomed before Sim. Chaos reigned around him as rioters, axthos, and Mystics all battled in different ways. For all their talk of peace and serenity, this was what came of meddling in the affairs of Mystics. Perhaps some, like Grandmaster Faywong, deserved respect, but only because he had seemingly rejected the very aspects of being a Mystic that brought trouble.

A horde of axthos burst from the western trees. They rushed toward him, quickly closing the wide gap. He turned toward them, Memory and Remorse held firmly in his grip. He did not want to harm any of them, no matter how cruelly they might present themselves.

A deafening roar rumbled across the grounds, pulling the axthos up short. They skidded to a halt, tumbling over one another. Sim followed their terrified expressions and saw a massive fay dragon, shaped just like the one on Shevia's shoulder, rise into the sky on the opposite corner of the tower from where he stood. The dragon flapped its wings and twisted into the sky.

The axthos fled. Sim sheathed his onkai and continued along the shining path leading to the tower. He found it surprisingly easy to remain calm. The path *always* led him the right way.

Kelt Apar's familiar stone tower stood where it normally did, but overlaid atop it was the larger, more imposing spire with carved runes covering every inch. The only entrance that Sim could see was the normal doorway from Kelt Apar's tower.

Tibron sat with his back against the doorframe. Blood covered his face, along with angry red burns. He tried to stand when he saw Sim but grunted in pain and collapsed.

Sim placed a hand on his shoulder. "Rest," he said.

"My sister . . ." Tibron said in Qina. Blood leaked from his swollen lip. "She's not herself."

Sim gave him the barest of nods and moved toward the

doorway. Tibron grabbed Sim's arm with a bloody hand. "Pomella," he said. "She's with her."

Sim's heart raced, but he forced himself to retain a calm demeanor. He didn't know how Pomella had returned to Kelt Apar, but he didn't have time to dwell on it.

Sim looked toward the tower's summit, then returned his gaze to Tibron. "The silver path leads me here," he said. He didn't know if other rangers saw that path, but more and more he was convinced Rochella had seen it. Perhaps Tibron could, and if not now someday. "I don't know what awaits me," he finished.

Sim could see Tibron studying him through his swollen face. They remained there calmly for a long moment as chaos rumbled around them. At last, Tibron spoke.

"I understand," he said.

Living in the highlands for years alone had bred in Sim an instinct to hear what was unspoken, to see what could not be observed. That, perhaps, had been Rochella's true lesson. Through loneliness, one learns to *hear*. Now, at the entrance to the tower, Sim could see Tibron was learning that lesson, too.

"Take care of Pomella," Sim said.

Tibron nodded. "I will, brother. What will do you do now?"

"We are rangers," Sim said, easily pulling out the familiar words and translating them to Qina. "We do what we always do. We move, and we survive."

A chill washed over Sim as he crossed the threshold of the tower, along with a strange feeling of remembrance. It was as though he'd done this before, although he'd never previously stepped foot in the tower. The wide double doors behind him closed with a heavy boom, and the sound echoed upward.

Nothing stirred within the tower except an odd mixed scent of holly and sandalwood, as bitter as some of his memories. The silver path still shone at his feet, although fainter, despite the foyer's dim illumination, leading up the narrow spiral staircase that hugged the tower's rounded wall. Each stone shimmered with silver light, and upon their surface he saw runes scratched in. He traced his fingers over some of these runes but could not read them. They were in an entirely different language than he knew.

Sim sheathed his onkai into walking sticks, and ascended the stairs. The first landing he came to held a door made of dark wood with the same unknowable runes etched upon it. Three thin slits, about as long as his hand, ran vertically through it at his eye level. Sim peered in and saw a nearly empty room with no window. The lone occupant was a man sitting with his back to the door. A lump formed in Sim's throat. He recognized him, even from behind.

The man turned, and Sim looked into the face of his long-dead brother. Sim's heart thundered. "Dane," he whispered.

Dane tried to rise, but Sim now saw he was shackled with thick iron chains to the floor. Dane opened his mouth to speak, then dissolved entirely into silver light, leaving the room empty.

Sim stumbled back from the door and nearly tripped down the stairs. His heart raced and he tried unsuccessfully to calm himself. Dane had been dead nearly twenty years now.

He gathered himself and called up the stairs where the path still led, "Do not haunt me!"

He wondered, not for the first time, who or what he would find at the top of the tower, if anything. He continued up the stairs, and found himself wondering where the silver path came from. Was it from the Myst? From Sitting Mother? Or something else entirely? As he ascended each step, he wondered whether the path's creator—if there was one—had an agenda for him.

More doors greeted him at each landing, and each one contained slits by which he could've peered through. But he ignored them, not wanting to find more dead loved ones. It would be too easy to see them again, too tempting and wonderful to gaze on their faces for just another moment. He willed himself forward, toward the uppermost chamber, leaving his past behind, unseen.

At last he came to the final door at the top of the staircase. A twisted dragon, tangled upon itself like a Mothic knot, was carved into the wood in place of the open slits contained by the previous doors.

Sim placed his hand on the door handle but paused. After a moment of reflection, he drew one of his onkai, then entered the room.

The door closed behind him. There was no handle on the inside. The room itself would normally be cramped, except that a portion of the wall and roof had been destroyed.

Sitting cross-legged in the center of the room, with her short hair trembling in the wind and her back facing Sim, was a woman Sim recognized.

"Sitting Mother," he whispered.

She turned, and Sim beheld an attractive woman in her late thirties. Her hair was red, with a dusting of freckles upon her pale skin. Had he met her anywhere else, he would have thought she was just another woman from Moth.

"You came at last to me," she said.

"Who are you?" he said. "Truly."

The woman faced forward again and stared out the gaping hole in the tower. "I asked that very question to the Nameless Saint once. I was unable to hear her reply, for she was old beyond aging, and, quite possibly, beyond names."

Sim walked in a slow circle around her, coming close to the open portion of the wall. Outside, he saw a mountainous landscape and a wide valley in which hundreds of humans and fay ran and fought.

"But *you* have a name," he said.

"Yes," said the woman. "I have had many. Two of them, you know, one of which you've already spoken."

"Saint Brigid," he said, naming the other.

The woman smiled but kept her attention on the landscape beyond the tower. "Yes."

"Shevia wreaks devastation in your name," Sim said, coming right to it. "People are dying. Come out of the tower, and bring peace."

"Have you forgotten the stories, Sim? You and your sister sang them every Springrise. By the reckoning of your world, I've been trapped in this tower for nine hundred years. I cannot escape."

Sim glanced at the shattered wall. A feeling of dread crept through him. "Until now."

"Shevia has allowed me to escape the tower. But I cannot physically leave. Not yet, anyway."

He heard something in her tone, and suddenly knew the truth. "I'm to be your replacement."

The woman finally faced him. Her eyes were the same color as his.

"Yes," she said.

An explosion of memories and emotions assaulted Pomella as she tumbled through Shevia's mind. Previously, when she'd descended through Lal's mind, it had been like strolling through the Mystwood on a clear morning. Lal had barely been alive at the time when Pomella had merged with him, and that, along with his lifetime of calm thinking, as well as his bond with her, had allowed her to travel through his mind with ease. But Pomella had none of those benefits with Shevia, so it was like falling through the thorn-filled branches of a hundred trees.

Memories from Shevia's life rained down on her. She struggled to find something, anything, she could cling to in order to find stability.

As each memory touched Pomella, it became part of her as if it had been her own. In a moment that lasted a lifetime, Pomella lived experience after experience. She was a little girl, just nine years old, peering over the ledge toward the Obai entourage arriving at her parents' estate in Qin. She felt her eldest brother's slap streak across her cheek. The wetness of her tears upon her pillow soaked onto her face. Her skin bled beneath the barbs of the Thornwood. The bitter scent of sandalwood and holly washed over her, bringing visions that foretold the futures of kings and queens, Mystics and commoners.

A thousand memories, all filled with pain.

She tasted poison hidden in a wine goblet, and felt the fear and pain of Bhairatonix breaking her. She saw herself through Shevia's eyes, and experienced the longing for her freedom.

Within a single heartbeat Pomella lived all of Shevia's life, and with those experiences came something she hadn't expected to find.

Understanding. Empathy. Unity.

And within every memory, Pomella found Shevia's friend, this entity she called Sitting Mother. Lagnaraste. Brigid. She lurked there, in the shadows or on her shoulders, waiting and watching and whispering. Slowly, over the course of a decade, she breathed power into Shevia, lifting her up when necessary, or nudging her forward.

And now Brigid ensnared Shevia, turning her into a wivan. The Saint's presence surrounded Pomella as well as Shevia, pressing her down. Pomella tried in vain to push back the unseen force, but the Saint was too powerful.

"It did not have to be this way, Pomella," said Brigid's sad voice from the darkness. "You could have been my apprentice and, eventually, my successor. Shevia served her purpose, but she is too fragile, too broken. And she killed my Janid. But now, by coming here, into her mind, I cannot save you. You will break with her."

"Help me," Pomella whispered, hoping Shevia could listen to her. She tumbled through memories without an anchor, unable to find solid ground. She reached for the Myst, but it slipped away from her as she scrabbled. She called to Lal, and her past masters, but either they did not respond or she could not hear through the chaos of imagery and sound that assaulted her.

"Please, Shevia," Pomella said, desperately trying to find something they could use together to press back against Brigid's overwhelming will.

Like the clouds parting, she realized what she needed. *Who* she needed. A memory, fresh in Shevia's experience, rose up, of her standing beside the waterfall that led to Fayün. A man stood there, with matching walking sticks and scraggly blond hair.

Sim.

His face was as fresh and clear as ever. As soon as Pomella saw him, her awareness within Shevia's mind stabilized. The tumbling stopped and she found herself floating in a sea of life and experiences.

"He is beyond you," Brigid said. "He is mine, too."

Without thinking, Pomella reached out to the formless voice that was Brigid, and merged with her as well. Another rainfall of memories roared by, but she clung to the image of Sim. Three lives—her own, Shevia's, and Brigid's—stormed through her. She could no longer see individual memories, but as long as she held on to Sim she maintained herself.

One memory from Brigid crashed into Pomella with such force that Pomella almost lost her grip on sanity. It was a fresh memory, in which Sim stood beside Brigid as she knelt in the upper chamber of a tower. So vivid that it wasn't a memory at all. It was happening at that very moment.

Pomella whispered a single word to Sim.

"We could leave together," Sim said to Brigid.

The Saint shook her head. "The Tower must always be occupied."

"Why?"

She replied, but Sim did not listen to her words. At that moment, a voiceless word filled his mind. He didn't know where it came from, or how it arrived, but in an instant he knew with certainty who the voice belonged to.

Sitting Mother. Not the woman before him in this moment. Sim didn't understand how, but the certainty that washed over him was deeper than any truth he'd ever known. The true Sitting Mother—the gentle voice of patient love that had called to him for years in the wilderness, the voice that had guided him back to life—was not Brigid. It was another that echoed perfectly with his heart.

It was Pomella.

The word she'd spoken echoed in his mind.

Strike.

Brigid was still speaking. "Crow Tallin is ending, but soon—"

Memory and Remorse flashed in Sim's hands, crossing each other, as he decapitated the Saint.

Untold torrents of power surged into Shevia. A heartbeat ago, she'd been falling deeper into a sea of darkness, with the only light she could see fading away. Pomella had been there, with Brigid, but Shevia had not been able to speak, or make herself heard in any way.

Her whole life had been that way. When she made noise that bothered her brothers' ears, she was slapped. When she'd voiced her interests to her mother, she'd been banished to her room. When she'd ask for instruction or for her Mystic name, Bhairatonix had beaten her to silence. And even now, when Sitting Mother had finally revealed herself to her completely, when Shevia accomplished all that she asked, her mind had been pushed back into the recesses of darkness, and taken over by the woman Pomella and other High Mystics had referred to as Saint Brigid.

But now, for reasons Shevia didn't understand, that woman's presence suddenly vanished, leaving her power behind. It flooded into Shevia, filling her with the might of ten thousand Mystics. The Myst itself became her world. Every life that ever existed, and ever would, was a thread in her fingers that would dance to her callings. They would all listen to her noise now, whether they wanted to hear or not.

She blinked, and found herself standing at the infinitely thin border of two worlds. In one moment she found herself standing in the middle of Kelt Apar, near the central tower. The grass was on fire around her. Rioting humans, panicked axthos, struggling Mystics, and even terrified goats ran in every direction. A heartbeat later the world refocused and she saw a mountainous landscape with the same human and fay world denizens running about. High in the sky, watching calmly over it all, hung a bloodred moon.

She held a staff in either hand. They had both been Bhairatonix's, although only one had been his actual Mystic staff. With a sneer, she used the barest fraction of her power, and incinerated his wooden staff. She clutched his backbone—*her* staff—tighter in her fist.

Back and forth the worlds cycled, and with every moment that passed more power surged into her.

A huge presence loomed behind her. Shevia turned and saw the massive fay dragon gaze down at her with dead eyes. As a test, she moved her hand slightly, and the creature shifted in reply. She controlled its every action. It was an extension of her power, like another Mystic staff.

A groan sounded from near her feet.

Pomella pushed herself slowly to her feet, holding a hand her to head. She still gripped her Mystic staff, which had somehow changed form since they'd last seen each other. Shevia remembered how Pomella had touched her mind, and lived her memories. It was like waking from a dream now, but a part of Pomella's experiences had come to her as well.

Pomella looked from Shevia to the fay dragon and back.

"Brigid?" she asked.

"Gone. I have inherited her power." There was nothing more Shevia could say. Even though she stood there, wearing robes and flesh, she could not find words in any language she knew to fully express the magnitude of power that coursed through her. She had become a living Saint. With this power she could do anything.

Pomella used a trembling hand to tuck a tangle of her hair behind an ear. "What will you do?"

For all her seemingly endless power, Shevia could not find an immediate answer to that question.

"People are frightened," Pomella urged. "Dying. You can help them."

"I want nothing to do with it," Shevia said. "I will not be used by you or anybody else again."

Pomella stepped toward her, and Shevia readied to destroy her. It would be as easy as breathing. But she held herself back when she saw the look of understanding on Pomella's face.

"I'm sorry," she said. "I've *lived* your memories, Shevia. Use your power. Set yourself free. You don't need Sitting Mother. Be yourself."

"Be myself?" she said, her anger rising. "I am fire. I am death. I am Lagnaraste. Even now, I'm enslaved to my own nature."

"Then change your nature," Pomella said. "My master once gave up his power. He stepped aside for something greater. I believed Brigid had done that, too, but I was wrong. Like you, she had power, but not freedom. And ultimately, the Myst is about freeing yourself, not about gaining power."

An unexpected tear welled in Shevia's eye but burned away from the heat radiating from her skin.

"I don't know how," she confessed.

Pomella took her hand. Shevia flinched but let her.

"I will help you. Just ask," said Pomella.

Shevia nodded. "Yes," she managed. "Help me be free."

"Then I declare you Unclaimed," Pomella said. "I withdraw all names you've ever held, and by the waters of this world and Fayün, may you be washed anew."

There was no discernible change, or shifting of the Myst, to accompany Pomella's words. The torrent of power still raged in Shevia. But she understood the point, and like a sword of indestructible metal it severed Shevia's fears, and eased her heart.

Pomella leaned closer to her and whispered in Shevia's ear, "If you would accept it, I offer you a new name. Lorraina, after my grandmhathir. She, too, gave up the life of a Mystic for something greater, something *honest*. She chose love and a simple life, and lived happily until her last days."

The name shone on to Shevia like the sun, and she basked in it. She stared at Pomella, and for a moment all the chaos and confusion of Crow Tallin slipped away. The woman before her became timeless, as though she stood at the central hub of a wagon wheel that ground to a halt. The past and future that she'd previously seen for this woman fell away, leaving her only to stand in the moment. Shevia might be the one holding all of Lagnaraste's might, but it was this other woman would who truly determine all of their fates.

"I accept," Shevia said, and this time her name, and immense accumulated power, fell away, leaving her humble, alone, and *free*.

The woman who had been Shevia kissed the center of Pomella's forehead. "Thank you. But go. Sim needs you. We all do."

Shevia—no,   Lorraina's—lips searing through the skin of Pomella's forehead, filling her with the unfathomable power of a Saint. When the other woman pulled away, Pomella had to steady herself. She saw the woman smile, and warn her about Sim.

Sim.

Pomella looked at the central tower. The Tower of Eternal Starlight stood in the same place but rose several times higher than Kelt Apar's stone structure. As she gazed upward she turned her attention to the moon hanging in the sky. She knew she only had moments. As quickly as it had come, Crow Tallin waned in its final moments. Already the Tower of Eternal Starlight had began to fade.

"Ena!" she called, and less than a heartbeat later the hummingbird was carrying her toward the tower's broken summit. She hovered beside the window and looked in.

Brigid's decapitated body lay in the center of the upper chamber. It phased out of existence, briefly revealing empty sky, but cycled back into existence, if less substantially than moments before.

Beside Brigid lay another body.

"Sim!" Pomella cried. "Wake up, Sim!"

The tower faded further as Crow Tallin took its final breaths. *"Sim!"*

He stirred and raised his face toward her.

"Come here, Sim!" Pomella called. "Come to me. Please!"

He grunted and pushed himself to his feet.

"Hurry!"

He ran and leaped for the window, but it was too late. The Tower of Eternal Starlight vanished from the human realm as Crow Tallin ended. His fingers brushed hers. She clawed them, holding on as tightly as she could, praying for every once of strength and time.

As their fingers touched, a flood of memories flashed into Pomella. Like Shevia's life, Sim's now became a part of her. She saw his childhood in Oakspring, his time with the Black Claws, his voyage to the Continent, his journeys with Rochella, the face of his lover Swiko, and his loneliness in the wilderness.

Above all, she inherited his memories of *her.*

His eyes met hers amid the storm of memories. "It was you who called me," he said.

"No! Sim!" she cried. "Come back! Come back to me!"

He opened his mouth to speak, and was gone.

Treorel emerged from behind the moon, and Pomella plummeted from the tower, alone.

At the moment her fingers parted from Sim's, the blended human and fay worlds tore themselves away from her, and the shockwave of that transition hurled Pomella's mind into itself.

She had come to the Crossroads, the normally thin place where the worlds converged. This time, she held the inherited might of Lagnaraste, Saint Brigid, and Shevia. As Pomella's body fell through the air beside Kelt Apar's central tower, her awareness stood motionless in a trembling, endless void surrounded by stars. The fear of the fall left her. The wretched sadness of losing Sim fell away. Nothing but peace surrounded her.

The stars surrounding her *sang* with a chorus of voices unequaled by anything she'd heard before. If she had eyes, she would have cried with blissful joy. They serenaded the song of her life, of every past that could have been hers, and of every possible future. She shifted within that endless void, and found that she could move the stars, and the Myst itself that was her destiny. Here, she was more free than ever before. Here, there were no limits.

Several shimmering points of light within the void pulsed in familiar ways. She recognized them as people. Her grandmhathir and her parents, distant and dim. Her brother, cold and alone. Sim's star shone bright and warm, but always behind her, and just out of sight. Lal, clear and joyful. And there, bound to her with a beam of light she only now saw, was a vibrant star that burned as only Shevia—now Lorraina—could.

Freedom and power, mixed in harmony.

Hovering in the Crossroads, with the veil all but torn away, and the Myst surging around her, Pomella found serenity. She let go of all her desires, her hopes, her expectations, and just let herself *reside* in that peace.

In that moment, when Pomella released the last of her limits, and let herself travel with the light of the stars surrounding her, going beyond the powers she possessed, she at last found herself in the Deep.

The Crossroads themselves collapsed, leaving the Myst, and the whole universe, to blossom within her. A thousand thousand worlds, with different skies numbered beyond counting, dawned in her heart as if awakening under the sunlight of her gaze.

She *was* the Myst, in its purest, most profound form. There was no longer a Pomella. No longer one world or two or a thousand. No thought. No emotion. Only the Myst existed just as Lal had said.

The formless emptiness around her *breathed, alive and conscious.* The pattern of life revealed itself to Pomella. Here in the Deep, harmony existed in all times and places. She saw order to the chaos reigning across Moth and the rest of the world. Rather than seeing division among castes, and between the worlds themselves, she saw the opportunity to unite. That same harmony could exist between Fayün and the human world, just as it could unite the separate aspects of her own life as a Mystic and a secular person living in society. Visions of the united world that Lal had spoken of drifted through her consciousness. It had been broken long ago, but now sought Reunion.

In that infinite moment, Pomella knew with perfect clarity what she had to do. The time had come to unite her worlds.

She moved in harmony with the Deep, allowing herself to submit to its will, and shifted the very fabric of time and space. With a thought, the foundations of the world moved at her urging. The veil dissolved, and burned away into the infinite void. Fayün and the human world synchronized, then *fused* together.

She breathed once more, in perfect unision with the Myst, and knew her task had been done properly.

Pomella's mind returned from the Deep, just as her body crashed to the ground. The first and last thing she saw was Treorel hanging in the silver-black sky above, sitting apart from the moon. The tide of Myst pulled away from the land, and from Pomella, leaving her to remember the strange experience like a dream, all but forgotten.

Vivianna's face blurred into existence. "Oh, sweet ancestors, you're alive," she said. "Are you all right?"

Pomella's body ached like a pummeled rice sack. She was still in Kelt Apar, with her back against the stone tower. Fires burned all around her, although early-morning sunlight had begun to outshine them. Above her, fay creatures glided through the air. She managed to sit up and catch her breath.

"Wh-what happened?" Pomella asked, still groggy.

"I don't know," Vivianna said, but there was wonder in her voice. "Look at the sky."

Blinking against the smoke, Pomella looked upward and beheld a new land. Fayün and the human world had merged—forever, it seemed. The fay crossing the dawn sky still glowed with silvery light, but they had weight and substance now. Motes of drifting light—silver and gold mixed together—filled the air like falling snowflakes. Nearby, a cluster of axthos and luck'ns looked around in disbelief beside commoners, nobles, and Mystics.

Pomella tried to find her feet, but wobbled and nearly fell, until a strong arm caught her. She glanced up and saw Tibron.

"I have you," he said.

"Thank you," she said. "I'm—" She couldn't find the words. Through Shevia's memories she suddenly knew him better. His presence comforted her in a way she couldn't yet explain.

With a sudden pang of fear, Pomella realized the Tower of Eternal Starlight was entirely gone, and Sim with it. Only the broken remains of Kelt Apar's central tower remained.

"Where's Shevia?" Pomella finished.

Vivianna's eyes widened. "I don't know. We should find her."

"No," Pomella said. "Let her go. She's free now."

Vivianna watched as a flock of fay birds circled the sky above them. One of them sounded a call, and to Pomella, it seemed like a mourning cry.

"Crow Tallin is over," Tibron said. "When will the fay vanish?"

Pomella took a slow breath. "They won't ever," she said.

Vivianna stared wide-eyed at Pomella. "What do you mean?" she asked slowly.

A dragon is one with the land, Lal had said. Pomella thought of her fall from the tower, of how, for mere seconds, she'd entered the Deep.

"The world is changed forever, Vivianna," Pomella said. "Let us hope we are ready to face it."

At her feet, a flower, golden and silver at once, had already pushed itself up from a pile of ash.

It was a lily.

ACKNOWLEDGMENTS

            This book was written during a time of great turmoil in my life. I am grateful and indebted to the many people who supported me throughout its crafting. To the amazing team at Tor, among them my editor, Melissa Frain, as well as Tom Doherty, Devi Pillai, Irene Gallo, Robert Davis, Patty Garcia, Zohra Ashpari, and Alexis Saarela. Thank you for your patience and willingness to let this book come alive in the time it was meant to. Thank you also to Eddie Schneider, my agent, for encouraging me and providing feedback on the earliest draft.

The members of my writing group once again proved indispensable. They are: Andrew Wilson, Laura Harvey, Andrea Stewart, George Hahn, Kris McCandless, DJ Stipe, Ryan Coe, Caroline Patti, and Nicole Vanderveer. Other early readers who provided feedback on this book include Leslie Annis, Brooke Coe, Diana Trent, Chris Lehotsky, Richard Fife, Jennifer Johnson, Ravi Persaud, Megan Kurteff-Schatz, Georgene Jansen, Sarramy Anderson, Robin Allen, Amy Romanczuk, Valerie Lauer, Sae Sae Norris, Thom DeSimone, Elizabeth Beattie, Meesha Lenee, Lisa Burris, Tina Pierce, John Monsour, Stacey Holditch, Laura-Gene Ryke, Courtney Lynn Leiphart, and the ever-reliable Gary Singer.

A special thanks goes out to Nicole Stephenson for her numerous read throughs, frequent brainstorming sessions, and overall love, support, and encouragement when I needed it most.

Finally, I wish to thank my family, especially my mother, brothers, and my sons, Aidan and Andrew. You were what kept me together when my worlds fell apart.

Jason Denzel
January 2018

7/18